SPLINTERED

JON McGORAN

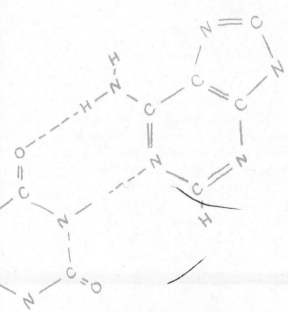

HOLIDAY HOUSE New York

For Will

Printed and bound in February 2020 at Maple Press, York, PA, USA.
www.holidayhouse.com
First Edition
3 5 7 9 10 8 6 4 2

Library of Congress Cataloging-in-Publication Data

Names: McGoran, Jon, author.
Title: Splintered / Jon McGoran.
Description: New York : Holiday House, 2019. | Sequel to: Spliced.
Summary: "Seventeen-year-old Jimi Corcoran continues her fight for
survival and equality in a near-future world where teenagers have
animal DNA spliced into their own"—Provided by publisher.
Identifiers: LCCN 2018039836 | ISBN 9780823440900 (hardback)
Subjects: | CYAC: Genetic engineering—Fiction. | Survival—Fiction.
Toleration—Fiction. | Science fiction.
Classification: LCC PZ7.1.M43523 Spp 2019 | DDC [Fic]—dc23 LC
record available at https://lccn.loc.gov/2018039836

ISBN 978-0-8234-4546-2 (paperback)

CHAPTER 1

The Lev train hummed as it surged away from the platform at Silver Garden, stirring up a thick cloud of ice and snow that sparkled and swirled in the darkness. Hundreds of tiny crystals peppered my face and melted on contact. I couldn't wait to get where I was going, but I paused to watch as the snow settled back to the ground and the train disappeared into the night.

Then I took a deep breath of frigid air and looked around at the old, brick warehouses that surrounded the station. To the south, the towers of Philadelphia glittered in the distance. A couple of blocks to the east, a freight train chugged along, comically slow compared to the Lev train. Then that was gone, too.

I grinned and descended the long, metal stairway that led to the street. The cold bit my cheeks and ears, but it was refreshing, a welcome change from the past week and a half. Christmas had been nice, but after days of eating too much and being stuck in an overheated house with my mom, Kevin, and Aunt Trudy, I was ready for the holidays to be over.

Now it was New Year's Day, which meant they almost were.

I'd spent New Year's Eve at my old friend Nina's party. I appreciated the invitation, but I kind of wished I'd stayed home, or had anywhere else to go. All her rich friends who never used to pay attention to me suddenly wanted to know me now—or, least, say they knew me—because I'd been on the news. It was a fifteen-minutes-of-fame kind of thing, and as far as I could tell, my fifteen minutes were just about up. Which was fine with me.

All my real friends had been away, some for the week, some for a lot longer. Tonight, though, most of them were finally back in town, and I'd spent the entire ride to Silver Garden smiling at the thought of seeing them. Even the fact that school was starting up again next week couldn't bring me down—much.

I wasn't dreading school like I would have not too long ago, but I was glad there were a few days left of vacation, and especially glad that my mom would be spending part of that time on a long ski weekend with Aunt Trudy. It had been my suggestion, since their relationship needed a little mending. I was kind of shocked Mom had embraced the idea—especially since *our* relationship was still mending, too, after what happened last time she left me on my own.

We'd had some deep heart-to-hearts about it, though; ones that included long hugs and more than a few tears. And eventually, she told me she understood why I did what I did that fall. After I'd offhandedly suggested she and Trudy could use a girls' weekend, she said going away for a few days would give her the chance to prove she still trusted me, and let me prove I could be on my own without any drama.

I guess we were making progress.

My feet crunched on the snow that crusted the pavement as I made my way up the hill and out from under the Levline station. Sheer brick walls on either side created a canyon that funneled the wind. When it finally died away, my footsteps echoed in a way that made it sound like there were two of me.

Or even three.

I whipped around, suddenly feeling like I was being watched. I didn't see anyone, but the sensation didn't entirely go away.

It wasn't the first time I'd felt like this lately. Ever since my face had been splashed all over the headlines, I wondered sometimes if strangers on the street were staring at me, if they had seen me on the Holovid and knew who I was. Or more disturbingly, if they knew because they were with Humans for Humanity.

H4H was the big anti-chimera group led by Howard Wells, the tech bazillionaire owner of the Wellplant Corporation.

They were behind the Genetic Heritage Act, which the state legislature passed and the governor signed a few months ago. GHA defined anyone whose DNA wasn't one-hundred-percent human—meaning chimeras—as legally nonpersons. It was totally absurd. I personally saw people try to use the law to justify killing chimeras, and I called them out on it in a pretty public way.

It was weird to think that just a few months ago, I didn't even *know* anyone who'd been spliced, and now H4H hated me almost as much as they hated chimeras. Maybe even more.

I looked over my shoulder again, then glanced up the hill toward Dyson Street. The coffee shop where I was meeting everybody was just around the corner. I felt silly getting so worked up, but I took off running anyway, my feet trying to find safe patches of dry pavement. I was almost at the top of the hill when I slipped on black ice. I planted one hand on the crusty concrete as I fell, and felt the bite of gravel and rock salt digging into my palm. I stretched out my other arm, preparing for impact, but I never landed.

Instead, another set of hands closed around me and scooped me up. They were so massive, I knew right away who they belonged to. But I fought out of sheer reflex, twisting in his grip and swinging my left hand hard. I couldn't see his face in the shadows, but I heard his voice, a low rumble that could only be Rex.

That should have been the end of it. I should have slammed on the brakes.

But he was laughing at me and I guess that pissed me off just enough to keep me from pulling my punch. It landed, then so did I.

"*Ow!*" Rex bellowed, releasing me as he clasped his nose.

The same word passed through my brain as I hit the ground. I was determined to keep it to myself, but it wasn't easy. He'd been holding me higher that I had realized. Sometimes I forgot how big he was.

"Damn, Jimi," he said as I got to my feet. "You punched me!"

"You snuck up and grabbed me," I said, brushing myself off.

"I didn't grab you, I *caught* you," he said, gently massaging his nose. "You were falling."

"Well . . . ," I said, "you were laughing." He was right, of course. But so was I.

He sneezed.

I laughed.

He glowered.

"Sorry," I said, stepping up close to him. He looked away, still angry, but I reached up and put my hand against his cinder-block jaw and turned his head back so he was looking at me.

I flashed him a big, exaggerated, sheepish grin to let him know how sorry I was. And to make him laugh.

He tried to resist, but it was useless. We both smiled.

I reached up and ran my fingers through the hair on the back of his head, then lingered, massaging behind his ear. He closed his eyes, reveling in it, then looked down at me, his eyes bright and his face slightly flushed. "Heya," he said.

"Heya," I replied. "Welcome back. How were your holidays?" I hadn't seen him since right before Thanksgiving.

"Better now. How about yours?"

"Same."

"Lacking something, though, you know what I mean?"

I smiled as he put his hands on my ribs and gently raised me to his lips. We kissed, parted, kissed once more for good measure, and then he put me down. I held onto him for another moment, wrapping my arms around the taut muscles of his midsection. Then I wedged my shoulder under his arm and he rested his chin on the top of my head, and we started walking. It was awkward, but neither of us cared. We stumbled a few times and laughed, holding each other that much closer.

As we turned the corner, I glanced back at the Levline station.

It was still deserted.

Up ahead, soft yellow light played across the sign for New Ground Coffee Shop, a carved picture of a small seedling breaking through bare soil. I smiled at the sight of it. New Ground was unofficially Philadelphia's official chimera hangout. I wasn't a chimera, but it had become like a second home to me over the past few months.

"How's everyone been?" Rex asked as he reached out to grab the door.

"Everybody's good, as far as I know," I said. "I mean . . . you know."

He paused and looked down at me with a sad smile. My eyes welled up, just for a moment, thinking of the friends we'd lost that fall. "Yeah, I know," Rex said quietly. He reached out to touch my face. "You okay?"

I forced a bright smile. "Yeah."

Then, arm in arm, we went inside.

CHAPTER 2

The coffee shop was bright inside, and warm in a run-down kind of way. Jerry, the guy who owned the place, was clearing a table when we walked in. "Hey, kid," he said when he saw me. Then Rex came in behind me and Jerry's face brightened even more. "Hey, Big Dog! Back from your travels, huh?"

I grinned at the nickname. Rex was a chimera, spliced with canine DNA. His size wasn't directly from the splice, but the splice had somehow activated the unsuccessful growth treatments he'd received as a kid—a very little kid whom I'd known as Leo Byron.

The splice had probably given Rex his especially strong jaw, slightly pointed ears, and incredibly thick brown hair. But his amazing, dark-brown eyes were pretty much the same as he'd always had.

Pell was behind the counter and Ruth was perched on a stool directly across from her, folding flyers. They were chimeras, too. They had the same curved nose, the same wide, dark eyes, and the same soft, elegant fawn-colored feathers covering their scalps. They'd gotten their splices together, with identical bird DNA, making them sisters, in a way. Pell had a new piercing since last time I saw her, a green stone in her bottom lip to match the one in her nose. I smiled thinking back to when I first met them, when that green stone in Pell's nose was the only way I could tell them apart.

Pell smiled and waved. Ruth jumped off her stool and ran over to us with a squeal.

"Jimi!" she said. "And Rex! Oh my God!" She gave me a hug, surprisingly firm considering her slight frame. Then she squeezed Rex and hugged even tighter and longer. Rex winked at me over her head.

"It's so great to see you both," she said, when she finally let go.

"Is Sly here?" I asked, looking around the room. He was another chimera I'd grown close to over the last few months, but hadn't seen in a while.

"No," Ruth said. "Haven't seen him since Thanksgiving."

"Me neither. Where is he?"

Ruth shrugged. "I don't know. He said he was going away, but he wouldn't say where. He was pretty cagey about it, actually."

I glanced at Rex, but he seemed to be making a point of looking anywhere but at us.

"Weird," I said.

"Yeah," she laughed. "All very mysterious."

I laughed, too. Rex was still looking away.

"How was Connecticut?" I asked Ruth.

Rex snapped around, shocked. "You visited your family?"

Ruth nodded and smiled. "Yeah, we did. My mom wrote me a letter after Thanksgiving."

"That's huge," he said.

"Yeah, it was good. There were a few rough spots, but it was a good start." Turning to Rex, she said, "When did you get back?"

"Just now," I said.

"Right," he said, glancing at me.

Ruth looked back and forth between us and grinned. "Oh! Well, I guess you have some catching up to do. We're actually getting ready for a meeting, anyway." Ruth had become heavily involved in Earth for Everyone, the chimera-rights group that had formed to counter H4H. Pell was involved with E4E too, although not as enthusiastically as Ruth.

Rex and I nodded and found a table in the corner.

Pell brought us some cocoa. "On me," she said. "We're heading out in a minute. Some big E4E meeting." I got the feeling she was resisting the urge to roll her eyes. "Do you want anything else before I go?" She lowered her voice to a stage whisper, "Or do you want to wait and take your chances with Jerry behind the counter?"

Rex and I laughed, but I'd tasted Jerry's chai lattes, so I thought seriously before saying I was all set.

We said goodbye as Ruth and Pell packed up and left, then I turned back to Rex.

"So," I said as he sipped his cocoa. "What's new?"

He laughed. "It's good to see you, Jimi."

"It's good to see you, too." I grinned and let a few seconds pass before asking, "So . . . what's it like?"

His eyes narrowed, confused and suspicious. "What's *what* like?"

I leaned forward and bobbed my eyebrows playfully. "Chimerica," I whispered.

His shoulders slumped and he rolled his eyes. "Jimi, come on. I told you I can't talk about any of that."

I was mostly messing with him—not that I didn't want to know all about where he'd been and what he'd been up to since the last time I'd seen him—but I could see he didn't think my question was funny. Before I could halfheartedly apologize, though, the door opened, and Doc Guzman came in.

Rex called out to him. "Doc!" Then he turned back to me. "Sorry. I forgot to tell you when I called. I was supposed to be meeting Doc here tonight, too. Earlier."

I held in a sigh and tried not to look annoyed. I hadn't seen or spoken to Rex in weeks, had only seen him twice since our crazy adventure months earlier. I considered him my best friend. And, I was pretty sure, my boyfriend. It sure felt to *me* like our relationship ran that deep. But I wondered if maybe I was misreading the situation.

Doc unwound the scarf from his neck, the static lifting random strands of his tousled gray hair. His glasses fogged up as he made his way over to our table.

Rex stood and they quickly embraced.

Physically, they couldn't have been more different. Rex was practically a giant. He was young and in amazing shape. Doc was about five foot four and in his late sixties, wiry and bespectacled, with a small belly.

But as different as they looked, they had a lot in common.

Doc was the local fixer, someone who could reverse a splice in the first forty-eight hours if someone changed their mind about it, or, more commonly, if the splice went bad. Technically, splices were legal to perform, but only by a licensed medical doctor—and only to treat some naturally-occurring genetic condition. Any doctor caught giving an "unnecessary" splice would lose their license. Since fixing a splice was considered the same procedure in reverse, the same rules applied. Give a splice or fix a splice, either way, you lose your license.

That's what had happened to Doc. He'd given up his legit medical career to treat chimeras, because no one else would. Insurance companies wouldn't cover them, so most doctors and hospitals wouldn't treat them if they were sick, beyond sticking them in beds and watching them die. Fixers like Doc were incredibly important to the chimera community. Although I don't know if there were any who were *quite* like Doc.

Rex, meanwhile, was the self-appointed protector of his friends, of chimeras in general, and pretty much anyone else in need. He looked out for everybody. It was one of the many things I liked about him.

Rex and Doc were both deeply committed to taking care of their people, and these days, that was more important than ever. Even though a judge had temporarily blocked most of GHA, there were all sorts of appeals and motions. Chimeras in a large part of the country were in legal limbo. A lot of people expected the courts to fully overturn GHA— but a lot of people had said it would never pass in the first place.

"Hello, Jimi," Doc said as he approached the table.

"Hi, Doc," I replied.

We didn't know each other all that well, but we'd been thrown together during some intense moments a few months ago.

"Sorry I'm late," Doc said.

"I was actually starting to worry," Rex said.

"Some idiot came by the clinic, one of these belligerent types making threats about what he'd do if I didn't help him find his girlfriend, or ex-girlfriend, who was apparently a patient of mine."

"That's scary," said Rex. "Any idea who it was?"

"He said his name was Brian Kurtz."

"Was he H4H?"

Doc shook his head. "I don't think so. I'm pretty sure this was strictly personal."

"What happened?" I asked.

"Eh, nothing. It's done. Just made me late, is all."

"So what's going on?" Rex asked, lowering his voice as he leaned forward over the table.

Doc glanced at me, then looked back at Rex, as if questioning whether he could trust me. I thought about asking if they wanted me to leave, but mostly I thought, *To hell with that.*

Rex correctly read my expression and gave him a slight nod.

Doc took a deep breath and shrugged. "I've been in my lab a lot lately. Working on something kind of big. And I think I just had a breakthrough."

"What is it?" Rex asked.

"You know there are a couple of different categories of gene splices used today, right?"

"You mean like somatic and germ-line?" I said, afraid of getting it wrong, but—I admit it—hoping to impress.

Doc gave me a tiny smile. "That's right, plus AAV, adeno-associated virus. Germ-line means the changes to the genes get passed down to your offspring, and somatic—the kind chimeras get—means they don't. AAV is temporary, impacting only the cells it infects, so as the cells die and are replaced, over the course of days or weeks or months, the tissue reverts to its previous state." He sat back and scratched his chin. "Been some fascinating developments lately. Some people are using tiny particles called nanospears to deliver AAV genetic treatments, keeping the viral media present and continuously inserting the gene splice into the new cells as each generation arises. In fact, a former colleague of mine now at Johns Hopkins—"

"Uh, Doc." Rex cut him off, and flashed me a look to let me know he was aware that this conversation was cutting into *our* time. "Is this what you wanted to talk to me about?"

Doc thought for a moment. "Um . . . oh no, not really." Then he leaned forward. "Okay, so as a fixer, I can only reverse splices in the first forty-eight hours at the most, right? Any longer and it's too late. Well, I've come up with a way, using a person's cord blood, the blood from the umbilical cord from when they were born, to reverse a genetic splice. It's germ-line, so any changes would be hereditary, but since we'd be using the person's own genome, which would have been left unchanged by their somatic splice, the effect would be no germline change at all. But the big thing is, we could do it at any time."

"Cord blood?" Rex cocked his head. "But what good is that decades after they've been born?"

"People save it," I said. "Sometimes."

Doc nodded at me. "Hospitals ask new parents if they want to freeze it. It costs, but not all that much."

"Why?" Rex asked.

"It's amazing stuff," Doc said. "It can be used to treat all sorts of things—cancers, genetic diseases, blood disorders. But you're missing the point. This could be huge."

I couldn't help thinking about Del, once my best friend, who had died from a bad splice, or from what followed it. I didn't know if his parents had frozen his cord blood when he was born. His dad probably thought it was an abomination against God. His dad thought a lot of things were abominations against God.

"And this works?" I asked, almost hoping it didn't—not yet, not so soon after it could have saved Del's life.

"I think I'm close. I mean, something like this would have to be tested out the wazoo. I've got some funding of sorts, nothing official, just people who support my work. But it's nowhere near the resources for any kind of legitimate testing. I still know some people who have that kind of funding, though, at Penn, at Drexel. But here's what I'm worried about—"

Before he could finish his sentence, the door opened and Ruth and Pell burst back inside with a third person propped up between them. I didn't recognize him. He had some kind of bird splice, but different from Ruth and Pell. More colorful. The feathers that framed his head were bright yellow, but they were also matted and filthy and dripping wet. So were his clothes. His head hung down on his chest.

Rex and I rushed over to them. Doc followed, slower.

"Who's this?" I asked, and Rex said, "What happened?" as we both helped them move him to a chair.

"We don't know," Ruth said, out of breath.

"We found him on the train tracks," Pell added.

"The *Levline*?" Rex said, alarmed.

"No," Pell said, "the freight train."

Doc was already examining him, gently lifting his head. He was young, our age or maybe younger. There was some sort of metal bottle hanging around his neck, with a plastic mask attached by a hose.

Doc looked at it, then up at Ruth and Pell. "What's this?"

"No idea," Ruth said.

Doc looked in the kid's pupils, felt his pulse, and then put an ear to his chest and listened to him breathing. The kid looked terrible.

"Is it a bad splice?" I asked, and I felt myself turning even paler than usual. I'd seen up close how devastating it could be when a splice went wrong.

Doc shook his head. He looked worried. "No, I don't think that's it."

Jerry came around from behind the counter, looking concerned but exasperated. "Should we maybe get him into the back?"

"No," Doc said. "We need to get him to my clinic. Now."

CHAPTER 3

Doc's van was parked out front. Rex and I carried the sick kid out and got into the back with him. Ruth and Pell followed, but when Pell started to climb in with us, Ruth put a hand on her arm.

"The meeting," Ruth said. "It's important."

Pell paused as Doc started the motor.

"It's okay," I said. "We got it."

What I meant was, Doc had it. Ruth and Pell weren't going to make much difference, and neither was Rex or I. Doc was the only one who really mattered.

Pell nodded. "Keep us posted." Then she stepped back and closed the door.

Doc drove away, fast but not reckless.

The kid was totally out of it, but I held his hand anyway, feeling strangely awkward. I hadn't seen Rex in so long, and now here we were, sitting with an unconscious stranger between us and Doc in the front seat. It didn't feel like the best time to resume our conversation. Not that we'd even really had a chance to start it in the first place.

The kid's sleeve had slid back, revealing a slender, dirty wrist with a white plastic band around it. I leaned in for a closer look in the dim light coming from the windows.

"What's that?" Rex rumbled.

"It looks like a hospital bracelet," I said. The interior of the van lit up as we passed some lights outside.

"A hospital bracelet?"

"Something like that. It says 'Patient name: Cornelius.' No last name. It doesn't say what hospital, either, just some numbers."

Cornelius looked like a nice guy, with a soft brow and a mouth that seemed like it probably smiled a lot. The splice suited him: the yellow feathers nicely offset his bronze skin, and his strong beak-like nose suited the angles of his chin and his cheekbones. Maybe it was the fact that now he had a name, but I felt a pang of intense sadness. He was not well at all. His breathing was shallow and fast, and his face was speckled with nicks and cuts and what looked like little burns. His clothes were torn and singed. I had a lot of faith in Doc Guzman's abilities, but I didn't think Cornelius was going to make it.

"He doesn't look good," Rex said softly. Then the back of the van was plunged into darkness, meaning we had left the city and crossed into the zurbs. No municipal electricity, so no streetlights.

"No, he doesn't," I said. "Do you think he needs this?" I held up the grimy metal canister around his neck.

"We'll be there any minute. We should let Doc decide."

A moment later, the van lurched and came to an abrupt stop. Rex opened the back door, and together we carried Cornelius out.

Doc was already unlocking the front door to the clinic, which sat in the middle of an abandoned strip mall in the zurbs, a half mile outside the city. The only light came from the van's headlights, but they were bright enough to light up the entire row of stores.

As Doc opened the door, a figure stepped out from around the farthest store. I could barely make him out in the darkness, but he looked like trouble.

"We have company," I said to Rex.

He nodded. "Hey Doc," he called out, just loud enough to be heard. "Is that your friend from earlier?"

Doc turned to us, then saw the guy approaching. His shoulders slumped and he nodded. "Brian Kurtz."

Kurtz stepped into the light, looking drunk and disheveled, with manic eyes set deep in a pale, freckled face under a blond buzz cut. He did look belligerent, but he also looked scared and confused. Like a little boy only slightly hidden under a thin veneer of whatever he thought a man was supposed to be.

"Look, kid," Doc told him. "Like I said before, I don't know where your friend is. But even if I did, I couldn't tell you."

"Right. Patient-doctor confidentiality," Kurtz replied with a sneer. His voice sounded even younger than he looked. "Like a real doctor would be set up in a crappy place like this out in the zurbs."

Rex met my eyes and whispered, "Put him down."

I slowly lowered Cornelius's feet to the ground. Rex moved him upright, handing him off to me so that I could lean him against the van. With his head closer to mine, Cornelius's wheezing sounded even worse. Some of his feathers were bent and broken. Rex stepped slowly away from the van and closer to Doc.

Kurtz froze for a second as he took in Rex's size. The sneer returned, but the fear didn't leave his eyes. "Oh, so you brought your mixie bodyguard to protect you, is that it?"

Cornelius was slipping from my grasp, and as I readjusted my grip, Kurtz looked over at me and laughed. "If that's your friend and he's sick, I'd be careful bringing him to this guy. You might not be happy with the result."

Rex took a step closer and Kurtz whirled on him, pulling a gun from his waistband. The tension in the air skyrocketed and my stomach clenched.

"Okay, kid, now let's calm down," Doc said, showing his open hands in a soothing gesture. "That's serious business right there. Deadly business."

Kurtz clenched his eyes for a moment, then opened them as he clumsily swung the gun in Doc's direction.

"Doc, look out!" I yelled.

Rex lunged, whipping out one long arm with extraordinary speed and snatching the weapon.

Kurtz seemed stunned, staring at his empty hand for several seconds before realizing Rex was now holding the gun.

"I told you before, son," Doc said gently. "I don't want any trouble."

Kurtz turned to Rex. "You . . . you need to give me that back."

Rex opened the gun's cylinder, shook the bullets into his palm, and flung them into the air. A moment later they pitter-pattered back to Earth in the overgrown, trash-strewn lot across the street.

Rex clicked the cylinder back into place, and as he was handing the gun back, an oddly smug, malevolent smile flickered across Kurtz's face. Then I realized why.

"He's got more bullets," I called out.

Kurtz flashed me a murderous glare as his hand moved to his pants pocket. I might have heard a faint *clink* as he did.

Rex snorted and pulled the gun back, then heaved it into the dark sky.

Kurtz tried to track the arc, but it had disappeared. "Hey . . . ," he said, pausing as a distant, muffled crash emerged from somewhere in the night, "that was my dad's gun."

Rex took a step closer and loomed over him. "Get out of here."

Kurtz took a step back. "You'll be sorry you did that," he said, his voice jagged with emotion. Then he turned and ran, disappearing around the corner. Rex, Doc, and I exchanged glances as a car door slammed and tires squealed.

Rex and I lifted Cornelius again as Doc opened the door.

"Does that happen a lot?" I asked as we carried Cornelius inside.

"It happens," Doc replied, slapping a switch to turn on the battery-powered lights.

"You shouldn't be out here on your own," Rex said.

Doc avoided Rex's eyes. "Just take him straight back and put him in the chair."

We carried Cornelius through the small waiting area and into the large treatment room in the back.

It felt strange to be at Doc's clinic again. I'd only been there a couple of times, several months earlier, all in the name of helping Del after his splice went bad.

A lot had gone down after that.

And worst of all was that I'd lost Del—again and again, it seemed—until the day he died, and I knew nothing would ever be the same.

Being at the clinic was bringing back a lot of memories for me, and Rex seemed to pick up on that. After we laid Cornelius into one of Doc's barbershop examination chairs, Rex put his arms around me and pulled me close.

"You okay?" he said as Doc bustled around Cornelius.

I nodded as we both watched Doc work. His expression seemed to support my grim prognosis. He picked up the canister and looked at it, confused.

"I was wondering if maybe he needed to use that," I said. "To breathe."

Doc glanced at me, then sniffed at the mask. He fiddled with a knob on the valve, then sniffed it again and jerked his head away. "I don't think so," he said, giving it a shake. "It's pretty much empty, but it doesn't seem like it was good air to start with. Maybe that's what made him sick."

He pressed a button on the bottom, and it made a loud, whirring noise.

"What is that?" I asked, as the noise faded out.

Doc turned it around, looking at it from different angles. "It's got a compressor. It's refillable. Probably meant for short-term use, I guess."

He sniffed at it again. "Smells better now." He shrugged and put it aside.

As he checked Cornelius's pulse again, I said, "He's got a bracelet on the other wrist. Like a hospital bracelet. Says his name is Cornelius."

Doc lifted Cornelius's other wrist and studied the bracelet. He nodded to himself, then began cutting off Cornelius's filthy shirt. The skin underneath seemed unaffected by his splice, but it was scratched and bruised. Doc listened with a stethoscope to his heart and lungs, poked his midsection, and thumped it with two fingers, listening to the sound.

"His condition is deteriorating," he said, as he turned to a drawer and took out a vial and a syringe.

I knew what it was: vitamins and stimulants meant to boost Cornelius's strength, keep him going while Doc figured out how to help him.

As Doc wiped Cornelius's arm with an alcohol swab and gave him the injection, I had a vivid memory of him doing the exact same thing to Del.

It hadn't worked then, and it didn't seem to work now.

Doc attached an oxygen monitor to Cornelius's finger, a glowing plastic clip connected to a machine the size of a toaster on a tall metal stand. When the digital displays on the monitor flickered to life and started cycling through numbers, Doc started drawing vials of blood. He took four of them, and put them into four slots on top of an ancient-looking white plastic apparatus that said DIAGNOSTICOMP. He flicked a switch on it, adjusted a couple of knobs, keyed in some numbers on a keypad, and then stood back as it began to whir and hum.

Apparently satisfied, he turned back to the oxygen monitor and frowned. He readjusted the clip on Cornelius's finger, then smacked the monitor itself. His frown deepened as he removed the clip.

"Either this thing is broken or his blood oxygen level is totally out of whack."

Rex gestured with his thumb toward the corner of the room and said, "What about the hyperbaric thingy you used on Del?"

Doc and I both followed his gaze to the hyperbaric bed, a rectangular platform covered with a plastic bubble that was supposed to help people heal using super-oxygenated air. It was connected to a bunch of hoses that snaked up to the loft upstairs. It used to be suspended from the ceiling up there. I was relieved to see it was now firmly attached to the floor.

"I doubt it'll help," Doc said. "But I suppose it couldn't hurt. We won't know much more until the blood tests are done."

Doc opened the lid and turned to Rex. "Would you mind?"

Rex lifted Cornelius's limp body out of the chair and laid him down in the bed.

Doc gently closed the lid and hit a few switches. The hoses stiffened, filling with pressurized oxygen, and the plastic bubble clouded up.

Doc walked stiffly over to the blood analyzer, suddenly looking tired and old. "We'll give him five minutes and see if that helps."

"Did you see his bracelet?" I asked. "It said he was a patient somewhere."

Doc tweaked a knob on the unit before nodding. "That bracelet is from an OmniCare hospital. I recognize the code."

OmniCare sounded vaguely familiar, a chain of for-profit hospitals. Except a hospital of any kind didn't make sense. "I thought hospitals wouldn't treat chimeras," I said.

"OmniCare's one of the rare ones," Doc said. "They just started to a couple of months ago. You may have seen their medical director making a big deal about it on the news."

"Wait," Rex said. "Charleston or something?"

"Charlesford is his name," Doc said. "He's pretty slick. A bit late to the party, as far as treating chimeras with any respect, but better late than never, I guess."

"Well, maybe we can take Cornelius there," I said hopefully.

Doc shook his head. "There are just a few OmniCare facilities that take chimeras. The only one in Pennsylvania is out near Gellersville."

"That's, like, two hours away," I said.

"Yes. And the state he's in, I doubt the kid would make it halfway." Doc looked at the hyperbaric bed and glanced at his watch.

"What about the cord-blood thing you've been working on?" Rex said. "Any chance that could work?"

Doc shook his head. "That's not close to ready for prime time. Besides, we don't even have this kid's birth name, much less his cord blood. Plus, I don't know if whatever is ailing him has anything to do with his splice. And even if we had the cord blood and were able to fix his splice, there's no way he's strong enough to sweat out a change."

"Then what are we going to do?" I asked.

Doc hooked a thumb at the blood analysis machine. "We're going to wait and see what the blood tells us, and then we'll go from there."

For a moment the only sound was the hiss of the hyperbaric bed and the quiet whir of the blood analyzer.

Then something occurred to me. "Doc," I said. "Is OmniCare one of the places Wells gave all that money to after Pitman?"

Just mentioning Pitman made my skin crawl. That was where Del had died.

Doc nodded.

Rex screwed up his face. "You mean *Howard* Wells?"

Doc nodded again. "Pitman was such a public-relations disaster for Wellplant and H4H, Wells tried to buy his way out of it by giving OmniCare money to help care for chimeras."

I'd seen *that* on the news: Howard Wells saying he and H4H were *horrified* at what happened in Pitman, and making a big show of funding medical care for chimeras, as if he wasn't personally responsible for putting them in danger in the first place.

Rex shook his head with a bitter snort. "Imagine that. You push through a law that dehumanizes people, and then you claim to be surprised that those people are suddenly treated as less than human. I hate that guy."

I was mildly stunned to hear that. There were plenty of good reasons to hate Howard Wells, but while Rex was big and bad in his way, he wasn't about hate. The word didn't sound right coming from him.

"I hear you," said Doc. "If it makes you feel any better, Howard Wells is getting thumped on a number of fronts."

"What do you mean?"

"As much as he condemns what happened in Pitman, a lot of people don't believe he had nothing to do with it."

"Yeah," said Rex. "I'm one of them. What else?"

"His company might be in trouble, too."

I laughed. "Are you kidding? Wellplant's one of the biggest companies in the world. Did you see their holo-ad right before Christmas? And everyone's talking about how powerful the new upgrade is. The company's got to be growing like crazy right now."

"Maybe too fast," Doc said. "Some people think they're overextended, that they've taken on too much debt and can't fill their orders."

Rex laughed. "Good."

The blood analyzer dinged and Doc went over and pressed a button to print out the results. His frown returned and he shook his head. "This thing must not be working," he mumbled.

I wasn't surprised. It looked at least thirty years old.

Doc shut off the hyperbaric bed and undid the latches on the plastic bubble. Rex and I gathered behind him as he opened the lid. I didn't need confirmation from Doc to know what I was seeing.

Cornelius was dead.

Doc let out a soft whimper of sorrow and frustration. Rex put his arm around me. We stood there for a moment, quietly looking down at Cornelius's body.

Then the silence was shattered by a sharp bang at the front door. A voice barked out, "Open up! Police!"

All three of us froze as a second bang shook the entire building. Then the door exploded into a thousand shards of glass.

CHAPTER 4

Two cops entered, guns drawn. I didn't recognize either of them, and I was struck by the absurdity that my life had taken such a weird turn over the past few months that I might expect to know them at all.

"Freeze! Right there!" said the first officer, holding his gun in front of him with two hands. His name tag said RETZLAFF. He was the younger of the two, and judging from the deepening flush on his ruddy cheeks and the look in his wild blue eyes, the more excitable.

His partner was older, heavier, and calmer, his eyes half closed. The faint wrinkles on his olive skin made him seem almost grandfatherly—but not quite. His tag said TERASOVIC and his gun was pointed at the floor. He put out a hand and gently pushed Retzlaff's weapon down as well. The younger cop looked annoyed, but he went along with it.

Terasovic looked at Doc. "Is this your place? You're Guzman?"

Retzlaff kept his eyes on Rex. His entire body seemed tense.

Doc took off his glasses and polished them with his shirt. "Yes, that's right."

Terasovic turned toward the front door. "All right," he called. "Come on in here."

We heard footsteps on the broken glass, then Kurtz walked in, looking as messed-up, scared, and defiant as ever.

Terasovic pointed at Doc. "This is the guy you said, right?"

Kurtz glanced around the room, then down at his feet. "That's him, yeah."

"Mr. Guzman, Mr. Kurtz here says that you kidnaped his fiancée, a Ms. Bembry. Is that right, Mr. Kurtz?"

This time Kurtz didn't even look up. "Yes."

Terasovic looked around the lab, then looked at Doc. "Is it okay with you if we search the place?"

Before Doc could answer, Kurtz said, "She's not here."

"What's that?" Terasovic sounded vaguely perplexed. "I thought you told my partner here that this man abducted your fiancée." He glanced at Retzlaff with a hint of a scowl on his face. Retzlaff looked confused. His hands squirmed around the grip of his gun, like they were sweaty.

"Well, yeah, that's basically what happened," said Kurtz. "She disappeared without a trace, and this guy," he said, pointing, "so-called *Doctor* Guzman over here, was the last person to see her."

Terasovic took a deep breath. "And when was this?"

"Well, I just found out about that part," Kurtz said.

"When did she disappear?"

"October 15."

Terasovic rolled his eyes, then paused, thinking. "The day of the GHA riots?"

"Yeah, I guess so."

"And this girlfriend of yours—"

"Fiancée."

"This fiancée of yours, did she belong to Humans for Humanity or any related groups?"

"No way," Kurtz snapped. "She was a mixie."

Rex stiffened at the slur and Retzlaff tightened his grip on his gun.

Terasovic turned to Rex and said, "Sorry about that." Then he turned back to Kurtz. "Watch your tone, son. So you're saying your girlfriend was a chimera, and she went missing the day of the riots, and you think her disappearance has something to do with Mr. Guzman here?"

"Well, yeah, she just got spliced the night before and she went to see him to get it fixed, because it was stupid. I never saw her again, and he won't tell me what happened to her."

Terasovic's face was darkening. "Well, that's not exactly what you told my partner right before we came in here breaking down doors." He turned to Doc with a forced smile. "I'm sorry for the misunderstanding, Mr. Guzman. I just have to ask, *do* you have any information on the whereabouts of Ms. Claudia Bembry?"

Doc squinted and tilted his head, like he was trying to remember.

I don't know if it was an act or not, but I sure remembered her. I felt myself staring daggers at Kurtz. I had met Claudia that day in October when we were both looking for Doc Guzman. The reason she was trying to get her splice fixed was that her boyfriend—*Kurtz*, I now realized—had been supposed to get spliced alongside her, but once hers was underway, he backed out and ran away, leaving her alone to deal with the huge life change they'd been supposed to go through together, and right as all hell was breaking loose.

"Maybe she just doesn't like you anymore," I said. "Maybe she came to her senses and realized what an asshole you are."

"That's not true!" Kurtz yelled. "She loves me! We were supposed to get married!"

I rolled my eyes. "What are you, like, fifteen?"

Terasovic turned to me and said, "Miss, please. Unless you have information to share, please don't escalate the situation." He turned to Doc. "Mr. Guzman, does the name ring a bell? Do you have any information about Ms. Bembry's whereabouts?"

"No. I met her. I tried to help her but couldn't. As far as I know, she's with her parents."

"Okay, that's all I needed to know. Thanks for your cooperation. And I'm sorry for the inconvenience."

"That's it?" Kurtz practically shrieked. "That's all you're going to do?"

"Mr. Kurtz," Terasovic snapped, "have you even *spoken* to Ms. Bembry's parents?"

Kurtz tried to scowl, but it looked more like a pout. "They don't return my calls."

"Because you're an asshole," I muttered.

Kurtz and Terasovic both glared at me. Terasovic took out a business card and approached Doc. "Like I said, Mr. Guzman, we're sorry for the inconvenience." He looked around the clinic, then handed over his card. "You can file a claim with the county to get that door fixed. Just call the number right here, and make sure you have your deed and your property tax ID number."

He gave Doc a fake smile. It was obvious to all of us that no one was paying taxes on the place. Doc took the card anyway and slipped it into his shirt pocket. "Thank you."

Terasovic turned toward the door, motioning for Retzlaff and Kurtz to precede him, but as he did he stopped.

There was an odd expression on his face. He glanced back at Doc, and it took me a second to realize he was actually looking past him. At the hyperbaric bed. The condensation on the bubble had cleared enough that Cornelius's foot was visible.

"What's that?" Terasovic asked.

Doc didn't answer. Terasovic stepped around him, peered into the bubble, then let out a loud sigh, part sad, part victorious, part weary.

"Hands," he said to Doc, pulling out his cuffs.

"Wait, what's going on?" I said, but I knew what was going on. Cornelius was dead, and Doc was about to be blamed.

"Were these two involved?" Terasovic asked Doc as he put the cuffs on him.

"You can't arrest him," Rex said, moving toward them. "He didn't do anything wrong."

Retzlaff pointed his gun in Rex's direction, his hands shaking. Kurtz smiled—a smug, infuriating little smile.

"No, they weren't," Doc said. He looked up at Rex and shook his head, telling him not to interfere.

"Sorry, folks," Terasovic said. "I know you fixers think you're doing the right thing, and maybe sometimes you are. But performing unlicensed medical procedures is unlawful. I generally don't give a crap about that, but if someone dies because of it . . ." He put one hand on Doc's shoulder, the other on his cuffed hands. "Mr. Guzman, you are under arrest. For murder."

"This is crazy," I said.

Terasovic pointed at Kurtz. "You. Leave. If Ms. Bembry's parents want to file a report, they know where to find us." Kurtz vanished as Terasovic turned to Retzlaff and pointed at us. "Names and addresses, then get them out of here and tape the front and back doors. I'll take care of the suspect and call the crime-scene unit."

Rex said, "Doc?"

"It's okay," Doc replied. "Just tell Jerry to get me a lawyer."

As Retzlaff took down our info, Terasovic gave Doc a gentle shove and started marching him toward the front door, reading him his rights along the way.

CHAPTER 5

Retzlaff took our info, then he said, "Now get the hell out of here," and pushed us toward the door.

We reached the parking lot just as Terasovic was stuffing Doc into the back of the patrol car, his hand clamped over Doc's head.

Rex sighed and scanned our surroundings. I knew he was searching for Kurtz, but I also knew that kid was long gone.

"Come on," I said, tugging gently at Rex's sleeve. "We need to go."

"This is bullshit," he said, resisting me, his muscles taut, his voice strained.

"I know," I said. "That's why we need to get going. We need to tell Jerry what happened so we can get Doc a lawyer and straighten this out."

From the backseat, Doc looked out at us and flicked his head, indicating that we should get going. Then the car pulled into the road, crunching ice under its tires as it picked up speed. It stopped at the end of the block, just as a white van with MONTGOMERY COUNTY MEDICAL EXAMINER on the side appeared from the opposite direction. The two vehicles flicked their headlights in greeting. Then they passed each other and Doc was gone.

"Come on," I said quietly.

Rex nodded. We walked quickly past a dozen empty storefronts and an old gas station that looked like it hadn't even been repurposed before it was abandoned. Doc's clinic was about two miles from the nearest Levline stop. It was cold and getting late, and we had to cover some distance.

We were both runners, and without a word, we broke into a jog.

"I've been thinking about running with you, ever since the last time," Rex said, with a wistful smile. "I'd pictured better circumstances."

"Me too," I said. "Still nice, though."

He glanced down at me "Yeah. Sure is."

We were cutting through what had once been an expensive neighborhood, with big houses only three or four to a block. We passed one that had been kept up, a stone mansion with an iron fence, landscape lighting, even a fountain. It looked like an old French estate, except for an acre of solar collectors next door and a pair of quadcopters parked in the courtyard.

Another house, a couple of blocks farther, was almost as big. It had been turned into what looked like a pretty nice squat. The yard was filled with a cluster of mismatched solar collectors and a greenhouse made of plastic sheets. A woman was standing on the side porch, scraping table scraps onto a compost pile as we jogged by.

The other houses we passed were a little less grand and had been left to fall apart completely. The road was in bad shape, too, and with the ice and snow, we had to be extra careful where we stepped in the darkness, so neither of us twisted an ankle.

We ran in silence for a mile or so. I was thinking a lot about what had just happened to Cornelius and to Doc, and I knew Rex was, too.

"Poor Cornelius," I said aloud.

"Yeah," Rex said.

"And Doc, too."

"Yeah."

We were quiet again. Rex's one-word answers got me wondering what was going on in his head.

I had never thought of him as the mysterious type—which was good, because I *really* wasn't into the mysterious type. But right now, he was being mysterious. And I was finding it annoying.

I glanced at him as he ran, his eyes looking straight ahead, and I wondered again about our relationship. We hadn't been together long, but we had gone through a lot when we connected back in the fall.

It was right when GHA passed statewide and the anti-chimera movement was getting really ugly. Some of our friends with splices had been lured to a remote compound in the mountains called Haven with the promise that they'd ultimately be relocated to Chimerica, a supposed permanent refuge. Rex and I had been pretty sure Chimerica was BS. But Haven was real—and it turned out to be a deadly trap for chimeras, set up by some very sick people.

Uncovering all that and then losing Del—it had been awful.

But it had also led to Rex and me reconnecting, discovering a shared past as well as some pretty intense feelings for each other.

And then Rex had disappeared. When he resurfaced in my driveway a few weeks later, he told me Chimerica existed, but he wouldn't tell me any more about it right then.

It was almost Thanksgiving before I saw him again. I'd gone for a run after school, and Rex appeared next to me, silently, matching my stride.

Then, suddenly, we weren't running. He was holding me and kissing me and I didn't want to let go of him. Because I knew he'd be leaving again. I could feel it.

"I can't stay long," he'd said, when our lips regained circulation.

"How long?"

I half expected him to say a few minutes, like last time, so I was actually relieved when he said, "Just tonight."

"Where have you been?" I asked. "Where are you going? What's the deal with Chimerica?"

I saw pain in his eyes, pain you couldn't fake.

"Are you in trouble?" I asked.

"No, it's just . . . I can't get into it."

In the moment, I let it go. I was just so happy to see him. That night we went out to dinner; I assumed we'd go to New Ground, but Rex said he didn't want to see anyone else. Just me.

We took the Levline into the city and back out to the Chestnut Hill historic district. The Night Kitchen was a restaurant that had been around forever, and it was magical. The food was amazing, and the people were super nice. No one judged us or messed with us.

We talked as if we'd never been apart—not for the weeks since I'd last seen him, or for the years since we were little kids and I'd known him as Leo Byron. It was unseasonably warm, and after dinner we sat outside, right on Germantown Avenue. A cop car drove by, and Rex watched it, unperturbed. He saw me looking at him, and he smiled.

"Just so you know, I'm no longer a wanted man," he said.

"What do you mean?" I asked. On top of everything else, Rex had been accused of robbing—*had* robbed—a deli for money to help me try to get Del's bad splice fixed.

"Genaro died, so the charges were dropped." Genaro was the mean and bigoted old owner of the deli.

"What? How did I not know this? He *died*?"

Rex nodded. "Peacefully. Or at least, in his sleep." He smiled sadly. "I don't know if he was ever really at peace. Hopefully he is now."

"What about 'flight from arrest' or whatever? Disappearing from the back of that police car?"

He shrugged. "If I ever get arrested for something else, they might throw that on top. But for all intents and purposes, it's done."

I grinned and poked his shoulder. "So I guess the crafty accomplice who helped you escape should have nothing to worry about?"

He laughed. "I will take the secret of my crafty accomplice's identity to my grave."

I hadn't actually been worried about my own arrest, but this was still a relief to hear.

"So . . ." I paused for a split second before deciding to try again. "Where have you been all this time, then?" I asked. "What have you been doing?"

He'd been smiling playfully almost the whole time we'd been there, but now his smile faltered. "Jimi, I—I can't say."

"What do you mean, you can't say? Says who?"

He slowly shook his head, and lowered his voice even further. "I can't say that either."

"So . . . you can't tell me where you're going next, either?"

"No. I'm sorry. I really wish I could. I hope you believe me." He looked stricken.

"Right." I wasn't going to beg or cajole or nag, but I couldn't resist the slight chill that crept into my attitude.

The rest of that evening was nice, but not as nice as it would have been if his secrets hadn't been hanging over us.

They still hung over us.

"Have you seen Sly?" I said as we ran through the icy night.

Rex turned to look at me, confused.

I glanced at him and shrugged, then went back to looking where I was going. "I just figured you've been gone, he's been gone, maybe you two had seen each other."

He turned to look at me in the darkness for so long that he almost stumbled. "I—I'm sorry, Jimi. You don't know how sorry. I'm just . . . I'm trying to do my part to help make the world safe for chimeras, and for everyone." He said it like he was reciting a pledge. "I wish I could tell you more than that, but I can't."

"Okay, whatever. It's fine," I said. I tried to sound nonchalant but I could feel my face growing hot. I started jogging a tiny bit faster, and Rex had the decency to let me run a few steps ahead, at least until my face felt like maybe it was back to its normal color.

Half a block later, he pulled up next to me. We didn't speak, and it felt awkward, like we were both trying to achieve the kind of comfortable silence we'd shared in the past.

We rounded a curve, and a few blocks up ahead I saw the light from North Avenue, which separated the zurbs from the city.

Rex turned to me and cocked an eyebrow. I didn't know what he was getting at, but then he started running faster. I matched his pace, and then he started running faster still. I caught up again, and then he turned, grinning, and took off like a shot. It was an obvious attempt to coax me out of my frustration, and I shook my head, but I also laughed and tore after him. I couldn't tell if he was running full out, but I was and it felt great.

Ahead of us, the blur of headlights and the whoosh of speeding cars on North Avenue stopped. The crossing light had turned green and the timer was ticking down. We were so far away there was no chance we would make it, but we were running flat out and neither of us slowed. By the time I caught up with him, we were just a few feet from the intersection. The crossing light turned red again and the cars shot forward. We both tried to stop, but Rex's feet lost traction on the ice and he went into a slide, his momentum propelling him toward the traffic.

For an instant, I thought he was going to die. My heart shot into my throat as I grabbed him under the arms, but I was standing on the ice, too, and his mass took me with him. I dug in my heels and pulled back as hard as I could.

Somehow I managed to stop our forward motion, but with my arms tangled in Rex's, there was nothing I could do to stop falling, or to stop Rex from landing on top of me. I braced myself for impact, doing my best to keep my head from cracking against the icy concrete.

I hit the ground hard, flat on my back, then Rex hit *me* even harder, smooshing the air out of my lungs. I struggled to regain my breath, and as he scrambled off me, I took a big gulp of air.

"Jimi!" he said, crawling over, and bracing his arms on either side of me. "Are you okay?" Cars were speeding past, inches from where we lay.

I took another gulp of air, trying to breathe and trying not to laugh.

He looked confused at my expression, until I managed to say, "Caught . . . between a Rex . . . and a hard place." Then the laughter won out, which really didn't help with the whole breathing thing.

Rex's head sagged and he groaned with a crooked smile. "I guess you're okay, then."

I held up my hand and teetered it back and forth.

"Thanks for the save," he said, tipping his head at the traffic that he had almost fallen under.

"I owed you one," I said.

Our smiles faded as we looked into each other's eyes, suddenly very serious.

We hadn't really had a proper "hello" since he returned. So, as the torrent of cars roared past us, I put my arm around his neck and pulled myself up to him, put my lips against his, and said hello. Properly.

A few of the vehicles honked at us, but they were moving so fast their horns were more like blips than blasts. I didn't care. Rex didn't either. Between us, in our little bubble, there was both absolute calm and absolute electricity.

I don't know how long we stayed there like that, but by the time we parted, the crossing light was green again.

Rex rose to his feet and lifted me to mine. I laughed and started running again, across the avenue. Rex laughed, too, as he ran after me, but I didn't look back and he didn't catch up until we reached the Levline station.

When I turned and plopped down on the cold steel steps, he was still twenty feet behind me, his face contorted with the effort of not grinning. He slowed for the last few steps, white clouds of condensation billowing with each breath, then he sat down on the steps next to me.

I leaned against him and put my arm around him.

"I've missed you, Jimi Corcoran," he said.

"I've missed you, too," I told him.

A high-pitched whine descended out of the black sky, and without a word we scurried up the steps to the platform as the Lev train pulled in.

It was late enough that fewer than a dozen people were in our car, most of them in their own little worlds. But with a dozen people, you were almost guaranteed to have a couple of jerks, and as we took our seats, I spotted them, directly across from us. One had tinted contacts and the other a patchy beard, both sneering and making a show of staring at us.

I looked away from them.

Across from me was a poster for a band called Menagerie. Their lead singer was a chimera with a snow leopard splice. They had a big hit with a song called "Earth for Everyone."

The music was a bit too pop for my tastes, and some people thought the band was just cashing in, but it had a catchy beat and a good message, and it was encouraging to see a major label getting behind a chimera band. It was less encouraging to see that someone had scratched out the lead singer's eyes and drawn an arrow going through her head, and someone else had written MIXIE MUSIC SUCKS across the rest of the group.

I looked out the window, instead, at the darkened buildings and lighted streets whizzing past. Rising above them a few blocks away, lit from below and gleaming in the night sky, was a huge golden cross with a garish H4H emblem at the center, taking up nearly half of it. My heart sank a little. The whole city had been talking about it, but this was the first time I'd seen it in person since it was erected on top of the Church of the Eternal Truth, otherwise known as H4H Central.

The church was already pretty unpopular among a lot of people who opposed their anti-chimera rhetoric. Now they were offending even more people in the mainstream religious community. Several denominations had spoken out against the way Eternal Truth twisted the Bible to suit the H4H agenda, but they were aghast at the giant H4H logo that now sat on top of the church, at least as prominent as the cross it was incorporated into.

But not everyone was unhappy with them. Since GHA passed, Eternal Truth had been bringing in money by the truckload. Enough to pay for the cross, as well as a huge addition to their building, a bigger and brighter sign out front, and anti-chimera Holovid commercials and billboards around the city.

The Genetic Heritage Act may have been partially blocked, but the people who supported it had revealed themselves. And there were a lot of them.

It seemed to me that the people who thought these H4Hers were ignorant bigots needed to show themselves, too. To stand up and be counted instead of quietly shaking their heads in disgust.

Reflected in the window I could see the two jerks still staring at me and Rex. I turned and stared back at them. Then I pulled Rex's head around, raised myself up off my seat, and put a wet kiss right on his lips.

Rex looked down at me, half smiling, half annoyed. He knew I had done it at least partially to aggravate the pair across from us. He didn't usually approve of provoking people like that, even obvious jerks. But I think the fact that it was in the form of a kiss helped.

The jerks looked away from us for the remaining few minutes of the trip. We got off back in Silver Garden, and hoofed it up the same hill I'd climbed less than two hours earlier.

The light over the sign in front of New Ground went out just as we got there. I ran up and found the door locked. I banged on it, hard.

"Easy," Rex said, coming up beside me. "Don't break it in."

After a brief moment of keys scratching the other side of the door, it was yanked open, replaced by Jerry's red face.

"*What?*" he demanded. "You almost gave me a heart attack banging like that."

"Doc's been arrested. He needs a lawyer," I said.

Jerry's shoulder's slumped. "What now?"

"It's serious," Rex said. "It's murder."

CHAPTER 6

Rex and I sat with Jerry in the back office while he called a series of people at Earth for Everyone. The E4E staff was transferring him to this person and that, trying to figure out which lawyer could take the case. Not surprisingly, the legal fight over GHA was taking up a lot of their attorneys' time. Finding someone who was free was going to be difficult.

At one point, someone put him on hold for what seemed like twenty minutes. In the lull, something that Doc had said came back to me. Jerry seemed to sense it. Maybe he saw a strange look on my face. He turned to me. "What is it?"

"You told me Claudia Bembry got her splice fixed."

"Who's Claudia Bembry?"

"The girl who was here after the riots last fall, when we brought Ryan."

"Oh. Yeah. So?"

"You told me she got her splice fixed."

"And?"

"She didn't."

"Huh. I thought she did. She seemed okay. She even fixed my espresso system."

"Doc said he tried to help her but he couldn't and then her parents came and got her."

"Oh."

"Oh?"

"Look, kid, there was a lot going on those days, including Ryan dying in my office and you guys heading out to Pitman. Sorry if my health updates on someone I barely met weren't up to your standards of accuracy. All I know is, Doc treated her, and when I got back from

Pitman, her parents had already come and gotten her. Oh wait, I do know one other thing: you're a pain in my ass."

Rex was looking anywhere but at me this whole time, mostly at his shoes or the ceiling. I don't think Jerry was done with me, but at that point, mercifully, someone picked up on the line.

"Yeah," Jerry said. "I'm waiting to be connected to a Marcella DeWitt. . . . Oh, hello, Ms. DeWitt, I'm very sorry to have woken you. . . . That's right, this is about Hector Guzman."

I could tell from what Jerry was saying that she was trying to deflect like all the others—this wasn't her specialty, she was too busy working on the GHA stuff in addition to her regular job. Maybe it was because she was groggy or maybe because Jerry was just getting good at his spiel, but I could tell based on his end of the conversation that she'd relented and would be going to the police station first thing in the morning.

I checked my watch, figuring it must be close to midnight, and was stunned to see it was barely ten o'clock. DeWitt had the right idea. I yawned, wide and long, and drew looks from both Rex and Jerry that seemed oddly appreciative, like they were impressed by the magnitude.

"Sorry," I said.

Almost immediately Rex and Jerry were fighting off yawns of their own.

"All right," Jerry said, exhaling loudly. "There's nothing more we can do tonight, but DeWitt's going to want to talk to the two of you tomorrow, since you were there when Doc was arrested. For now, you need to get the hell out of here so I can finish closing up."

We were quiet walking back to the Levline, and after we got on the train, too. There were only three other people in the car with us, and none of them were H4H jerks.

"Where are you staying?" I asked Rex after a couple of stops.

"Near Doc's place. Jerry set me up." He reached over and took my hand in his. It was massive, but it felt just right.

"Then why are you coming all the way out here? You're going to have to get right back on the train and double back."

He shrugged. "It's late. You're alone."

"I can take care of myself."

"Okay. Well . . . it's been a while since I've seen you, and I want to spend more time with you."

I reached over and patted his knee. "See? Now *that's* a good reason."

I slid a little closer and leaned my head against his shoulder. We'd be at Oakton in just a few minutes, but I closed my eyes anyway, enjoying the feeling of Rex by my side. As I did, though, a flood of images from the previous few hours washed over me.

"Did you know about Claudia?" I asked suddenly.

"What, that she was still a chimera?"

"Yeah."

"I don't think so. I don't know. I never met her, so if I heard anything, I probably wouldn't have thought about it."

"Right." I felt bad having gotten on Jerry's case about it, but it was upsetting. I'd seen how badly Claudia had wanted to get her splice fixed, and all this time I thought she had, and that she had gone back to her old life, the one that she'd been so afraid of losing. I thought she was happy.

I allowed myself a slight smile. At least she wasn't still with her idiot ex-boyfriend, Kurtz. I wondered what she could possibly have seen in him in the first place.

I thought back to when I first met Claudia, just hours after she'd been spliced—scared and alone, wandering through the city looking for Doc Guzman just as all those morons were out there rioting, threatening chimeras. But she was a rock. She was upset, sure, but she kept it together even when it looked like getting her splice fixed was hopeless—which, as it turns out, it was. And she didn't miss a beat when we found Ryan, bleeding and dying, or when we had to carry him back to the coffee shop.

The girl had an inner strength. I felt reassured by it. Claudia would be okay no matter what. I just wished her life had been more like what she hoped it would be.

As the train slowed to a stop at Oakton, we got to our feet. Rex put his arm around my shoulder, holding me close. We walked down the steps to street level, then walked along the sidewalk, under the tracks, to the steps on the other side.

I started up, but Rex didn't seem like he wanted to.

"Aren't you going back?" I said.

"I'll walk you home first."

"It's just a few blocks," I said, reaching up to touch his face. "I'll be fine, and you've got to go all the way back."

"But—"

"Besides," I said, biting back a smile, "you had a long day, coming back from . . . where was it again?"

He started to hedge, then he realized that this time I was messing with him. He started to laugh. His eyes sparkled.

I laughed, too. "I'll see you in the morning, okay?"

He stifled another yawn. "Yeah, okay."

A far-off whine announced the approach of the Lev train coming the other way.

"Well, thanks for a memorable evening," I said.

"You, too." He came in for a kiss, and lingered with it, long enough that I was worried the train would arrive and leave without him. We parted as the train pulled up to the platform above.

Rex added one last kiss and said, "See you tomorrow." Then he dashed up the steps, each footfall sending a wispy cloud of ice particles cascading from the steps.

Then the train pulled away, and I was alone.

CHAPTER 7

It was late and it was cold and I was just a few blocks from home, but suddenly I felt creeped out. Again. And it wasn't because I was alone, it was because I felt like I *wasn't*. Just like earlier, when I felt as if I was being watched. I knew it was ridiculous, but I still couldn't shake it.

Well, if there's really no one watching, I thought, *then no one will see me running home scared*. I took off, resisting the urge to look over my shoulder until I came to a stop in front of my house, four minutes later. Warm light spilled from the windows, painting the icy ground a soft, pale gold. I paused before I went inside, standing in the driveway that separated our house from the one next door.

The windows there were black and empty. The house screamed of vacancy.

For my entire life, it had been the home of my friend Del. Now it was empty.

As far as anyone knew, the house still belonged to Stan Grainger, Del's dad. But no one had seen Stan in three months—apparently not even the police department where he used to work, out in the zurbs. No one had seen him since the night he shot and killed his own son.

He hadn't even been arrested. Some tried to turn him into a hero—Howard Wells, H4H, even some of the same media that called me a hero. He was an off-duty officer of the law who shot his own son rather than let him endanger the innocent people of Pitman. That account might have been partly true. But it was still murder.

I was glad Stan had disappeared. I couldn't have lived there knowing he was still next door. The thought that he could return any day was bad enough.

I jogged up our back steps, through the back door, and into the kitchen.

I could see my mom in the living room, engrossed in a book. A cup of tea sat by her elbow on the end table. If the book was any good, the tea had probably gone cold hours earlier.

I went into the living room and paused at the bottom of the stairs, leaning on the bannister. The room felt kind of cramped with the Christmas tree still up.

"Hi, sweetie," Mom said, looking up. "Did you have a nice time?"

"Yeah, I did," I said, feeling guilty not saying more, but absolutely confident I did not want to get into what had just gone down, at least not now. "It was fun."

I retreated into the kitchen for a glass of water, thinking about how hard we'd been working to rebuild the trust between us after the events of that fall. The lies I'd told were bald-faced, meant to protect my friends. Hers were more lies of omission about our family, meant to honor my father's wishes.

I wouldn't have even found out about them if Aunt Trudy hadn't spilled the beans that I had an aunt I didn't know of—Dymphna Corcoran—whom I was *named after*.

I had been furious when I confronted Mom about it, but she explained it was my dad's idea to cut his sister out of our lives, to pretend she didn't exist. When I was two, there'd been a big family fight, and Dymphna had become persona non grata. I grew up not remembering anything about her.

When Mom finally talked to me about Aunt Dymphna, she actually couldn't hide the admiration in her voice. Dymphna sounded like quite a character: a scientist and perpetual student, with degrees in everything from microbiology and epidemiology to chemistry and information technology. She was also an activist—an environmentalist and animal rights advocate. Apparently, Grandma and Grandpa weren't crazy about that. Then she got arrested—my mom swore she didn't know what for, and Trudy backed her up on that—and she went into hiding.

My grandparents were furious and heartbroken. They both died within a couple of months, and my dad never forgave Dymphna. She didn't even come back for the funerals, and he never forgave her for that, either.

From that point on, no more Dymphna.

Mom said that after Dad died, she just kept on honoring his wishes.

I was still mad, but I kind of understood. Mom had been in a tough spot, and my dad had been pretty clear about what he wanted.

But between my lies and her lies, our relationship had suffered.

Now that we were finally pretty much back on track, I felt guilty all over again about not sharing more about tonight. But apart from anything else, it was late and I was tired.

"It was fun" was about as much detail as I had energy for.

I came out of the kitchen and started to say good night, but Mom closed the book around her finger and slid it between her thigh and the arm of the chair. That was okay: a finger meant a short conversation. A bookmark would have meant a long one.

"How about . . . Rex?" she said. "Was he there?"

She paused every time she said his name, but at least she was saying it. That was progress. Up until recently, she had insisted on calling him Leo.

My mom wasn't sure about Rex, and I really couldn't blame her. I knew she was a little put off by his decision to get spliced. I understood—I mean, just a few months earlier I had tried pretty hard to stop Del from doing the same thing. But I know a lot of her concerns had less to do with Rex's splice and more to do with the fact that, in her mind, Rex was also the guy who'd robbed Genaro's Deli. Rex was the guy who, after all he and I had been through together, and everything we supposedly felt for each other, practically disappeared for three months, without telling me where he'd been or why he'd been gone. That worried her, and I understood.

I trusted Rex, the way you trust someone because you believe the best about them, and everything they do confirms that belief. But all that trust notwithstanding, I shared some of my mom's concerns. Not that I would ever say it aloud. And frankly, I found it annoying having to defend the very things about Rex that were currently bugging the hell out of me.

"Yeah, he was there," I told her. "It was really good to see him."

"I bet. It's been so long. How did he seem?"

"He was good. He was Rex." When I said it I realized it was true, and I smiled. He was Rex, and as messed-up as the night had been, it still really *had* been amazing to see him.

"Okay," I said. "I'm gonna read and then get some sleep."

"Good night, sweetie," she said, opening her book. "Don't forget, I'll be leaving first thing in the morning."

I hadn't forgotten, but it had been quite a night, and for a moment maybe it had slipped my mind.

"Skiing, remember?" she said when I paused. Her smile had a vaguely accusatory cast to it. "With Aunt Trudy? Because *someone* thought it would be a good idea for us to do something together?"

I laughed. I loved Trudy, and I think my mom did, too, in a way, but they were very, very different. Plus, as much as my mom apologized for not telling me about Aunt Dymphna, I think she was irked at Trudy for not keeping the secret.

My mom scowled at my grin.

"Oh, come on," I said. "It'll be fun."

"Well, it'll be nice to get away for a bit," she said. "Kevin's in charge until I get back, but you need to make sure you're ready for school on Monday morning, okay?"

"Kevin's 'in charge'?" I laughed again, but this time with more of an edge. My brother was a good guy and I loved him, but he was a bit of a meathead. "So, if I want to eat some cookies or watch a scary movie I should ask his permission?"

"Oh, Jimi, of course not. Don't be silly. Just let him know what you're up to so someone always knows where you are. He should do the same for you."

"Yup, you're right," I said. "That is silly."

She waved her hand, dismissing the comment. "Anyway, we're leaving at six thirty. If you're up, you should come down to say hi to Trudy."

"I'll check with Kevin and see if I'm allowed."

"Jimi . . ."

"Okay, okay. See you in the morning."

I turned and went upstairs, passing Kevin's room on my way to my own.

He was lying on his bed with his ear buds on, drumming his hands on his belly with no apparent rhythm or pattern. Clothes, gym bags, grimy balls of used athletic tape, and at least three empty Gatorade bottles littered the floor. There was a smudged glass on his bedside table with a couple of inches of discolored orange juice at the bottom and several rings above from where it had evaporated away. The glass had been there since the beginning of winter break.

And this was the guy who was in charge. This was the guy who, just a few weeks ago when I had asked him about the whole Aunt Dymphna thing, said, "Oh yeah! I forgot about her."

I couldn't believe it. "You *forgot* you had another *aunt*?"

To be fair, if I'd been two, he'd only been three, but then he said, "I didn't know she was a *real* aunt. I thought she was one of dad's work friends, like Uncle Bill. Remember Uncle Bill?"

When we were little, my dad's boss had insisted we call him Uncle Bill, which even then I thought was kind of weird. But Kevin was missing the bigger picture.

"So the fact that her name and my name are both Dymphna . . . ," I said. "You thought that was just . . . a coincidence?"

"What? It's not that unusual."

Dymphna was *totally* that unusual.

I was shaking my head at the memory of it when Kevin looked over and took out an ear bud. "What?"

"Nothing." I rolled my eyes and went into my room. To be honest, it didn't look much better. But I had an excuse. I'd been redecorating, taking down all the little-kid stuff that had been cluttering my walls and surfaces, and putting it all in a box.

I hadn't decided what to replace it with yet. At this point the only thing on the walls was a framed antique David Bowie poster Aunt Trudy had gotten me for Christmas. I loved it, but now I really felt the pressure to get some other stuff up there, quick, so it didn't seem like that was my only interest.

On the floor by my desk, there was a huge Earth for Everyone sign I'd bought at a fundraiser after Thanksgiving. It had the E4E logo on it, and behind that, the H4H logo with a red line through it. I liked the sentiment, but the poster was kind of ugly. I'd probably put it up anyway, eventually.

As I changed into my pajamas, I thought I caught a whiff of Kevin's room, but I realized, to my horror, it was me. After all that running, I needed a shower before bed. By the time I finally climbed under the covers, I was too tired to concentrate on a book. Instead I lay there, staring at the blank walls, and at David Bowie, who seemed almost disapproving that I'd left him alone up there. My eyes found the box of old posters and photos and figurines I'd taken down. Part of me wanted to pull it closer and look through it all. But I'd already decided I was moving on. Instead, I turned out the light and went to sleep.

CHAPTER 8

I woke up in the early morning darkness to the sound of my mom's suitcase banging against my door. Twice. I'd told her I'd get up to see her and Trudy off, but I suspected she'd *thunk*ed my door to make extra sure of it.

I pulled on a sweatshirt and hurried downstairs so I wouldn't miss them. If I was getting up this early, I wanted to get credit for it.

Mom and Trudy were sitting at the kitchen table, drinking coffee. When she saw me, Trudy glanced at my mom over her mug with an impish look that confirmed my suspicions that Mom had been intentionally loud.

"Oh, you're up," my mom said, feigning surprise.

"Yes, I heard you," I said, pouring myself a cup of coffee. "I'm surprised Kevin's not awake too."

"Oh, you know Kevin," Mom said. "He'd sleep through a herd of elephants."

"Yeah, I know," I said, sipping my coffee. "I'm pretty sure I just heard one."

Trudy snorted. "Well, I'm glad you're up. Full confession: I told your mom I wanted to see you before we left. And she said she'd wake you."

My mom rolled her eyes. "Thanks, Trudy."

"That's okay," I said, "it's not like I only have a few days of winter break left to sleep in, or anything." I offset my sarcasm with a kiss on Trudy's cheek.

"Any big weekend plans?" Trudy asked.

"Not really," I said, flashing my mom a sidelong glance. "I'll probably just watch some scary movies and eat lots of cookies."

Trudy looked at my mom, curious.

"Rex is back," my mom said, ignoring me.

"Oh," Trudy said, then, "*Ohhhh*," as if some deeper implications were sinking in.

I had to fight back a laugh as my mom blanched, as if she was suddenly realizing that Rex was in town and she was about to *not* be.

"When did he get back?" Trudy asked me.

"Last night."

"Did you see him?"

"Yup."

"And how was that?"

"Good."

She paused, as if weighing whether she could get away with one more question before we crossed the line from conversation into interrogation. "He's been gone awhile. Where has he been, anyway?"

Mom lowered her coffee cup, looking at me expectantly.

"I don't know," I said, trying to sound casual.

Trudy glanced at my mom, and seemed to realize she'd stepped into the middle of something. "Oh. Well . . . sounds very mysterious."

"Yup."

After an appropriately awkward moment of silence, they both finished their coffees and started making noise about how they really should be hitting the road.

I wholeheartedly agreed.

Mom hugged me and told me to stay out of trouble. Trudy hugged me and told me to have fun. Then they were gone.

I took my coffee back to my room and snuggled back under the covers, thinking about Rex, and how after the quiet normalcy of the past few months, and all of my efforts to reestablish trust with my mom, almost immediately after his return I was involved in drama: fights, guns, arrests, and even death. And I was essentially lying to my mom by not telling her about it.

None of it was Rex's fault. I knew that. But trouble sure seemed to follow him.

I realized that sometimes trouble came from not running away from a fight. From standing up for what you believed in. From sticking up for your friends. The kind of trouble that followed Rex was the same kind of trouble that had found me three months ago. And maybe it was all part of him being the kind of guy I liked as much as I did.

I set my mug on my bedside table and closed my eyes. When I opened them again, the sun had risen. I could tell by the light coming in through my window that it had snowed again. A glance outside confirmed it.

I went downstairs and emptied the cold, burnt coffee in the coffeemaker and put on a fresh pot.

Kevin was in the living room watching Holovid Sports. A panel of middle-aged former athletes were arguing about what the current crop of athletes would achieve later on that day.

"Hey," I called out. "I'm making coffee. You want some?"

"There's a pot in there," he called back. "Mom made some."

"It's cold and gross."

"Just microwave it."

I stepped into the dining room so I could see him. Sure enough, he was drinking a huge cup of the sludge.

I ate a banana while I waited, and when the coffee was done I poured myself a cup. Kevin came into the kitchen as I was savoring my first sip.

"See?" he said. "It's fine."

He poured himself the rest of it, microwaved it unnecessarily, and headed back into the living room, slurping as he went. "You're crazy," he said over his shoulder. "This tastes great."

"Amazing," I said.

I went upstairs to get dressed, and the phone rang as I was coming back down. Kevin answered it just as I reached the bottom of the steps.

"Hello?" he said, then glanced up at me with a smirk. "Well, I'm not sure if she's here," he said, his voice gravelly in an exaggerated imitation of Rex. "Can I ask who's calling?"

I stormed toward him, scowling, and he held the phone out to me.

"It's Rex," he said, trying to maintain the low voice while cracking himself up.

I snatched the phone and mouthed the word *asshole* to him before taking a breath and putting the phone to my ear. "Hello?"

"So that's Kevin, huh?" Rex said.

"Afraid so."

"He's every bit as charming as when we were little."

"Yes," I said, projecting my voice into the living room, "He *is* a total jerkwad with no redeeming qualities."

Kevin flipped me off in reply.

I looked at the display on the phone. "Is this your new number?"

"Yeah. For a little while at least."

I entered it into the phone's memory, then turned toward the kitchen and lowered my voice. "So how's it going?"

"Okay, I guess. Jerry talked with that lawyer, DeWitt. She wants to meet with us here at Doc's place. Can you make it?"

"When?"

"In an hour."

"Yeah, I can do that."

"Good. You okay?"

"Me? Yeah, I'm fine. Look, Rex, about last night, asking you where—"

"No, don't apologize," he said. "I'm sorry I have to keep so many secrets right now."

"So many? How many others are there?" I half laughed, because I was only half joking.

He chuckled in reply, as if I were completely joking. "Okay. I'll see you then, right?"

Hahaha. "Yeah, I'll see you then."

I went to grab my jacket, hat, and gloves. When I returned to the living room, Kevin was still sitting on the couch.

"I'm going out," I said.

"Where?" he said without looking up.

"Oh, please."

Kevin just shrugged, which got him partial credit. "I'm out tonight," he said, "so you're on your own for dinner." Then he went back to his sports show, and I went out the back door.

The sun was bright, the sky was a clear, cold blue, and the fresh snow was sparkling. I took a deep, bracing breath, and set off for the Levline.

A couple of houses I passed already had Christmas trees out, waiting to be recycled.

These days, I was ambivalent about Christmas. It used to be my favorite holiday, but ever since my dad died, there had been an undeniable sadness to it, as well. At this point it felt like part of the tradition.

I always felt a slight relief when Christmas was over, but in a way that was the saddest part: one more Christmas without my dad. One more year of me growing up without him. Deep down I felt guilty, as if somehow I was responsible for letting the time go by without him.

New Year's was easier. It always felt kind of arbitrary—how do you decide the beginning and end of a circle?—but I appreciated the idea of a new beginning.

The sun disappeared behind a low, fast-moving mass of gray clouds that brought with it a squall of snow, suddenly transforming everything I could see. I looked around to make sure I was alone, then I caught a snowflake on my tongue, like my dad had taught me to do.

The squall continued as I walked the next three blocks, even as the sun broke through a few times, which only made the display more dazzling. As I turned the corner and saw the Lev station up ahead and a couple of cars dropping people off, the snow abruptly stopped. The entire time it had been falling, I hadn't seen a single soul. I couldn't help smiling at the thought that it had been just for me.

CHAPTER 9

When I got off the Lev train in Silver Garden just a few minutes later, the new snow was already turning to gray slush. As I walked from the station, I recognized parts of the neighborhood from the one time I had been to Doc's house before. His entire block sat in the shadow of an old factory converted to apartments. I found his house without too much trouble, a tiny brick bungalow with an equally tiny porch that somehow managed to wrap around the side.

I kicked the slush off my boots and knocked on the door.

Rex opened it almost immediately. "Hey," he said, with a gratifying grin. "Come on in."

"Hey," I said, squeezing passed him.

I was shocked to see Doc himself sitting at a small dining room table with a woman I didn't recognize—presumably the lawyer.

"Doc!" I said. "You're out!"

He gave me a slight, weary smile and tipped his head. "Thanks to Ms. DeWitt over here." His face was bruised and he had a cut on his lip and another one over his eye.

"What happened to your face? Did the police do that to you?"

He shook his head. "Some of the more vehement chimera-haters in the prison population."

"Are you okay?"

He nodded. "Again, thanks to Ms. DeWitt."

She shook her head and waved away the compliment. "I just got him bail. But it was a fight. The prosecutor went on and on saying some shadowy network of chimeras could be poised to whisk him away at any moment. That's why the bail was so high. They're going to fight us on everything, so we've got a lot of work to do."

She looked about forty, with dark skin, hair styled into a short bob, and a no-nonsense intensity about her. She also seemed exhausted.

"Well, I'm just glad to be out of there," Doc said. He seemed kind of stunned, and I wondered how scary it had been, in jail. I knew it wasn't his first time, but this was for murder.

Rex put a hand on his shoulder.

"Ms. DeWitt has been working with Earth for Everyone on getting the Genetic Heritage Act thrown out," Doc said. "She took time away from that to do this."

"It's still blocked, right?" I asked.

"The injunction is still standing," she said, "but there's a lot of political pressure on the judge to reverse it. We're trying to get the whole thing thrown out." She laughed bitterly. "Never thought I'd have to argue points that were so *self-evident* in a court of law. . . . But back to the matter at hand. Mr. Guzman here—"

"Doctor Guzman," Rex said, correcting her.

Doc held up a hand and DeWitt gave Rex a stern look. "No," she said sharply. "*Mister* Guzman was decertified eleven years ago."

"Well, yeah, but—"

"He is not *Doctor* Guzman, and presenting himself as such goes to the heart of the government's case against him—practicing without a license. Each time you call him Doc or refer to him as a doctor strengthens their case. Call him Hector, call him Guzman, call him Mad Dog, I don't care. But do not call him Doc. Is that understood?"

Rex and I turned to Doc, and he nodded. "Don't call me Hector," he said. "I hate that name. Guzman is fine."

DeWitt picked up a few folders and rearranged them, pulling one to the top and opening it. "Okay, we should get started. You kids can come and sit right here." She motioned us toward two empty chairs.

"Did you contact that OmniCare place?" I asked. "To find out what happened to Cornelius there?"

DeWitt paused for a second, closing her eyes and taking a deep breath, like she was summoning patience. My mom did the same thing when she was being patronizing, usually right before she explained to me why whatever I had just told her—but that she hadn't really listened to—was ridiculous.

"Yes, we did," she said. "The police contacted them last night and I followed up this morning. We sent them a scan of the bracelet and a photo of Cornelius." She put printouts of both on the table. "They said they have no record of him being there, no history of any patient named Cornelius, and no such ID number in their system. A dead end. Now then, shall we get started?" She took out what looked like a pen, but when she clicked it, a line of light appeared running along the length of it and I realized it was a virtual keyboard. When she laid it down, a rectangular display appeared in the air above it and a pretty convincing keyboard appeared on the surface of the table. It was top of the line. Her fingers hovered above it. "First, your names. Jimi Corcoran, is that the name on your birth certificate?"

"No, it's Dymphna Corcoran," I said. Then I spelled it out, because that's what you do when your name is Dymphna Corcoran.

DeWitt raised an eyebrow, but she got points for typing it in without asking me what it meant or anything. She turned to Rex. "And Rex, what is your full name?"

He shrugged. "Just Rex."

She nodded slowly. "Is that the name on your birth certificate?"

Rex glanced at me, then looked at DeWitt and said, "No. It's Leo Byron."

"Okay, technically, we should be doing this separately, but I simply don't have the time. I want you both to tell me exactly what happened the night Cornelius died."

I went first, starting with Doc arriving at the coffee shop. I didn't mention his breakthrough with the cord-blood thing. When I got to the part about what happened at his clinic, I paused and looked over at him. He nodded and I continued, telling it exactly as it went down.

When I was finished, Rex recounted pretty much the same story. He added that he had arranged to meet Doc a half hour earlier, but that Doc had been late, because Kurtz had been harassing him.

When he was done, DeWitt sat back with a sigh. "Well, clearly Mr. Guzman did perform medical procedures on the deceased. It's going to be a very tough case to defend."

A silence settled over us, part thoughtful, part defeated.

"I could lie," I said, and everybody looked at me.

"I beg your pardon?" DeWitt said, sounding as if she hadn't heard me, but looking as if she had, and really didn't like what I'd said.

"I could lie," I repeated. "I could say Doc—I mean Guzman—didn't do the things he shouldn't have done, according to the case. Rex—Leo, I mean—we both could."

DeWitt sat back and rubbed her eyes, careful not to smudge her makeup. "No," she said, shaking her head. "No, no, *no*. Apart from the fact that perjury is illegal and as an officer of the court I could never condone it, lying is hard. And don't take this the wrong way, because it's a compliment, really, but frankly I don't think either of you would know how to do it. As hard as it is for one person to lie, it's almost impossible for two people to lie about the same thing and get away with it." She laughed, wearily. "That's the basis of probably three-quarters of the successful criminal convictions out there: figuring out the inconsistencies in two sets of lies. Besides, whether or not Mr. Guzman's actions contributed to Cornelius's death is almost irrelevant unless we can point to another cause."

"Which gets us back to figuring out what happened at that Omni-Care hospital," I said, looking at Rex and Doc. "Doesn't anyone else think it's strange that this guy shows up wearing a bracelet from OmniCare, dying from some unknown cause, and they deny he's ever been there?"

No one replied.

"So what did they tell you, that Cornelius was wearing a fake hospital bracelet?" I went on. "That's ridiculous."

"Maybe he switched the bracelet with someone else?" Rex said, thinking aloud.

"No," I snapped, a little too harshly. "*This* bracelet is the one they checked, this number, and they said it wasn't in the system." I turned to DeWitt. "Right?"

She put her hands flat on the table, and said, "Look, I don't know why someone would have a fake bracelet. Maybe to get drugs or something, though I'll grant you it does seem far-fetched. Regardless, for the moment, we're at an impasse. The law takes patient privacy very seriously, making it next to impossible to subpoena medical records for someone whose legal birth name we don't even know. If they say they don't have a record of him, we pretty much have to accept it. We can't subpoena all of their records to see if one of their patients matches Cornelius's description. The hospital would be breaking the law if they granted such a request."

"Well, someone should at least go out there in person," I said. I knew DeWitt was doing Doc a favor by helping, and she was probably right, but her negative attitude was getting on my nerves.

"No," she said flatly. "We can't just go out there making demands. That's what subpoenas and the legal process are for. The last thing we want is to interfere with the investigation, or risk accusations of obstruction of justice getting thrown into the mix."

"But—"

DeWitt cut me off with an upraised hand. Rex reached under the table and squeezed my knee. I couldn't tell if he was being supportive or telling me to shut up.

Doc shook his head. "You don't want to get Charlesford and his lawyers involved in this anyway," he said. "He's a brilliant doctor, but he's a tough businessman, brutally tough. I've seen what happens to those that go up against him, and well, I wouldn't trade places with them. Not even now."

"There *is* one other strategy I want to discuss," DeWitt said.

Doc looked up at her, tense, like he was bracing himself for something he knew was coming.

"As we well know, even though parts of the Genetic Heritage Act have been blocked by an injunction, the law itself is still nominally on the books." She paused to give Doc a meaningful look. Then she looked at Rex for the briefest instant before lowering her eyes, as if she were almost embarrassed. "One strategy that might be successful is if we argue that no crime was committed since, according to GHA, Cornelius was not a person."

I gasped.

"*No*," said Doc, shaking his head in disgust. "No, that's preposterous. It's reprehensible."

DeWitt leaned forward, softening her voice. "I know . . . I *know*. But it could be our only—"

"No." Doc cut her off again. "That would go against everything I stand for. Howard Wells and H4H, they'd *love* it if someone like me helped set a precedent that supported all the worst things they're trying to accomplish."

Rex looked pained. "Yeah, but Doc—"

"No, dammit." Doc got up and walked into the tiny kitchen, then turned and came back into the dining room. "Look, I appreciate your help, all of you, but I'm too tired to think straight. Can we continue this later?"

DeWitt stared up at him as if she were calculating something—somehow assessing him, or maybe mentally rearranging her schedule. After a moment, she said, "Sure." She picked up her pen and the keyboard and display disappeared, then she scooped her papers and folders into a pile. "That's probably a good idea."

After a quick thank you, goodbye, talk to you tomorrow, Doc

deposited the three of us on his porch, closing the door gently but firmly behind us.

It happened so abruptly that for a moment we just stood there together.

Rex peered back in through the glass around the door. "Poor guy's exhausted."

"Listen to me, you two," DeWitt said, her tone making us stand up straight. "This is a serious charge. A *murder* charge."

"I know," I shot back. "And that hospital has something to do with it."

Her eyes burned. "I do not have the time to go chasing after bogus leads like that. This is not the only case I have, but I am doing everything I can that makes sense and is *lawful* to get Mr. Guzman off. Frankly, I'm surprised I was able to get bail for him, even as high as it was."

"Who put up Doc's bail?" Rex asked suddenly.

"Do *not* call him Doc," she snapped, then she took a deep breath and continued, calmly. "I couldn't say even if I knew. But I'm glad they did. With what happened after one day, it looks like prison would be a very inhospitable place for *Mr.* Guzman, which is why we need to do everything we can not to screw things up on a technicality. This is a delicate case, and if we're going to win it, we need everything to break our way. The tiniest error could turn things against us. That means you two need to do as you're told. Do you understand?"

Neither Rex nor I said a word. She was probably a good person, and she was definitely working for a good cause—two of them, really: Doc and E4E. But she sure knew how to piss me off. Rex, too, judging from the way he was breathing.

I didn't say anything because I couldn't trust myself not to say something I shouldn't. So instead we just stood there, staring at her.

She rolled her eyes and shook her head, probably thinking something about sullen, pain-in-the-ass teenagers. I decided to play into it, cocking my hip and my chin in opposite directions. After a moment of uncomfortable silence, DeWitt let out an exasperated sigh and stormed off, slipping a little bit on the ice as she approached her car. It was a nice one. She might have been fighting the good fight, but she was doing okay for herself, too.

She opened the door and paused, looking over at us. "Don't screw this up."

Then she got in and sped off with a spray of slush.

CHAPTER 10

Rex looked down at me. "You're pretty good at that, the hip thing. And the death glare."

I gave him the same treatment. "Yeah, that's what my mom tells me."

He glanced back through Doc's window. I put my hand on his back and gently turned him away from it. "Come on," I said. "Let's go."

He nodded. "You know she's only trying to help, right?"

"Yeah, I know," I said as we both started walking. "And it's great that she's willing to take this on even while she's doing all this other stuff...."

"But?"

"But she's doing all this other stuff. She's obviously swamped with the GHA case, along with whatever other cases she has that are paying for that car. How much time is she going to have for Doc? How much digging is she going to do?"

He nodded, hearing me if not yet agreeing with me.

"Do you know how Doc—how *Guzman* lost his license?" I asked. "I know it was for treating chimeras, but do you know the details?"

"Yeah, he told me about it once. He was a medical doctor, but he did research, too. This was years ago, around the end of the flu epidemic. Chimeras were still new and there weren't many around. And even though the epidemic started before splicing became a thing, a lot of people blamed them—us—for the flu. Even back then, scientists were saying it was BS, but you know how it is."

"People wanted to blame someone," I said.

"Exactly. And it kind of made sense, right? That chimeras could provide a way for a virus to jump from some other species to humans."

"But they proved that never happened, right? Like you just said, the epidemic started before there even were chimeras."

He nodded and raised a finger. "Fun fact: did you know there are no documented cases of chimeras getting the flu during the epidemic?"

"Really?"

"That's what Doc said. He said there weren't enough of them around for anybody to do a study, but it turned out later that there were no recorded cases of that flu in chimeras. Anyway, when a few chimeras did get sick, no one would treat them. But Doc did."

"Wait, I thought they couldn't get flu."

"They couldn't. It wasn't flu. It was bad splices, things going wrong with the viral medium, the stuff that delivers the splice. And it was killing them."

"What did Doc do?"

"He talked to some of his colleagues, and found out there was a theoretical procedure that could reverse a splice. He figured out how to do it."

"So Doc invented fixing?"

"He says he just . . . improved it. And he doesn't actually like that term. He calls it reversal. Anyway, he saved people's lives, but it cost him his medical license."

"Wow. Poor Doc."

Rex nodded. "He says he's happier now—well, not *right* now, I imagine, but you know what I mean. I don't know if I believe it or not."

"He does a lot of good."

"Yeah, he does. Still, I can't help wondering how much more good he could have done if they hadn't taken his license."

A light, freezing rain began to fall, making a ticking sound against the frozen ground.

"Do you want to go to the coffee shop?" he asked.

"No." I stopped walking and waited until Rex did the same. "I want to see your place. Where you're staying."

"What?"

"I want to see where you're staying. You said it's near here, right? I want to see it."

"It's kind of a dump, Jimi. I mean, I'm grateful Jerry's letting me stay there, but—"

"Then that's what I want to see. I don't care what it looks like. I just want to see it."

He opened his mouth to protest again, but I didn't let him.

"Look, you've got all these secrets and you say that's how it has to be, and I'm trying to be okay with that. But *everything* can't be a secret, right? So let's not keep any more secrets than we already have to, okay?"

Rex stood there with his mouth still open. I almost felt bad for him, but mostly I felt relief at having gotten that out there.

He closed his mouth, then nodded, slowly at first, then with a little more gusto, as if what I had said made sense. "Sure."

"Okay then," I said. "Which way?"

"This way," he said, hooking his thumb to the left.

I started walking, and he fell into step beside me. I veered a little closer to him and looked up. "Sure is cold out," I said, pressing my shoulder into his ribs.

He looked down and smiled at me, like he was struggling to keep the smile from going wider. Then he put his arm around me.

It was nice.

We walked like that for a few blocks, then turned onto a street of run-down stores—carpets, wigs, nail salon, a falafel place—each with a few stories of apartments above.

We crossed the street diagonally, toward an almost invisible door wedged between the falafel shop and the nail salon.

"How's the falafel?" I asked as he fished his key out of his pants pocket.

He laughed. "It's really good."

He opened the door and stepped aside so I could go in ahead of him. On the other side of the door was a steep, narrow set of stairs, with worn plastic treads and metal edges. It creaked as I started up, then creaked louder as Rex followed me.

As we approached the top of the steps, he said, "To the left and up again."

The next set of steps creaked even worse. At the top, he said, "To the right."

Turning, I found myself in a narrow hallway with a door on either side and one at the end. "All the way down," he said.

I walked to the end of hallway and turned to let Rex go by, but there wasn't really room. I looked up at him and we both laughed. I flattened myself against the wall, and he reached past me with his key to open the door.

He tried to wait for me to go in first, but we ended up kind of spilling into the room together.

And inside, it was . . . nice.

It was tiny, yes, and it was humble, but it was neat and clean and it seemed well cared for.

It was pretty much one room, with a kitchenette to the right, a sleeping area to the left, and past that, a sitting area with a small but sturdy-looking sofa, a coffee table, and a pair of windows. The only thing remotely out of place was a book lying open and facedown on the sofa.

The bed was made. The sink was empty. If it hadn't been my idea, and if he hadn't protested, I would have thought maybe he had been expecting me. I smiled at that thought.

"What?" he asked.

"Nothing," I said.

"I know. It's tiny," said Rex.

"No, it's nice. I really like it."

"You want a cup of tea?"

"Sure," I said. "That'd be great."

A single step put him in the kitchenette. He filled an electric kettle from a filter spout and turned it on, then grabbed a couple of mugs from one cabinet and a box of tea bags from another.

I walked over to the seating area and looked out the windows at low gray clouds over dark rooftops, and a cluster of supertowers, hazy in the distance. Much closer, just a few blocks away, I saw a glint of gold, from some kind of spire. I realized it was a side view of the new H4H cross atop the Church of the Eternal Truth.

I snorted, and Rex said, "What?" suddenly right behind me.

I looked at him over my shoulder. "Kind of a cool view, but it's got to suck having that H4H cross poking up right in the middle of it."

He laughed. "A lot of people in Silver Garden are mad about it—the other churches more than the chimeras, I think. It doesn't bother me that much. Although it does sometimes feel like they put it there just to mess with me."

The kettle clicked off and Rex went to make the tea.

I sat on the sofa and he returned with our mugs. He put them on the table and sat on the corner of the bed, across from me. I patted the sofa next to me and we both laughed, our eyes locked.

I just wanted him to be close. I hadn't really thought past that.

"That sofa's smaller than it looks," he said. "And I'm—"

"I know what you are," I said. I started to say it was more of a love seat than a sofa, but thought better of it.

He came over and eased down next to me. It was a tight fit, but I didn't mind at all. I reached over and picked up his tea, then handed it to him and picked up my own.

"Thank you for inviting me over, Rex," I said formally.

"Well, thanks for inviting yourself over," he said with a grin.

I sat forward and looked back at him, pretending to be offended.

He laughed. "No, seriously. I mean it. It's nice to have you here. I'm glad you suggested it."

"Well, me too," I said, leaning back against him and sipping my tea.

He put his arm around me and we were quiet for a minute or two, listening to another round of rain and sleet clicking against the windows.

"So," I said lightly. "I know there are things you say you can't talk about, but I bet there's a lot of stuff you can."

I could feel him tense up beside me. "Like what?"

I shrugged, keeping it casual. "I dunno. Like . . . whatever happened to Leo Byron?"

"Um . . . you mean why did I get spliced?"

"Well, yeah, but before that, too. What happened to Leo, my friend who moved away from the neighborhood and never got in touch with any of us again?" I squeezed his knee, to reassure him that I was asking, not accusing.

Rex set down his mug, looking thoughtful. "Well . . . I'd been intrigued by chimeras since the first time I saw one," he said. "At first I couldn't understand why someone would get spliced, but the more I thought about it, the more it made sense to me."

"How?"

"It just did. I never really felt like I fit in anywhere—"

"Not even in the old neighborhood, with Nina and Del and me?"

"No, you were all great. But after that. When we moved away. I felt like an outsider constantly. Plus I was tiny, *really* tiny, and that didn't help either. It never occurred to me that a splice would make me bigger, but I wondered if getting spliced would help me lean into the whole outsider thing. If like, being a chimera, I could *own* it, have more control over it. And then . . ." He made a soft grunting noise, as if part of him didn't want to say whatever was next.

"What?" I said gently.

"You're going to think this is really corny, but when I did get spliced, it was like I discovered who I was all along."

I nodded slowly. "So . . . what did your parents think about it? I remember they were pretty protective when we were little."

"Yeah, they were. It got worse after we moved."

"Really?" Mr. and Mrs. Byron had never been my favorite parents growing up, partly because they had so many rules, but also they seemed really cold. They kind of smothered Leo, but not with affection.

"Sometimes I felt like I was a little boy action figure," he said, "like they were keeping me in all my original packaging to maintain my value. They worried about me because I was so small. They wanted me to be healthy and happy, but my dad . . . I think on some level he was embarrassed by it. By me."

I craned my neck to look up at him. "Are you serious?" I felt a swell of emotion at the thought of it. Leo was the sweetest, smartest, cutest little kid. The idea that anyone could be ashamed of him was hard to contemplate.

Rex shrugged and looked away. "I know they loved me. . . . Anyway, they'd already—they died long before getting spliced ever crossed my mind. But you're right, they wouldn't have been happy about it."

I sat up straight, shocked. "Rex, I had no idea."

"How could you have?" he said gently. "I'm only telling you now."

"How did they die?" I asked softly.

"In a plane crash. My mom had a business trip to Antarctica."

I picked up his hand and squeezed it.

"Her company was developing a lot of properties there, making a fortune on all that newly uncovered terrain. She brought my dad. They used to go away a lot, and leave me with my grandparents. Then one time they didn't come back. The plane had a multiple engine failure."

"How old were you?"

"Ten."

"So . . . you stayed with your grandparents permanently after that?"

He nodded. "Yeah. Well, there and boarding school. Which was its own special brand of hell."

I pictured Leo back then, tiny little Leo. Del had also been a misfit, and he'd had a rough time, but Leo would have been a *tiny* misfit. If anyone was going to be mercilessly teased, it would be him.

Rex laughed again, such a sad, tired laugh. "I don't know which was worse, actually. Boarding school was bad, but at home, I was clearly in the way. The only one really glad to see me was Juniper."

"Juniper?"

"The dog."

"I didn't know you had a dog."

"Well, *they* had a dog. They made it clear that Juniper was theirs. But she was *my* pal. They didn't show her much affection either, so she was pretty happy to have me around."

"I just can't understand why your grandparents wouldn't be happy to have you around, too," I said.

"Well, let's put it this way: I think my grandparents had been *very* happy empty-nester retirees. Like, they were always happy to see me when I came home from school, but within a day or two, they'd get antsy. I'd hear them on the phone with their friends sometimes, how they couldn't do this or that or how they had to cancel plans because I was there. They were not one-hundred-percent overjoyed to have me there permanently."

"I'm sorry."

"Yeah, me too." Rex drained his tea. "In hindsight, it actually made me feel closer to my dad, realizing how he grew up. It's a wonder he wasn't more screwed up."

"You're not screwed up."

He laughed. "Everybody's screwed up."

I cocked an eyebrow at him. "Am I screwed up?"

He grinned at me, fully aware that I was messing with him. "Less than most."

CHAPTER 11

When Rex put more water on to boil, I got up to look outside. "I missed you, you know," I said over my shoulder. "When you moved away."

Rex was quiet. "I missed you, too," he said finally. "And that made it all so much worse. It's so hard in this world to find your people, you know? And I'd found them. You and Del and Nina. But mostly you. You were my people." His voice was thick with emotion.

"And then I lost you," he continued, walking back from the kitchenette. "All three of you. Instead, I was living with two cranky grandparents at home, or with a bunch of really awful guys at school." He let out a sigh. "I never felt like I had people again. Until I got spliced."

"So when was that, exactly?"

"When I was thirteen."

I turned to look at him. "Thirteen? That's so young. I didn't think genies would splice anyone that young."

"They're not supposed to. The good ones won't."

"So who did it?"

"I guess it was like the fourth genie I found. A guy named Walden. He left town right afterwards. But I remember lying there in this abandoned house, with this chimera I didn't know who I'd just given all my money to, and I'm looking up at the IV bag hanging over me, and it was filthy. There were, like, fingerprints and smudges on it, and I was thinking, 'Leo, what have you gotten yourself into?' In the end, I actually think the splice he gave me was okay. But I had some sort of odd reaction. You remember how my parents used to send me to all those growth specialists?"

"Yeah, I do."

"Well, after we moved, as I got older, they tried harder. I must have seen every endocrinologist on the East Coast. They gave me all sorts of injections and treatments intended to jump-start my growth. None of them ever worked. Or not until later."

"Until you got spliced?"

"While I was sweating the change, actually." He laughed, thinking back on it. "So, I'm there with Walden, who I barely knew, and a couple of other people I didn't know at all, and the fever hits me, and the shakes, and he's telling me it's all normal, it's all part of it. So I'm like, 'Okay, he's done this before.' But then the pain hit, and it was like nothing I ever felt. I tried to stay quiet, but after a while I couldn't help it, I start whimpering, and then full-on groaning and crying, in and out of consciousness. I wake up at one point with Walden yelling in my face to keep it down, that I was bothering everybody else."

It sounded awful, but Rex was laughing as he told me. "Finally, I come out of it, and I see Walden standing there with some other guy, another chimera, and they're looking down at me, both of them like this."

He half folded his arms, leaving one hand free to pinch his bottom lip, and furrowed his brow as if he were appraising something, thinking hard. "Finally the other guy shakes his head and says to Walden, 'Nope. Never seen anything like it.' And Walden says, 'I know, right? He's, like, doubled in size.' I tried to ask them what was going on, but then the pain started up again. Apparently I was screaming, because they both started telling me to shut up."

"Oh, Rex."

"I know," he said, laughing again. "It was terrible. Next time I wake up, the house is quiet and dark and empty. There's a case of water next to me and a box of protein drinks, and a piece of cardboard leaning against them with the word *drink* written on it."

"You must have been so scared."

"I was mostly too hungry and thirsty to even think about it. I drank six bottles of water and three or four of the protein drinks."

"And were you okay after that?"

"I was only halfway done."

"What do you mean?"

"I was still growing and changing for two more days."

"Two more *days*?"

The kettle boiled and Rex took our mugs over to refill them. "Yeah. It was crazy. I'm wandering around this empty house, sucking down water and protein shakes, and just as I'd start to kind of get a grip on what was going on, another 'growth spurt' would hit me, and the pain would knock me out."

He came back with our fresh tea and I joined him on the couch again. "You must have been terrified," I said, cradling my mug.

He paused, thinking back. "I mean . . . yeah, I must have been. But the whole thing was so bizarre, it's almost like I was too freaked out to be scared, you know?"

"No, I'm pretty sure I could do both."

"Sometime early on the third day, this guy hears me in there yelling—it was Sly, that's when I met him. He told me later that when he found me, my pants were split and digging into my skin, and I was covered in bruises from all the internal rearrangements. But Sly and some friends somehow got me to Doc's place, and that's how I met Doc. He saved my life."

"Did he try to fix your splice?"

"No. It was probably too late, anyway, but Doc knew I *wanted* to be a chimera. He kept me calm, kept me hydrated, and kept an eye on me in case anything went wrong. He said at one point he was afraid I was going to just keep growing, like a monster or something." He paused to wipe his eyes with his shirt.

"It sounds terrible," I said.

"Ah, I was unconscious through most of it. Anyway, finally, on the fourth day, I was done."

I could hear the laughter drain out of him with those words. "What happened then?" I asked.

Rex let out a sigh. "I was just waking up from it all, on this double cot in a back room, and I could hear voices out front, angry voices. I realized right away something was wrong. There was this guy, this chimera-hater."

"H4H?"

"I don't know. They weren't so big yet. Probably, though. Anyway, he's there threatening Doc, saying he's going to smash everything up. I don't think this guy had any idea I was there. But I hear the sound of breaking glass, and the guy says he's going to break Doc's legs. I could barely move, but I knew I had to do something. So I kind of heave myself up, and stumble out there, and this guy turns and sees me and he screams." He looked down at me, reading my face, seeing how I was taking it. Deciding how much he was going to tell me.

"Go on," I said.

"He had this metal pipe, and he swung it at me. Somehow I caught it, reflex, or luck, really, but he didn't know that, and now he looked horrified. Then I shoved him, just to get him away from me, the flat of my hand against his chest—and Jimi, it was like he disappeared. One second he was there, the next he was on the other side of the room, spitting out blood." He paused, took in a breath and let it out. "I was scared then, terrified," he said quietly. "I thought I'd killed him."

"But he was okay?"

"Okay enough to get up and run away."

"How about you? Were you okay?"

"Well, yeah. What do you mean?"

"I mean, I know you were different physically, but what about mentally? Emotionally? Did you feel different?"

"A bit, yeah, but I was still the same person. I mean, as much as anyone is from one day to the next."

"I've heard chimeras say getting spliced changed the way they saw the world. Did that happen?"

He shrugged. "Kind of, I guess. But not all at once. I think that comes from *being* a chimera, not the process of getting spliced."

I nodded, then shook my head. "Still, the whole thing sounds crazy. I mean, even if I wanted a splice, I couldn't see putting myself through what you did."

Rex looked thoughtful. "I know Del had a bad time, and I did, too. And it's never fun, no matter what. But it's usually not *that* bad."

"Really?" I said, dubiously.

"It's really not, Jimi. But even if it were, think of the good that can come of it. Think of what happened to me. Getting spliced was how I met Doc, and he's one of my closest friends. Sly, too. And through them I met Ruth and Pell, and a bunch of other people. I'd do it all over again in a heartbeat. Especially now that I have . . . I mean, now that I have you back in my life, too."

I looked up at him and our eyes met. There had been so much distance between us, and for that I'd been blaming the secrets about where he'd been and what he'd been doing the last couple of months, but I realized maybe it was more about where he'd been the past ten *years*, since he'd disappeared from my life. I suddenly felt like a big part of the wall between us had been smashed, obliterated.

I reached up and put my hand on the back of his neck, ran my fingers through his hair, and pulled his head down to mine.

As I pressed my lips against his I heard a sound like a clap of thunder. The building shook and the windows rattled. We both looked outside as an angry-looking ball of black smoke rolled up into the sky.

CHAPTER 12

We couldn't quite tell where the smoke was coming from, at first. Then the gold H4H cross gleaming atop the Church of the Eternal Truth shuddered. We both held out breath, watching, and after a brief moment, the cross slowly pitched forward, twisting to reveal the H4H logo at its center, gaining speed as it fell. It disappeared behind the other buildings, then the sound of it crashing echoed off the surrounding structures.

"Oh my God," I said. "It looks like someone bombed the church."

A chorus of sirens began to wail, seemingly from everywhere. A police quadcopter streaked across the sky, right over the roof, lights flashing as it rocketed toward the smoke.

Rex's jaw clenched and his eyes smoldered. "Idiots," he said.

"Who?"

"Whoever thought something like this would do anything other than make things a million times *worse*."

We watched for a second as the black smoke smudged the bottom of the cloud cover. The sirens were growing louder.

"We need to get you home," Rex said.

I looked up at him. He was scared. "I'll be okay," I said. "I can stay here." An image flashed through my mind of Rex and me, huddled together in his tiny apartment, safe and warm as the world raged outside. I felt a deep sadness as the image faded, and anger at the thought that we couldn't even get through some tea and a few kisses without the world conspiring to keep us apart.

"I wish you could," Rex said. "But you can't. There could be riots after this. You saw what happened before. We need to get you out of Silver Garden. And we need to go now, so we don't get caught out on the street if things do get ugly." He cupped my face in his hands and kissed me. Slowly. As if he wanted me to pay attention. When he was done, he pulled back, just a couple of inches, his deep brown eyes looking into mine.

"We only just got together," I said.

"I know," he said. "It sucks. But this time I'm not going anywhere. I'll see you tomorrow, okay?"

I felt a twinge of fear, as if he had jinxed things simply by saying those words. He started to pull his hands away, but I grabbed his wrists and held them in place. "Do you promise?"

He kissed me again. "I promise."

As we tromped down the stairs, I pointed out to Rex that maybe Silver Garden wasn't the safest place for a giant chimera, either. That maybe he should come home with me, to Oakton. To his credit, he thought about it, or at least pretended to, before he said no. He needed to be here, with his people. To my credit, I didn't point out that while I wasn't a chimera, I was his people, too.

Then we were out the door and sprinting across the street.

The cross hadn't been visible from ground level here, but the black smoke was. Surrounded by a trio of police copters and a swarm of drones, most of them blinking red and blue in the gray sky, the column of smoke looked like some kind of giant monster under attack.

The police sirens were now accompanied by the slower, louder wail of fire trucks. Traffic was light, but as a fire truck came around the corner two blocks up, the emergency systems took control of all the cars and pulled them over to the side of the road.

I covered my ears against the noise as the fire truck passed us, but we didn't slow down. People were coming out of buildings and looking up at the smoke in the sky. Some of them watched us run by, their faces suspicious.

At the Lev station, we hustled up the steps to the platform. There was no sign of a train coming, so we ran to the end of the platform, where the view was better.

The dark smear of smoke had stretched across the bottoms of the clouds moving by, but only a thin wisp was still rising up, as if the fire had been extinguished.

The Lev train appeared in the distance, followed by its familiar faint hum.

We hurried back to the center of the platform, where the train would stop.

"Last chance," I said. "Are you *sure* you won't come with me? My mom's out of town until tomorrow. . . ." I let that hang.

Rex grinned. "And what about Kevin?" he said.

"To hell with Kevin," I said, and we both laughed.

Rex groaned and shook his head. "You have *no* idea how much I'd love to come with you to Oakton, Jimi," he said. "But I need to be here, just in case, you know . . . anybody needs me."

You mean in case anybody else *needs you,* I thought. But I understood. I knew how seriously he took the other chimeras' safety. I grabbed him by the shirt and looked up at him with my gravest, most serious expression. "Be careful."

"Come on," he said, tugging my arm. "You're going to miss the train."

I kept my feet planted. "Say you will."

"I'll be careful," he said. "Come on."

The train pulled up just as we reached the boarding area. As the doors slid open, I pulled Rex close and kissed him again.

"You be careful, too," he said as we pulled away from each other. "Call me when you get home."

I nodded, then turned to step onto the train. I was greeted by the disgusted grimace of a middle-aged guy in work overalls, making clear what he thought of me kissing Rex. As the train pulled out, I looked around and saw other passengers staring at me as well, including a woman in her thirties in Italian boots and a fur coat that must have cost a fortune. I knew the fur had been grown in a lab, but it still creeped me out. She also had a Wellplant, so she was probably watching or listening to coverage of the bombing. Her stare soured into a sneer as I looked back at her.

None of them looked like they would harm me physically, but I realized how much easier it was to be brave when Rex was with me. I thought back to my realization the night before about how important it was for chimera supporters not to hide. I flipped my collar down, making sure my E4E button and the chimera pin Ruth had given me were proudly on display.

Ruth had said the pin made me an honorary chimera. It didn't, but it at least made my position known: I was an intelligent, open-minded, and compassionate person who took the time to get to know someone before judging them. *Except for the guy in the overalls and the lady in the fur,* I thought with a snort. I felt okay judging them.

It was three o'clock when I got off the train in Oakton, and the sky was already darkening toward night. I flipped my collar back up. There was no one around to see my buttons anymore, and it had gotten colder. Before I left the platform, I looked back toward Silver Garden. There was no longer any sign of smoke or police copters. I hoped that meant the fire was completely out, that the damage was minimal and no one was hurt, and that Rex was home safe, warming up his tea and reading his book.

Halfway down the steps, I passed a man just standing there. He was dressed for the weather, but his coat was open. His fedora was pulled so low he could have had a Wellplant. He was in his forties, with pale, chapped skin and gray eyes that locked onto mine in a way you don't do with strangers. *But maybe we weren't strangers,* I thought. I was sure I saw recognition in his eyes.

He smiled but didn't say anything. I didn't either. I continued on my way, trying not to let on that he was creeping me out.

I hit the sidewalk at a brisk pace, and made it half a block before giving in to the urge to look behind me.

He was at the bottom of the steps now, staring at me. I quickened my place, telling myself he was probably just some kind of creeper, then wondering why I thought *that* should make me feel better. My senses were on high alert for any hint of footsteps behind me.

When I reached the corner, I looked back again, but there was no sign of him.

I stood there and scanned the street, wondering where he could have gone. There were no cars, no side streets. It started to snow again, with a hush similar to when I'd been walking to the station in the snow that morning. This time it felt different, though. This time, I didn't feel like I was truly alone.

I hurried past houses lit from within, emanating warmth and good cheer, but locked up tight against the cold and the wet. I couldn't see anyone looking out through any of the windows, but I couldn't shake the sensation that I was being watched.

My brain began compiling a list of who might be following me: Brian Kurtz, Stan Grainger . . . maybe some random crazy H4Her?

As the new snow blanketed the street, my footfalls disappeared. The only sound was my breathing.

There was nothing else. There was no one else.

But I started running anyway.

CHAPTER 13

I kicked the snow off my feet as I ran up the back steps to my house, then let myself in through the kitchen door.

Kevin was in the living room, sitting on the sofa, watching the Holovid. I smiled at the sight of him, reassured by the familiarity of it, with the knowledge that he likely hadn't moved from that spot since I'd left, hours before. Kevin was one hell of an athlete, but sometimes I was more impressed by his ability to waste an entire day sitting on the sofa *watching* sports.

Turning to close the back door, I paused for a few seconds and watched the snow coming down. When I turned back around, Kevin was standing right behind me, his arm raised over my head.

I let out a startled yelp, and he screwed up his face at me as he grabbed a bag of chips from the shelf over my head.

"You're such a weirdo," he said, shaking his head as he walked back toward the living room.

"Don't sneak up on me like that!"

"And your weirdo friends are weird, too," he called back as he plopped back onto the sofa and pointed at the Holovid. "You know some whack-job chimeras blew up that H4H cross? The news keeps cutting into the game."

"Is it still on?" I asked, hurrying into the living room.

He looked at me, confused that I cared. "Yeah, Villanova's up by six."

"Not the game, idiot, the news."

He shrugged. "Oh, I don't know, they've been breaking in every—argh, not again. There's only four minutes left!"

I hurried over to the sofa and whacked his knee with the back of my hand. He slid over a few inches and I sat down next to him and turned up the volume.

The local news guy had on his most serious expression. In front of him, the words BREAKING NEWS throbbed in red letters. Behind him, a computer-enhanced clip of the H4H cross toppled in dramatic slow motion in front of a wall of flame.

"Was anybody hurt?" I asked, dreading the answer.

He shook his head. "No, they don't think so. Just that big, stupid cross." He shook his head. "Dumbass chimeras."

I gave him a sidelong look.

"Look," he said. "I totally get it. The H4Hers are even crazier than your weirdo friends. But this was dumb, Jimi. I mean, things were just calming down. Don't your buddies know when to give it a rest?"

The broadcast cut to dramatic holo-feed footage of the incident. It began with a flat, two-dimensional image from a single camera drone, shaking and jerking as it rapidly panned across the sky to capture the explosion a microsecond after it happened. Within seconds, as more camera drones joined the swarm, the image deepened into three dimensions. Before the initial ball of smoke had fully risen, the image was crisp and solid and detailed. Even from the drones' vantage point above, there wasn't any visible fire—just that first ball of smoke trailing up into the sky, and the golden cross teetering and falling as the police drones started showing up, followed by the actual copters. Then it looped back to the beginning and started all over again.

"You don't know it was chimeras," I said.

"Really?" He snorted. "Church of the Eternal Truth? Gathering place of haters? Who else would it be?"

He had a point. The Eternal Truth congregation disapproved of all sorts of people and lifestyles that didn't conform to their values, and they might have viewed all of them as less than people, but chimeras were the only ones they were trying to *legally* define that way.

The news anchor echoed Kevin, openly speculating that chimeras or chimera sympathizers were responsible for the blast. He recounted the events of the past several months—the marches and the anti-chimera riots, the passage of GHA and the resulting court battles. "Of course," he added, "the structure damaged in the blast had been the subject of other controversies, as well."

They cut to a slender man with sad, gentle blue eyes. The bottom of the screen said REV. BRIAN CALKIN OF ST. PETER'S CHURCH, SPRING CITY – RECORDED EARLIER.

"Yes, I disagree with some of the teachings of the Church of the Eternal Truth, and some of their political initiatives, but differing opinions are to be expected in a world of many faiths and denominations. What I simply cannot abide, though, is this altering—this *desecrating*—of the cross that our savior Jesus Christ died on for our sins. I . . . I simply cannot. . . ."

An unseen interviewer said, "Surely lots of groups use the cross in their imagery."

"Absolutely," said Calkin, regaining his composure, his voice gaining strength and gravity. "And if Humans for Humanity wants to use the cross as part of theirs, well, so be it. But to include their *brand* as a part of the cross, their logo, and to put it on top of their church, well, I'd call that idolatry. I'd call it sacrilege!"

They cut back to the holo-feed loop of the explosion and the fire as the anchor said, "Nevertheless, Pastor Gordon Kerns of the Church of the Eternal Truth says he knows exactly who is responsible."

Pastor Kerns was in his mid-fifties, with reddish hair and pale cheeks dramatically streaked with soot. His eyes were wide and intense, which could have been because his church had just been bombed, but I'd seen him speaking at rallies and marches—usually blocking off some street between me and where I was going—and as far as I could tell, his eyes were always like that.

"This is undoubtedly the work of those filthy, ungodly chimeras," he said, his voice trembling with rage, his breath visible around the microphone held in front of him by the field reporter. I winced as the holographic spittle that accompanied his words seemed to arc through the air toward our coffee table. In reality, it had probably landed on the reporter. "They choose to poison themselves, to live in squalor, outside of normal society. Howard Wells is right: they've ruined their own lives, and now they want to ruin everyone else's. And Church of the Eternal Truth and all the other churches in the Humans for Humanity family, we're not going to stand for it. And we're not going to let these activist judges get in the way of the human race protecting itself. We knew this day was coming. We knew the chimeras would turn vicious, like the wild animals they are, that they would attack humanity, whom they've abandoned, and that they would attack God, whom they blaspheme by their very existence, and—"

The feed abruptly cut back to the anchor in the studio, catching him as he let out a deep breath. "And speaking of Howard Wells, be sure to join us thirty minutes from now as Alenka Bogdan interviews Wells tonight on *60 Minutes*, America's longest-running news show. Meanwhile we now return you to our regular feed."

The scene abruptly changed to a basketball court, where two teams were casually slapping hands at midcourt as thousands of fans wearing red and white chanted and yelled and waved handheld holographic cartoon badgers over their heads. Fans wearing blue were heading for the exits. The scoreboard read 71–68 and a commentator was saying, "Well folks, that was, without a doubt, one of the most *exciting* games of the last five years."

"Absolutely," said an almost identical voice. "We'll be watching highlights from this one for years."

"It's *over*?" Kevin said with a growl. "Damn chimeras," he said, shaking his head as he stalked out of the room.

I watched him go, stunned, as I occasionally still was, by his lunkheadedness.

"You still don't know it was them," I called after him, then raised my voice even louder as he thumped upstairs. "But I'm sure if whoever did it knew you were watching basketball, they would have postponed the bombing till after the game!"

I didn't get a reply. The credits scrolled for a few seconds, then it was time for the regularly scheduled local news, with the lead story being the bombing, of course.

I went into the kitchen and called Rex. He answered on the first ring.

"You're back safe?" he said as soon as he knew it was me. "How was it getting home?"

I decided not to mention my encounter with the creeper at the Oakton station. "It was fine. Uneventful. How about you? Run into any problems?"

"No, it was fine. I came straight home, just to be safe, but it wasn't bad. Lots of blinky lights and dirty looks, but not much more than usual. It's quiet around here and everyone seems fine."

I looked into the living room and up the steps to make sure Kevin wasn't nearby. "Was it a chimera, do you think? The bomber?"

"Most likely, I guess. I'd like to smack whoever did it."

"I hope it doesn't make things worse."

"Well, it's not going to make things better, that's for sure."

"I was hoping we'd get to hang out more today. Hoping some maniac wouldn't blow up a church and stir up a hornets nest."

"I hear you," he said. "But . . . I'll see you tomorrow, right?"

"Absolutely. Do you want to just hang out at your place?"

"We could, but I was thinking maybe we could walk down by the river or something. Get out of Silver Garden and keep some distance between us and the cleanup at the church. Just in case."

"That sounds good. Should we meet at New Ground first? Ten-ish?"

"Perfect."

"Great."

"Well . . . I hope you have a nice, quiet evening."

I laughed.

"What?"

"Howard Wells is on *60 Minutes* tonight. I'm probably going to watch it, but it could be pretty infuriating."

"Oh, right! Thanks for reminding me. We can compare notes tomorrow."

How romantic, I thought.

He chuckled, as if reading my mind. "Or not!"

We said our good-nights and got off the phone. I looked up at the clock and sighed. It was getting late. I had three more days of winter break, and I didn't want to spend it worrying about getting ready for school. That meant I needed to get ready now.

I put in a load of laundry and got my stuff together, then gave a final read to an essay I'd written about the impact of energy policy on depopulation of the zurbs. I put on some pasta and threw some fresh spinach into a pan with some jarred sauce. When the pasta was done, I served myself a big bowl—rotini topped with lots of sauce and plenty of Parmesan. I left enough for Kevin, even though he was being particularly annoying.

The Holovid had shut itself off, but when I came into the living room with my dinner, it lit up again, and I grinned at the ancient *tick-tick-tick-tick* of the *60 Minutes* title segment. It was kind of adorable, in a way.

Then there was Howard Wells, right up close.

The sight of the guy made my skin crawl: his unnaturally tanned, unnaturally smooth face, and his unnaturally white teeth. Creepiest of all was the signature glassy disc over his left eye—his Wellplant, the computer implant that bore his name and had made him trillions of dollars.

The clip they showed upfront had Wells grinning in an aw-shucks kind of way, humble and self-effacing while flashing a smile that cost more than our house.

I felt vaguely depressed as I mixed the Parm into the pasta. As the feed cut to a commercial, I went back into the kitchen.

If I was going to watch Howard Wells, I needed more cheese.

CHAPTER 14

I got back to the sofa just in time for the introductory montage that recounted Wells's rise to prominence, including some 2-D footage of his young adulthood and his early career working in pharmaceuticals, public health, and computers, among other things. That was followed by a brief history of Wellplant Corporation, and then Wells's involvement in H4H, how he transformed the organization from some fringe joke into a serious political force that was driving anti-chimera legislation. There were some hints at Wells's political aspirations, and the voice-over also mentioned the events in Pitman. They were careful to point out that Wells was never directly connected to Pitman and that he had personally condemned what happened there, but they also described how it had damaged public perception of the anti-chimera movement, H4H, and Wells and his company.

As a commercial played in the background for Wellplant's new 10.0 model, considered its most ambitious and powerful yet, the voice-over turned ominous, referring vaguely to production and other challenges facing the company, and quoting some famous economist as saying that with its expanding pharmaceutical and medical-care divisions and its ambitious new implant products, Wellplant Corporation might be overextended.

Alenka Bogdan, the interviewer, was in her late sixties, with spiky gray hair, a half smile etched on her mouth, and fierce gray eyes. The interview was taking place at Wellplant's global headquarters, a campus of towers in West Philadelphia, south of the University of Pennsylvania. Bogdan and Wells were both perched on stools in a white room with large windows. The towers of Center City were visible over Wells's shoulder, somehow looking fragile and small from that angle.

Bogdan welcomed Wells to the program and congratulated him on the release of Wellplant 10.0.

"Thank you," said Wells, flashing his teeth. "We're very excited about it."

"And why exactly is that? What's so special about this upgrade?"

Wells leaned forward, tilting his head downward, as if to show off his Wellplant. I leaned forward, too, to get a better look. The previous versions were black, but this was a smoky gray. The skin around the disc seemed faintly discolored, and I realized there was makeup covering redness.

"This technology is nothing short of revolutionary, with significant upgrades in connection speed, computing power, wetware connectivity—"

"And by that you mean the connections to the user's brain, is that right?"

Wells held his head up straight. "Yes, that's right."

"It's also substantially more expensive."

"And worth every penny."

"What do you say to critics who complain this technology is out of reach for most Americans and others around the world, and that it gives an unfair advantage in schools or the workplace to those who can afford it?"

As she spoke, he tilted his head again, as if showing off his Wellplant. He flashed his teeth once more and pursed his lips, as if he was thinking. But I got the distinct impression that the pause was purely for effect, that he knew exactly what he was going to say.

"Look," he began, "it's no secret that wealthy people have nicer things than people who aren't wealthy. You can argue whether that's fair or not, whether we should have a capitalist society or a socialist society, but right now, this is a capitalist country. I think that's the best system, and I won't apologize for a system that makes it possible for people to become rich, even if it doesn't make everyone rich. I think that's better than a system where everyone is poor. And as for an unfair advantage in universities or the workplace, well yeah, sure. If it didn't give an advantage, it wouldn't be performing as advertised. But frankly, if someone can afford one of these babies"—he paused to lightly tap one finger against his Wellplant—"they've already got an advantage. And as for anyone else . . ." He paused, holding his head up straight as he looked right into the camera. "There is financing available, and with the professional advantages and increased earning potential provided by your new Wellplant, you'll be able to pay it off in no time." He smiled, looking confident, but it also seemed fake. Forced. Calculated for effect. "Plus, Wellplant has programs, both in the US and around the world, to make Wellplants affordable, and in some cases even free, to those who are working hard to make the world a better place."

"I hadn't heard about that program. Can you tell me more about it?"

"Well, we don't like to talk about it, frankly, because we're not doing it for the PR, we're doing it to give back, and do our part. I shouldn't have mentioned it in the first place. Next question."

"Okay. I understand advance orders are already well beyond your company's projections."

The fake smile widened by a quarter inch. "That's correct."

"I've also read some analysis suggesting you may be struggling to meet demand due to scarcity of materials, including this." She held up a glass vial containing a small, silver nugget. "Yttrium, one of the rare metals essential for production."

Wells laughed. "That's ludicrous. Some people may have to wait longer than they'd like for delivery because the 10.0 is so popular, but I assure you, there is no shortage of yttrium or any other essential components—in fact, we have new domestic sources coming online."

"Really? Where is that?"

"Trade secret," he said. Wells kept smiling, but now his frustration was barely concealed. I realized I kind of liked this Alenka Bogdan person.

She moved ahead. "Some have expressed safety concerns over these so-called domestic sources—"

"Look," Wells said. "I've told you I can't comment on that, but I will say that in any of our extraction operations around the world, wherever there is undue hazard, we can always rely on robotic equipment."

"Yes, and robotic equipment is also heavily dependent on yttrium, isn't that right?"

"Like I said, there is no shortage."

Bogdan sat back and took a breath, changing her focus. "What is it that makes you so vehement in your dislike of chimeras?"

Wells didn't miss a beat. "I don't dislike chimeras. I feel sorry for them that they would willingly abandon humanity. *Willingly* make themselves less than human."

"Some people have argued that you're the one trying to make them less than human, given your enormous financial support of Humans for Humanity and getting the Genetic Heritage Act passed."

"I'm simply advocating that the law mirror reality, and recognize these creatures for what they are."

"The law has been blocked by the courts—"

"*Parts* of the law have been *temporarily* blocked. And similar laws are being legislated in twenty-seven other states, as well as the US Congress."

"Where do you see it going from here?"

"I think the judges will come to their senses and reinstate GHA in its entirety, and other states and the federal government will emulate our success and make it the law of the land."

"Really?"

"Absolutely."

"Do you accept any responsibility for what happened in Pitman?"

"I have condemned what happened in Pitman in the strongest terms. I have nothing further to say on the subject."

"You have devoted much time and energy to condemning chimeras as being less than persons, and vilifying them for altering themselves so they are not human. What do you say to those who argue that Wellplants are an alteration as well, and that those who have them, who have computers implanted into their brains, are themselves not entirely human?"

Wells's face showed a flash of anger, then he got it under control. He tipped his head down again, as before, but this time I got the impression that instead of doing it to give Bogdan a better view of his new Wellplant, he was giving *it* a better view of *her.* "Alenka," he said, with a friendly smile as his eyes looked up at her, "people have been using tools since the dawn of humanity. Some believe that's part of what *made* us human. Wellplants are the next generation in tools. If anything, they make people even *more* human, not less."

"Interesting. What do you make of the recent flood of chimera references and depictions in popular culture, including songs, Holovid feeds, even T-shirts?"

"Popular culture in this country has a long and tawdry history of flirting with dangerous and self-destructive character archetypes. Look at the Old West gunfighters, the Depression-era bank robbers, and the gangsters at the turn of the century. It's no surprise mixies would become a part of that shameful legacy."

"I believe chimeras consider the word *mixie* to be a slur."

"Do they, now? Well, I consider them debasing their humanity to be an affront against God. So there you are."

CHAPTER 15

When the phone rang at eight the next morning, somehow I knew it was Rex. And somehow I knew it wouldn't be good news.

"Hello?" I said, glancing up the stairs to see if Kevin was in earshot.

"Hey," he said, and I could hear from the tone of his voice that I'd been right about something going wrong.

"What's going on?"

He took a deep breath. "Doc's bail has been revoked."

"What?"

"That explosion yesterday kicked up a major shit storm. Doc's judge revoked his bail."

"On what grounds?"

"On the grounds that the judge is up for reelection next year." He let out a sigh, and I could feel his deep disappointment, not just in what had happened but in what it said about the people involved. "There's more in the spineless politician judges department. The injunction against GHA might be revoked."

"Are you serious?" I said, slumping against the doorjamb.

"Yeah," he said quietly. "And now DeWitt's so busy on that front, she won't be able to do much for Doc."

"So what are we going to do?" I said, struggling to keep my voice even and strong.

"Well, you're going to stay where you are. I don't know what's going to happen today, but after what went down when GHA passed in the first place, who knows what the streets will be like. We're going to need to change our plans. Maybe I can come out there or we can meet somewhere else, but we're going to have to push things back today. I need to meet with Jerry and try to figure out what to do next."

"Don't you think I can help with that?" I added annoyance to the list of things I was trying to keep out of my voice.

Rex started to say something, then stopped, apparently thinking better of it. "I know you could be helpful," he said slowly. "Very helpful. I just worry about you, that's all."

"Right. So you're meeting Jerry at New Ground, I'm guessing?"

"Yeah."

"What time?"

"In an hour."

"I'll see you there."

The streets were quiet and empty. Maybe it was too cold for idiots to riot. Or maybe it was just too early. New Ground was empty as well, except for Ruth sitting at the counter and Pell standing behind it.

Ruth slid off her stool and came over to me, crying silently on my shoulder as she put her willowy arms around me. I squeezed her back and smoothed the feathers on her head, like I had seen her and Pell do to each other.

"Thanks," she said, laughing as she wiped away a tear. "And sorry."

"Don't be sorry about that," I said quietly, as she stepped back toward her stool. "Hey," I said, turning to Pell.

She nodded at me, her eyes angry and her forehead creased. "They're in the back."

When I opened the door to Jerry's office, Rex got up from the chair facing the desk and crossed the distance between us in two steps. He grabbed me by the upper arm and gave me a kiss that dissipated my need to lecture him on making assumptions about what was best for me and disregarding my contributions to the fight against GHA and H4H, and several other things that, by the time he pulled away from me, I had temporarily forgotten.

Jerry, sitting behind his desk, raised an eyebrow. "You about done?"

Rex ignored him. "I'm sorry," he said to me, with an earnestness that, as far as I had seen in the world, only he was capable of. "I worry about you sometimes, that's all."

"Yeah, you said that already."

"Well, it's still true. But I'm also really glad you're here. We can definitely use your help."

I put my hand on his cheek and nodded.

Jerry cleared his throat, and Rex and I turned to look at him. He looked terrible. Then I realized Rex did, too. They were both pale and haggard, with dark rings under red eyes.

"You two look awful," I told them. "Were you both up all night?"

They exchanged a glance, then Rex nodded. "We were with Doc. Trying to get the bail thing sorted out. Then going with him to turn himself in."

"Oh, wow. Sorry."

"Yeah, so we've got a lot of stuff to figure out," Jerry said.

Rex gestured toward a second chair facing the desk, and I sat in it as he eased himself back onto his. There was a platter of muffins on the desk; he gestured at those, too, but I shook my head. "We were talking about how the hell we're going to get Doc out of jail," he said.

Jerry looked at his watch. "Yeah, and we were doing it in a hurry because I got to get out of here."

"Where are you going?" I asked.

Jerry huffed impatiently, but Rex said, "He has to go get the case files from DeWitt, to hand them off to whoever we get to take over this case."

"Is there another lawyer ready?"

"Not with all this GHA stuff," Jerry said. "We had a hell of a time finding the first one." He pointed at Rex. "Which reminds me, you were saying something about using GHA as part of Doc's defense?"

Rex shook his head. "No, I was saying we couldn't. DeWitt suggested we could argue that there was no crime because of GHA, that Cornelius wasn't . . . a person, as far as the law is concerned."

"Yeah, but Doc said no way," I cut in. "That was when he kicked us out. He said it was against everything he stood for."

"Exactly," Rex said. "*That's* what I was saying."

Jerry shook his head. "Look, I feel you. I really do. And Doc, too. I love the guy and what you just said is a big part of why. But you saw him yesterday. They beat the crap out of him in that jail. How much more of that do you think he can take? We need to get him out of there. Now."

"We need to go out to that hospital," I blurted out. "OmniCare. The one from the bracelet."

"What are you talking about?" Jerry asked, looking back and forth between Rex and me.

"The hospital bracelet," Rex said. He moved around a few papers on Jerry's desk and pulled out a photocopy of the bracelet. "The one Cornelius was wearing. Doc said the code was from an OmniCare hospital, and there's only one in the whole state."

"You have a copy of it?" I reached out and took it from him. "How did you get this?"

"DeWitt. She got her copy from the police and made a copy for Doc." He turned back to Jerry.

"Yeah, yeah, I remember," said Jerry. "But DeWitt said the police called there, and she called there, and they said they didn't have this Cornelius kid in their system, right?"

"Yeah, but what if that's BS?" I said, holding up the photocopy. "We need to go out there. To the hospital. Show them this, at the very least. And see if we can find—"

"Ach." Jerry shook his head dismissively. "We don't have time to be chasing down false leads."

"How do you *know* it's a false lead?" I shot back.

"Look, I'm not saying a lot of police aren't corrupt, or stupid or hateful, but they followed the lead. It didn't pan out. And DeWitt called, too. She got the same result."

"So *what*?" I looked to Rex for support, but he was staring at the floor in front of the desk, listening, hearing us out. "Whatever," I said, looking back at Jerry. "Why would he have a bracelet from that hospital, then?"

Jerry rolled his eyes. "I don't know. Maybe it's fake, to get drugs or something."

"Did he have any drugs in his system?"

Rex shook his head without looking up. "No," he said. "Doc told me they checked."

Before Jerry could continue, I said, "Isn't it conceivable that maybe this hospital is lying?"

"Why?" Jerry said, but then his face changed, as if he started actually wondering about it. Then he looked at his watch and shook himself out of it. "Shit, I got to go get those case files."

My heart sank as he started pulling his coat on.

"Look," I said. "Maybe you're right. Maybe the bracelet was fake and it was about drugs, and maybe he sold them instead of taking them. But that would mean he got his drugs from OmniCare illegally, right? Wouldn't that make them look bad? That could be something they'd lie about, isn't it?"

"And what would that prove?" he said. "Nothing."

"Unless we can figure out what else might have killed him, they're going to pin it on Doc. And that bracelet is our only lead."

I could see Jerry was thinking about it, but he was also headed for the door. As he yanked it open and hurried out of the office, I followed close behind.

Ruth was standing outside the door, startled as Jerry barreled past her. "There's someone here to see—"

Jerry waved her off. "Can't. I'm already late."

I followed him, with Rex close behind us. "And what if he *was* a patient there?" I said. "What if they treated him and did something wrong and that's why he died? What if they killed Cornelius and they're letting Doc take the fall?"

Jerry paused, his face conflicted. "Look, all I know is, the lawyer said it was a dead end."

"Right, and now *she's* a dead end, and Doc is in jail."

Jerry opened the door and paused halfway through it as the cold air rushed in. "Look, I'll ask DeWitt's assistant if we can get the ball rolling on filing a subpoena."

"A subpoena? DeWitt said that could take weeks, and it was hopeless anyway. She said the hospital can just say there's nothing to subpoena."

"Sorry, kid," he said. "I'm as worried about Doc as you, more even, but that's the best we can legally do."

Then he was gone.

I turned to face Rex. "We need to go out there. Now. Doc needs our help."

"We can't, Jimi," he said, shaking off a yawn. "DeWitt was clear about that. Us getting involved like that could screw everything up for Doc."

"What she was *clear* on was that she didn't have time to do it herself," I snapped. I felt bad badgering him. He looked so tired. But he still looked a hell of a lot better than Doc. "And Doc was out on bail when she said that. Now he's back inside. Things are *already* screwed up for Doc—now. And we need to help him, *now*."

He took a deep breath, then nodded as he let it out. "Okay. Maybe. But Gellersville is in the middle of nowhere, with no Levline or anything. We have no way of getting out there right now."

"I'll drive," said a vaguely familiar voice, coming from behind Rex. When he turned around I saw who it was, and I gasped.

CHAPTER 16

C *laudia?"* I said, stunned. "Oh my God!"
      The last time I'd seen her, she was just about to have her splice reversed by Doc. Except, as I'd just discovered the day before— and as I could see for myself, now—it had been too late after all.

In ways, she looked just as I remembered her: slim and achingly pretty, with large, gray-green feline eyes and a spray of spots from her forehead into her hairline. But the last time I'd seen her, she'd been traumatized and afraid, drawing on an impressively deep well of strength, but close to exhausting it. Now she looked strong and confident—happy, even. But worried, too.

She smiled when she saw me, broad and bright, adding an extra sparkle to her crystalline eyes. "Hi, Jimi."

She slipped around Rex, glancing up at him as she did, and hugged me tightly.

"You look great," she told me as she stepped back.

"You, too," I said. "Really." She had on a tight blue sweater and jeans under a smartly tailored Nanoma overcoat that matched her eyes. "I just found out your fix didn't take. All this time I'd thought . . ."

She put her hand on my arm. "It's fine," she said. "It's good, really. I'm glad it didn't take." She shook her head. "I was . . . freaked out, at first, alone and then with GHA and the riots and everything. But I got spliced because I *wanted* to. I'm happy."

"Good," I said. "Then I am, too." I stepped toward Rex and put my hand on his back. "Have you two met?"

"No," she said. "I'm Claudia."

She put out her hand and Rex's enveloped hers.

"Rex," he said.

"Doc has told me a lot about you."

"You know Doc?" he said.

"Yeah. We've kept in touch the last few months."

"Really?" I had not seen that coming.

Her face turned serious. "That's why I'm here. I heard he was in trouble and I want to do whatever I can to help." She pulled out a set of car keys. "You want to get to Gellersville? I've got a car out front. Fully charged. If Doc needs help, let's go."

It was the last Friday of winter break, and my mom had just left town until Sunday night. Gellersville was a hundred miles there and a hundred miles back. This could work.

I turned to Rex. "Are you coming with us?"

The look on his face made it clear he had misgivings. But he nodded.

As we headed for the door, Pell called out, "Hey!"

We stopped and turned to see her coming up behind us with a white paper bag. "Might as well take the muffins."

"Thanks," I said with a smile.

When we got outside, Claudia headed for a very nice, very new Jaguar. "Holy crap," I said. "This is yours?"

She smiled, bashful but not embarrassed. "It was a birthday present from my parents."

Rex grunted. "Wow. That's quite a gift."

"So . . ." I paused, trying to process this new information about Claudia's family's financial situation.

She gave me a shrug, unapologetically acknowledging that yes, she was kind of loaded. "So, hop in."

I turned to Rex. "You want shotgun?"

He yawned and shook his head as he reached for the rear door. "Actually, do you mind if I stretch out in back?"

As we took the Roosevelt Smartway to the Schuylkill Smartway, the car was virtually silent except for the soft sound of the tires, like two pieces of paper barely touching.

Rex was less silent. By the time we were headed west on the Pennsylvania SmartPike, he was snoring lightly.

Claudia kept one hand casually resting on the wheel, even though the car was in Smartdrive, like she enjoyed the feel of it. She reached the other hand into the paper bag and started eating one of Pell's muffins.

Rex let out a soft groan as he adjusted his position, and Claudia looked over her shoulder at him.

"I guess he was really tired," she said.

"He and Jerry were up all night trying to keep Doc out of jail," I said, grabbing a muffin, too. "Then they went with him to turn himself in."

"That must have been intense."

"Yeah, I think it was."

She shook her head. Then, after a few seconds, she looked over at me, smiling. "So . . . how long? You and Rex?"

I looked back to make sure he was sleeping. "Hard to say, really. How much do you know about what happened after you and I parted ways?"

"I saw you on the news. And Doc filled me in on a few things."

"So you know what happened at Pitman? What Haven really was? And what happened to my friend Del?"

"Yeah," she said, her voice dropping to a whisper. She put a hand on my arm. "I'm so sorry. That must have been awful."

"It was." I looked away, for some reason embarrassed about this next part.

"What?" she asked, nervous laughter creeping into her voice.

I let out a sigh. "So, Rex and I got close out there. And right when everything was coming to a head, I found out I actually knew him from before, from when we were little. His name was Leo Byron, and he was one of my best friends. He moved away from our neighborhood and I never saw him again. Well, not until he was Rex."

"*What?*" Claudia looked incredulous. "And he didn't tell you right away?"

I shook my head. "Nope. It was only a few days, but he actually didn't tell me until after I'd already found out."

"That's . . . that's kind of awkward. Why?"

"I don't know. He says he was embarrassed at first, or just weirded out. And I guess I understand that. Then, after we got to know each other, it was just too awkward, and I guess I understand that, too. But it's bizarre. I mean, we were, like, best friends. At least as close as Del and I were."

"Wow. So . . . how's it going now?"

"Good. I guess. Great. " I peeked over at him. His breathing had quieted, but I was pretty sure he was still asleep. "I've only seen him a couple of times since then, briefly. He's mostly been out of town."

"Where?"

I could feel myself blushing. "Well, interesting you should ask. He says he can't tell me."

She turned and stared at me with one eyebrow raised, long enough that even though the car was driving itself I started to get nervous. "Really?"

I nodded. "He's a really nice guy," I added quickly. "And I'm sure if he says he can't tell me where he was it's for a very good reason, but . . ."

"Hmm." She moved the rearview mirror and studied him in it. After a few seconds, she grinned. "Well, he's hot. I'll give you that."

We started laughing, but trying to keep quiet, which made it even funnier. When we finally stopped, I whispered, "Yeah, there is that."

For a few minutes we didn't talk, then Claudia turned and looked at me solemnly. "My name has always been Claudia, and I promise you: we've never known each other before."

We laughed some more. Then I said, "So, um . . . I met Brian."

She looked at me, truly embarrassed this time. "I know. I know," she said, shaking her head. "Ruth told me what happened at Doc's clinic."

I nodded. I wasn't surprised word had traveled.

"Ugh. He's the worst. Manipulative, controlling, deceitful, and a coward, too." She shook her head. "Just so you know, it wasn't obvious at first. He seemed like a nice guy. We'd been going out for a few months when I told him I was thinking about getting spliced." She laughed. "He freaked out about it at first, saying stuff like 'What about college?' and 'You'll never get a job.'" She shook her head at the memory.

"Well, he probably didn't know any chimeras," I said quietly as I remembered saying those exact same things to Del. "Maybe all he knew was what they tell you in health class. And he was worried about you."

"You're too easy on him." She laughed, then caught herself. "Sorry, I forgot. You didn't want your friend Del to get spliced. And I know it didn't . . . work out."

"It's okay. Sorry I was so judgy back then," I said—even though it crossed my mind that if he hadn't gotten spliced, Del might still be alive.

"No," she said. "You weren't being judgy. You didn't think your friend should get spliced, and maybe you were right about that. But you didn't judge the other chimeras. You didn't judge me. You tried to help me. I wish more people were like you."

"I was judgy. I might have hidden it, but I was."

"Well, you hid it pretty well, as far as I could see. Maybe that's just as important." She paused. "I think Brian was worried about losing me, maybe. Which he should have been, really. I was already starting to realize he wasn't the guy I thought he was, you know?"

I nodded.

"Anyway," she went on, "he decided he was going to get spliced with me. I told him he shouldn't do it just because I was, but he insisted, said he wanted to do it for him. I asked him if he would still want to do it even if we ever broke up, and he said yes. And I asked him about his parents, you know? Because my parents were pretty cool about all this, but his parents . . . I mean, I don't think they're H4H or anything, but one thing they're *not* is cool. He said he didn't care what his parents thought. I was starting to think maybe I was wrong about him again. Maybe he *was* more like who I thought he was to begin with. And then we went to the genie."

She got quiet for a moment, remembering. "I went first. And after I got my splice, after I'd already started sweating it out, when it was his turn, he freaks out and bolts. He said he changed his mind and he left me there. And then with GHA and the riots, I freaked out, too, started second-guessing everything." She shook her head, her eyes welling up. "The genie was great, though. Alfredo. He tried to help, but he wasn't a fixer or anything. He just did what he could, you know? He gave me a splice, and took good care of me while I finished sweating it out. And at the end of it, I mean . . . it was a pretty good splice, I think."

"It was a fantastic splice. You look amazing."

"Well, thanks, but I mean I felt good, physically. I felt strong and healthy. It's a big adjustment, for sure, and it was really upsetting to find out the law had passed just as I was coming through the other side. But . . . I think if I had gone to get spliced on my own in the first place, the way I had planned, I think I would have been okay. I would have been upset about GHA and the riots and all, but I don't think I would have freaked out like I did."

She leaned over and squeezed my hand. "I know that in the end I didn't get my splice fixed, and I'm glad I didn't, but that doesn't lessen how much I appreciate what you did for me that day. You saved my life from those H4Hers, and you kept me calm, enough that when the fix didn't take, I had it together enough to realize I never actually *wanted* it to."

"I'm really glad you're happy," I said, putting my hand over hers. I glanced out the window, watching the patchy brush whizz past us. "So, you've been keeping in touch with Doc? What's that about?"

She nodded. "After Doc gave me the fix, I figured if I had to sweat it out, I'd rather do it at home than in Jerry's basement, you know? Doc said it would be a little while before things kicked in, and he was busy trying to save poor Ryan. My dad was back home by then so I called him to come and get me. When I got in the car, he just looks at me and says, 'Hey, you got spliced. Looks awesome.' Then I told him I had changed my mind and was having the splice reversed, and he looks at me again and says, 'Right. Well, that's awesome, too.'"

"Wow," I said. "He sounds kind of great."

"Kind of," she said, with a tiny bit of an edge. "It can be a bit much. Luckily, my mom's not quite as laid back, so they mostly balance each other that way. But she was in Switzerland giving a lecture while all this was happening. Anyway, so I'm lying on the sofa, exhausted and starting to notice that nothing's happening. I had told my dad about Doc, about where he lived, and after a couple of hours, my dad goes and sees him. The next day, Doc came to our house and he looks me over and he frowns. He's clearly upset. He puts a hand on my shoulder, and says, 'I guess we were too late after all.' I didn't know what to think. I was already having second thoughts about my second thoughts, but mostly I was just tired. Anyway, my dad smiles down at me and says, 'Don't worry, pumpkin, it's a good splice. You're healthy and you look great. It's all good.' And then he starts asking Doc more questions about his research."

She saw the expression on my face and said, "I know, right? I love him to bits, but in case you're wondering: yes, there is such a thing as *too* chill."

We both laughed.

"So, as Doc's leaving, he and my dad get into this deep conversation about some new procedure Doc is working on, with, like, stem cells and umbilical-cord blood and stuff."

"Yeah, Doc told us about that."

"Well my dad was kind of geeking out over it. He's mostly into computers and engineering, like me, but he's interested in all sorts of other stuff, too. He's oblivious sometimes, but he's really smart. They stayed in touch after that. Anyway, my mom got home that afternoon, and she decided that between my splice and Brian and all the craziness here with GHA, we needed to head out to the West Coast for a couple of months, take some time to *recalibrate*, as she put it."

I grinned at the annoyance in her voice. "You know, Claudia, a lot of people would be just fine with a little recalibration like that."

"Yeah, I know," she said. "And she was right. I kind of needed it."

"What about school?" I asked.

"They set me up with a tutor. Dad and Doc kept in touch the whole time we were away, though, and I'd chat with Doc when he called. He mentions the big guy a lot," she said, tipping her head back toward Rex. "Doc thinks he's pretty impressive."

I smiled. "I think so, too."

CHAPTER 17

For most of the trip, Claudia and I listened to music, a mixture of oldies and newer stuff. After an hour, though, she opened a map on the dashboard and turned the music off.

"So the SmartPike goes pretty close to Gellersville, which is in two exits," she said. "But OmniCare is actually slightly closer to Belfield, which is the next exit. Either way we have to drive a few miles of local roads to get there, which could be a little rough going."

"Well, what's faster?"

"Belfield should be a little quicker. Just wondering if you have a preference about which exit we take."

I glanced back at Rex, wishing he were awake to weigh in. "Um, not really," I said.

As we approached the exit, her face turned serious. The sign said GELLERSVILLE 5 MI with an arrow pointing straight, and BELFIELD / BOGEN ROAD with an arrow pointing to the exit.

Claudia gripped the steering wheel tightly as she took the car out of Smartdrive, which isn't really programmed to drive on bad roads. The exit ramp was as smooth as the SmartPike, but just past the bottom it changed abruptly to a cracked patchwork of asphalt, punctured here and there by dead, snow-covered stalks of weeds.

A rusted sign had two arrows pointing left, one for BELFIELD 1 MI and below it, on a new panel bolted over whatever had been underneath it, one for OMNICARE GELLERSVILLE 4 MI.

The snow had held off while we were on the SmartPike, but it started falling as we turned onto Bogen Road, toward Belfield. The roads were already icy, and even with the Jaguar's advanced traction, we skidded a few times. We drove by several dilapidated houses and an abandoned diner, half covered with vines. The brush thinned and fell away completely as we passed several working farms, the fields striped with snow between the rows of stubble.

There was also a wind and solar farm, with a couple of acres of ice-encrusted panels and a handful of wind turbines spinning vigorously as if to make up for it. After that was Belfield, a quaint little town, too small to have a fence, like some towns did. The main street was lined with brick storefronts decorated with planters of dead, icy mums and lights in the shape of Christmas bells.

I watched it go by, feeling a moment of trepidation as I wondered what kind of people lived there, if it was full of chimera-haters, like Pitman. I looked back at Rex, still asleep, then at Claudia. It occurred to me that, especially with GHA back on the books, it probably wasn't a good idea for them to be out here.

We drove under an old railroad bridge as a couple of other cars came the other way, off-road types with high suspensions going faster than we dared.

The Jaguar's heated windshield did a good job of vaporizing any snowflakes that actually landed on it, but visibility was getting worse. Claudia seemed to know what she was doing. She also seemed stressed, which was somehow reassuring. I was stressed, too.

We hit a pretty bad pothole, and Claudia cursed under her breath. She turned to me with a forced smile. "Well, that knocked some rust off."

The car didn't seem to have a speck of rust on it. I hoped it hadn't knocked off anything else, instead.

The snow was coming down even harder now, and Claudia and I were leaning forward, squinting through the snow, when a deep voice behind us said, "Where are we?"

We both jumped and turned to see Rex rubbing the sleep from his eyes.

"We just got off the SmartPike," Claudia said. "We should be there in a half hour."

As she said it, the car lurched, worse than before, and scraped bottom with a wrenching screech. Rex's head hit the ceiling and mine probably would have if I hadn't been wearing my seat belt.

"*Shit!*" Claudia called out. "Sorry. Didn't see that one."

I couldn't tell if she was apologizing for the pothole or the language.

The snow eased up and the road got a little better, but it seemed that as the road got flatter, it got slipperier, too. Rex and I exchanged glances each time the rear of the car started to slide.

A faint, metallic grinding noise started coming from the undercarriage, and after half a mile, a red light appeared on the dashboard. Then it started blinking.

Claudia rolled her eyes and pulled over to the side of the road. She seemed more aggravated than worried.

"What is it?" I asked.

"The charger plate. There seems to be a minor short."

"What does that mean?" Rex asked. "I mean, practically?"

She sighed. "It means the battery is discharging into itself."

"Can the car still go?" I asked.

"Not for long. The battery won't last, and if it starts to run hot it'll shut itself off." She opened her door and got out.

"What are you going to do?" I called after her. Snow swirled in through the open door.

She looked back at me and said matter-of-factly, "I'm going to fix it."

Rex shrugged and I got out the passenger side. Claudia was rooting around in the trunk. "Crap!" she said.

"What is it?" I said, coming up next to her.

"No tools. Argh! My dad must have borrowed them and not put them back."

"Does that mean you can't fix it?" Rex said.

Claudia straightened, holding a voltage meter in one hand and a crowbar in the other. "Well, these aren't the *ideal* tools. But they'll have to do."

I must have looked skeptical, because she pointed the crowbar at me and said, "It's just a charging plate, Jimi. If you're going to drive, you better know how to fix a dinged charging plate." She glanced at Rex and said, "Right?"

As she dropped onto the icy ground, wriggling under the car, Rex looked at me and shrugged, shaking his head. "I don't know how to do that," he mumbled.

As we stood there in the cold, Rex and I looked at each other, but wordlessly resisted the urge to cling to each other for warmth.

"You hungry?" I asked.

He put his hand on his midsection and nodded. "Now that you mention it."

I reached into the car and handed him the bag with the muffins. "This one's got your name on it."

As he started eating, a truck approached, bumping over the rough road on its high suspension. It slowed as it passed us, enough for someone inside to lower the window and shout, "Mixie trash!"

Rex rolled his eyes and shook his head, still chewing.

"I'm sorry," I said.

He swallowed. "You don't need to apologize for every idiot in the world."

"I know," I said. "I just—"

"I know." He stepped up close and rubbed one hand up and down my back.

Metal clanged against metal under the car, followed by a flash of bright blue light as a handful of sparks skittered across the ground. A moment later, Claudia wriggled back out. She got to her feet and tossed the crowbar and voltmeter back into the trunk, then took off her coat and shook off the worst of the dirt and ice.

"Well, that's as good as I can do without a socket set. It was a pretty bad ding, but we should be fine getting out to OmniCare and back."

As Claudia got back into the car, I turned to Rex and said, "Full of surprises, isn't she?"

"Seems like it, huh?" Rex said, putting the last of the muffin into his mouth.

As we got back into the car, it occurred to me that maybe I was the only one of the three of us who *wasn't* full of surprises.

Claudia started up the car again, and the red light started blinking. Then it went solid, then it went out.

"There you go," she said, smiling. The car rocked and wobbled as she eased it back onto the road. The metallic grinding noise hadn't gone away entirely, but we didn't mention that.

We'd gone about half a mile when a bright light in the shape of the rearview mirror appeared on Claudia's face. She squinted as she looked into the light. I turned and saw Rex already looking out the back window at a pair of headlights, bright, high off the ground, and approaching fast.

None of us said anything, but the vibe in the car, already tense, grew even more so.

As the headlights got closer, I felt an ambiguous mixture of relief and dread that it wasn't the police. Instead it was a truck, like the one that had passed us when we were on the side of the road. Maybe even the same one.

The truck came right up behind us, close enough that it had to be intentional, and flashed its high beams.

"There's plenty of room to pass, you jerk," Claudia said under her breath.

It seemed pretty obvious they were more interested in harassing us than passing us. Claudia's eyes flickered back and forth from the road ahead of us to the morons behind us. Then the truck slowed slightly, easing back to a safe distance.

Claudia opened her mouth to say something, but before she could, the truck accelerated again with a screech of tires, rocketing straight at us before braking hard with another screech and a blast of its horn right behind us.

Claudia gasped and the car slid just a little.

Rex and I watched as the truck receded behind us again. The muscles in his neck and his jaw were taut. When he turned around, our eyes met. His were filled with anger, resentment, and fear, and a heartbreaking disappointment that I'd seen in them too often, especially considering how little time we'd actually spent together. Humanity continued to let him down, again and again, no matter how much he lowered his expectations.

"Assholes," he muttered. Strong language, for Rex.

We were approaching the top of a slight hill, and the truck was well behind us, but its tires screeched again as it sped toward us once more. This time, instead of braking, it swerved around us, missing the Jaguar by inches. Its brake lights lit up in front of us, just for an instant, and Claudia slammed her own brakes—hard.

The anti-lock system kicked in, keeping us straight, but the road curved to the left. Between the ice, the hill, and the uneven asphalt, the tires couldn't get a grip. The rear of the car swung out as we slid toward the edge of the road.

To her credit, Claudia turned into the skid and regained control of the car, but not before we slid over a huge chunk of asphalt. A terrible sound came from under our feet, like a ship hitting an iceberg. Claudia wrestled the car back onto the road, and as she eased to a stop, all three of us exhaled.

As the truck shrank in front of us, its horn beeped twice, an oddly friendly sound, then it disappeared around the bend.

"Is everybody okay?" Rex asked.

Claudia nodded. She looked like maybe she wasn't ready to talk yet.

"Yeah, we're okay," I said.

Claudia took a deep breath and let it out. She looked in the rearview, then took her foot off the brake and eased down on the accelerator.

The car rolled forward and started picking up speed, but we hadn't gone fifty yards before the red light on the dashboard came back on and started blinking. Then it went out, along with all the interior lights, the headlights, the motor, and apparently the power steering. Claudia had to crank the steering wheel hard to coax the car to the side of the road as it coasted to a stop.

She was quiet for a moment, then she assaulted the steering wheel with a flurry of punches and a blistering stream of obscenities.

I agreed with every word of it, including a few words I would have to look up later.

In the silence that followed, a gust of wind pelted the car with snow and ice.

"Can you fix it?" I asked.

She let out a dubious sigh. "Let's find out."

Rex and I got out with her. It felt colder than before.

She got her crowbar and voltmeter out of the trunk and got back down under the car. Rex and I looked up and down the road, keeping an eye out for morons as Claudia cursed and clanged under the car. A minute later, she climbed out from under the car and shook her head. "Not this time," she said, apologetically.

"We must be almost there, right?" I said.

She nodded. "Yeah, a mile or two."

"All righty then," said Rex, clapping his hands and rubbing them together. "Guess we better start walking, right?"

CHAPTER 18

The road curved sharply to the right, but straight ahead of us, a path cut through the woods. Claudia looked at the map and said we could save some time by going straight. Rex and I agreed, relieved to be off the road anyway.

As we entered the woods, the air filled with the sharp, dry cracking of the frozen leaves and twigs under our feet.

The path narrowed, and Rex ended up in the lead, but he came to an abrupt stop.

Coming up next to him, we saw a road, or what was left of it. It wasn't just crumbled, like the streets in the zurbs. It was buckled, or heaved, like something had pushed it up from underneath, an explosion or some subterranean monster. It looked dark, too, like the snow and ice had left it alone.

"This road isn't on the map," Claudia said.

"Well, there's not much left of it," Rex said. "It was probably closed long before that map was created."

As we crossed the road and continued on, the brush grew thicker. Vines hung from the trees, and although the trees were bare, the vines were still mostly green, despite the ice and the cold.

A light fog was settling in.

We came upon a tiny house, covered with mats of thick green vines. "It looks like topiary," Rex said, and it did.

Continuing on, we passed a few more buildings, all draped in green. As the foliage grew denser, the crisp, frozen air took on a vaguely stuffy smell, like a closed-up room. We exchanged glances as we crossed another jumble of asphalt chunks and descended into a shallow valley.

To my left, I noted another row of leafy mounds that might once have been houses. One had steam rising from it, blending with the fog. There wasn't a speck of snow or ice on it. I slowed, looking around, and saw several other faint columns of steam rising from dark spots on the ground where the thin layer of snow and ice had melted away.

"Do you see that?" I said. My voice sounded thick, my words almost slurred. Before the others could answer, I saw a dull flash of color through the brush to our left.

We all turned to look, but nothing was there.

"I saw it," Claudia said. She sounded far away.

From the corner of my eye, I saw a similar flash between two trees to our right. I spun around, but my eyes wouldn't focus. My feet weren't working right either. I tried to make sense of what was happening, but the synapses in my brain seemed sluggish. The movement in the trees solidified into something—some*one*—watching us, but by then my vision was starting to fade.

I turned my head, looking for Rex. He was standing behind me, his head tilted, like he was listening, so still it seemed as though time had stopped.

"Rex?" I said. My voice sounded like I was in a tunnel or down a well.

The first tendrils of fear penetrated the confusion as I realized that whatever was happening, it wasn't good.

Rex turned to look at me in slow motion. His body started to move toward me but his feet were rooted to the ground. His eyes rolled up and he toppled like a tree.

"Rex!" I cried out, barely able to hear myself through the rushing noise that filled my ears.

He hit the ground hard, sending tiny twigs and crumbled leaves tumbling out from under him. I looked around for Claudia and saw her already on the ground.

I started to call her name, too, but my voice was no longer working. Then neither were my eyes. Then everything else was gone, except the sensation of falling.

CHAPTER 19

I woke up with a start and with a headache, lying on my back in the frozen woods, looking up at bare trees and a flurry of snow falling through them. I was afraid for Rex and Claudia, afraid that I was all alone. But when I looked around, I saw them lying on either side of me, both coming out of whatever unconsciousness had overtaken us.

We were at the side of a crumbling road, similar to the one we had crossed before, but I was pretty sure it wasn't the same one. To our left there was a cluster of two or three houses, looking vacant but remarkably intact. A ways beyond them was a blue VW, relatively new, smashed up against a tree.

I sat up, trying to figure out where we were in relation to where we had been, and saw a wide furrow that ran through the leaves and the snow. It ended at the spot where Rex was lying on the ground, and led back down into the woods, to a place where the foliage was thicker and greener.

Once I saw the trail Rex had made, I made out two fainter trails next to it, one leading to Claudia and one to me.

"Someone dragged us up out of there," I said, as my head cleared. They both looked at me, confused. I pointed to the trails. "You can see where."

Behind us, on the side of the road, was a rotted wooden sign, sagging where one of the support posts had given away completely. WELCOME TO CENTRE HOLLOW it had once said. HOME OF THE FIGHTING BOBCATS.

Or at least, I'm pretty sure that's what it said. Another sign had been posted across it, diagonally, saying THIS TOWN HAS BEEN CONDEMNED BY THE U.S. GOVERNMENT DUE TO TOXIC EMISSIONS. NO TRESPASSING.

"Centre Hollow," I read aloud. It sounded vaguely familiar.

Claudia followed my gaze. "Centre Hollow?" she said slowly. "Jesus, no wonder."

"What?" Rex said. "What is it?"

"It's Centre Hollow," she repeated, as if that explained everything.

"Wait." Rex shook his head, as if to clear a fog. "Is that the town that was on top of that huge underground coal well?"

"That's it," said Claudia.

"Right," Rex said, rubbing the back of his neck. "And all the gases started coming out of the ground."

"That was, like, twenty years ago," Claudia said, peering back into the woods we'd been dragged out of. "My dad told me about it. The whole town was condemned. Forcibly evacuated."

Rex winced as he removed a handful of leaves and twigs that had gotten wedged in the waistband of his pants. "We could have been killed back there."

"Yeah, well, someone dragged us out," I repeated. "They saved us."

"Not *too* creepy," Claudia said sarcastically.

"Right? I wonder who it was."

Rex looked back, then squinted up at the sky, like he was tracking the sun through the thick clouds. I couldn't tell if he was creeped out, too. "Well, I'd love to thank them," he said. "But we need to get going."

Claudia pointed in the direction away from the Centre Hollow sign. "I'm pretty sure that's west."

Rex and I nodded and we started walking, up a gentle incline. Looking back, I saw that on the back of the Centre Hollow sign someone had spray-painted E4E 4-EVER.

Claudia looked back too, and said, "Chimeras."

Rex smiled. "They're everywhere."

"Do you think that's who helped us?" I asked.

"Maybe," Claudia said. "But how could they survive if we couldn't?"

"Maybe they had breathing masks, like Cornelius had."

"Maybe," Rex said.

The brush thinned out the farther we went, and a few minutes later we pushed past a wall of brittle vines and out onto a road. There were no signs, but it looked rough but functional, like Bogen Road, where we'd left Claudia's car.

With a group shrug, we unanimously decided to take it.

As chewed-up as it was, I was still happy to be walking on pavement.

The road curved along and a sign came into view, partially rusted out, displaying a blue rectangle with a white H in it, and an arrow.

Just past it, we slowed down as we came upon an unpaved driveway on the side of the road. Twenty feet in from the road, there was a kiosk with a big green button, and beyond it a gate with black and yellow stripes.

"Is that it?" Rex asked.

A small, bulky-looking box truck appeared on the road, coming from the opposite direction. It pulled into the driveway, and the driver reached out and pressed the green button. The gate rose and the truck continued on, up an access road toward a sort of notch cut into the hillside.

"I don't think so," I said.

We angled to the far side of the road, cautiously eying the gate and the access road leading past it. As more of the dirt road came into view, we could see it was wide and flat, and at the end of it, set into the side of the hill, there was a massive steel door, like a garage door but bigger. A simple sign above it said CENTRE RIDGE – MAIN BRANCH.

The door slowly started to rise as the truck pulled up in front of it and two men got out. The driver stood by his door. He was tall, with bleached hair shaved on the sides and a matching blond patch on his chin. His partner, short and heavy with shaggy dark hair, went around and opened the back of the truck.

Behind them, two figures emerged from the darkness beyond the big door, each carrying a stack of gray boxes. Their movements were strangely jerky. For a moment I wondered if they were chimeras of some sort. But as they got closer, I realized they were a lot bigger than the figures by the truck.

"They're wearing exosuits!" Claudia said. "That's so cool!"

"What's an *exo*suit?" Rex asked.

"They're, like, semi-robotic steel frames, but incredibly strong and fast and maneuverable. Like a forklift that you wear. They're used for, like, really high-end industrial work. I tried a few out when my dad was buying one for an assembly plant his company owns. They're pretty badass."

The frames had big gaps all over, where you could see the yellow fabric of the coveralls the operators wore.

"Wonder what they're doing out here," Rex said quietly.

Claudia shook her head. "Don't know. This looks like a mine entrance, but that doesn't make sense, this close to Centre Hollow. I thought all the coal around here had been liquefied and pumped out a long time ago."

As the two guys in the exosuits put the boxes into the back of the truck, it sank down low on its tires. Each of the boxes was marked with an orange square surrounding a bold, black letter Y.

"Let's keep moving," Rex said, but as we resumed walking, a smaller figure ran out of the darkened entrance, then abruptly stumbled and fell, just past the truck. A third guy in an exosuit appeared just inside the entrance.

"Did they just *shock* that person?" I said as we stopped to look.

"I didn't see," Claudia said.

"He sure fell hard," Rex said as the third exosuit reached down with one hand and picked up the figure on the ground. The other two exosuits joined him. Together they walked back into the garage or whatever it was, then the huge door began to slowly close.

The dark-haired guy closed the rear of the truck, and the one with the little beard paused at the driver's-side door and glanced over in our direction.

Without a word, we looked away and quickened our pace.

"What the *hell* was that about?" I said.

"Don't know," Rex said. "Maybe the mine is still operational?"

Claudia shook her head. "Like I said, there's nothing left to mine around here. It'd just be slag. And the carbon dioxide they pump down there to force out the liquid coal."

Rex tilted his head. "Slag?"

"The stuff that's left behind from the coal liquefaction," she said. "They pump the chemicals and steam into the coal and break it down, then force out the liquid fuels with carbon dioxide. It totally destabilizes the mines. Miners used to leave columns of coal to hold up the ceiling of the mine. But when they liquefy and suck *that* out, all that's left behind is a bunch of byproducts from the process—the slag—and a lot of carbon dioxide and other unbreathable gases. I'm sure that's what seeped up and killed Centre Hollow."

"How do you know this stuff?" I asked.

She shrugged. "My dad says if I'm going to go into the family business, I need to know this kind of stuff. But it's pretty interesting anyway."

"What is the family business?" Rex asked.

She shook her head. "All sorts of things, actually. My mom says my dad has the attention span of a fruit fly."

I looked at her. "All sorts of things, including . . . coal drilling?"

She scowled at me. "Of course not! But we are involved in environmental remediation, cleanups and stuff."

"Maybe they're here cleaning it up, then," I said. "Or fixing it so the gases aren't seeping out."

"I doubt it," Claudia said. "It's expensive, and I imagine this would be low on the list of priorities for rehabilitation."

Rex nodded. "Because there are so many places that are much worse off, contamination-wise. And closer to population centers."

Claudia pointed at him. "Exactly. I doubt Centre Hollow would make the top ten thousand."

CHAPTER 20

Once the coal mine or whatever was a little ways behind us, the road got better. We passed a few cross streets and began to see more cars and trucks coming and going. No one hassled us, but we moved off the road anyway. Better safe than sorry.

"There it is," Rex said, pointing. "OmniCare."

My stomach lurched. I'd been lost in thought, still unsure of exactly what I planned to do when we got there, or even what I hoped would happen when I did it. I had done some crazy things just a few months ago, and it all had turned out to be important, so I was glad I did. This time, though, I suddenly wondered if the whole venture was half-baked and ridiculously naïve.

The big metal-and-plastic sign said OMNICARE in white letters against a blue background. Below that, blue letters against a white panel listed the different departments—EMERGENCY, RADIOLOGY, OUTPATIENT, ADMINISTRATION. Each panel had an arrow pointing left or right.

"Okay," Rex said to me. "What's your plan?"

I had been thinking about that since we'd left the coffee shop. "We go to the emergency room," I said.

As we crossed the road and made our way up the driveway toward the ER, I explained my plan a little more. There wasn't much to it.

A guard nodded to us as the automatic door to the hospital slid open.

I'd only been in a handful of emergency waiting rooms in my life, but they all seemed to have the same vibe: a combination of pain and fear and anxiety, all somehow smothered under a thick blanket of boredom.

There were maybe a dozen people, in twos and threes, scattered in chairs across the room. Several were filling out paperwork. Roughly half were chimeras, which made me feel better about the place.

A guy not much older than me was mopping the floor. He was handsome, with shiny black hair trimmed neatly on the sides but topped with unruly curls that fell onto his forehead. He stared at us in a way that made me wonder if he somehow knew what we were up to. When I met his eye, he looked away and went back to his mopping, working his way out of sight down a hallway.

Claudia and Rex sat by the exit and I got in line at the check-in window, clutching the scanned copy of Cornelius's bracelet. My "plan" involved a lot of me bullshitting the intake nurse, but as I waited, I noticed a second window on the other side of the room with a sign that said BILLING. It gave me an idea.

As I turned toward the billing window, I overhead the chimera in front of me at the check-in counter saying, "Sorry, I don't have anyone for the emergency contact." He was holding up a clipboard with a form that said in bold across the top: ALL CHIMERA PATIENTS MUST FILL OUT A SPLICE DISCLOSURE AND EMERGENCY CONTACT FORM.

"That's okay, honey," said the intake nurse. "Just put 'NA,' for 'Not Applicable.'"

Unlike the check-in desk, the billing window was essentially a hole in the wall leading to a cramped office. A small ledge ran across the front of it, with pamphlets about flu shots and hand-washing.

The woman behind the window—her name tag said MAUREEN— glanced up at me. She looked bored and standoffish, like she was expecting a challenge or an argument or an excuse. Or some bullshit.

"Hi," I said, opening with a smile, trying to come off as young enough that she might want to cut me a break, but old enough that she should take me seriously.

She gave me a dubious look, but I kept smiling, waiting. Eventually she said, "How can I help you?"

I let my smile falter. "We're trying to find my brother. I know he was a patient here—"

"Name?" she said, cutting me off and turning to her computer.

The kid with the mop appeared over her shoulder. His name tag said DANIEL. His head was down, his eyes on his mop, but I got the distinct feeling he was listening in. That didn't help my nerves.

"Well, that's just it. His name is . . ." I froze for an instant, realizing I hadn't come up with a random name. "Bruce Johnson," I said, hoping that wasn't some Hollywood star or famous athlete. "But I'm not sure what name he used when he checked in here." I paused and looked around, then leaned forward and lowered my voice. "He's been involved in some . . . bad stuff. Drugs and . . . getting spliced. He's using different names. And running up debts. I know he was here because he had on this bracelet." I held up the copy. "My parents can pay whatever balance he left. They just want to know if he's okay. And what name he's using. So we can find him. And pay his debts."

She looked at me, maybe even more dubious than before, but she took the copy and ran it under the scanner next to her keyboard. I could just barely see her computer screen, enough to perceive it flicker and change. Her eyes widened, just for an instant, then she glanced at me again, her face different than before. She tapped a few keys and waited, tapped a few more and waited again. It seemed to be taking forever, and my heart was pounding.

Finally, she turned to me and shook her head. "Sorry, we have no record of that person here," she said, her voice flat and her face blank.

I glanced from her to the monitor. I wanted desperately to reach out and turn it so I could see it. Scratching my head, I turned to look behind me. Rex and Claudia were sitting by the exit. There didn't seem to be any security, other than the guy in the uniform standing outside. My new plan was to reach over and look at the monitor, see what it said, and then run.

Unfortunately, when I looked back at Maureen, there was a man standing behind her. He had appeared out of nowhere, a tall white guy with gray hair and a neatly trimmed beard, maybe sixty but with an athletic build. He looked like a doctor from a pharmaceutical commercial or a holo-show. He had a Wellplant, one of the new ones, and his head hung low so his chin was on his chest. He stood there like he owned the place, staring down at me in a way that was both eerily calm and frighteningly intense.

"Hello, Dr. Charlesford," Maureen said, flustered. Then I was flustered, too. If this was Charlesford, he really did own the place. He owned the entire company.

"What seems to be the problem, Maureen?" Charlesford asked. His eyes quickly scanned her computer screen, then darted back at me, as if he had his answer before she opened her mouth.

"This young lady—" she began.

"And what is your name?" he said, turning to me.

Good question, I thought, still flustered. "Mary," I said. "Mary Johnson."

"And how old are you, Mary?"

"Eighteen," I said.

His eye twitched.

"And you say this is your brother you're asking about?"

"That's right," I said. I hadn't told him that, and I wondered how he knew, if he'd overheard or if he knew because of something Maureen had typed into her computer. "His name is Bruce," I said, although I got the feeling he already knew that, too.

He asked me everything Maureen had asked, plus a dozen other questions: about the fictional Bruce's birthday, what school he went to, his medical history.

I tried to stay calm and casual, looking into his eyes and not at his Wellplant, but I got the impression he was studying my reaction more than listening to my answers. I briefly wondered if the Wellplant gave him some sort of built-in lie-detecting ability. I was pretty sure I'd heard somewhere that the new generation were sensitive enough to read *other* people's biometrics, not just the wearer's.

When he finally stopped asking questions, he continued to stare at me for a moment, then he said, "Well, I'm very sorry, Ms. Johnson, but your brother has never been a patient here."

He had an odd way of speaking. Flat and measured, almost robotic. It was hard to read his emotions, and I didn't have a Wellplant to help *me* read his micro-expressions or whatever. Even so, I was certain of one thing: he was lying just like I was.

"Okay, thanks," I said briskly. Then I reached through the window to grab my printout from Maureen's desk, leaning far enough in that I could see the computer screen.

In that brief second, I saw Cornelius's picture, complete with his brilliant feathers. He didn't look happy, but it was definitely him. Underneath it was the name Bennett Thompson—so Bruce Johnson hadn't been too far off. Two other things jumped out at me. It said he'd been transferred to something called the Chimeric Conversion Unit. And at the bottom of the page, in bold red letters, it said RESOLUTION: UNAUTHORIZED RELEASE.

Cornelius had been here. And he had run away.

CHAPTER 21

As soon as I realized Cornelius had escaped, it occurred to me I needed to do the same. When I had leaned through the window, Maureen had backed away, shocked by the intrusion into her space. Before she could lean forward or even say anything, Charlesford's hand shot past her and clamped onto my wrist. I looked up at him and when our eyes met, he smiled.

He was fast and probably stronger than me, but I had leverage and I was scared. I braced my other hand on the side of the window and wrenched free. Staggering back away from the window, I spun around and ran.

Rex and Claudia were already on their feet, but my heart sank as I looked past them and saw three guards pulling up in some kind of cart just outside the door. As I paused, another guard came at me from the side, holding a shock baton. Rex flattened the guy with his shoulder. Another guard came at us from the same direction, his shock baton already spitting blue sparks. I could smell the ozone coming off it. As he closed on Rex, Claudia threw herself onto his back and raked his face with her fingers. He screamed and tried to get her with the shock baton, until Rex punched him, once in the gut and once in the face.

Claudia jumped off him as he fell, landing on her feet at the same moment the guard's face hit the floor.

In the moment of quiet that followed, as the rest of the people in the waiting area sat up and stared, Rex flashed me a glare, letting me know that all his misgivings about coming out here were coming true.

The guards outside were running for the door.

"This way," I said, and took off running toward the far corridor, away from the guards at the entrance, away from Dr. Charlesford and Maureen in the billing office.

I pushed through the swinging metal doors and heard Rex and Claudia come through them behind me. I had no idea where we were headed, but I figured first things first: get away from the bad guys, *then* figure a way out of the building.

We were in a long corridor with doors on either side. None of them were open, and there was no sign of anyone else. At the far end there was a set of double doors, much like the ones we had just come through. As we drew closer, however, I realized one crucial difference.

"They're locked," Claudia said, before I could.

There was a keypad with a card slot next to the door, and a big red light next to the word LOCKED.

We'd barely had time to slow down when Rex reached between us and swiped a card through the slot. Claudia and I both stared as he pushed open the door.

"Picked it up off the floor. I think I knocked it off that guard back there. Figured it might come in handy."

The next corridor wasn't empty; there were doctors and other medical staff coming and going from room to room. A few of them looked up at us like we didn't belong in there, but apparently they were too busy to bother with us. At the end of the corridor was a single swinging door and a red EXIT sign. We headed toward it.

Just as we reached the door, a man in nurse's scrubs approached us and said, "Excuse me, can I help you?"

"No, we're good," I said, pushing the door open with my back. Through the doorway I saw stairs going up and down, and on the opposite wall, another door that hopefully led outside.

"But you're not—"

"It's okay," I said as Rex and Claudia moved past me. "I just need to get my card."

I let the door close in his face and turned to see Rex swiping that card through another card slot. He pushed the door open and we stepped into the outside air. It was cold and wet, smelling of rain and leaves and something else, too. I took a deep breath and was about to start running when I realized that other smell was ozone.

Then the world disappeared in a shower of sparks and pain.

When I came to, Rex was already conscious. Claudia was just waking up. Our wrists were bound with plastic cuffs threaded through steel loops attached to the metal bench we were sitting on.

"Are you okay?" Rex said, his face creased with concern.

I nodded, although I wasn't too sure. My shoulder felt bruised and burned where I'd been shocked. I looked at Claudia. "You okay?"

She nodded, testing her cuffs against the steel loop.

"Don't bother," Rex said, lifting his wrists. They were red around the cuffs. He'd obviously tried pretty hard to get free already.

"Are we still in the hospital?" I asked.

Rex nodded. "I'm pretty sure."

"What kind of hospital has a room like this in it?"

Before anyone could answer, the door opened. I was expecting one of the guards, or maybe Charlesford, but instead it was the kid with the mop. Daniel. He was still holding the mop as he came halfway through the door.

"Who are you people?" he said, his voice hushed. "Charlesford himself came down to see you. He never leaves the fourth floor."

"Who are *you*?" Rex, said, defensively.

"We're looking for information about a friend of ours," I said. I could feel Rex staring at me, like he didn't want me to give anything away, but I got a good feeling from Daniel. We needed a friend, and of all the people we'd encountered so far here, he seemed most likely.

Daniel looked at each one of us, then said, "Me, too. Was he a chimera? Your friend?"

I nodded.

Daniel thought for a moment, looking at his watch. Then he stuck his mop in the door to keep it open, and came over and started cutting through my plastic cuffs with a pen knife.

"The security cameras are on a twenty-minute cycle," he said. "There's a . . . hiccup when it resets. Be ready to go in five minutes."

Rex looked dubious. "The security system glitches up every twenty minutes?"

Daniel glanced at him. "No. But if you know which way the cameras look, and when, there's a few minutes when you can sneak past them." He paused in his cutting and looked up at me. "You looked at the computer screen back there. What did it say?"

I looked at Claudia and Rex, leaning forward and listening. I hadn't had a chance to tell them what I saw. "It said our friend was sent to the Chimeric Conversion Unit. Do you know what that is?"

He shook his head. "That's what I've been trying to find out." He finished cutting through my cuffs, and as I rubbed my wrists he moved to Claudia. "I know it's in the basement. Or one of the basements. I can't get down there. Not with a janitor's card."

He finished cutting as he said it, and as soon as he was done, Claudia said, "What about one from a security guard? Do you think that would work?"

"A security card?" He nodded. "Yeah, it should. But where would we get one?"

She smiled and pointed at Rex, kind of cocky. "He took one from one of the guards."

"Seriously?"

Rex held up the card.

Daniel moved over to him and started cutting, ignoring or oblivious to the suspicious frown Rex was giving him.

"How do we know you're not part of this, *Daniel*?" Rex said, making a point of looking at Daniel's name tag. "After all, you do work here."

He stopped cutting and looked up at Rex. "Look, do you want to stay in here or do you want to get out?"

They stared at each other for a moment, then Rex looked at his cuffs and said, "Keep cutting."

"My name's not Daniel," he said as he did so. "It's Kiet. My boyfriend Devon is a chimera, and he came here just to get a few stitches. He called me before he went in, all excited because they were going to treat him for free. But he never came out. He got sent to the conversion unit, too, and that's all I know. I've been trying to find out what happened ever since. That's why I took this job."

I felt a tingle in my spine, a chill at the possibility that whatever had happened to Cornelius was more than a one-time medical error that they were trying to cover up. Rex and I shared a look that made me think he was wondering the same thing.

"The rest of the hospital seems to be more or less a normal hospital, but the CCU . . . I've seen other chimeras sent down there, and I've never seen any come back. I know a bit about computers, and I've been able to sneak onto their system a couple times, but there's almost nothing about the CCU. Apparently Charlesford keeps his important files on paper, in his office. It's up on the fourth floor, and even the security cards can't access that. Only senior medical staff."

He finished cutting, and as Rex rubbed his wrists, Kiet put his knife away and looked at his watch. "One minute," he said, then he turned to Rex. "I'll get you out of here, but then I need you to give me that card. Soon they'll realize it's missing, so it won't be good for long anyway. If I have it, I can get down there and figure out what's going on."

Rex looked at Claudia and me.

"No," I said. "We're coming with you. Or at least I am. We need to find out what's happening, too."

"Or I could just go with him," Rex said. "You and Claudia could get word to Doc and Jerry about what we know already."

I shook my head. "We know next to nothing. And OmniCare will just deny it anyway."

Claudia looked back and forth between Rex and me. Kiet glanced at his watch. "Thirty seconds."

"Maybe you should get out of here," I said to Claudia.

"Screw you," she said, sounding half serious. "Doc's my friend, too. And you're right. We don't have proof of anything. As far as anyone else is concerned, it would just be the same suspicions we had before, except crazier."

Kiet looked us each in the face again. "You're sure?"

Claudia and I nodded. Rex paused, frowning, then he nodded, too. "Yeah, okay."

Kiet eased the door open and grabbed his mop, then peered out. He checked his watch, bobbing his head with each second, then silently counting down from five. When he got to one, he looked up and said, "Let's go."

CHAPTER 22

We stepped into a hallway that looked exactly like the one we'd escaped down earlier. As we hustled along, I rubbed my shoulder, which still ached. This wasn't the first time in my life that I'd been shocked, and it hurt as much as ever.

We followed Kiet to the end of the hall, where it made a ninety-degree turn. He held up a finger, and we froze. My skin crawled with the absolute certainty that we would be discovered. Then Kiet waved at us to continue.

We followed him into a small utility room filled with cleaning supplies. He held up one hand as he stared at the watch on his other wrist, once again bobbing his head, almost imperceptibly, as he counted the seconds. Then he lowered his hand and nodded, opened the door and started through it.

I was following close behind and almost crashed into him when he stopped short. As Rex bumped into me from behind, Kiet waved us back.

Suddenly, I heard voices out in the hallway and I caught a glimpse of two figures in white lab coats passing by. I pushed back at Rex, and as Kiet closed the door in front of us, I picked out a snippet of conversation: " . . . I don't know what they're so upset about. We can always use more . . ."

Then the door clicked shut and I heard nothing.

Claudia looked out from behind Rex, confused and annoyed. She mouthed the words *What's going on?*

I mouthed the words *Someone's out there*, and made walking motions with my fingers.

I could hear Rex breathing, each exhalation a miniature sigh of exasperation.

After a few more seconds, Kiet popped his head in the door and whispered, "Come on."

We followed him out into the hallway, through a heavy swinging door marked EXIT, and into a dimly lit stairway, similar to the one we had tried to escape through before. On the opposite wall was a heavy door with a security panel and card reader next to it. A sign said AUTHO-RIZED PERSONNEL ONLY. UNAUTHORIZED USE WILL SOUND ALARM.

"This leads outside," Kiet said. He pointed to the card in Rex's hand. "If you want, you can swipe yourself out and leave right now."

Rex flashed me a doubtful look.

I looked down the stairway, which seemed to get darker as it descended. I had a very strong feeling that I was making an irreversible decision, and that the ramifications could be terrible.

Rex put his hand on my shoulder, looked into my eyes. "Go," he whispered, barely audible but so emphatic I think I would have gotten the message if he hadn't spoken at all. He turned to Claudia. "You, too."

For an instant, she seemed to be thinking about it. I was too, but *only* for an instant.

"This is going to be dangerous," Kiet said. "I don't know what these people are doing. I don't know what they did to Devon. I have no reason to think they won't kill us to keep us from finding out. But I'm going to find out, no matter what it takes."

I looked at Claudia and she nodded. I nodded back at her, then squeezed Rex's hand on my shoulder. "Let's go."

We crept down the next flight of stairs. At the bottom of the stairwell, Kiet turned to Rex and whispered, "I need the card."

He looked at me and at Claudia, then he handed it over.

Kiet pushed the door open, just a crack, revealing a hallway similar to the ones upstairs, but dimly lit and with a distinct "basement" vibe. He looked each way, then pointed across the hallway at a massive freight elevator, its doors extra wide and extra tall.

"You all wait here," he said. "Keep the door open so you can see me. I'm going to press the button for the elevator. When it comes, I'll give you a thumbs-up if the coast is clear."

He slipped through the door and Rex held it open just enough so we could watch Kiet cross the hallway, press a button on the elevator, and swipe the card.

He stood there nonchalantly, looking alternately at his shoes and at the indicator light above the elevator, waiting. After a couple of seconds, he started humming, too, quietly at first, then louder, some vaguely familiar melody. The humming grew even louder still, and I was starting to wonder if Kiet was losing it when someone in a white smock walked by, just inches away from us, rubber-soled shoes padding silently on the tile floor. My heart jumped into my throat, and I tried to swallow it back into place as the humming faded.

Kiet glanced over at us, looking the way I felt. He bobbed his eyebrows and rolled his eyes, then went back to his studied nonchalance.

A few seconds later, a bell sounded. Kiet looked up at the indicator, then over at us. He held up a finger, telling us to wait.

Finally, the large doors started to open. When they were wide enough for Kiet to confirm no one was already on it, he looked up and down the hallway one more time and gave us a thumbs-up.

We slipped across the hallway and onto the elevator. It was huge, maybe twenty feet wide, with a ten-foot ceiling at least. The buttons were oversized, too, old-fashioned mechanical ones that you actually had to press. There were five floors, with BASEMENT at the top, then CCU-A, CCU-B, CCU-C, and IMPLEMENTATON. Below them were DOOR OPEN and DOOR CLOSE.

Kiet hit the button for CCU-A, the next floor down, and we flattened ourselves against the sides of the elevator until the doors closed.

None of us breathed until the elevator actually began to move.

Kiet scanned the ceiling. He had an elastic surgical cap in his hand, and I wondered why. Then he said, "No cameras," and shrugged, stuffing it back into his pocket.

As we descended, I wondered what we were about to find, what was about to happen, and, in the back of my mind, whether this was going to turn into a Mom-kills-me-when-she-gets-home kind of thing or a too-late-I'm-already-dead kind of thing.

The elevator stopped and the light next to CCU-A went out. The four of us exchanged nervous glances, then the doors slid back, and we were looking out onto a short hallway or vestibule. There was a gray door with a security panel to our left, and an identical one across from us, next to a window looking onto a room with two long rows of hospital beds. I counted them: ten on one side, twelve on the other. Each bed was occupied. They seemed to be chimeras and they seemed to be unconscious, attached to monitors and IV bags. At the far end of the room were two other doors, both closed.

"Devon," Kiet said, dashing out of the elevator and over to the window. His eyes scanned the row of beds and filled with disappointment.

Behind us, the elevator started to close. As Rex stepped back and stopped it with his arm, I noticed there was a second elevator next to the one we'd been riding.

"He's not here," Kiet said. He swiped the card through the slot between the door and the window. The display flashed red and said CCU MEDICAL STAFF ONLY.

He tried the door to our left, but got the same result.

"What now?" Rex asked, as the elevator gently closed on his arm and opened once more.

If we couldn't get past either of the doors, there didn't seem to be much point staying where we were. "We should check the next level down," I said.

Kiet looked at me, his face stricken.

"Devon could be down there," I said, gently. "And we're not going to learn anything else here."

"She's right," Claudia said, putting her hand on his arm, comforting him.

Kiet nodded and we got back onto the elevator.

He pressed the next button: CCU-B. Once again, the doors closed and we resumed our slow descent. When the elevator lurched to a stop and the doors opened, they revealed that CCU-B level looked a lot like CCU-A: the same setup with the doors and the window, the same rows of unconscious chimeras attached to IVs and monitors.

But there were differences, too. Little ones, like the floors and the walls were visibly dirty and the two rows of beds were the same length, twelve on each side. A bigger difference was that the chimeras seemed an odd grayish color.

The biggest and most pressing difference was the three medical staffers standing over the chimeras, going from bed to bed. They had on some sort of breathing apparatus, clear plastic masks over their noses and mouths, with hoses that trailed down under their lab coats. One of them, a woman with a fake tan and even faker-looking red hair who seemed to be in charge, was poking and prodding one of the chimeras, looking at his pupils and listening to his chest. Her manner was cold and detached, maybe even disgusted, more like a meat inspector than a medical professional.

There was also a smell, stale and vaguely chemical.

We flattened ourselves against the sides of the elevator, out of sight, but Kiet peered around the edge, scanning the figures in the beds. As he ducked back in, his shoulders sagged and he shook his head. Devon wasn't here, either.

Rex and I reached out for the button panel at the same time. I got there first, pressing the button for CCU-C, the next level down. I was surprised to see his finger headed for the BASEMENT button, which would have taken us back up.

I looked at him questioningly as the doors closed, but before he could respond Claudia said, "What the hell was that about? What's with the breathing masks?"

I wondered if it had anything to do with Cornelius's breathing device.

"I don't know," Kiet said as the elevator descended. He seemed despondent.

"Maybe it was an infectious-disease ward," Claudia said.

"Maybe," Rex replied, unconvinced.

I turned to him. "You wanted to go all the way back up," I said.

"Yes." He pointed up. "*That* was dangerous." Then he pointed at the floor. "Who knows how bad this next place will be?"

I stared into his eyes. I was about to remind him that Doc was depending on us, and that Kiet's boyfriend Devon was still missing, and that obviously something strange was going on down here. But he knew all that. And I knew that Rex was the bravest person I'd ever met. He might have been as scared as I was about what we were headed into, but that wasn't why he didn't want to go. I felt a growing annoyance as I realized the reason he didn't want to go was me. It wasn't fear for himself, it was worry for me. I was touched, but also pissed off.

"I *said* I wanted to do this," I told him, my voice tight but even. "It's important."

He looked hurt, and I felt bad about that, but I was angry. I wasn't something he needed to save or protect.

He opened his mouth to respond, but then the elevator stopped, and the doors opened.

CHAPTER 23

The CCU-C layout was the same as the previous two levels, but once again, it was the differences that were most striking. The stale smell was stronger. All but two of the chimeras were sitting up, some even standing. And in addition to a doctor, there were two guards in exosuits, each armed with at least two guns and a shock baton. The guards and the doctor wore those clear plastic breathing masks. I could see the guards' faces through them. One had a ridiculous mustache that hung down his face like a horseshoe, twisted in a sneer. The other had a pinched face and cold gray eyes.

The doctor was injecting a syringe into the arm of one of the two chimeras still lying down. Almost immediately, the chimera shot upright, his eyes wide open, looking around, confused. She did nothing to comfort or reassure him, just moved to the next bed, the last unconscious chimera.

"What the hell is going on in this place?" Rex asked in a terse whisper, his face twisted in disgust and distress.

Once again, we all ducked out of sight, except Kiet, who was peeking out with one eye, looking for Devon.

"Is he in there?" I whispered, across the open door. He started to shake his head, then his eyes widened and I took a peek myself.

The armed exoguards were lining up the chimeras, facing the door directly in front of us, as if they were getting ready to march them out—right toward us.

I hit the DOOR CLOSE button, and Kiet flashed me a distressed look. As the elevator doors closed, the light on the security panel next to the door across the hallway blinked from red to green.

There was one more floor: IMPLEMENTATON. My heart was pounding. But we'd come this far, and we hadn't really learned much to show for it.

I put my finger over the button and paused for a microsecond, looking at Rex, Claudia, and Kiet. They all nodded and I pressed it, sending the elevator even lower.

I couldn't tell how fast we were descending, or how low we were going. My ears didn't pop, but I could feel them adjusting to a change in the air pressure.

"Man, did you see those exoguards or whatever?" Claudia said.

"Yeah," I said, "and I saw their weapons."

Kiet nodded. "Lots of weapons."

"They looked like the same exosuits we saw outside the mine," Rex said.

The elevator stopped, and I fully expected the doors to open onto another version of the previous three levels. Instead, we were in a massive, dimly lit cavern of rough-hewn rock. Enormous stalactites hung from the distant ceiling, and where the floor hadn't been cleared away, stalagmites rose up to meet them. They were a glassy black stone, weirdly iridescent. The same stuff coated the ceiling and walls, and chunks of it littered the floor.

The smell was even stronger. There wasn't a soul in sight. We stepped off the elevator, our footsteps echoing in the distance.

The opposite wall of the cavern, maybe sixty feet away, was lined with huge steel doors, labeled NE1, E1, E2, and SE1.

"CCU-A, CCU-C, NE1, E2," Claudia said. "They sure like their codes around here."

"Are they mine shafts?" I asked. I had a hard time hearing myself speak over a whooshing noise I hadn't noticed before.

"I don't know," said Rex, his voice rumbling.

The main cavern continued to the right, past the doors, narrowing into a tunnel that curved into the distance. A sign hanging from the ceiling said CENTRE RIDGE MAIN BRANCH. "This is the mine we saw from outside," I said, pointing at the sign. "Centre Ridge Main Branch."

"But . . . there shouldn't be anything left to mine, remember?" Claudia said. Her voice sounded funny and slow.

Kiet seemed to be in shock. I was about to ask him if he was okay, when I sensed movement behind us and I turned to see the elevator door closing. Rex saw it, too, and he dove for the door, but it was too late. The door was closed.

"No!" Rex yelled, his voice echoing around us.

Kiet seemed to snap out of his trance and swiped the card to recall the elevator. The panel lit up and he pressed the call button, but the elevator was already on its way back up.

I felt strangely confused, and vaguely panicked. The four of us stood there, watching the numbers on the panels detailing the elevator's progress. Still going up.

"It's okay," I said, pointing. "There's another elevator." As if on cue, the bell chimed to announce its arrival. I started to say "Come on," but two thoughts penetrated the thickening fog in my brain.

First was a sense of alarm about that fog, a realization that something about it was terribly wrong. The second thought was that the elevator might not be empty.

"Wait!" I called out, and the others looked over at me sluggishly. The closest thing to a hiding spot was an indentation in the rock wall to our left, where it curved away from the elevators. "Over here!" I cried, beckoning them to follow me.

Claudia and Kiet came over, but Rex paused. "But—"

"Now!" I snapped, startling him into movement. He stumbled as he came over, and I grabbed his arm, jerking him around behind the outcrop.

He started to ask "What?" but was interrupted by the sound of the elevator doors opening, audible even through the growing background *whoosh*.

We ducked farther back, and looked on as the two exoguards from CCU-C emerged from the elevator. One stopped and the other continued walking across the cavern. With the breathing masks and distance, I couldn't see the face of the first one, but I could clearly make out the horseshoe mustache on the one waiting by the elevator.

Two dozen chimeras emerged from it. I recognized a few from the level above us. Their skin was definitely gray, and they looked groggy, but they weren't wearing breathing masks of any kind.

I didn't know what to make of that, but I knew it was important. I knew it had something to do with the panic I'd felt just a few minutes earlier. The explanation was just outside my grasp, and I screwed up my face with the effort of trying to think of it.

The last chimera off the elevator was lagging, and the exoguard with the mustache gave him a savage kick in the small of his back. I almost cried out, but Rex somehow anticipated it and put a hand over my mouth. The chimera tumbled across the stone floor, stopping in a twisted heap. The exoguard that had kicked him grabbed him by the arm without slowing down and dragged him across the stone floor.

A dull tone reverberated through the cavern as the set of massive doors marked NE1 began to open. It first revealed a tunnel almost as high and wide as the cavern itself, sloping downward into the distance. The ceiling was clear for a little ways, but after that it was thorny with stalactites.

As the doors opened wider, I could see clusters of chimeras every twenty or thirty feet along the wall, swinging picks and wielding shovels. Some were chipping away at the glassy rock that coated the floors and hung from the ceiling, others were shoveling it into metal carts.

Rex's hand fell away from my mouth, and I whispered, "God. That's horrible."

As the guards marched the chimeras inside and the doors began to swing closed behind them, one of the stalactites splintered and fell, bringing with it a large section of ceiling. The miners below tried to scatter, but two or three disappeared under the rubble. As the doors continued to close, other miners began frantically digging them out. The exoguards watched, and kept their weapons at the ready, but none moved to help.

A loud *ding* rang out, almost immediately swallowed up by the thunderous clang of the massive door closing. I was struck by two thoughts almost at once: that the *ding* sounded a lot like the elevator, and that the lightheadedness I was feeling was awfully similar to how I felt before I passed out in Centre Hollow. We had to get out of there, fast.

I stepped out from our hiding spot and saw that indeed the elevator we had come down in was open, its light spilling out across the stone floor, beckoning.

As I turned back to tell the others we needed to go, I heard a sharp percussive *thwap* as Kiet's mop handle hit the stone floor. Kiet and Claudia were crumpled next to it, unconscious, and Rex was down on one knee, visibly struggling.

For a moment, I tried to process the situation. I knew that if the elevator doors closed, if we got stuck down there, we'd probably die from whatever poison we were breathing before we were even captured.

Rex looked up as I took two shuffling steps toward him.

"Get up," I said, my voice thick as I reached down to grab the mop, my hands feeling around on the ground for it as my eyes refused to focus. I turned and shoved the mop through the elevator doors, just in time for them to lightly close on it, then open again.

When I turned back, Rex was on his feet, swaying back and forth.

I grabbed his shirt, struggling to look into his eyes. "Got to get out of here," I said, " . . . get them out of here."

He looked like he was straining to focus on me, but he nodded and reached down to grasp Kiet by the arm. I grabbed Claudia by her shirt and we dragged them both onto the elevator, past the mop, still lying across the threshold. Rex pulled Kiet into one corner, then collapsed against the rear wall with a loud thud that shook the elevator car. I slumped against the side wall. Reaching out with my fingertips, I grabbed the strings on the mop head and pulled it inside the elevator.

The doors closed and I shut my eyes, letting the sickly lethargy wash over me as I waited for the lurch of the elevator to take us away from this nightmare.

CHAPTER 24

The headache was worse than when I woke up outside Centre Hollow. A lot worse.

I opened my eyes, still on the elevator floor. Rex and Claudia and Kiet were next to me, and with a jolt of panic I threw myself onto Rex to make sure he was breathing. He let out a snort when I landed on him, and I kissed him on the cheek and held his head to my chest, fighting back tears of relief.

I checked Claudia and Kiet to make sure they were breathing, too. I had no idea how much time had passed or if I had actually reached the button before I passed out, or even if the elevator had gone up and then come back down. For all I knew, we were still down in the mine, with armed exoguards waiting on the other side of those doors.

I jabbed my fingers on the top button, BASEMENT, the one I'd been aiming at before, but the doors opened with a *ding*, revealing that we were already there.

There was no way of knowing how long we had until someone could come along and discover us. And there was no way I could get the others off that elevator myself—at least not Rex. I wouldn't know where to hide them or myself even if I did.

I was frozen with indecision. Any second, someone below could summon the elevator and bring us all back down into that hell. And if I pulled the knob to stop the elevator, an alarm would surely go off somewhere. I hated the idea of being exposed while I was trying to rouse the others, but that seemed to be the best option.

I put the mop between the doors again. Then I started slapping everybody. Gently, but insistently. I started with Rex—left, right, left, right—then moved on to Claudia and Kiet, "Get up, get up," I said, my voice hushed and urgent at the same time. "You've got to get up. We've got to get out of here."

I went from one to the other several times until they were all awake. My headache had largely subsided, but I could tell they were waking up with doozies. The doors closed on the mop, then opened again.

"What?!" Rex said. He sat upright, then winced, holding his head. "Where are we?"

"What's going on?" Claudia said, looking pained.

"We're back in the basement," I said, gently shaking Kiet. "You'll feel better in a minute."

Kiet groaned, squinting up at me and screwing up his face.

"We've got to get out of here," I told him. "Can you get us out?"

He propped himself up on his elbow, thinking. Then he nodded, his eyes clearing and his face resolved. "Yes. I know a way."

I turned to Rex and Claudia. "Are you ready?"

They both nodded. Rex still seemed a little sluggish.

"Are you sure?" I put my hands on his elbows and looked into his eyes.

"Yeah," he said. "Yes. Let's go."

"Okay." I turned to Kiet. "What's the plan?"

"I'll go first and signal when it's clear. We're going back up those stairs across the hallway. On the first landing, there's one door that leads out to the lobby, and another that leads outside." He thought for a second. "The building is L-shaped, with a south wing and an east wing. That exit is right at the bend. It's going to let you out onto a grassy area between the two wings of the hospital. Stay to the left. Go past the dumpsters at the end of the building, cross the driveway, and you'll see an empty lot they've cleared for construction. To the left of that is the edge of the woods." He looked at his watch. "I'll meet you there in the woods."

"Wait, you're not coming with us?" Claudia said.

He shook his head. "My shift's done in twenty minutes. If I'm not here to punch out, they'll know something's up."

"But what if they already know you helped us?" I said. "What if they arrest you or . . . or worse?"

He shook his head. "I have to risk it. I can't lose this job. It's the only lead I have on finding Devon."

It made sense, I knew. He was our inside man at OmniCare. We needed him to keep his job, too.

"Where in the woods should we meet you?" Rex asked.

Kiet didn't hesitate. "There's a creek a little ways in. Follow it upstream until you come to an abandoned fishing shack. I'll come find you there in an hour."

"Are you sure it's abandoned?" I asked.

"It's falling apart. I stumbled across it on a hike. I don't think anyone's used it for years."

"Nothing to fish," Claudia said grimly.

"Okay," Rex said. "Thanks." Then he turned to Claudia and me. "We better go."

Kiet nodded and went out into the hallway, nonchalantly looking left and right. He opened the door to the stairway and poked his head through, listening for a moment, then beckoned us to follow.

We hurried after him, and as I bent to grab the mop, a button on the panel lit up, for the IMPLEMENTATION level. My stomach lurched as I thought how close we had come to being sent back down there.

I caught up with the others across the hallway and we hurried up the steps to the first-floor landing. Kiet swiped the card through the panel next to the exit and pushed the door open. Cold, fresh air hit me like a slap in the face, blowing away the remaining cobwebs.

Outside was just as Kiet had described. One wall extended straight away from us on our left, and another wall extended away at a right angle to it. In front of us was a square of frozen grass and mud, dusted with snow and crusted with ice.

"That way," Kiet said, pointing to our left. "Driveway, woods, creek, fishing shack. I'll find you there. You'll be fine."

He turned to Rex and handed back the security card. "Probably best if I don't get caught with this."

Rex smiled and took it from him.

Somewhere above us, a door opened and footsteps started coming down the stairs.

Kiet mouthed the word *Go*.

Rex patted him on the shoulder. Claudia and I gave him a quick hug, then we stepped outside.

I turned back to wish Kiet good luck, the but door was already closed behind us.

CHAPTER 25

The wind swirled around us, angry and cold under a wintry, blue-gray sky.

The walls on either side were plain concrete with evenly spaced windows. The ground floor was slightly elevated, so as we crept along the south wing, even Rex could easily stay beneath the lowest windows. But there was no cover from the windows in the east wing, which all seemed to be staring at us.

We ran low and close to the wall. *Like rats*, I couldn't help thinking.

I kept waiting for someone to start yelling or alarms to go off or something, but the only sounds were our breathing and our feet on the frozen ground. At the end of the wing, we paused next to a trio of blue dumpsters. It was so cold, they barely stank.

The driveway was in front of us, a few feet below ground level, sloping away from the parking lot to our left and down to Bogen Road, which curved back around toward the front of the hospital. A second driveway branched off the far side of the first, leading up to a muddy construction area. Beyond that were the woods. Just like Kiet said.

Claudia looked back at Rex and me, and whispered, "I'm going to take a look."

We nodded, and she crept forward with feline grace. I wondered briefly how much of it was because of her splice and how much she'd always been like that.

She came back and shrugged. "It looks clear, as far as I can see."

The longer we waited, the more likely we'd be caught.

I nodded and Rex nodded back. He held up his fist and mouthed the words *On three.*

Then he silently counted, raising a finger each time: one ... two ... three ...

And we took off.

The ground was slick, and as soon as I started down the short slope to the driveway my feet began to slide, but somehow I kept them under me.

Claudia looked to her left, and as her eyes widened, I could see the twinkling of blue and red lights reflected in them. I looked over, too, and saw three police cruisers, lights flashing, and a cluster of cops standing around them.

Behind me, Rex's voice rumbled, "Oh, shit."

The cops were too far away to have heard him, but all at once they turned and looked right at us.

"Go!" Rex grunted, but he didn't have to. Claudia was already halfway up the embankment on the other side of the driveway, scampering toward the open lot. I crossed the driveway and sprang, planted a foot on the steep slope, and vaulted up to the top. Claudia was already sprinting across the lot, kicking up little clumps of mud with each step. I took off after her, but almost before I started running, I realized something was wrong.

There was no low, heavy breathing or footfalls behind me. I skidded in the mud and looked back.

Rex was running back across the driveway.

"Rex!" I called out.

"Go!" he called back. "I'll catch up!"

"Come on, Jimi!" Claudia cried, her voice jagged. She was practically across the cleared lot.

The police cruisers were already screeching in tight circles as they turned in our direction.

Rex kicked the blocks out from under the wheels of the closest dumpster. "Go!" he thundered again as he pulled the dumpster toward the driveway.

I realized at once what he was doing. If the cops made it to the driveway leading up to the dirt lot, they would easily chase us down in their cars.

"Go," he said once more, quiet this time, but emphatic, clear as a bell even though he was so far away. Then he twisted his body, grabbed the edge of the dumpster, and shoved it onto the driveway.

It tipped over and landed with a massive *clang,* blocking the driveway and sending trash bags tumbling everywhere. As Rex took off across the driveway, the first cruiser slammed into the dumpster, almost pushing it into him. He sidestepped the dumpster and kept running.

I ran, too. Fast.

I glanced back and saw Rex pounding across the lot, maybe fifty yards behind me. Behind him, the second police car was trying to go around the first, the tires on one side grinding their way up the embankment before the car slid down and got wedged between the dumpster and the embankment, completely blocking the driveway.

The cops climbed out of their cars and started running, but there was no way they could catch us. We were too far ahead of them. Even Rex.

I was almost at the trees when I glanced back and saw the third police car speeding down Bogen Road. It must have gone out the front entrance and come all the way around.

"Faster," I screamed at Rex.

The third cruiser skidded up the main driveway from the street, then turned onto the second driveway, up onto the muddy lot. It shot past the cops running after us, its tires spraying mud.

We still had a good lead on it, but it was going to be close.

Claudia plunged into the woods. A moment later, I did, too. I glanced back at Rex, who was churning up huge clods of mud as he ran.

As I scrambled into the trees after Claudia, I heard Rex crashing through the brush behind us. I had just allowed myself to think that maybe we were going to make it, when I looked back again and saw his body go rigid and his eyes roll up.

"Rex!" I cried. "*Rex!*"

A hand grabbed my arm, and I started to flail, but it was Claudia, dragging me away. Tears filled my eyes as two cops set upon Rex, cuffing his hands and feet. They kept the current running through him as they did it, not wanting to take a chance with someone so big—and maybe enjoying it, too.

Claudia pulled me along and I stumbled halfheartedly after her, part of me still considering going back. Then suddenly we were splashing in icy water. It soaked into my jeans and seeped into my boots. We were at the creek.

We looked at each other. In seconds they'd be after us again, too. And if they caught us, there'd be nothing we could do for Rex at all.

"We need to go," Claudia whispered, and I knew she was right.

Blinded by tears, I stumbled along the stream after her, deeper into the woods. Farther away from Rex.

CHAPTER 26

The fishing shack was disgusting. The tiny porch out front was stained with God knows what from years of anglers cleaning their catches. It was dusty and mildewed and so overgrown with vines that it was almost invisible in the fast-falling darkness. It was cold and filthy and smelly. To be fair, I was, too, but that just made it worse.

Miraculously, we'd found an old chemlight stick in a cupboard with enough left in it to fill the tiny room with a weak green glow.

I looked at my watch, for the tenth time since we'd been there. Kiet should have been there an hour ago, and I was jumping out of my skin. Part of me wanted to go back and try to free Rex from the cops, who were obviously working for OmniCare. Part of me wanted to rush home and rally Ruth and Pell and my mom and Aunt Trudy and Jerry and the lawyers at Earth for Everyone and the rest of the so-called civilized world, and get them to help Rex. At this point, there was zero part of me that wanted to sit in that smelly shack, doing nothing but wait for Kiet.

"Kiet's not coming," I said, looking into the night through the dust-caked windows. It must have been the tenth time I'd said it. Each time, Claudia had replied, "Yes, he is." This time she said, "I know he's not."

I turned and looked at her. She was sitting in a saggy wooden chair with her elbows on her knees and her chin in her hands. She had been arguing the point with me for so long, I was a little stunned that she'd given up, too.

"Well, he might," I said, walking over to her. The fact was, he had to. We needed to get back into OmniCare and get Rex out. I didn't know how we were going to do that without Kiet.

Claudia shook her head without lifting it. I couldn't tell if it was her neck doing the work, or her hands.

I pulled an old plastic crate closer to her and sat on it. The grid bit into my thighs and butt. The partial remnants of a second chair were piled on the floor by the woodstove—a pair of legs and a couple of slats from the seat. The rest of it had apparently been burned. Claudia had suggested starting a fire, but I was already worried that the weak glow from the chemlight would give us away.

I leaned back against the wall, hugging myself against the cold. "What do you think was going on down in those sub-basements?" I asked.

I had ideas—terrible ideas—and I was hoping to hear a theory that was less ghastly and more reasonable.

"I don't know," she said quietly. A tiny round wet spot appeared on the dusty floor beneath her head, soon followed by another, an inch or two away. "But they were doing something really, really bad to those chimeras. They were altering them somehow, and making them work in those awful mines." She wiped her eyes and looked up at me. "What do *you* think was going on there?"

I got the feeling she knew I'd been thinking the same thing.

"Well . . . ," I said, "they're mining *something* down there, right?" She nodded and I continued. "But the air isn't breathable. That's why we all passed out. The guards had breathing masks, but not the chimeras, the miners. They didn't have anything like that. They didn't seem to need it." Maybe to reassure myself that I *could*, I took a deep breath and let it out. "I think they put out word that they'll treat chimeras—like Kiet's friend Devon and Cornelius—but instead of healing them, they're . . . you know, altering them or whatever, maybe even splicing them again, I don't know. But changing them so they can breathe down in those mines."

"It's *horrible*," she said, her voice ragged and thick.

"I know," I said quietly. "And they've got Rex." I'd been mostly keeping it together up until that point, because as dark as my thoughts had been, and as much as they centered around that one fact, I'd avoided saying it out loud. Now that I had, I started making some of my own wet spots in the dust.

Claudia put her arm around my shoulder. "He'll be okay," she said. "I know it."

"You don't know it. You can't. And we're just sitting here doing nothing instead of helping him."

I pulled away from her and stood up, pacing. "We have to go back. We have to find out what happened to Rex and help him. We need to get out of here and get help, for Rex and for all those others down in that hole."

"I know," she said. "But we can't right now. We can't do anything out there other than get ourselves killed or break a leg in the darkness. If Kiet's not here by sunrise, we'll sneak back, and we'll do whatever we can."

"Okay," I said quietly. A wave of exhaustion came over me, so intense that for a moment I almost wondered if I'd been breathing toxic fumes again.

"Let's get some rest," Claudia said, taking my hand.

We lay on the bare floor, huddled together for warmth. As I shivered, I thought about home. The feeling was not unfamiliar—once again I had big things to worry about, and people's lives could be at stake, but I also had to worry about my family.

I'd put Kevin in a tough spot. He was going to have to decide between contacting my mom at the ski lodge and telling her I hadn't come home tonight—and to be fair, he had no idea if I was okay—or *not* tell her and risk catching hell for it later.

I'd never wanted a Wellplant—and I still didn't, not even a little—but I couldn't help thinking how much easier some things would be if I did, or even if I just had a cell phone, like my mom did when she was my age. Things would be so much simpler if I could get in touch with Kevin or my mom or Aunt Trudy, even just to lie about where I was.

I felt like I was being inconsiderate and irresponsible. Again.

I didn't like it. For so long—until Del got spliced, really—I'd thought of myself as responsible and levelheaded. But even when Mom and I had that talk a few weeks ago, when she finally said she understood why I did what I did in Pitman, and that she was *proud* of me, I knew she was seeing me differently. In her eyes, I was no longer the sensible, responsible, dependable one.

After tonight, I never would be again.

As I slipped into sleep, I told myself maybe that was okay. Maybe responsible and dependable wasn't who I was anymore. Maybe it wasn't who I'd ever been.

CHAPTER 27

I woke up abruptly. It was still dark, but maybe marginally less so, like a drop of white had been mixed into the blackness coming through the windows, punctuating the dim green of the dying chemlight. Claudia was awake, too; her head was tilted, listening. I couldn't tell if I'd been roused by a sound or by her reaction to it.

For a long moment we both lay there, the air prickly with intense concentration. Then a twig snapped outside. It couldn't have been an animal—there weren't any animals out there.

Claudia slipped into a crouch against the wall, under the window and next to the door, both hands clutching a chair leg. I grabbed the other leg and scrambled to the other side of the door, my feet scuffing loudly against the floor.

We looked at each other across the door. Claudia's eyes flashed in the darkness.

Another twig snapped outside, louder. Closer.

I was holding my breath to stay silent—and beginning to realize that wasn't a long-term strategy—when the porch creaked.

Every muscle in my body was rigid with fear and stress and anticipation, ready to spring into whatever action was necessary as soon as some goon stepped through that door and—

Tap, tap, tap—my plans were interrupted by a tentative knock on the door.

It was such a soft sound, I wondered if I'd imagined it. But as my eyes met Claudia's I could tell she had heard it, too.

The knock came again—*tap, tap, tap.*

Before we could reply, or even react, a soft voice whispered, "Jimi? Claudia?"

It sounded like Kiet. We exchanged a quick nod in the dim light, but as Claudia reached out for the door handle, I stepped back and kept my chair leg raised, just in case.

The chemlight barely reached through the door, but the sky had another drop or two of white mixed in, enough to see Kiet, and to see he looked scared.

"Come on," he said, his voice quiet and rushed. "We need to get out of here."

"What's going on?" I said.

"The OmniCare people are still combing the woods. I've been trying all night to get past them. I doubt they'll keep searching much longer, but if they do, they'll be here soon."

"Where are we going?" Claudia asked.

"Belfield, I guess. I have to be back at work in a few hours, and we need to figure out what's next. But before anything else, we need to get a little farther away from them."

"What about Rex?" I said.

"The cops have him."

"We need to go back for him. We can't just leave him there."

"Are you kidding me? You saw what was going on in that mine. He's safer with the cops than we are with OmniCare after us."

"Wait . . . ," I said. "Aren't the police working with OmniCare?"

Kiet looked confused. "No. They actually had a bit of a dispute about your friend. The police arrested him and OmniCare insisted *they* should keep him, claiming he stole trade secrets or something." He leaned back and looked to his left, off into the distance. "Look, we can talk about it later, but we need to go. *Right now.*"

I paused one more second. "Wait, so . . . is it safe to go to the police?"

He looked at me like I was insane. "Oh, *hell* no. Just because they're not on OmniCare's payroll doesn't mean they'll take our word for anything, or even that they wouldn't just arrest us. They're still cops."

I knew he was right, that there was nothing we could do for Rex right then—and if we got caught by OmniCare, we might never be able to help him. I could only hope that what Kiet was saying was true, and Rex was safer where he was than we were.

We kept our chair legs, just in case, and filed out onto the porch.

"They're up that way," Kiet whispered, motioning with his head.

We nodded and fell in behind him as he started walking in the opposite direction.

The sky continued to brighten, casting everything around us in a pre-dawn blue that was the absolute color of cold. We hiked without talking, a tense and scared quiet fueled by the awareness that people with guns were fanning across the same woods we were in, searching for us.

But as the gray sky continued to brighten, so did our moods. None of us spoke—we still didn't dare—but it seemed as though we all felt we were out of immediate danger.

It started to snow. For days it had been snowing on and off, but this was different: big, soft, pillowy white flakes that floated in the air. They almost defied gravity, like we were inside a snow globe.

It had warmed up considerably, and didn't feel cold enough to be snowing, and yet there it was. A thin dusting became an opaque layer as we walked. I turned back and saw Claudia skipping through the deepening flakes, and Kiet, behind her, looking on and smiling.

It was the first time I had actually seen him smile, and it made me smile, too. But even as I did, I had a slight but insistent feeling that something was somehow wrong with this picture.

We were just rounding a pile of debris from an old mudslide when Claudia opened her mouth and stuck out her tongue to catch a particularly fat snowflake.

"Claudia," I said. "Don't."

But she was too quick, looking triumphant as she caught it. Her face froze, then fell, her grin dissolving into a grimace. She stopped in her tracks, her tongue extended, the snowflake still on it, mostly intact.

"It'th not thnow," she said.

"What?" Kiet asked, confused.

"It'th not thnow," Claudia said again.

Past the rocks, I saw the source of the flakes. "Spit it out," I said sharply.

Kiet looked confused, as Claudia frantically spat, trying to clear her mouth.

"God, that was disgusting," she said, working her tongue around her mouth, spitting some more. "What the hell is it?"

"That," I said, pointing at a concrete ring maybe two feet wide, barely jutting above ground level and partially obscured by fallen rocks and a deep ring of white powder, with a steel grate leaning against it. It was belching out a steady geyser of smoke or gases, almost invisible, but along with it was an inverted blizzard of thick white flakes. Our eyes followed the column as it rose high into the air, then followed the flakes as they settled back down to earth.

"But what *is* it?" Kiet asked.

I pressed my foot down on the stuff. It flattened but didn't melt.

"I don't know," I said, looking back at the vent pumping more and more of the stuff into the air.

"It tastes like . . . burned chemicals," Claudia said, spitting again.

It was settling on her head. Kiet's, too. I shook out my hair. They did the same.

"Whatever it is," I said, "we should get the hell away from it."

CHAPTER 28

As we ran, the snow that wasn't snow slowed to a flurry, but we didn't stop until it had quit completely and the cloud cover had thinned almost to blue.

We shook out our hair and clothes, getting as much of the stuff off us as we could before we continued on. Looking back, I saw a cloud behind us, a dull white mound, billowing almost imperceptibly and falling in on itself. I still didn't know what it was, but it gave me a chill.

"Everybody okay?" I asked.

They looked at each other and nodded.

"Do you think we lost them?" I asked Kiet.

"Yeah, I imagine," he replied. "We've probably put enough distance between us and anybody looking for us."

"Where the hell are we?" Claudia asked.

Kiet looked around. "We must be close to Belfield, I'd think. From there, we should be able to get a ride back to my place in Gellersville. Before I go back to work, we should compare notes about what we saw in that subbasement, and hopefully come up with some ideas about where Devon might be. And your friend, too."

Claudia and I exchanged a quick glance. I felt guilty, realizing I might have accidentally misled Kiet about Cornelius.

"Kiet . . . our friend isn't down there," I said quietly.

"What?" he turned to look at me. "How do you know? What did you find out?"

Claudia stayed silent, letting me take the lead.

"He was never down there," I said. "Or he was, I think, but hasn't been for a while. And actually, he wasn't really our friend."

Kiet's eyes went flat and hard. "What do you mean?"

I told him everything, about Doc and about Cornelius, and how

Cornelius had an OmniCare bracelet, but they denied he'd ever been there. As I spoke, Kiet's glare lost its edge.

"So he's dead?" he said softly.

"Yes," I said. "But that doesn't mean Devon is," I added quickly. "I mean, this was back in Philadelphia. It seemed like Cornelius had hopped a freight train to get there. Who knows what happened to him after he left the hospital. Plus . . ."

My voice trailed off as a thought began to assemble in my brain.

Kiet looked confused. "Philadelphia?"

I was only half listening as Claudia explained, "Yes, we drove out here yesterday. We hoped to confirm Cornelius had been at Omni-Care, find out whatever else we could, then drive home."

"Wait, you have a *car*?" he said, shocked and maybe a little annoyed. The going was easier now, with the ground sloping gently down, but we'd been trudging through the frozen woods for what seemed like hours. "Where?"

Claudia put up her hands, calming but defensive. "It's down on Bogen Road, but it's broken down. Bent charger plate. I need to fix it."

Kiet gave her a dubious look. "You're going to fix it yourself?"

Claudia bristled. "Yeah, if I can get my hands on a decent socket set."

Kiet looked at me, as if for confirmation.

"I've seen her in action," I said. But I was distracted by several thoughts coming together in my mind at once.

"Cool," he said, with a shrug. "Didn't mean to doubt. I know a guy in Gellersville who might lend me some tools."

"Great," Claudia said, smiling until she turned and saw the frown I could feel dragging down the bottom of my face. "What's wrong, Jimi?"

Our surroundings seemed familiar to me. The woods around us were still dusted with ice and snow—the real thing, not that other stuff—but they seemed greener. The air had a slight haze of fog.

"Cornelius had that breathing mask, remember?" I said, still thinking things through. "Doc said it smelled toxic, like the air inside it was bad. But if Cornelius went through OmniCare and got sent into the mines, if he could breathe the atmosphere down there, maybe he couldn't breathe the air up *here*. Maybe the only way he could escape was to bring some of that bad air with him."

Claudia put a hand over her mouth. "That's horrible. It's bad enough they're being imprisoned in those mines, but to be left unable to survive in natural air?"

"It's monstrous," Kiet said. He looked devastated, obviously thinking about Devon.

"Kiet," I said. "Where *exactly* are we?"

"I don't know *exactly*. Just what I told you, that we're heading away from OmniCare. Toward Belfield."

Claudia and I had followed him into a clearing where the gentle slope grew steeper. I stopped, taking in my surroundings even more closely. Taking stock of how I felt, whether I was confused or groggy. "Are we anywhere near Centre Hollow?" I asked.

Claudia shot me an alarmed look.

"I have no idea," Kiet said, oblivious to our sudden tension. "Why? What's Centre Hollow?"

"Do you feel okay?" I asked Claudia.

"I think so," she said, but she didn't seem sure.

"What's Centre Hollow?" Kiet repeated, walking back toward us.

Before I could tell him, a blur of color flashed between two trees down in the woods on the far side of the clearing, so fast and so far away I couldn't be sure it was really there. "Did you see that?" I said, pointing.

Claudia turned and followed my gaze, staring intently into the woods.

"See what?" Kiet asked, looking around. "What's going on?"

A voice called out from the distance. "Kiet?" It was faint and far-away, but the emotion in it was loud and clear.

Kiet froze. "Devon?" he said, the name catching in his throat as he spun around, trying to place the voice.

A figure emerged down in the woods on the other side of the clearing. It looked like a boy, but he was too far away to make out much in the way of details other than his dark hair, oddly gray complexion, and grimy, disheveled clothes. I couldn't even tell if he was a chimera. But somehow I could see the emotion in his eyes, a roiling mixture of pain and fear and love and joy and sorrow. I could have seen that from a mile away.

"*Devon!*" Kiet cried. He started running down the hill, but Devon held up a hand.

"Stop!" he called out sharply as Kiet approached the middle of the clearing. "Stay back!"

"What do you mean?" Kiet said, slowing but not stopping, as if his feet wouldn't follow the command.

"You can't come any closer. It's not safe."

"You come here, then," Kiet said, still inching forward.

"I can't," Devon said, the sorrow in his eyes more acute than ever. "I'm farther from town than I should be. And you're closer than you should be."

"What are you talking about?" Kiet said, his feet finally stopping.

"Is this Centre Hollow?" I asked, stepping up next to Kiet.

"The outskirts," Devon said. "You should be okay where you are, but you shouldn't stay long. And you can't come any closer."

"What the hell is Centre Hollow?" Kiet demanded, looking back and forth between me and Claudia and Devon, confused and angry, the only one in the dark.

"Was it you who saved us earlier?" I called out.

"Me and my friends." He looked to his left. "Rajiv," and then to his right, "and Georgie." Two other guys appeared on either side of him, one spliced with raccoon to his left, the other, spliced with lion, to his right. They were grimy and disheveled, and had the same gray cast to their skin.

"Thank you for helping us," I said.

"You shouldn't have come back," Devon said.

"We didn't mean to."

Kiet threw his head back and yelled at the sky, "What the hell is going on?"

I didn't know that much more than he did, and probably none of the part he cared most about. I kept my mouth shut and met Claudia's questioning look with a tiny shrug.

Kiet took a step forward, but Devon cried out, "Stop! I mean it."

For a brief moment, they stood staring at each other, tears rolling down their cheeks. Then, without warning, Devon gave his head an exasperated shake and ran up across the clearing. Rajiv and Georgie both reached out for him and followed a few steps trying to stop him.

One of them called out, "Devon! No!"

But Devon sprinted across the snowy ground, toward Kiet.

Kiet took two steps forward, then they met, practically tackling each other, but staying on their feet, twirling around, hugging, whispering into each other's ears.

Despite his gray pallor, Devon was beautiful. I thought at first he was spliced with fox, but as he got closer, I suspected it was red panda. It was a subtle splice, mostly a faint blush of fur, white, black, and russet over white skin. He had soft blue eyes, full lips, and prominent cheekbones.

I wondered if he'd been as good-looking before the splice, or if red panda simply agreed with him.

They pulled away from each other, just enough to kiss, lingering long enough that I could tell that as far as they were concerned, the rest of us—the rest of everything—had disappeared.

But then it all came rushing back.

Devon pulled away first, running a hand through Kiet's hair, his eyes scanning Kiet's face, as if he was memorizing every detail.

"You look so thin," Kiet said.

"You look perfect," Devon replied. He smiled, and so did Kiet, just for a moment. Then Devon's smile faltered, followed by the rest of him. His breathing became shallow and fast.

"Devon?" Kiet said, growing alarmed. "Are you okay?"

Devon smiled feebly and said, "You always did . . . take my breath away." Then his knees buckled.

Kiet caught him. *"Devon!"*

Rajiv and Georgie ran up and skidded to a stop on either side of Devon. They looked like they were holding their breath as they grabbed him by the arms and hauled him back down across the clearing.

Kiet began to follow them until Georgie coughed and said, "Stay there!"

Rajiv said, "We'll be back in a minute."

CHAPTER 29

K iet watched, stricken, as Devon's friends dragged him off into the brush. Then the woods were silent around us. For five minutes, we stood there silently waiting and watching and hoping. Finally, we saw and heard movement in the distance. Devon returned, walking on his own, flanked by Rajiv and Georgie. They came just to the edge of the clearing, then Devon sat heavily on the ground and leaned back against a tree.

"I'm fine," he said, barely audible from where we stood. He was looking directly at Kiet, whose face was etched with worry and fear, his body leaning forward as if straining against an invisible leash.

"Devon?" Kiet said, his voice sounding even farther away, though he was standing right next to me.

"I'm fine," Devon repeated, louder, followed by a raspy cough. "Sort of," he added. He stared at Kiet for a moment, then he said, "I've changed a bit. I've *been* changed."

"What happened?"

Devon looked down at the ground between his outstretched legs. "You remember when that cut on my arm got infected, and I went to OmniCare to get it stitched?" He bent his elbow to look at his forearm. "They did a good job with that, actually," he said with a snort. "But they sedated me to do it. I woke up, briefly, in a big room half filled with chimeras sleeping in beds. When I woke up the second time, the room was full, twenty or thirty of us, all chimeras, all sleeping, all strapped to our beds. I was so weak I couldn't have gotten up anyway. There was a doctor carrying this big tray, taking notes or something, a few beds down, and I tried to ask what was going on, but I was too tired. I don't know if she noticed that I was awake. If she did she ignored me.

"As I watched, she leaned over one of the chimeras and covered his mouth and pinched his nose with one hand. In the other hand, she was holding an inhaler. One of her assistants called it a splinter inhaler. After a few seconds she slipped her hand off the chimera's mouth, stuck in the inhaler, and blasted it."

"A splinter inhaler?" I said.

"That's what they call it and that's exactly what it feels like, too. It's kind of like an old asthma inhaler. I was barely conscious when she did me. The mist tasted sweet, but it burned my lungs like I was breathing in needles. We all got the treatment, then her assistants came into the room and started moving us. I was in and out, but they seemed to be hurrying."

Kiet and Claudia were staring at Devon with eyes as wide as mine felt.

"When I woke up, I couldn't tell if it was the same room or not," he continued. "It smelled different. The others all looked gray and washed out. I guess I did, too. I felt different. My chest was raw, like I'd had a really bad cough. I was still tied down—this time even more securely. Someone came in to examine us, but I couldn't tell who because they were wearing a breather.

"When I woke up after that, I wasn't tied down anymore, but two guards in exosuits and heavy-duty breathing masks were poking us with rifles, telling us to get up. They also had shock batons and clubs, dart guns. They marched us all onto this giant elevator and took us down into the mine. There were all these other chimeras working away with picks and shovels and they put us to work. We were still dazed, but I recognized some of the other chimeras, from when I checked in."

He started crying, but no one said anything. It was clear he wasn't finished. Rajiv, the raccoon chimera, squeezed his shoulder. Kiet and Claudia were crying, too.

Devon took a deep breath and continued. "There was this girl I'd met in the waiting room. She was smart and funny, kind of tough. She said no." He paused and wiped his eyes with his sleeve. "She said they were crazy and they needed to let us all go. The guard shot her, practically tore her in half."

Devon stifled a sob, then got himself under control. "The rest of us were terrified . . . so we got to work."

"But you got out," Kiet said.

Devon nodded. "Kind of, I guess. When they splintered us—with the mist they made us breathe—it didn't just make us able to breathe the gases down in the old mines. It also left us so we couldn't breathe regular air, at least not for long."

I felt sick. It was pretty much what I had feared, but hearing it from someone who had lived through it was a million times worse than I had imagined.

Devon paused and looked at Rajiv and Georgie before continuing. "Every now and then, someone would run for it, up through the main gate. It wasn't even that hard, either. The guards were careless, because they knew once we'd been splintered we couldn't survive outside, and they knew we knew. The guards use oxygen tanks, because they're down in the mines for hours at a time, but the medical staff don't come in for long, so they use refillable breathers with built-in compressors, so they can just go anywhere with regular air and refill them. We figured maybe we could fill it with whatever it was we were breathing."

"Is that how you got out?" Kiet asked.

"Kind of. The breathers didn't hold much, so we knew they could only get us so far. But there was a guy in the mines named Henry. He grew up around here, and knew about this ghost town, Centre Hollow—he called it Creepy Hollow—that had been condemned and evacuated, not just abandoned, like the zurbs, but forcibly evacuated because the air was poisoned."

"Poisoned how?" Kiet asked.

"The town was built in a little valley, on top of an old coal mine.

The mine companies pump all those chemicals into the mine to liquefy the coal they couldn't mine, then they pump in CO_2 to force it out. It turns out the coal they liquefied had been holding the mine together, so cracks started forming and the CO_2 and other gases seeped up through the ground."

"Enough to displace the air?" Claudia asked.

He nodded. "It's like a little valley, protected from the wind. The gases would just kind of sit there and collect. Anyway, Henry figured maybe we could breathe there. He figured the vents should let out close enough to Centre Hollow that someone with a full breather could get there." He smiled sadly and a haunted look seeped into his eyes.

"So it worked?"

"We were only in the vent for ten or fifteen minutes, tops." He smiled sadly. "On our way out, we saw . . . well, actually, we saw a lot, but we actually found the master controls that could open all the doors, even the main gate. There was even a master for the cameras, all right there. But we knew it was useless because it wasn't the gates that kept us trapped in there, it was the air. The main entrance would have been way too far from Centre Hollow. Luckily, Henry was right and the vent let us out close enough that with breathers, we made it here without passing out. Luckier still, he was right that we could breathe once we got here."

"The vent you came through. Was that the one with the . . . snow or whatever?" Claudia asked.

Devon turned grayer. "Yes. But . . . that's not snow."

"How many people got out?" I asked.

"There were six of us in that first group. Three more groups came later, the same way. Rajiv and Georgie slipped out the main entrance and managed to steal a car and drive it here. They passed out while driving and crashed on the edge of town. Luckily, we heard it and got them here before they suffocated. That brought us up to twenty."

"You could have been killed," Kiet said.

Devon tilted his head, looking at Kiet fondly but almost conde-scendingly. "I'd probably be dead by now if I'd stayed."

"Are they doing this to all the chimeras who go to OmniCare?" I asked.

Kiet started to speak, but Devon said, "Just the ones that had no family, no emergency contact." He smiled bitterly. "The ones no one would miss."

"Don't say that," Kiet said.

"Not you," he said. "But my family . . . they're not going to miss me."

Claudia looked around. "What have you people been eating?"

"A couple of the gardens are still producing," he said with a smile. "Kind of amazing, they've been reseeding all these years. Maybe it's the CO_2. But mostly we've been eating canned goods we found in the elementary school basement. Past its prime but we'd have been screwed without it. There's not much left, actually."

"We'll get you more food. But why didn't you tell us all this when you found us earlier, so we could help?"

He smiled dismissively. "Well, you were unconscious, for one, and if we'd waited for you to wake up, we would have been unconscious too. Or worse. Rajiv actually came back with a note, but you were already gone."

"We were down there yesterday," I said. "In the mine."

"What?" Devon said, horrified.

"And in the hospital basement, too. We saw it."

"It was terrible," Claudia said.

"How the hell did you manage that?" Devon asked.

"We stole a key card from one of the guards," I said. "Then Kiet showed us how to get down there."

Devon looked even more confused at that.

"I got a job mopping floors," Kiet explained. "To look for you, try to find out what happened." He smiled. "I've been there two months, but I hadn't made much progress until these two showed up."

"Three," I said. "There were three of us."

"Right," Kiet said. "I'm sorry, I didn't mean—"

"It's okay," I said. I didn't want him to feel bad about it, I just wanted to make sure we didn't forget about Rex for a minute.

"Their friend Rex was the one who got us the card," Kiet explained to Devon. "He's spliced. He was arrested as we were leaving."

Devon sat up. "By the guards?"

"The police," Kiet said.

Devon nodded and relaxed slightly, which I found reassuring.

"We need to get him released, though," I said. "And we need to get everyone out of that mine, too. We need to get word out about it, and shut it down."

Devon seemed excited by the thought and yet somehow dismissive, like it was a great idea but he didn't think it possible. And I knew he might be right. Ever since GHA and the whole Humans for Humanity movement, there were people who thought they could get away with anything when it came to chimeras.

"Devon, what were you mining?" I asked.

Kiet frowned at me like I was being insensitive, and maybe I was, but I was also trying to figure out what was going on.

"What?" I said, feeling defensive. "I want to know. The coal's all gone, isn't it? I'm wondering what's so valuable someone would do this to get it."

"Yttrium," Devon said. He seemed to be getting tired again, but this was important.

"Yttrium," I repeated.

He nodded. "It's a rare metal."

"Yeah, I know," I said, distracted. "I think we saw them loading it onto a truck outside the mine." I leaned against a tree as I considered the implications of Devon's words.

"Well *I* don't know," Kiet said. "What is it?"

"It's used in high-end tech," Claudia said. "I think they used to mine a lot of it in China."

Devon nodded. "Yeah, but they've pretty much run out, so there's a shortage. There's deposits on the ocean floor, but too deep to get to." He patted the ground. "Turns out, though, that there's also trace amounts of it in coal. And in me, too, for that matter. I probably absorbed thirty bucks worth of yttrium when I was down there. It's supposed to be harmless, but I have my doubts."

"But the coal's gone, right?" Claudia said.

He nodded. "Every drop. But when they liquefy the coal and pump it out, the yttrium is left behind in the residue."

As the pieces assembled in my brain, I slid to the ground, shocked but not surprised. It seemed like any time you came across something really evil in this world, chances were it led back to one person.

"But why don't they just use more exosuits?" Claudia was asking. "Each of those exosuits could probably mine five times as fast as a person without one. Who would go to all that trouble—kidnapping all these chimeras and altering them and forcing them to work down there? Why not just get a bunch more of those exosuits?"

"We wondered the same thing," Devon said. "I think they must be really expensive. OmniCare has tons of money, but they only have eight of those exosuits—we counted. It only takes four well-armed pairs—they always work in pairs—to brutalize and control eighty or ninety chimeras."

"It's not because they're expensive." I said it quietly, but everyone turned to look at me. "The exosuits are semi-robotic. That means they use yttrium, right?"

Claudia nodded. "Yeah, probably."

"That's why they're not buying up a ton of exosuits," I said. "For the same reason they're going to such terrible lengths to get the yttrium out of the mines. Because Howard Wells needs every last speck of it he can find. This is all about him and his new generation of Wellplants."

CHAPTER 30

For a long moment we were each on our own, dealing with our individual reactions of horror and disgust and anger and sorrow. I wanted to curl into a ball and sob. But instead, I got to my feet, brushing the dirt off my pants and my jacket.

Kiet looked up at me. "Where are you going?"

"We need to get a move on," I said, wiping my eyes. "We need to get to Gellersville and get tools so we can fix Claudia's car, and tell the world what's going on here, and stop it before anyone else gets hurt." I turned to Kiet. "Maybe we can get one of those inhalers as proof."

Kiet thought about it and nodded.

"You need tools?" Devon asked.

"A socket set," Claudia replied. "For a bent charger plate." She took a few steps closer to Devon and explained about her broken-down car.

"We've got some tools you can borrow," Devon said. "As long as you don't mind them being a little rusty."

Rajiv got to his feet and said, "I'll get them."

Devon called him over and spoke into his ear, then called out, "Thanks, Rajiv!" as his friend ran off into the woods. While we waited for Rajiv to return, Kiet started walking into the clearing again.

Devon held up a hand and said, "Close enough."

Kiet looked miserable. "So this is it?" he finally said.

"I don't know," Devon replied lightly. "I hope not. . . . I never did like the idea of a long-distance relationship. But they say boundaries are important. Maybe this will be good for us in the long term."

Claudia and I both smiled at that. Kiet did, too, even as he shook his head in disapproval. "That's not funny," he said.

Devon held up his thumb and his forefinger an inch apart. *A little.* "It's really good to see you," he said.

"You, too. But . . ." Kiet waggled his hand, indicating the space between them. "This?"

"I was afraid I'd never see you again," Devon said. "Were you afraid I was dead?"

Kiet nodded, tearing up again.

"Then you should be happy." Devon smiled, but he didn't seem happy either.

I liked Kiet, and I found myself liking Devon even more. And at my core, I felt a rage at the people who put them in this predicament. At Howard Wells and that Dr. Charlesford, and everyone else who was a part of it.

I had known already that this was no longer just about Doc. Down in that sub-basement under OmniCare, it had become clear that something huge and terrible was going on. But somehow, seeing Kiet in such anguish, seeing him and Devon torn from each other, seeing people physically separated from those they love, and in such a ghoulish way, and for such a base, materialistic reason, it made putting a stop to it that much more urgent.

Rajiv ran back through the woods, carrying a dented toolbox in one hand and a breather in the other. He set the tools on the ground next to Devon and handed him the breather.

Devon stood up and pulled the mask around his face, then he picked up the toolbox and walked up across the clearing, toward Kiet.

He held out the toolbox toward Claudia. "Just bring them back when you're done," he said as she took it, his voice only slightly muffled by the breathing mask. "Or don't. I don't know."

"Thanks," she said, dropping to one knee and looking inside. "These are perfect."

Then Devon reached out his arm to Kiet. "I've got five minutes on this thing. Want to go for a walk?"

Kiet took his hand and nodded. As they turned and walked up the hill away from us, Devon looked back at Claudia and me. "We'll be back in a few minutes."

They walked off, hand in hand, then arm in arm, making a circle through the woods, never completely out of sight for more than a minute.

Claudia was engrossed in checking out the tools. I leaned against a tree, trying to keep an eye on Devon and Kiet without *looking* like I was keeping an eye on them, trying not to think about how much I missed Rex, how worried I was about him.

When Kiet and Devon made their way back down to where Claudia and I were waiting, Devon pulled up his mask and they kissed once again. Afterward, he held the mask to his face and took a deep breath, then he shook the can next to his ear, listening to it. He pressed a green button on the side and held it as it let out a soft gasp.

He tossed the breather to me, and trotted back down across the clearing. "I want you to take a walk with me, too," he called out. "Just press the blue button to fill it, then put the mask over your face and press the green button to breathe."

Kiet seemed pensive, probably thinking about whatever they had discussed. But he still looked up at me, quizzically. So did Claudia. I replied to them both with a shrug as I pressed the blue button.

It was louder than when Doc had pressed the button on the breather Cornelius had been wearing, sounding halfway between a clogged vacuum cleaner and a spoon in a garbage disposal. After about ten seconds, the noise trailed off to silence.

My hands fumbled with the mask as I put it on. I was nervous about being summoned and about trying to work the breather while walking into an environment that I knew could kill me.

I got the mask into place and pushed the green button. The can vibrated softly and the mask filled with air as I walked across the clearing.

Devon smiled as I approached. "Thanks for coming," he said, holding out his arm to indicate where he wanted to walk. We both looked back at Claudia and Kiet as we set off.

"You're the girl from Pitman, aren't you?" he said.

I wasn't *from* Pitman and I didn't want anyone thinking I was, but I knew what he meant. "Yes," I said. My voice sounded muffled in my ears.

"That was impressive what you did out there." He turned and looked at me, studying me. "Are you spliced?"

I shook my head.

"Just wondering," he said. He glanced back at Kiet again, through the trees, then at me. "Look, I don't know you, but I know a little bit about you, so I'm going to tell you something that I can't tell Kiet right now. He's too upset as it is."

"Tell me what?" We were walking down a slight incline, past a tiny, sagging little wooden house. It wasn't until we stepped past it and out of the trees that I realized it was sitting next to the remnants of a wide avenue.

Devon gestured to our left and we turned to walk along it. Ahead, the road was lined with the remains of a small town—little houses, a few stores, and an old gas station on one side, and a school on the other—all of them sagging, every single window broken.

"We're dying," Devon said as we walked.

"What?" I asked. "What do you mean? Who is?"

"All of us here. Everyone still down in the mines, too."

"H-How do you know? Is it from the yttrium?"

"No. It's this thing they did to us. You don't live more than a few months with it. Down in the mines, most of us don't last that long anyway. But some do. The tough ones. After three months or so, though, they all get sick. They start to cough, they get weak. Within a couple of weeks, they're dead."

My head was spinning.

"Are you sure it's not from whatever they were mining?" I said. "The other toxic chemicals?"

He nodded as he stepped up onto the porch of one of the houses, opening the door and motioning for me to follow.

"How do you know?" I said, as I entered after him.

The house was tiny, but in better shape inside than I expected. We stepped into a living room with a jumble of mismatched furniture: an armchair, a coffee table, a sofa. The windows were all broken, but heavy curtains hung in front of them blocking out the worst of the cold.

On the sofa, trembling under a thick layer of blankets, was a chimera, a lion splice. He seemed to be unconscious. His breathing was shallow.

"This is Henry. We thought—we hoped—just what you said, that it was something about the mines that was killing us, and that when we escaped, we'd escape that, too. It's not much of a life here, but it's a life, and we could work on making it better, work on stopping what they're doing to us at that place. But Henry is our senior citizen. He went into the hospital and ended up in the mines just over three months ago." Devon paused to frown down at the figure on the sofa, then lowered his voice. "He's not doing well. In the mines, by the time they got to this point, they only had a few days left."

Henry's eyes opened a slit. "I can hear you, you know." His voice was raspy and thick. He coughed after he spoke.

Devon sat on the bed next to him. "Sorry, buddy. I was just—"

"No worries," he said, feebly waving him off. "You're not saying anything I don't already know." He looked up at me, and then turned to Devon. "Is she that girl from Pitman?"

He nodded.

Henry snickered, then coughed. "Things must be getting dire if I'm getting bedside visits from minor celebrities."

I could feel my cheeks light up. "Oh, no, that's not it at all," I said. "We were just—"

He snickered again and waved me off, too. "Just messing with you."

"She came with Kiet," Devon said. "They discovered the CCUs."

"We're going to get help," I said. "We're going to shut it down."

Henry looked at Devon. "Kiet's here?"

Devon nodded. "Just outside the safe zone."

Henry's hand flopped on top of Devon's and gave it a limp squeeze. "He okay?"

Devon smiled, but a teardrop fell from his cheek onto Henry's blanket. "He looks great."

"Good," Henry said. "That's good."

They stared at each other for another second, meaningfully. Then Henry turned to me, suddenly looking exhausted. "You're going to get help, huh?"

"We're going to try. Me and Kiet, some others. We're going to shut that place down."

He smiled and yawned. "Good," he said. "Too late for me, I'm afraid, but I hope you do." He closed his eyes. "Not going to be an easy thing in the kind of a world this one has turned into. But I guess if anyone could change things it'd be the girl from Pitman and her friends."

Again I resisted the urge to say I wasn't *from* Pitman, but I realized it didn't matter. He was already asleep.

I was horrified and heartbroken, but in the back of my mind, I couldn't help wondering how much air I had left in the breather. I was glad when Devon nodded toward the door and said, "We should get you back."

As we stepped outside, I took a deep breath of the canned air. Georgie and two other chimeras were sitting on a porch a few houses up. We waved and they waved back, watching us.

"There's something else," Devon said as we walked quickly back the way we had come, uphill this time. "After Henry, I'm the one here with the most seniority."

I turned to look at him, not quite sure what he was getting at.

"I'm just a few days behind him," he said. "A week at the most. So that's what I have to look forward to. I . . . I don't know why I'm putting this on you, other than that I can't tell Kiet, not now, and I have to tell someone. Someone who can tell him . . . later."

"He needs to know."

"Not yet, he doesn't."

I would have argued further, but by then we were approaching the clearing. Kiet was on his feet, watching us. Claudia was sitting on the toolbox, waiting.

The breather let out a faint beep.

Devon smiled. "Good timing. Looks like you're almost out of air."

CHAPTER 31

Kiet watched us intently as we approached. Devon bent close to me and said, "Kiet has to get to work so they don't suspect he's involved with you two, but do me a favor. Give him this breather, tell him how to fill it, and send him over here to say goodbye to me properly."

I ran across the clearing and gave Kiet the breather. He filled it, put it on and ran over to Devon for one last embrace.

"You're sure you can fix the car?" I asked Claudia, as we turned away from them. I think we both wanted to give them some privacy, but for me, knowing what I now knew, it was also just too tragic to look at.

"Piece of cake," she said lightly. Then she squinted at me, studying my face. "Are you okay?"

"No. I'm freaking out. I'm worried about Rex and Doc, and about the people here, and everybody in that damned mine."

She nodded. "Yeah, I hear you."

I glanced over at Kiet and Devon, standing with their foreheads touching, whispering to each other. I wasn't going to rush them, especially since I knew they only had so many goodbyes left. But I could feel my anxiety growing to start doing something, anything, to help them and Rex and everyone else.

After one last, quick kiss, Kiet ran toward us and Devon turned and walked briskly back toward Centre Hollow.

"Okay, let's go," Kiet said without looking at us as he walked past us and into the woods. We followed him for a few minutes, until he stopped at a break in the trees. He looked to his left and right, his eyes wet and pained. "Devon said this is Main Street."

I looked each way, too, the way you're supposed to do when

crossing a street, I guess. To our left was the WELCOME TO CENTRE HOLLOW sign where Devon and his friends had dragged Claudia, Rex, and me to safety. Across from it was the small cluster of houses that somehow hadn't been claimed by the vegetation, and farther down was the wrecked VW.

"This should take us back to Bogen Road, where your car is," Kiet said, pointing right. "When we get there, I'll go back to OmniCare."

He started walking along the road. We both hurried after him, but he made no effort to slow down. Claudia and I exchanged a glance, realizing he wanted to be alone. We stayed back, matching his pace but keeping our distance, taking turns carrying the toolbox.

After a while he slowed, almost to a stop. As we stepped up next to him, he said, "Sorry," and resumed his pace.

"Nothing to apologize for," I said.

"Absolutely," Claudia said.

"I can carry that for a while," he said, taking the toolbox from Claudia.

"Kiet," I said. "Are you sure you want to go back to that place?"

He laughed. "I'm sure I *don't*. But I have to. And I need to be there on time, too. There's this one big delivery truck that arrives at ten every morning. It's huge: paper goods, food for the cafeteria, linens and stuff, all together in this one huge truck—"

"Is that how the splinter inhalers come in?"

He shook his head. "No, everything but the medicine. Anyway, we have a half hour to empty it. If we're not done by ten thirty they get all bent out of shape. And if I'm not there to help, they'll fire me, but more important, they'll know I'm involved somehow. Having me there gives us a better chance to fight them, especially if I can get my hands on one of those inhalers."

We continued to trudge along, not saying a word until a new road appeared in front of us, more intact than the one we were on.

"This is Bogen," Kiet said. He pointed down the road, to the right.

"Your car should be down that way." He turned to us. "I hope it's still there."

"It is," Claudia said, before I could start to worry. "If anybody fixed it up enough to run, it'll be fixed enough for the security system to kick on."

"Okay. When you get it running, take this road back a couple miles and you'll hit Belfield."

"Yeah, we passed it on the way in," I said.

"And Gellersville is farther that way?" Claudia asked.

He nodded. "Yeah, a little ways past the hospital. I live upstairs from Frank's on Main Street—best pizza in Gellersville," he said, with an exaggerated wink. "It's actually the only pizza in Gellersville. But it's an okay little town, chimera-wise, that is. Belfield, too. More E4E than H4H, if you get me."

"Okay, cool," Claudia said.

"Where's the jail?" I asked, "Where would they have taken Rex?"

"That's in Gellersville. Next to the police station."

I nodded. "You going to be okay, going to work after being up all night?"

He nodded, stifling a yawn. "Yeah. As long as I punch in on time and get the truck unloaded, it should be cool. So . . . I'm going to try to get my hands on one of those inhalers. What are you going to do?"

"After we fix the car?" Claudia said.

"We're going to get E4E up here," I said in a rush. "We're going to get Rex out of jail and shut down that mine. And if you can get one of those inhalers, we can expose OmniCare, and get our friend Doc out of jail, too."

Kiet nodded solemnly. There was a lot on his shoulders. "I get done work at five. I'll be home by five thirty. How about we meet at five thirty at Frank's?"

We took turns hugging him, then Kiet turned and started jogging one way and we started walking the other.

We didn't talk much as we walked, both lost in our own thoughts, but the toolbox clanked with every step.

Seeing Kiet and Devon together made me think about Rex. Our circumstances were way less dire, but there were undeniable similarities. It seemed like the universe was conspiring to keep us apart.

Half an hour later we saw the car up ahead. At first it looked exactly as we'd left it. As we got closer, we saw what looked like dried soda on the windshield and a Dairy Queen cup on the ground next to it.

"That's just great," Claudia muttered, but she didn't pause as she took off her coat, pulled a socket wrench set out of the toolbox, and slid under the car.

I had warmed up from all the walking, but it was still cold out, and as I stood there, feeling useless and hoping whoever had thrown the soda didn't come back to cause more trouble, the chill began to work its way back into my bones. I thought about getting into the car, but it wouldn't have seemed right with her underneath, fixing it.

By the time Claudia slid out from under the car and brushed off her hands, I was hugging myself for warmth.

"Helps to have the right tools," she said as she got in. The car started right up and she bobbed her eyebrows at me through the driver's-side window, kind of cocky, but she'd earned it.

She popped the trunk and I put the tools in and closed it, then I hopped in next to her.

"Oh my God," I said, holding my hands in front of the vents. "Heat!"

Claudia laughed. "I know, right? I'd almost forgotten what it felt like."

Together with the plush upholstery, the warmth seeping into our bones felt incredible, and I could feel my exhaustion trying to lull me to sleep. We indulged in a moment to savor the luxury, then we drove off.

Claudia drove slowly and carefully, taking pains to avoid every crater-like pothole and dislodged chunk of asphalt.

When we reached Belfield, we turned into the center of town. Two blocks down there was a charging station next to a diner. Claudia pulled in and paid with a card, declining my offer of a few bucks.

As she dealt with charging the car, I went to the pay phone at the charging station. A decal on the door of the diner said there was a pay phone inside, but I didn't want to be overheard.

First, I called Jerry.

"Where the hell did you guys go?" he said when he found out it was me.

"OmniCare."

"Goddamn it, the lawyer specifically said not to! And I said—"

"How's Doc?" I interrupted.

That stopped him. "He's okay," he said with a sigh. "He *says* he's okay. I don't know. It's hard. He's having a hard time."

"Jerry," I said. "There's some crazy stuff going on out here."

"There's crazy stuff everywhere these days."

"Not like this." As quickly as I could, I told him about OmniCare and the mines, and about Centre Hollow and what Devon had told us. Then I told him about Rex getting arrested.

"God*damn* it," he said again, breathlessly. I heard a sound like a wooden chair scraping against the floor, like he was sitting down. I was glad of that.

"We have a friend who works at OmniCare. He's trying to get proof, one of the inhalers, but we've seen this with our own eyes. We need to get word to E4E," I said. "They need to get on this right now."

He made a growly, grunting noise but didn't respond.

"What?"

"Ah, just that E4E has their hands full with the GHA stuff. They've got all hands on deck as it is."

"Jerry, didn't you hear what I said? People are being killed! They're being held against their will and having . . . *medical experiments* done on them."

"I know, I know, I hear you. I get it. It sounds terrible. I'm just saying E4E is overextended and—"

"Well, we need them," I interrupted. "And they need to get Rex out of jail, too."

"Okay, okay. I'll do what I can. What's your plan?"

"Right now? We've got to eat something and try to get to Rex. Can you call the police and find out if they've set bail for him, or what the charges are?"

"Yeah. Where is he?"

"A town called Gellersville, we think. Rex said the charges from Genaro's Deli got dropped when Genaro died, but I'm not sure what'll happen if they put that together with this. Hopefully he hasn't told them his birth name, so don't ask for Leo Byron."

"Yeah, okay," he said. "I'll just ask what's the bail for the biggest dog they got in there."

By the time I got off the phone with Jerry, Claudia was leaning against the car, waiting for me. Unfortunately, I still had another call to make.

I took a deep breath and called home, holding my breath as the phone rang at the other end. I knew this wasn't going to change anything, but I figured I had to at least let Kevin know I was okay, and maybe even somehow put off or minimize whatever trouble I was in.

As the phone continued to ring, I started to hope the voice mail would pick up.

My heart sank when I heard a thick "Hullo?" on the other end. Kevin sounded almost confused, as if he'd never encountered a phone before and just happened to be passing by it when he was enticed by the ringing noise.

Crap, I thought, wondering if he'd been home the night before, and if he had, if he'd noticed I wasn't.

"Hey," I said. "It's me."

He paused, then said, "Hey."

I racked my brain, trying to remember if I'd left my bedroom door open, trying to figure the odds that even if he'd been home, he hadn't noticed whether or not I had been.

"Where are you?"

"Out with friends."

He let out a heavy sigh, like he was yawning and stretching. Like he was bored. "Whatcha do last night?"

I couldn't tell if he was anxious to get off the phone, didn't really care about my response, or was setting me up.

"Hung out at the coffee shop."

"What time didja get home?"

I didn't know what to say. I didn't know if he had been home. If he had been, and had gone to bed, I needed to say I got home late. If he got home *late*, I could conceivably have gotten home early and gone to bed. I took a gamble, guessing he'd been at his friend Malik's house playing Holo-Box basketball all night.

"Not too late," I said.

He yawned again. "Bullshit."

"No, it's—"

He cut me off, laughing. "I can't believe you're doing this again. You're off somewhere with your crazy friends, aren't you?"

"Kevin, this is important—"

He was laughing again, a super-loud, forced laugh. It grew fainter and farther away, and I could picture him, doubled over, fake-laughing so hard he had to hold the phone down while he did it.

"Kevin, stop it!" I yelled into the phone. *"I said this is important, asshole!"*

Claudia winced and half whispered, "I'm going to call my folks from inside," then she hurried into the diner.

I wanted to hang up, but I needed to talk to him, and he *knew* that, or else I wouldn't have called.

"You know . . . ," he said, still getting over his big laugh, "Mom thinks getting through high school without a criminal record is important, too."

"Please don't tell her," I said quietly.

"Don't tell her you didn't come home last night, or don't tell her you're mixed up in more chimera craziness?"

I growled. "Either."

"And when whatever it is you're involved in blows up, and she asks me why I didn't tell her, what am I supposed to say?"

"They're killing chimeras," I said quietly.

"Again?"

"Come on, Kevin."

"Oh, I'm sorry," he said, his sarcasm turning to anger. "So, someone's killing chimeras again. That's terrible. It is. But you know what? Most people, when they find out a crime is being committed, they call the cops and let them deal with it. Why is it that *you* have to save them?"

"Oh, please. You know what the cops can be like!"

"Jimi, you're not spliced! You're not one of them. Why is it that out of everyone else in the universe, sixteen-year-old Jimi Corcoran—"

"I'm seventeen, moron. My birthday was last month."

"—has to step up and save the chimeras of the world from evil? Who appointed you?"

"No one! I'm not and I don't. Look, I'm *trying* to get help, I'm *trying* to tell other people, lawyers and whatever, but . . ."

My voice trailed off, like I had just run out of energy, right at that moment. Kevin was never going to understand, not ever. I wanted to tell him *that* was exactly it: no one would understand. And sometimes it's easier just to do whatever needs to be done than to try to explain the situation to the people who were supposed to be taking care of it in the first place. Because those people just weren't going to, and *that's* what was wrong with the world.

"Please don't tell Mom," I said, my voice even and flat.

He sighed again, and this time I could tell that even if he didn't understand, he really did care. "I'm not going to call her. But she's going to find out anyway, you know, when you get arrested or hurt or when whatever crazy bullshit you're involved in ends up on the news again." He was quiet for a few seconds. "When are you coming home?"

His reasonableness took me by surprise. "What? Um . . . soon. I'm going to get home soon."

"Okay, well I'm crashing at Malik's tonight. Mom's supposed to be home tomorrow night. So, what I'm going to do, as a *responsible big brother*, I'm going to write Mom a note. I'm going to say you didn't come home last night—"

"*Kevin!*"

"—and if you don't come home tonight, I'm going to write that, too—"

"I just said—"

"—and I'm going to put it on the kitchen table. If you get home before Mom does, and if the note's somehow gone when she walks in, well, as far as I'm concerned, I tried."

"Kevin, don't—"

"Look, you said you were on your way home right now. If you are, then great. If I were you, when I got home I would *totally* tear that note into tiny bits."

"Kevin, just—"

"But I'm telling you, Mom was worried sick about you when all that stuff went down three months ago. Hell, so was I. She's just about gotten over it, but if you think she's going to get over it again, you really don't know Mom."

CHAPTER 32

The diner had a big E4E sticker in the front window. The guy behind the counter was watching an old-fashioned flat screen, with a BREAKING NEWS banner across the bottom and a couple of talking heads. But he turned and gave me a big, friendly smile. "You can sit anywhere you like."

His name tag said DOUG.

As he turned back to the news, his smile fading, I spotted Claudia waving at me from one of the booths.

I sat in the seat across from her, exhausted from the night we'd just had and from my conversation with Kevin. She held up a menu. "Buy you breakfast?"

My stomach answered before I could, growling loudly enough that Claudia's eyes widened and she laughed. "Sure, that would be great," I said.

The menu was massive, and I was engrossed by all the choices. When I looked up, Claudia was staring past me, at the flat screen.

"What is it?" I said, turning around to look.

"Another bombing."

The TV showed a cluster of news drones and police copters circling a square brick building with its windows blown out and black soot staining the bricks above them.

"Where?"

"Baltimore," she said. "Regional H4H office."

"Damn," I said. "Like we didn't have enough trouble."

She looked back at her menu, shaking her head. "Yeah, that's not going to help things. But I can't say I don't get it."

I didn't reply. I felt like it wasn't my place to disagree with her, and in a way I didn't. But I couldn't condone bombing, the same way I couldn't condone what H4H was doing.

"Was anybody hurt?" I asked.

She shook her head. "They don't think so."

Doug came over to take our order. It was still breakfast time, but we both ordered vedge burgers, fries, and shakes. When he left, I whispered to Claudia. "Do you think it's chimeras?"

Claudia nodded. "I think it has to be, right? When it was just the church, it could have been about something else, but this . . ."

I nodded, then she said, "Oh, great."

I looked over at the TV, and there was Howard Wells, being interviewed outside the damaged H4H building. Doug turned the volume up, shaking his head.

"I know some of you out there want to retaliate for these vicious attacks," Wells said, looking directly into the camera. "And I totally understand that urge, I do. Frankly, I want to as well, but Humans for Humanity can't. We have more important things to do, like winning the fight to save that which makes humanity special."

The reporter pulled the microphone back and said, "Wait, are you saying you would condone retaliation from those not affiliated with Humans for Humanity?"

Wells smiled wide. "No, no, of course I can't condone . . . cruelty to animals or anything like that. But at the same time, humans have their own free will, and I certainly can't condemn them for exercising it."

Doug turned the TV back down, shaking his head as he worked on our orders.

The food showed up minutes later, and it was delicious. We were halfway through before we paused long enough to speak.

"I talked to my dad," Claudia said, hooking her thumb at the pay phone by the entrance. "He's back in California. You know what he told me, though?" She took a quick sip of her milkshake. "He's thinking of getting a Wellplant."

"Really?"

"He's on the wait list."

"But . . . you're a chimera. And Howard Wells is . . . Howard Wells."

She shrugged. "He says all his competitors have them. He feels like he's at a disadvantage."

I didn't know how she felt about it all, so I didn't want to lay it on too thick. "Maybe he'll rethink when you tell him what's going on at OmniCare."

"Yeah, maybe." She ate a fry and picked up another one. "He wants me to get one, too. So we can keep in touch."

"*Ew!* Really? That's so creepy."

She dropped the fry she was holding. "You think everything is creepy."

"No, I don't."

"You think chimeras are creepy."

"No, I don't. I used to, but I don't anymore. Not at all."

"Okay. But it's not like you'd ever consider getting spliced."

"I might."

She sat back and raised an eyebrow at me.

"I might," I said again. It surprised me to hear myself saying it out loud, but I wasn't lying. The thought had crossed my mind a few times over the past few months. If I had to choose teams, well, pretty much all of my friends were chimeras. And Rex, of course.

But it also bugged the hell out of me—why should I have to choose teams? Why were there even teams at all? It wasn't like the people with splices were marching around hating on everyone else.

"Really?" Claudia leaned forward, her eyes sparkling with mischief. "What would you get spliced with?"

I couldn't tell if she was messing with me, but I hadn't given that part of it a whole lot of thought, or at least not enough to give her an answer. It was not a conversation I especially wanted to be having, but when I suddenly realized it was over, I didn't feel the slightest bit of relief.

"What?" Claudia asked, studying my face.

It was there again—that feeling of being watched. But suspicion quickly turned into fear as I realized that this time, it wasn't my imagination.

Two men were walking toward us across the diner. They were both white, both had Wellplants. One of them was in his forties, blandly good looking but also vaguely threatening. He reminded me of an unhinged version of the salesman that sold my mom her car. The other one I recognized right away. It was the guy who'd been staring at me with his creepy gray eyes at the Lev station back in Oakton. He wasn't wearing his fedora.

Doug had been intently watching the news coverage the whole time, but he turned to watch these two approach us.

Before I could warn Claudia about any of this, they were standing next to our table, looking down at us with smiles that were half-phony and the rest of the way evil.

"Dymphna Corcoran?" said the younger one, the car salesman.

The creeper from the Lev station smiled wider.

"Who are you?" I said.

"We just want to talk to you," said the creeper.

Doug glanced over, did a double take, and was now giving the two of them a hard stare from behind the counter.

"Why are you following me?"

"Like I said, we want to talk to you."

"About what?"

He smiled again. "It's kind of complicated. Perhaps we can go someplace quiet."

"Seems pretty quiet right here," Claudia said.

His smile faltered. "Somewhere quieter, then."

"Are you cops?" I said.

"Not exactly," he said.

"Then I don't *exactly* want to talk to you," I said. At this point, Doug had left the counter and was coming over.

"It's about your friends," said the car salesman.

"Which ones?"

He grinned wide and it gave me chills. "All of them."

"Everything okay here?" Doug said, hands on his hips, making a point of just talking to Claudia and me.

"No, it's not. These men won't leave us alone," Claudia said.

Doug turned to them and they stared back at him for a few seconds.

"If you gentlemen would like to sit up front, I can get you a couple of menus. Otherwise, I'm going to have to ask you to leave."

They continued staring at Doug with a sort of malevolent condescension, like they had all the power but they were going to go along with his game for now because they wanted to. The car salesman moved his arm to reveal a bulge on his hip, like he had a gun or a shock baton or something, and he wanted to let everyone know it. They let a few seconds tick by to make it clear they didn't have to do anything they didn't want to.

"No, that's okay," said the creeper, grimacing at our food, as if it didn't look good. "We were just leaving."

They waited another few seconds, then they turned and slowly walked away, looking back one last time as they went out the front door.

Doug stayed where he was, watching them through the glass door. "Do you know those guys?"

"No," I said. "And I don't want to."

They stayed right outside the front door, one of them leaning against a dark green sedan. Waiting.

"Do you want me to call the police?" Doug asked.

"No!" I said, maybe a little too quickly.

He gave us a dubious nod. "Okay."

I looked at Claudia. "We should probably get going anyway."

She looked sadly at the remains of her burger. "Yeah, I guess."

"Can we have these to go?" I asked Doug. "And can we use your back door?"

CHAPTER 33

We were in danger. I knew it. Claudia did, too. But sneaking out the back door of the diner clutching our to-go bags and tip-toeing back to Claudia's car at the charging station, for some reason it struck us both as absolutely hilarious.

As soon as we'd eased her car doors open and quietly pulled them shut behind us, we started snickering. It was a dangerous kind of laugh, seeing as how we needed to focus on getting away. But it wouldn't stop.

As Claudia started up the car and slowly drove around the back of the charging station and out the far side, we took turns taking deep breaths, trying to get ourselves under control even as the other kept laughing. The laughter didn't fully die until we turned onto the on-ramp for the SmartPike and I noticed her staring into the rearview display, her face filled with dread.

I looked behind us, but I knew what I was going to see. The men from the diner, right behind us in their dark green sedan.

"Crap," Claudia said.

We were approaching the place where the ramp split off, east or west.

"What should I do?" she asked.

"I don't know." The sign directly in front of us had two arrows. The one pointing left said PHILADELPHIA 102 MILES. NEXT EXIT: DURINGER 37 MILES. The one pointing right said PITTSBURGH 221 MILES. NEXT EXIT: GELLERSVILLE 7 MILES.

We were headed straight toward the white triangle painted on the road between the two sections that curved away on either side. The green sedan was closing on us, and Claudia said, "Jimi? What do I do?"

"Right!" I yelled, at the last second. She jerked the wheel hard and our tires screeched as we crossed the white paint onto the westbound ramp. Behind us, the green sedan screeched across it as well.

Claudia snuck a glance in the rearview mirror and pressed the accelerator to the floor, ignoring the flashing red speed-limiter warning light. She slid into the passing lane and started hurtling by other cars.

We were already doing ninety-five, way faster than you were supposed to go unless you were in Smartdrive.

"You disabled the Smartdrive detector?"

She grinned. "And the speed limiter." Then her grin disappeared. "Why did you say *right*?"

"We had to go one way, and I figured better to go the way with the nearest exit, so we can try to lose them, and maybe turn around and go back the other way." Also, because the plan, after eating, was to figure out how to get to Rex. And as far as I knew, he was in Gellersville.

She stared at me for a disconcertingly long moment, considering we were going almost one hundred miles an hour and the car was under her manual control.

"That's pretty smart," she said, turning her attention back to her driving, weaving through traffic so fast the cars we were passing were blurs going by. But the green sedan was keeping up with us. We passed a sign saying the exit to Gellersville was in one mile. The next exit after that was in twenty miles.

We both saw the sign and immediately looked at each other.

"What are you going to do?" I asked.

"I don't think we want to get trapped on the SmartPike."

"So what are you going to do?"

We were almost at the exit.

"Hold on," she said, and she jerked the wheel hard, swerving between two cars and rocketing down the exit ramp. We almost slammed into the Smartdrive pylon, a thick steel pole bristling with electronics that served as the ground traffic control, making sure all the Smartdrive systems played nicely with each other.

"That was close," I said. The pylons are kind of a big deal. Every couple of years, one goes out for one reason or another and it's traffic hell for hours.

Claudia eyed her rearview. Just as we reached the bottom of the ramp, the green sedan appeared at the top of it, coming after us. She barely slowed down, screeching into a hard left that took us back under the SmartPike, then jerking the wheel again, onto the eastbound on-ramp.

"We're going back to Belfield?" I said.

"I don't know. I don't want to get trapped on those back roads."

We drove in silence for a minute—sixty seconds that took us two miles closer to the next exit. The only sound was the soft *zip, zip, zip,* as we passed car after car.

"Okay," Claudia said. "I have an idea." She turned and stared at me, again for way too long. "Can you drive?"

"Yeah, I can drive," I said, quickly, so she could get back to looking out through the windshield.

She barely glanced at the road before she returned her stare to me.

"I mean can you *really* drive. Not 'My mom took me to a parking lot to practice three times' or 'I watched a Holovid on how to use Smartdrive in driver's ed class.' Can. You. Drive?"

"Yes," I said, with more confidence than I felt. My plans to get my license had been sidetracked the past year, but my mom had taken me to a parking lot to practice at least half a dozen times, and more to the point, I had also stolen *three* cars—which was vaguely distressing to think about, especially since only one of them was my mom's. I had also driven a truck through a fence three times, and a car through a different fence once. *That ought to count for something*, I thought, although I didn't know exactly what. "Yes, I can."

"Good. Because you're going to have to do it well."

CHAPTER 34

Claudia's plan was insane. Unfortunately, I was too terrified to come up with anything better. We rocketed those last couple of miles to the Belfield exit, then repeated the maneuver we had done in Gellersville: speeding down the off-ramp, screeching through the underpass and up the on-ramp, and heading west again, weaving through traffic back to Gellersville.

That's when it got really, really tricky.

Claudia gained as much of a lead as she could, driving as fast as she dared. My knuckles were white from holding on, and my fingernails were white from digging into the armrest.

The green sedan was actually falling behind, and part of me thought, since Claudia's car was obviously top of the line, maybe we could just keep driving like that and lose them on the highway.

But that wasn't the plan.

Halfway back to Gellersville, Claudia maneuvered the car into the slow lane. Making sure there was no one directly behind us, she turned to me and said, "Ready?"

Then she turned on the Smartdrive.

Red lights began flashing and beepers and alarms sounded as the car's Smartdrive system came online and realized that something not right was going on. As Claudia and I scrambled past each other, switching places, the car immediately began to decelerate.

As soon as I was in place, Claudia shouted at me, "Hit it!"

I had one hand on the steering wheel, my foot over the accelerator, and one finger aimed at the Smartdrive button. I paused, just for a moment, and Claudia shouted again, *"Hit it!"*

I glanced in the rearview and saw the green sedan angling through gaps in the traffic, making its way toward us. My finger jammed the

Smartdrive button, turning it off and mercifully killing the alarms and warning lights as my foot pushed the accelerator down to the floor. The tires wailed, spinning until they caught some traction and we shot forward. The back of the car slid from side to side as we picked up speed.

I started passing the other cars, then shooting past them, the rears of the ones in front of us coming at me like some terrifying Holo-Box game. I bobbed and weaved, trying to avoid them, knowing it wasn't a game at all.

Claudia was halfway in the backseat. She had pulled one of the seat backs down and was rooting around in the trunk.

I was going too fast to look in the rearview. "Where are they?" I asked.

She looked out the back windshield. "Falling back but still too close. We need more distance."

"Okay," I said, which was a lie. Nothing about this was okay.

"What are you doing?"

It took me a second before I realized what she meant. I glanced at the speedometer.

"One-thirty." *Holy crap, 130!*

"You can do one-forty, no problem."

I realized there was a good chance that Claudia might be insane. But I pressed the accelerator harder, and the needle icon crept toward 140.

Claudia pulled the toolbox out of the trunk and checked the back window. "Okay, good. They're falling back."

She wiggled her way back into the passenger seat with the toolbox clutched to her midsection. She looked out the window at the rapidly approaching Gellersville exit, then she turned to me. "You ready?"

I nodded without looking at her. From the corner of my eye I saw her nod back. The exit was still almost a quarter mile away, but at 140 miles an hour, that was, like, six seconds.

I pulled into the exit lane, and she shouted, *"Now!"*

I took my foot off the accelerator and jammed the brakes as hard as I could, bracing my back against the seat, pulling on the steering wheel, while at the same time trying to keep the car straight enough that it didn't slide off the road or back into traffic, or even worse, go into a roll.

Finally the car came to a stop, just ten feet away from the Smart-drive pylon.

Claudia opened her door, slipped out, and closed it without a word. Just like that, she was gone. I could smell burning rubber as I hit the accelerator once more, picking up speed along the off-ramp, through the underpass, and back up the on-ramp toward Belfield.

I was getting more comfortable driving at such a high speed, or maybe just more used to being terrified. But when I got to the Belfield exit, things got even scarier. I had to try to keep my speed up while doing the whole off-ramp, underpass, on-ramp maneuver. Somehow I managed it, and even allowed myself a slight smile, though I knew the trickiest part of the plan was just ahead. I looked in the rearview mirror. The green sedan was quite a ways back. But just behind it was a mass of blue and red lights on top of a rapidly approaching police car.

Instinctively I took my foot off the accelerator, but then jammed it back down again. The plan was still the plan. Now it was even more important that it work.

The Gellersville exit was approaching. I tried to do the calculations in my head. I was going faster than before, and aiming for a different place. I was still working on my estimates when I pulled into the exit lane and flew past the place where I'd hit the brakes the first time. I waited one more second, then did it again, punching the brakes as hard as I could, trying to maintain control of the screaming, smoking, bucking car, and at the same time trying not to think too hard about the fact that Claudia was out there, and that if I lost control, it was entirely possible I could squish her like a bug. I skidded past the

Smartdrive pylon, saw a flash of color through the window that might or might not have been Claudia.

The car skidded to a stop, and I looked out the back window just in time to see a tiny arc of sparks spewing out of the base of the pylon, and Claudia backing away from it.

The air filled with the incredibly loud and bizarrely sonorous tone of hundreds or thousands of tires screeching in unison as every car on that stretch of the SmartPike came to a halt.

Claudia stood in the middle of the ramp, her back to me as she looked over her handiwork. I couldn't see the green sedan, but I could see the police lights, a quarter mile back, hopelessly mired in the frozen sea of gridlocked cars.

Claudia turned, ran toward me, and got into the passenger seat.

As I drove away at a safe, lawful speed, she turned to me with a manic grin and said, "That was freaking awesome!"

CHAPTER 35

Gellersville seemed like a slightly bigger version of Belfield. I was so focused on the rearview mirror, I didn't notice too much of it at first. I kept to the speed limit, even though part of me wanted to be doing 140 again, putting as much distance as possible between us and the mayhem behind us. But when I stopped at a stop sign in the middle of town, across from a dull concrete building with a big American flag out front, I kept my foot on the brake.

After a few seconds, Claudia looked around nervously and said, "Um, we need to keep moving and find someplace inconspicuous."

"That's the police station," I said, staring at the concrete building. "That's the jail. Where Rex is."

As I said it, a couple of drones flew by, low and fast, headed for the SmartPike.

"Yes, and that's also where the police are. We can't just stop here staring at it. We need to get out of here."

A pair of drones lifted off the roof of the police station, red and blue lights twinkling, and zipped across the cloudy sky in the same direction as the other two, toward the SmartPike.

I drove up the block and turned into the Dairy Queen parking lot. It was closed for the night, but the sign was still lit up. In the rearview, I saw a pair of patrol cars pull out of the lot next to the station. Their lights started flashing as they headed back the way we'd come.

I pulled all the way into the back of the parking lot, by a pair of dumpsters. Then I turned the car off and let out a heavy sigh.

"You did good," Claudia said, punching me in the arm. "But maybe I should drive now."

"I need some air first," I said, getting out of the car. I took a few unsteady steps, and took a deep breath, trying to fend off a vague jittery feeling that I suspected could turn into a case of the shakes.

Claudia got out the other side of the car and came over to me. "We need to keep moving," she said, grabbing my elbow. She pulled me farther behind the Dairy Queen and glanced up as the sky filled with the sound of quadcopters. "We just shut down the SmartPike. They're going to be looking for us—not just those creeps that were following us. Everybody. And it won't take long before everyone turns off their autodrive and they get those cars moving. We need to figure another way out of this place and we need to use it, fast. . . . Jimi, are you okay?"

She was leaning over and looking up at my face, checking.

"I'm fine," I said.

"Who were those guys?"

I shook my head. "I don't know. I saw one of them before. Back in Philly, at the Lev station near my house. He seemed like he was watching me. Maybe waiting for me."

"Seriously?"

"I think so. I . . . I've had this feeling lately, like I'm being watched. First I thought it was from being on the news, after Pitman. My fifteen minutes of fame, you know? Then I thought I was going nuts. But with that guy showing up out here, saying he needs to talk? Maybe I'm not nuts."

"Well," she said with a smirk, "I wouldn't rule that out just yet. But they're definitely after us now, so we need to get out of here."

"I know, but . . . Rex is right across the street."

"I know. And our best chance to help him is to get home, get help, and . . . oh, crap. . . ."

Her voice trailed off as she looked past me. I turned and saw the car salesman and the creeper, two menacing grins coming toward us, one on either side of the Jaguar.

"Well, that was a cute trick," said the creeper.

Claudia and I looked around, but we were trapped. We both took a step back, which put us right up against a tall wire fence.

"Very cute," said the car salesman, above the noise that increasingly filled the air. "But unfortunately, it wasted all our doing-things-the-easy-way time."

The creeper took out a stun gun. "I almost felt bad, you two being such innocent young ladies and all. But you're not so innocent, are you?"

The car salesman took out a stun gun, too, but he fumbled with it, his hands looking clumsy. "And . . . you're not . . . ladies, either," he said, his voice sounding sluggish, too.

The creeper scowled at him. "What hell'za matter with you?"

Both of their guns were sagging, aiming at the ground in front of us.

Claudia snuck me a glance that seemed to say *Something's up with these two. Should we make a break for it?*

I honestly didn't know, so instead of replying, I looked back at the two goons, still staring at each other. The creeper grabbed the car salesman's shoulder and looked at his back. "What the . . . ," he said, turning his head to try to see over his own shoulder. "Aw, goddamn it." He turned and glared at us, his face angry and red even as his eyes went dull. He raised his gun again, slurring, "You little . . ." Then he pitched forward onto his face.

The car salesman watched him fall, squinting at the little piece of gray fluff on his shoulder, ruffling slightly in the breeze.

"What the fff . . ." he said, then his eyes rolled up and he pitched over, too.

Claudia and I shared a brief, incredulous laugh, no idea what the hell was going on.

We stepped around the car and the two guys on the ground, and peeked around the corner of the building, but there was no sign of anyone who might have fired the darts.

We were still looking when we heard a *zzzzip* sound behind us.

Spinning around, we saw a large woman dressed in tactical black. She looked like she was spliced with some kind of bear, with a black nose and coarse brown hair stark against the white skin of face. Her feet were just hitting the ground. One hand held a clip attached to the rope she had just descended. The other one held a dart gun. "Jimi and Claudia, right?" she said.

Claudia's eyes narrowed suspiciously. "Yeah, who are you?"

"My name's Roberta."

Before she could continue, another chimera, half her size, came down a second rope. His landing was a little rougher, but I was still infinitely more delighted by it. I dove past Roberta and wrapped my arms around him. As I squeezed him tight, I heard his strangled voice telling Claudia over my shoulder, "You can call me Sly."

I let him go and stepped back.

"You two know each other?" Claudia said.

"Hell yeah," Sly said, pulling me in for a second hug.

I was surprised Claudia didn't recognize him, but then I remembered their paths had missed crossing by five minutes.

"Sly's a really good friend, and a good friend of Doc and Rex and the others," I told her. "He was with us throughout the whole thing at Pitman."

Claudia introduced herself, and they each said hi. Before I could ask Sly what he was doing there, Roberta cleared her throat, interrupting the pleasantries. "We're here to get you out of here," she said. "We're from Chimerica."

CHAPTER 36

C himerica?" I said, turning to Sly. "What's she talking about?"
"I'll explain later. Right now, she's right—we've got to move.
Wells's people are all around here. Looking for *you*."

Roberta was peering around the edge of the building, just like we
had done.

"Howard Wells?" Claudia said, her voice edged with a faint serra-
tion of fear.

"Looking for *me*?" I said, somehow having a hard time mustering
the disbelief.

Roberta looked back at Sly and gave him a thumbs-up.

He put an arm around my waist and looked up at me. "Hold on.
Tight." His tone told me there wasn't time to argue, so I held him as
tightly as I could.

Across from us, Roberta still had one arm wound with the black
rope. She wrapped the other arm around Claudia, who didn't look
entirely comfortable about it.

The alley darkened and the ambient buzz rose to a roar as a quadcopter drifted out from above the roof of the Dairy Queen and into
the air above us. Apparently it had been hovering up there, just out of
sight. The ropes jerked, and suddenly all four of us rose through the
air and into the belly of the quadcopter.

The inside was sparse, like an old cargo plane or maybe military
surplus. Instead of the car-like interior of a regular quadcopter, this
one had a large empty cabin with a short passage to the cockpit, where
the pilot and copilot sat. It smelled of metal, ozone, and old-fashioned
lubricant, more like a truck than an aircraft. As soon as we were safely
inside, the hatch slid shut and the copter surged forward.

"We can't leave yet," I shouted, bending my head close to Sly's so he could hear me above the din from the rotors. "Rex is in jail down there, or at least I think he is. We have to find out for sure and get him out of there!"

Sly shook his head. "He's down there, all right, but he's safe and secure and E4E is working on getting him out. Right now, we need to focus on getting you to safety, too!"

We were rising steadily and picking up speed when the police station—and the jail—came into view below. I pressed my forehead against the window.

"He'll be okay," Sly shouted over the motor. "They'll have him out of there in no time, and meanwhile, don't you worry." He grinned. "Big Dog can take care of himself."

Claudia turned to him and said, "But . . . what about my car?" Sly didn't seem like he had an answer for that, but then the copter began to bank, and for a moment the SmartPike came into view, a ribbon of stalled cars stretching from one horizon to the other, with a slow trickle coming off the exit ramps. The air above it swarmed with police drones and copters. But as we continued to bank and pick up speed, that all disappeared, too.

Two other chimeras were piloting the quad. I didn't get their names. Nobody talked at all, though my thoughts were churning, wondering what Roberta meant when she said they were from Chimerica. After half an hour, the engines dropped from a whine to a throatier roar. I looked out the window and saw the trees rising to meet us, but ahead of us, they abruptly stopped. There was a tiny sliver of ice-covered beach, and beyond that water, as far as the eye could see.

Claudia joined me at the window. "What the . . ."

I thought we were coming in for a landing, but I realized that we were just descending, not slowing down. In a flash, the beach disappeared beneath us and we were out over the cold, gray water. *Right* over the cold, gray water. Low enough that the downdraft from the rotors was kicking up spray.

Sly was avoiding my gaze, but I decided to take advantage of the change in the engines' pitch and try again. I grabbed his collar to bring him close enough to hear, and maybe for a little emphasis as well.

He looked at my hand, then up at my face.

"Where are we?" I shouted into his ear.

He pointed down and shouted back, "Lake Erie."

"*What?* Where the hell are we going?"

He shook his head. "I'm not supposed to tell you till we get there."

Claudia came up next to us and shouted, "Did you say Lake Erie? Are we going to Canada?"

He glanced at Roberta, then gave us a slight nod.

"How?" I asked. "It's a closed border."

I knew that what I'd been doing, what I was trying to do, for Doc, for Rex, for the miners, was all important, for real. But leaving the country illegally, without a passport, without telling my mom, that was a different order of magnitude. And we were still flying.

"This thing's a bucket of bolts," he said, twirling his finger at the copter, then pointing it at the cockpit. "But Dara's a magician. When we get close to the shore, she'll find a Canadian to track." He paused as the copter banked sharply to the right. Then he smiled. "I guess we're close to the shore."

Outside the window, another copter came into view, startlingly close. It looked nice and new, with white paint and red trim. We were close enough that I could see the pilot, his hands gesturing at us to back off. In the rear window, two little kids were waving at us. Our copter dipped its wing, presumably to the kids.

"What the hell is she doing?" Claudia shouted, alarmed at how close we were.

Roberta was giving Sly a cold stare, like she didn't approve of him telling us anything.

"We get close enough that our radar signatures merge, then Dara clones their beacon. As far as Canadian air traffic is concerned, we're a Canadian craft that flew out over the water to see the sights, then came back ashore."

Claudia paused, suddenly more impressed than alarmed. "That'll work?"

Sly shrugged. "Worked every time so far."

"What about when we get to the other side?" she asked.

"We're just another quadcopter coming and going."

"And where are we going?" I said again, casually.

He opened his mouth, but caught himself. "You'll see soon."

Moments later we banked again, peeling away from the other copter. Minutes after that, we were over land again, in Canada.

We flew northeast along the shoreline for a few minutes, then veered left and headed northwest.

Once I got over my shock at having left the US and entered Canada—and stopped wondering how I was going to tell my mother that, in addition to everything else, I had done so without permission from her or either government—I stuck by the window to take it all in.

Ever since we hit land, we'd been flying over grids of farmland and suburbs. There were still suburbs in Canada. I knew that from school. They hadn't been so hard hit by the flu epidemics, so there hadn't been the same depopulation as in the States. Plus, people had been moving northward for decades as things got warmer, so Canada's population had actually been growing. While most American suburbs had become the zurbs, in Canada they were still just . . . suburbs.

It was weird looking down on them, thinking about how different they were, probably still kids playing in the streets, just like when my parents were young.

Then they were gone, and once again we were skimming over water, this time flecked with ice.

"Where are we this time?" I asked.

"Lake Huron," Sly said.

Roberta sat up and looked out the window for a moment. "Georgian Bay, technically."

Sly rolled his eyes and leaned closer, lowering his voice. "Lake Huron."

"Okay, Sly, enough is enough," I said. "Where are you taking us?"

As if in reply, the copter started to bank, tipping so the window on one side showed only sky, the other side only sea. We circled as we descended, over and over. At first sky and sea were all that we saw. Then an island appeared beneath us, a squarish patch of white and green in the middle of lots and lots of cold, gray ice and water. The island grew as we descended, enough that I could make out a dozen wind turbines spinning madly, painted green to match the trees around them on a ridge overlooking the water. But by the time we landed, the island still hadn't grown by much.

The engines slowed and quieted, and Sly opened the side door. As frigid air filled the copter, he grinned and said, "Welcome to Lonely Island."

CHAPTER 37

Lonely Island?" Claudia said, smirking at me like I was a co-conspirator. "Are you serious?"

But as we stepped off the copter, her smirk faltered. We weren't alone at all. The place was bustling with dozens of people, all dressed in gray-and-white camo fatigues, all chimeras as far as I could tell. But the place still seemed so desolate that the name made perfect sense.

We had set down at one end of a large, snow-covered field surrounded by thick woods that whistled with a steady, cutting wind. The top of a lighthouse peered over the treetops.

The far end of the field was carpeted with more white-and-gray camouflage—tents, maybe fifty of them. The place had the feel of an army camp from the Civil War, and I felt a chill deeper than the cold as I wondered if that was where things were heading.

The pilot and copilot came out of the copter after us, and for the first time I saw they had names written on their headsets. Amos, the copilot, was spliced with something feline. Dara, the pilot, was spliced with a hawk or falcon. She looked vaguely like Ruth and Pell, in some ways. But whereas they were graceful and almost delicate, Dara seemed absolutely fierce.

"Thanks," Sly called over to them. They both gave a thumbs-up, then they each grabbed a corner of a large, heavy-duty gray tarp that was anchored to the ground on one side.

"Thanks," I said, not sure how grateful I should be. Amos didn't seem to hear me, but Dara replied with a curt nod and a clipped smile.

As soon as the copter's rotors stopped, they shook the snow off the tarp and lifted it over the copter, clipping the loose corners to hooks sunk into the ground. I then realized that some of the larger tents in the camp were actually quadcopters under similar cover.

A tall, slender, strikingly handsome chimera walked up to us. I couldn't tell what he was spliced with, but the deep brown skin on his face and neck was covered with silky fur, a lighter brown, that blended into the close-cropped black hair on his head and his beard. His heavy green army jacket was open at the neck, revealing a patch of gold fur at his throat. He smiled and held out his hand, but his smile faltered as someone behind him muttered, "Who's the nonk?"

Nonk was a slur for nonchimera. Looking around, it hit me that I was, in all likelihood, the only one there who wasn't spliced. I'd never been called a nonk before. None of the chimeras I knew were the type to use the term, but they'd told me what it meant. Made sense, I guess. The nonks sure had slurs for chimeras.

The tall chimera seemed to be fighting the urge to glare or snap at whoever had said it. Then the smile was back, and he said, "You'll be Jimi and Claudia. I'm Martin."

"I'm Jimi," I said, " . . . but you know that already. Right." I turned toward Claudia and said, "And this is . . ." But he already knew that, too.

"Hi," Claudia said, shaking his hand as well.

I was about to ask him where we were when Claudia said, "So . . . this is Chimerica?" She looked around as she said it, making it plain that if it was, she'd be disappointed.

Martin's smile faltered again. "Not exactly," he said. "But it's part of Chimerica."

"So where are we?" I asked.

"Lonely Island," he said. "Canada. Ontario. Between Lake Huron and Georgian Bay."

"And why are we here?"

"Wells's people have been after you. They've been following you. They were closing in."

I laughed, but it sounded fake even to me. "Why would they be spying on me?"

"Because of Pitman, we're guessing."

"How do *you* know they were following her?" Claudia asked.

I looked at her, then back at Martin. She had a point. "Were *you* spying on me?"

His eyes rolled a little—annoyed, exasperated, but a little bit busted, too. "We've been keeping an eye on you, that's all. For your safety. But we lost you when your car broke down. Seems like we found you again just in time."

I looked at Sly. "Who's 'we'?"

Martin spread his arms out wide. "Chimerica."

"So, where is Chimerica?" Claudia asked. "The rest of it, I mean."

"And more important, *what* is Chimerica? What is it *really*?" I added. I looked around at the tents and the snow. It sure didn't look like the utopia people built it up to be.

"Chimerica is all over," Martin said, his eyes shining. "Wherever chimeras are being oppressed, somewhere nearby there's a bit of Chimerica, or there will be. There's probably a dozen camps like this, some a lot bigger, all around the world."

"Okay . . ." I tried not to sound as dubious as I felt.

"What do you do?" Claudia asked.

"We step in and do what we can to protect chimeras from persecution, or other threats."

"Are you part of E4E?"

"No." Martin smiled. "We value E4E's contributions and share many of their objectives, but . . . well, they do their thing and we do ours."

"Who's in charge of it?" I asked.

He gave me a look I couldn't read. "In this camp, I'm in charge."

Claudia rolled her eyes. "Yeah, but who's in charge of *you*?"

Martin's eyes flickered at me again, so quick I wasn't sure I'd seen it. "There's a council," he said. "We try to keep its existence quiet. For security purposes."

I pointed south. "Well, if you're supposed to be protecting

chimeras, we need to go back where we just came from. There are a lot of chimeras in danger." I turned to Sly. "And Rex is one of them."

"We know about Rex," Martin said. "E4E has lawyers on the way to help him."

"They'll have him bailed out in no time," Sly added.

"It's not just Rex," I said. "There's lots of other chimeras back at OmniCare, and they're all in danger. We need to go back and help them. Or send someone else if you've got someone closer."

"No," Martin said gravely. "We're the closest." He glanced at Sly and Roberta, then lowered his voice. "Let's go for a walk."

He turned and headed for the trees. Claudia and I looked at each other, then at Sly. Then the three of us started walking, too, over snow that had been packed into solid ice.

Roberta hung back by the shrouded copter for a minute, watching us, then she followed, too, twenty paces back.

Once we entered the woods, Martin stepped aside and waited for us to walk alongside him. Roberta maintained her distance.

"We've been wondering about OmniCare ever since they announced they were going to start treating chimeras," Martin said. "Funding from Howard Wells is a pretty big red flag, even if it's intended to take people's minds off his other misdeeds. And that Dr. Charlesford is hard to figure out." He shook his head. "Put those two together and I can't imagine there isn't something else going on. But we haven't had the resources to look too closely. Tell me what you know."

I glanced at Claudia and she nodded, so I explained what we'd seen inside the hospital, and in the mines below it. About what they were doing to the chimeras in the CCUs. I told them about Rex being arrested, and then about Centre Hollow, about the chimeras living there and about Henry and what Devon had told me about what happens after three months.

"And they're doing it all to obtain yttrium," Claudia said. "So they can make more Wellplants."

Martin whipped his head around. "So it is Wells? You know that for certain?"

"We can't prove it," I said.

Sly looked horrified. Martin must have been, too, but he didn't show it. He ground his jaw and looked down at his feet.

"So we need to get back there," I said for what felt like the millionth time. "*Now.* We've got to shut that place down. Save those chimeras down there. We have to help them. "

"I'll contact E4E," Martin said. "I'll get them to send investigators to check it out."

"Investigators?" I snapped. "We investigated already. We *saw* what they're doing. We talked to people who escaped, who've been altered permanently and can't breathe air anymore. Who are dying." I could hear my voice rising, and I paused to get it back under control. "Look, we don't know for sure who's behind it, other than Charlesford, but we know what they're doing down there, and where the yttrium eventually ends up. And the longer we spend talking about it or waiting for *investigators*, the more people are going to be . . . *altered* against their will. And the more people who will die."

He nodded, hearing me, but I could tell somehow that I'd be disappointed by his response.

"I'll contact my superior in Chimerica then, and see if we can activate agents Stateside." He didn't sound hopeful.

"You just *had* agents stateside. And you just said we are still the closest. Let's go back the way we came with a few more people. That's all it would take. There's easily enough people in this camp."

"No," he said, his voice flat and final. Sly looked down and away. "It's not our mission and I can't risk exposing the camp, or violating the very uneasy peace we have with the Canadian government. Frankly, it was provocative enough bringing you in."

"Well, we didn't ask you to. I mean, thanks for getting us out of a tight spot, but we didn't ask to be *exfiltrated* out of the country. If you're going to take your time kicking everything upstairs while people are being murdered, then just take Claudia and me back where you got us and we'll do it ourselves."

I looked at Claudia and she nodded.

Martin looked at her, too, and said, "Do you want to go back?"

"Yes," she said, folding her arms resolutely.

Martin nodded. "All right," he told her. "We'll have to wait until morning, in case anyone noticed you coming in, then Dara will take you back and make sure you get to your car okay."

I was starting to get annoyed, and I didn't try too hard to keep the tone out of my voice. "We can't go until *morning*?"

Martin took a breath and let it out. "Actually, *Claudia* can't go until morning. For the time being, *you* have to stay here."

CHAPTER 38

For a moment I just looked at him, not quite believing what I'd just heard. Then my voice erupted in something close to a shriek: "*WHAT?*"

Martin didn't look at me.

"Are you insane?" I said, stepping where he was looking. "You can't keep me here against my will."

"Those are our orders," he said, his voice quiet and even. "And they're for your own safety."

Claudia looked stunned. Sly appeared confused and mortified. Clearly, he hadn't known this was coming. Which was lucky for him, because I was livid. Roberta seemed to be wrestling with a smirk.

"This is *bullshit*," I said. "Orders from *who*?"

"From my superiors."

"You mean your secret *council*? And who are they, exactly?"

I could tell Martin wasn't enjoying this. But I didn't much care.

"Look," he said. "All I can tell you is that it has been decided that it's too dangerous for you in Pennsylvania right now, and you're too important to the movement."

"And what movement is that, exactly? What do you mean, too important?"

"Too important to risk letting Wells get his hands on you."

That gave me a chill, but I didn't stop to think about it. "Important how?"

He wriggled his shoulders in a movement that was halfway between a shrug and a squirm, or like maybe he just wanted to slip out of the conversation altogether. "As a symbol, I guess."

"Because I was on a *T-shirt*, for God's sake?" In that speech I made in Pitman, which was more of a diversion than anything else, I talked about equality and human decency and a bunch of other things that shouldn't have been necessary to say. But then it went on the news, and struck a nerve. People made T-shirts with quotes from what I'd said, things I didn't even remember saying because, while apparently it needed to be said, it was just the most basic, obvious right-and-wrong kind of stuff. Someone also made T-shirts with a picture of Rex and me kissing, and the words DOG MEETS GIRL. They at least used a cool font. But still, a couple of T-shirts didn't add up to *important*. Not even close.

Martin looked away, and I got the distinct feeling that it was something more than that. But he squared his shoulders and took a deep breath. "Look, I'm sorry about any inconvenience. I've got my orders, and I intend to carry them out. This is all in your best interests, and in the best interests of chimeras everywhere. If you care about chimeras, if you care about *people* the way you say you do, you'll support what we're doing."

Then he walked past us, his feet crunching the snow as he headed back toward the camp.

"And what *exactly* is it you're doing? While people are being killed down in those mines?" I called after him. "Because it looks to me like a whole lot of *nothing!*"

He just kept walking, and I growled in frustration.

Sly came forward and put a hand on my arm. "Jimi, I'm sorry. I didn't know this was going to happen."

I nodded, then turned to him. "Did you know they were spying on me, too?"

He took a step backward. "They weren't really spying, just . . . like he said, keeping an eye on you. For your own safety."

I shook my head, letting out a grunt of frustration because I didn't have the words.

"Hey, nonk."

I turned and saw Roberta smirking at me.

"I heard about Pitman, and that's great and everything," she said. "But here's what I wonder: Why is it you feel the need to be the savior who comes in and fixes everything?"

"I don't . . . I'm not trying to fix everything."

"Yeah, you are. You think we don't know what we're doing up here. You think you know what's best with this OmniCare place, but you don't know the bigger picture. How could you? You're not even one of us. And you never will be."

"I'm not trying to be a savior. I'm trying to help my friends, goddamn it," I said, feeling a rush of emotion that I didn't understand and couldn't quite control. "And how do you know I'll never get spliced? You don't know me."

A tear rolled down my cheek and I was furious at myself for it, and even more furious at Roberta for causing it and for seeing it.

Claudia put her hand on my back. "Jimi, it's okay."

I turned to Sly, pointing at Roberta. "What is her problem?"

Sly stepped up to Roberta. "Hey, hey," he said, putting up his hands. "Lighten up, Roberta, all right? Don't you think you're laying it on a little thick?"

Roberta glared at him, and then at me, then she stomped back toward camp.

I took a deep breath and got myself under control. "I do not like her," I said, wiping my eyes.

"Really?" Sly said in mock surprise. "Would never have guessed it."

"Seriously though," Claudia said, watching Roberta through the woods. "What's her problem?"

"I don't know," he said. "She can be a little bit . . . well, like *that* sometimes. . . . Most of the time."

"Yeah," I said, "well, if that's a little, I'd hate to see a lot."

A gust of wind howled through the trees, peppering us with tiny shards of ice. We hunched our shoulders against it and started walking back to camp.

"This is ridiculous," I said. "I can't believe I'm a prisoner here."

Sly kept quiet. I know he didn't agree with my being held there, but I got the impression he didn't feel like he could speak out against it.

"Tomorrow, when I get back to civilization, do you want me to tell anyone you're here?" Claudia asked. "Jerry? Your mom?"

"Pretty sure they don't want you telling anyone this is here," Sly said quietly.

I rolled my eyes and looked at him. "Oh, for God's sake. Another secret for the good of chimeras? That's what they told us in Pitman."

"I know, I know," he said. "But this is different."

I cocked an eyebrow at him.

"It is," he insisted.

I paused to shake my head at him, and as he walked on, Claudia elbowed me and gave me a look that seemed to be full of some meaning I couldn't grasp.

As we approached the camp, I got a better sense of the layout. At one end there were half a dozen quadcopters of various sizes and types, all under tarps. Thick power cables ran from under them into the woods, toward the wind turbines.

At the other end were the tents, mostly simple pup tents, but with a couple of bigger dome-types, and one elaborate frame tent that was larger than the others. They were all the same grayish-white color. Behind them was a row of composter toilets. Scattered among the tents were a handful of dark patches of bare ground, where the snow had melted within rough circles formed by thick logs. A few of the logs had chimeras sitting on them, and I realized there was a Hotblock dimly glowing at the center of each circle.

Hotblocks were kind of like chemlights, but generated more heat than light from the chemical reaction. People could sit around them and keep warm. It was like a campfire, but without the carbon emissions. Or much of the charm.

As we stepped into the clearing, Martin emerged from the frame tent. He spotted us and came directly over.

"What is it?" I said as he approached.

"I contacted our people Stateside. They said Rex has already been bailed out."

I felt wobbly for a second, I was so relieved, but I tried not to show it.

"That's great!" Sly said, clapping a hand on my shoulder.

"By *whom*?" I said, making sure he heard me say "whom."

"Earth for Everyone, it appears. Anyway, I thought you'd want to know."

"Any word on Doc Guzman?" Claudia asked.

"Still in jail, I'm afraid." He turned to go.

"What about OmniCare?" I said. "Are they doing anything about that?"

He paused. "They said someone named Jerry had been in touch, and that they'll look into it." Then he went back to his tent.

"Thanks," I said, not making much of an effort to be heard.

Any points Martin had gained for following up on things so quickly were nowhere near enough to make up for the fact that I was his prisoner.

CHAPTER 39

Sly showed Claudia and me to our tent on the edge of the clearing. "The tents are pretty warm, and there are a couple of sleeping bags inside. Dinner's in a couple minutes, and I have to go help get it ready. You might want to warm up for a minute, but night comes early, so you might want to enjoy the daylight while it lasts."

We thanked him and slipped inside, then zipped the flap closed behind us. It wasn't too cold in there. And it gave us a chance to talk in private.

There were chemlights attached to each of the tent poles, and two rolled-up sleeping bags. Claudia tapped one of the chemlights and sat on one of the sleeping bags.

"So what do you think?" she said quietly, as I sat on the other sleeping bag facing her.

"I think it's nuts that I can't leave here. I mean, I'm all for doing what's best for the team, but I don't like being held here against my will."

"No," she said. "This is messed up."

"I also don't like the fact that while they're holding me here—supposedly for my own safety—all those other people are stuck in those mines. And Doc is stuck in jail."

"I know. At least Rex is out."

"Yeah. That's a relief."

The dinner bell rang out, but neither of us moved for a second. Claudia looked up at me, her face serious but her eyes mischievous. "I can fly a quadcopter, you know," she said.

"Really? Cool." Somehow that didn't surprise me.

She held my gaze, nodding very slowly. "Yeah, Jimi. It is cool. Especially if maybe you don't feel like staying here until they let you go."

I laughed, more out of shock than amusement. "You mean take one of their copters?"

"We'll give it back."

"But you're leaving in the morning."

Her eyes sparkled. "Only if I haven't already left tonight."

"You're serious."

"Unless you'd rather stay here until spring. Or whenever *they* say it's safe. I'm sure your mom would love that."

The idea was still sinking in when we were interrupted by Sly's voice outside the tent. "Knock, knock. Didn't you hear the bell? Dinner's ready. And it goes quick around here."

We slipped outside and Sly led us toward the closest of the log circles. The sky had grown darker during the few minutes we'd been in the tent, and the glow of the Hotblock was brighter in the gathering gloom. Steam billowed from a large pot suspended above it, and a dozen chimeras sat around it, eating stew from mugs.

We followed Sly to a space on one of the logs, and the chimeras on either side moved to make room for us without looking up.

Sly filled mugs for Claudia and me. The pot sounded close to empty when he filled a mug for himself.

He handed us each a spoon, and sat so he and Claudia were on either side of me.

"Not bad, right?" Sly said, elbowing me.

I nodded. It seemed to be some kind of lentil stew with carrots and celery. At home I would have picked out the celery, but I was hungry and I didn't want to waste food, or come off as picky or spoiled. Plus, it actually wasn't all that terrible.

"So, how long have you been here?" I asked Sly. Claudia leaned forward so she could see and hear him around me.

"A little over a month." He lowered his voice to a comical stage whisper to add, "But we're not supposed to say."

"Does Chimerica have anything to do with the H4H bombings?"

He scowled at me. "No! Of course not. Do you think I'd be here if they had anything to do with that?" He shook his head. "Like Martin says, 'We're doing our part to help make the world safe for chimeras, *and for everyone.*'"

I'd heard those exact same words before. I gave him a sidelong glance before asking, "Rex was here, wasn't he?"

Sly smiled. "Like I said, we're really not supposed to say." Then he nodded.

The way Sly had been hurrying us—and from the sound of the pot when he served us—I figured the three of us would have been the last to eat. But several of the chimeras around us finished and left and a couple of others took their places.

Among the late arrivals was Roberta. She glared at me as she helped herself to stew, then sat on the other side of the Hotblock from me. I couldn't see her in the darkness, but I could feel more heat from her stare than I could from the Hotblock.

The other late arrival was Dara, the pilot. She helped herself to a mug of stew, then came and stood directly in front of me, looking down her beak-like nose.

"Jimi Corcoran," she said, as if that meant something on its own.

I sighed. I was almost finished eating, and all I wanted to do was slurp down the last of my stew and get back to the tent to talk to Claudia. I didn't want another fight.

"Yes," I said. "Dara, right?"

She nodded. "I was at Haven," she said. "In Pitman." Her face was hard to read, but her voice caught as she spoke. A couple of the other chimeras sitting around the Hotblock looked over at me. "A few of us were," she continued. "We would have been hunted down if it weren't for you and your friends."

In the dim light from the Hotblock, her eyes glistened.

"I'm glad you got out," I said, my throat constricting.

From the darkness, Roberta's voice said, "She's still a nonk."

The look in Dara's eyes hardened and she whipped her head around. "Why do you have to be such an idiot?"

Roberta shot to her feet and came halfway around the Hotblock. "Why do you have to be such a kiss-ass?"

Dara shook her head. "It's asshole chimeras like you that make H4H's work easy."

Roberta came closer. "It's an asshole chimera like me that's going to break that stupid beak of yours."

Sly got to his feet, not quite between them but dangerously close. "Hey, let's calm down," he said.

Claudia was suddenly standing behind the log, out of harm's way. She put her hand on my shoulder and as Roberta turned on Sly, looming over him, Claudia's hand tightened on my jacket, like she was about to yank me back.

"Shut up, Sly," Roberta said with a snarl, "you little—"

She was cut off by a thunderous "*ENOUGH!*"

It was Martin, standing at the edge of the Hotspot, his chest heaving and his eyes flashing. "I won't have this. I'm teaching you to fight so you can protect each other, not so you can brawl amongst yourselves."

He glanced at me, and I wondered if he thought I was at least partially to blame. Maybe I was. Maybe everybody had gotten along fine before I got there. But the glares Roberta and Dara were throwing at each other didn't seem like anything new.

"You're taking watch tonight, both of you. Dara, first shift. Roberta, second. Any more of that from either of you and you're out. If you can't be civil, we're better off without you."

Roberta gave him a murderous look, but Martin simply stared back, as if daring her to test him. She turned and stomped off into the darkness.

Then he turned to me. "Jimi, can I have a word with you in my tent?"

He turned without waiting for a response and walked off.

I looked at Sly, then Claudia, and got shrugs from both of them.

Thanks, I thought, as I slurped down the last of my stew.

CHAPTER 40

Martin was sitting in a folding chair in front of a folding table, reading a piece of paper. He didn't look up when I walked in, and it occurred to me that anytime I had ever been summoned—whether it was to the principal's office or by some paramilitary chimera commander—they didn't look up when I arrived. Maybe they really were that busy, but I always suspected it was some kind of lame tactic to assert that they had the upper hand. Either way, it was rude.

I figured I'd count to five and if he still hadn't looked up, I'd leave. While I was counting, I looked around the tent. There was a cot instead of a sleeping bag, an electric lantern instead of a chemlight, and a satellite phone. On the floor next to the desk was a metal bowl, and inside it, a little mini-Hotblock.

I realized as I was looking at it that Martin had finished whatever he was doing, and was now waiting for me.

"Oh *hi*," I said casually. I'm not sure if he got my point.

"Sorry about that out there," he said. "Roberta's been through a lot. She has a lot of anger. She and Dara seem to bring out the worst in each other."

I nodded but didn't reply. Frankly, I hadn't seen anything too terrible in Dara's behavior.

"I apologize also for insisting that you stay here for the time being. As I explained, those are my orders and they are for your own good, but I certainly understand if you find the situation less than ideal."

That didn't even get a nod.

He paused a few seconds until he realized no response would be forthcoming. Then he took a deep breath and continued.

"I've heard again from E4E. There seems to be some confusion about Rex."

"What kind of confusion?" I said, keeping calm until I knew more. "Is he okay?"

"Well, it turns out they didn't post his bail after all."

"He's still in *jail*?"

"No, no, he's not. That's just it. Someone *did* post his bail. We're just not sure who."

"Well, where is he?"

"I'm sure it's just a miscommunication. E4E has been growing rapidly and they've never been particularly well organized. Plus they have a lot on their plate right now, so—"

"*Where is he?*"

He took another deep breath and shook his head. "We don't know."

"*What?* What if OmniCare has him?"

He held up his hands, as if that would calm me down. "There's nothing to indicate that's the case."

"And has E4E *looked into* OmniCare yet?"

"In the past hour? I doubt it very much. Look, Jimi, everything is under control. I'm sure we'll locate Rex in no time."

"That's easy for you to say! He's not your friend."

"You don't know that."

That stopped me. Of course, Rex had been there. For the first time, I noticed the worry in Martin's eyes, and that scared me more than anything else. Maybe he and Rex were close friends. I had no way of knowing. I wondered if Martin knew about Rex and me, if Rex had talked about me. Or if, instead, he'd kept me a secret from Martin and the others here—just like he'd kept them a secret from me.

"Then I'm sure you agree we need to go and find him," I said.

The worry in Martin's eyes disappeared, replaced by a flat, disciplined lack of emotion, like a mask had descended over his face. "I have my orders," he said. "Rex would understand. He'd be disappointed in me if I disobeyed them."

I don't think he meant it as a dig, but it sure felt like one, like maybe he knew Rex better than I did. I left the tent without another word, marching through the darkness, torn between hot emotions and cold determination.

Everyone had left the circle except for Sly, Claudia, and Dara. They looked up as I stepped over a log and sat down.

I met Claudia's eye and gave her a tiny nod.

She did a bad job of hiding her smile as she nodded back.

"What?" Sly said, looking back and forth between us.

"Nothing," Claudia said.

"They've lost Rex," I said.

"*What?*" Dara exclaimed, taking me by surprise. I hadn't expected a reaction from her at all, and I felt a momentary petty jealously that she, too, had been part of this secret segment of Rex's life.

"He'll be okay," Sly said.

"What happened?" Claudia asked.

I sat down, feeling suddenly cold and achy. "Someone bailed him out, but now it turns out it wasn't E4E. They don't know who it was or where he is."

Sly snorted. "Just because E4E's left hand has no idea where he is, doesn't mean their right hand isn't holding him. You know how it goes. Someone at E4E probably got sick of waiting for the brass to take action and went and bailed him out."

I hoped he was right, but I didn't share his confidence. "Yeah, maybe."

The temperature had dropped and the last light in the sky had disappeared while I was in Martin's tent. Around us, the circle of dark earth thawed by the Hotblock was shrinking inside an advancing line of frost. Inside my jacket I was still comfortably warm, but below it and above it, the cold was biting.

Claudia looked at me in the darkness, then squinted as a gust of wind sprayed us with ice crystals. When the wind died down again, she said, "We'd better get some rest, huh?"

I nodded.

"Yeah," Sly said. "I guess it's that time."

"Yeah for some of us," Dara said. "I have to take first watch, thanks to Roberta."

"Thanks, Dara," I said. "For sticking up for us."

She smiled and said, "I'll see you tomorrow."

I gave Sly a hug, squeezing tight as I told him how good it was to see him.

"You too, Jimi," he said. "I'll see you in the morning, and it'll all work out. You'll see."

When Claudia unzipped our tent flaps, a thin coating of ice came off the fabric in flakes. We shook them out, then climbed inside and zipped the flaps behind us.

I found the chemlight at the top of tent pole and the tent filled with a pale glow.

Claudia was already grinning at me. "You ready for this?"

I nodded. "You sure you can do it?"

She gave me a smug look. "Piece of cake."

I hoped she was at least half joking. I was glad she was confident, but I didn't for a second believe it was going to be easy. "Okay," I said. "What's the plan?"

CHAPTER 41

Claudia held up four fingers and ticked them off as she spoke. "We need to disconnect the charger under the copter, get the tarp off, get inside, and then lift off. I figure we should be able to do the first three before anyone has the slightest inkling. And even if the entire camp wakes up when I start the motor, we'll be in the air before they can get to us."

"And you're sure you can fly these?"

"My dad had one. He taught me how."

I cocked my head at her. "I mean can you *really* fly one? Not 'My dad took me to practice three times' or 'I watched a Holovid once,'" I said, throwing her words back at her. "Can. You. Fly it?"

She smirked and gave me a withering stare that frankly wasn't as confident as I would have liked. "Okay, look, the one I flew wasn't as big as these, but they're all pretty much the same. We'll take the one we came in on. I can definitely fly that one."

"Okay," I said, thinking, *I guess that will have to do.* "You're sure it'll be charged up?"

She looked at her watch. "If we wait a few hours."

"What if they come after us? In another copter."

"We'll have a pretty good head start. And I doubt they're going to shoot us down."

I nodded, although I wouldn't have put it past Roberta. "If we wait until after three a.m., the battery will be charged and Roberta will be on watch," I said. "I'd hate it if she caught us, but she seems like a dim bulb. I think our chances would be better against her than against Dara."

"Agreed."

"But still, at least one person isn't going to be asleep. We have to be quick."

"Yeah, it sure would suck to get caught by Roberta. What do we do about her?"

"She'll be walking the perimeter, right?" I said. "If we wait until she's at the far end of the camp, would that give us enough time to lift off?"

"Yeah, it should only take a few seconds." She thought for a moment. "Unless she starts shooting."

"That's a pleasant thought."

"Could happen. But that copter's pretty heavy duty. We'll be okay even if she does."

I nodded, only mildly reassured. "I should let Sly know we're going."

"Are you *crazy*? Absolutely not. I know you two are friends, but he's taking his orders seriously. We can't risk it."

I couldn't argue with that. "I still feel bad, though."

"He'll understand. Plus, you'll see him again soon enough, and you can explain, tell him you're sorry."

I nodded. "We should talk about what we're going to do when we get there."

"I've been thinking about that, actually," she said, flashing a mischievous smile. "I have a few ideas."

"Yeah," I said, with a strange mixture of hope and trepidation. "Me, too."

We pieced together the outline of a plan, then a backup plan, too, and went over them both several times. We synchronized our watches—which was not as easy as it sounds—and put our alarms on vibrate, set for 3:20.

Then we tried to get some sleep.

It wasn't easy. My head was spinning with worry and fear: about Rex, about the chimeras in the mine and in Centre Hollow, about Doc, and about whether either of our plans would work. I even wondered how much trouble I was getting myself into at home, and whether the excuse that I'd been kidnapped/rescued and taken out of the country against my will would make things better or worse.

I slept fitfully, and I was awake before my watch quietly buzzed at 3:20.

"You awake?" Claudia whispered.

"Yeah."

"Do you hear anybody outside?"

I listened for a few seconds, then said, "No. But let's give it a minute to be sure."

We stayed silent and I counted to sixty in my head, but there was no sound other than the wind rustling the sides of our tent.

"Shall we?" I said.

"Yeah, okay. Slow and quiet, right? Stay in the shadows, and let's not make a move until we know where Roberta is."

In the darkness, I saw the outline of Claudia's hand reaching out, but just before it closed on the zipper, I heard a sound outside and I grabbed her wrist.

She turned to look at me, and I shook my head, finger to my lips.

We held perfectly still, and as the seconds dragged out, I wondered if my nerves had been playing tricks on me, but then I heard it again, barely there, the faint *crunch* . . . *crunch* of footsteps on the ice.

They grew slowly louder and louder, steadily closer and closer, until I began to suspect they were coming straight toward us.

I was still holding Claudia's hand when a silhouette appeared on the tent wall, cast by the moonlight outside.

It was clearly Roberta and she was clearly holding a gun. She stopped right outside our tent and stood there, listening. I suppressed a vague shudder, wondering how many times she had stood outside our tent as we slept.

Finally she moved away, the *crunch* . . . *crunch* . . . *crunch*ing of her footsteps slowly receding into the distance. She'd be headed toward the copters, on the opposite side of the camp, but it was impossible to tell if she was moving clockwise or counterclockwise, to our right or to our left.

After another minute, Claudia pulled her hand from mine, leaned in close, and said, "Now?"

"Yeah. Now."

As Claudia eased up the zipper and we climbed out, ice flaked off the fabric and wind whipped at the flaps.

The sky was clear and the moon was startlingly bright, casting an electric blue glow across the snow. It was way colder than before. I pulled my hands up into my sleeves, but the air bit into the skin on my neck and face, and clawed at my legs through my jeans.

We crept between the tents, keeping to the shadows. As we approached the clearing between the tents and the copters we paused, scanning the trees along the perimeter. There was no sign of Roberta.

We needed to know where she was before we moved to the copters, but we hadn't counted on this kind of cold, or this kind of delay. We were only standing there for a couple of minutes, but it felt like forever.

Finally we spotted her against the trees, slowly walking the perimeter in the darkness, still headed toward the copters. That meant we had to wait for her to get to the copters, inspect them or whatever she was going to do, and then move far enough past them so we could do what we needed to do.

"Damn, she's slow," I whispered.

Claudia replied with a shivery nod.

I thought about how embarrassing it would be to freeze to death out there and be found the next morning, frozen solid behind a tent. I almost suggested we go back to the tent to warm up for a minute. But finally Roberta got to the copters. She looked them over and moved on, slowly but deliberately. As soon as she disappeared behind the tents to our right, we took off, running as fast as we could while keeping low and trying not to crunch too loud.

I quickly outpaced Claudia, but with the copters all covered with tarps, I couldn't tell which was the one we'd flown in on. I looked over my shoulder at her, and she pointed at one to my left, the one with the least ice buildup. I slid to my knees and grabbed one of the clips holding the tarp down. The metal was so cold it burned my skin. By the time I had it unclipped, Claudia had wriggled under the copter to disconnect the charging cable.

As I worked my way around the tarp, my fingers felt dead, clumsy and useless. The wind whipped the tarp out of my grasp and I clawed at it frantically. When I finally managed to wrap my fingers around it, I heard a strange sound, sort of like laughter, but stupid, vindictive, and cruel.

Looking up, I found the source of it.

Roberta.

CHAPTER 42

She was wearing a thick parka, snow pants, and gloves. I hated her for that alone. Then she opened her mouth.

"Oh, this is too good."

I stood up straight, or as straight as I could—my back and shoulders wouldn't unhunch in the cold, and my hands were frozen into claws. I couldn't tell if Claudia was watching from the shadows under the copter, and I didn't know if my hands were capable of signaling anything comprehensible, but I did my best to wave them behind me, telling her to stay back.

I didn't know if I could even speak at this point, either—but before I could try to say anything, another voice said, "What's going on?"

Sly came around the copter, hands thrust into his pants pockets, eyes squinting against the cold.

"Your friend here is sneaking around, messing with the copters. I'm going to have to have her restrained."

Sly looked at me. "Jimi, is that true?"

"I—"

"Do you even know how to fly these things?"

"I—"

He glanced at the ground behind my legs, then back up at me. He knew what was going on. He knew Claudia was down there. I gave him a frozen half smile, both fessing up and begging for his help.

"She's just out for a walk," Sly said, turning to Roberta.

"At three thirty in the morning?"

He shrugged, but it became a shudder. "Why not? I am."

"The only legit excuse for *anyone* being up right now is if you've got to pee, so you'd better go do that, then get straight back to your tent before I have to restrain you, too."

Sly cocked an eye at her and tilted his head. "I'm sorry, what?"

She stepped closer to him. "You heard me."

She had a rifle over her shoulder and a dart gun in her holster. She was twice our size—combined—and I could barely move. But I wondered, if it came down to it, whether Sly and Claudia and I could take her.

"What's going on out here?" said yet another voice, and Dara stepped around the copter as well. It appeared Claudia and I had awakened the whole camp. "What's everybody doing up?" she asked.

She was dressed and armed just like Roberta, but her hood was down. Her eyes gleamed in the moonlight, and I wondered if it was from the cold or something else.

"What are *you* doing up?" Roberta replied, saying it like a challenge.

"Just wanted to make sure you were okay out here."

"Yeah, right. Well, I have everything under control. And your watch is over, so you can go back to bed."

"What exactly do you have under control?" Dara said.

"Look, Dara," I cut in, before Roberta could answer, "I know Martin has his orders, but Rex could be in danger, and there are dozens of other chimeras *dying* in those mines. More will be coming through OmniCare to replace them. One of them could be Rex."

"So, what, you were thinking you were just going to fly away?" She frowned. "Do you even know how to fly a quadcopter like this?"

"No," I admitted.

"But I c-c-can," said a voice, and Claudia crawled out from under the copter. "We'll bring it b-back." Her teeth were chattering and her face looked blue—I hoped it was at least partly from the moonlight.

Roberta laughed. "Oh my God, you are both in so much trouble."

"Well, here's the way I see it," Dara said.

Roberta cocked her head. "How's that? I'd love to know."

There was a faint spitting sound, like someone trying to get a speck of paper or something off of their tongue. A tiny piece of gray fluff appeared on Roberta's shoulder.

For a second we all stood there: Roberta with that smug, belligerent look on her face, everybody else looking at the dart embedded in her shoulder.

Finally she seemed to sense something wasn't quite right. She looked down at the dart, then back up at Dara. As her hand reached toward the dart, she said, "You little shhhh . . ." Then her eyes rolled up and she started falling.

Her face was headed straight for the rock-hard ice, but Dara's arm flashed out and she grabbed a wad of Roberta's hair, halting her fall with her face just inches from the ground.

Dara took a deep breath and let it out in an icy cloud. She eased Roberta to the ground and rolled her onto her back, then looked up at the rest of us.

"You get that thing decoupled and ready to go," she said. "I'll stash this one back in her tent."

Claudia clambered back under the copter while Sly and I carefully pulled back the tarp. By the time we were done, Dara had returned, carrying Roberta's rifle and dart gun in addition to her own. She was rolling a gray dart between her fingers.

"You took the dart?" Sly said.

Dara nodded. There was an odd expression on her face, and I realized she was trying not to smile.

Sly's brow furrowed. "What if Martin thinks she slept through her watch?"

Dara nodded again. "Yeah, what if?" She seemed to be trying even harder now.

Sly shook his head. "But—"

Dara's smile disappeared as she cut him off. "Look, Sly, Roberta is bad news in general, but she's especially bad news for Chimerica. If Martin expels her, it will be the best thing for all of us."

Sly nodded grudgingly.

Claudia looked at me and wrinkled her nose, making it plain she was totally on board with Roberta's comeuppance.

"Okay, let's get out of here before anyone else sees us," Dara said.

"You're coming with us?" I said, surprised.

She gave me a wink. "If Rex is in trouble, I'm not going to stop you from borrowing a copter to help him, but I can't let you steal it. Someone's got to bring it back."

We all climbed into the quadcopter.

"You're *sure* you're okay to fly this thing?" Dara asked as she and Claudia headed for the cockpit.

Claudia nodded. "Yeah, I was telling Jimi, my dad used to have one just like it."

"Just like it . . . ," Dara said, just this side of condescending. "Okay, great, so you're good with ramjet thrusters? And you know how to clone a beacon?"

"No . . . I guess I don't."

Dara grinned and edged past her, toward the pilot's chair. "We've made a few modifications. How about I take the lead this time and show you how they work."

Claudia nodded, intrigued. "Yeah, okay."

The lights came on, the motor clicked and groaned, then the rotors started spinning, two in the front and two in the back. The buzz became a whine and then a scream as the rotors built speed, and in moments we were rising into the sky.

It was not a smooth ascent. The wind was even fiercer above the trees. In the cockpit, Dara grinned at Claudia, clearly enjoying the ride.

As we rose into the night sky, the copter turned slowly clockwise. The rest of the camp came into view, and a lone figure standing in front of the big frame tent. Martin, watching our ascent. He didn't seem to be doing anything to stop us. I wondered how long he'd been there.

The copter dipped hard to one side. It might have been a gust of wind, but it seemed like a gesture, one wing tipping at Martin. Then we shot forward, past the trees, past the old lighthouse, and out over the moonlit water.

CHAPTER 43

S ly pulled headsets out of a compartment, put one on, and handed the others to Claudia and me. Dara kept her microphone on and gave us a running play-by-play. We saw a couple of other copters as we flew south across Lake Huron, and a few planes above us, as well. Dara explained that she was still using the beacon signature that she had cloned on the previous flight, so anybody observing us from a distance would think we were a small, Canadian-registered family craft, carrying a small Canadian family. The flight remained uneventful until we passed over the strip of land separating Lake Huron from Lake Erie. Then Dara said, "Crud."

The sky above us, ahead of us, and to the east remained calm and clear, dazzling with stars and a bright full moon overhead. To our right, however, a gray line on the horizon was rising quickly into a wall that seemed to be racing to head us off before we reached land. Dara adjusted course, edging east, explaining that she was trying to keep some distance between us and what looked to be a rapidly developing cold front.

"Well, that's a nasty looking storm system to our west, but we're halfway across the lake," Dara said. "With luck though, I should be able to get you where you're going and get back across before it hits."

As soon as she finished speaking, a bell-like tone rang through the copter, followed by Dara's voice once again. "Double crud," she said. "We have a little visitor on our port side asking for clarification because our beacon ID's not matching our radar signature. Just a drone, so it's no big deal, but I'm going to have to shake things up a bit to confuse it while I switch our beacon ID. Hold on to something."

I grabbed one of the slats that ran along the inside of the cabin. To the east, I could see a tiny blinking light, alternating red and blue and getting closer with each blink.

Then it disappeared. With a lurch, we decelerated and dropped, seemingly in free fall. My stomach rose into my throat. Seconds later, we lurched again, rolling to our right, then corkscrewing to our left. By the time we stabilized, the blinking light was between us and the storm front.

"That ought to do it," Dara announced. "We are now using the beacon signature of an American-registered commuter craft. Canadian Rescue might send a search party for that disappeared Canadian family, but they shouldn't give us any more trouble."

She had barely finished speaking when the cockpit filled with a flashing red glow that spilled out across the cabin. Sly and I looked at each other as a screechy buzzer alarm blared through the speakers.

"WARNING," a semi-robotic voice blasted through the headsets and the copter's speakers. "YOUR CRAFT IS USING A BEACON SIGNATURE THAT HAS BEEN REPORTED CLONED OR MISAPPROPRIATED. MAINTAIN YOUR PRESENT COURSE AND AWAIT POLICE ESCORT. FAILURE TO COMPLY WILL RESULT IN SIGNIFICANT CRIMINAL CHARGES."

A trio of red and blue lights appeared to our left, spreading out and approaching fast.

"Crap, those aren't drones," Dara said. "I guess you better hold on a bit tighter."

This time we dipped to the right and dove toward the water. The buzzer alarm resumed and the red glow coming from the cockpit began flashing twice as fast.

"Just . . . keep holding on until further notice," Dara said. "I'm killing the speakers. And the beacon."

With that, the headsets and speakers shut off and the cabin went quiet except for the whine of the motors and the roar of the air outside. We rolled into a corkscrew, turning over again and again and again. When we finally pulled out of it, the water was a lot closer and neither the drones nor the police copters were anywhere in sight.

Pressing my face against the window, I spotted them, above and behind us, three copters and a drone, all tailing us. I was puzzled for a moment, wondering how we had managed to get past them so quickly. Then I realized we hadn't. We had turned away from them. To the west. Toward the storm.

"We're headed into the storm!" I shouted in Sly's ear.

He looked confused for a moment, then his eyes went wide with alarm.

The copter shook like we'd hit a wall, then it bounced around like we were tumbling down steps. The windows went opaque and gray.

Behind us, I caught glimpses of red and blue smudges as the police lights tried to penetrate the snow and fog.

The whole time we bobbed and weaved, I was terrified we were going to end up in the water. Eventually we evened out, but the cockpit was still flashing, and when Dara turned the speakers back on, the buzzer alarm was louder than ever.

"I haven't been able to shake them," she announced. "I've got exactly one last trick up my sleeve. Hold tight."

We slammed into a steep climb, flipped around and doubled back, this way and that. I was totally disoriented, surrounded by dense gray, until a flashing blue-and-red smudge appeared in front of us, and then two more, one on either side. They were flying in a tight formation right toward us. And we were flying right toward them.

"DISENGAGE! DISENGAGE!" boomed the voice over the speakers, and in seconds the police copters were crystal clear and right in front of us. "DISENGAGE IMMEDIATELY OR WE WILL BE FORCED TO CONSIDER YOU A HOSTILE CRAFT."

At the last possible second, the three of them peeled off, two to the left, one to the right. Dara pulled us into a sharp turn, and suddenly we were out of the storm, the wall of clouds receding behind us. A single police copter remained alarmingly close. I could see the pilot do a double take at us. For several moments we stayed close and kept pace, and I felt queasy as I realized Dara was cloning his beacon. Impersonating a police officer.

"Got it," Dara said, and immediately we fell away, back toward the clouds.

Dara informed us we'd be riding under cover of the storm for a while, cycling several beacon signatures: the cop she'd just cloned, some other American copters she had on file, and at times none at all. They were all highly illegal, but even I knew using a cloned police signature was by far the most egregious.

The ride was bumpy but relatively uneventful after that. Sly asked what our plan was for when we landed. Claudia and I told him about Plan A as best we could over the noise. We tried to include Dara at first, but she made it plain her focus was flying the craft. As one point Sly asked her a question and she shook her head and tapped her headset, saying, "Gotta fly!"

After fifteen minutes without seeing any law enforcement, Dara announced, "I think we've lost them. We are now under the guise of a Pittsburgh-based courier service." As we reemerged into the clear ahead of the storm front, the eastern horizon was beginning to pale. Dara turned to Claudia. "We're about thirty minutes out. You want to drive the rest of the way?"

Claudia shook her head. "Um, no, that's okay."

"Okay, good," Dara said, maybe a little smug. Then she turned to look back at me. "So what's this plan of yours again?"

CHAPTER 44

Plan A was pretty straightforward. It consisted of finding Kiet, who had hopefully gotten hold of one of the splinter inhalers, then finding Rex, who was hopefully safely ensconced with a bunch of E4E lawyers somewhere. Then, all together and with the inhaler as proof, we would hopefully get law enforcement to shut down OmniCare and the mines and get Doc out of jail.

But that was a lot of "hopefully," and deep down, neither Claudia nor I truly believed Rex was safe with E4E, or that E4E was even following up on OmniCare, or that Kiet would likely be able to get an inhaler. When we said as much aloud, Sly shared our concerns. Dara seemed to, as well.

That's why there was Plan B. But that brought up concerns of a whole other magnitude.

I wasn't even going to tell Dara about it, but when I finished detailing Plan A, she eyed me as if waiting for more.

Claudia looked at me and shrugged. So I told them about Plan B, too.

When I was done, Dara thought about it for a moment. She and Sly exchanged a look, then she nodded to herself and said, "Well, let's hope Plan A works."

She turned back around in her seat and announced, "Okay, kids, we're about two minutes out. Our beacon says we're totally legit, but it's five a.m. and these are interesting times, so I don't want to hang around too long. I also don't want to put down across the street from the police station, so I'm going to drop you on the edge of town, if that's okay with you."

The Dairy Queen and the police station had just appeared ahead of us, but they disappeared once more behind the trees as we dropped down into the parking lot of a machine shop away from the center of town. It felt great to be back on the ground.

We all took off our headsets. Dara turned to face us and looked somberly at Claudia and me. "I'm not crazy about your plans," she said. "I wish I could stay and help, but like I said, I can help you borrow this, but not steal it. I need to get it back."

"Of course," I said quickly. "I know it. And I can't tell you how much we appreciate your help."

"Well, from what Rex has told me, you're the type who'd do the same for me. Tell the big guy I said hi when you see him. And tell him I said to try to stay out of trouble."

I managed a smile and said, "Will do."

"We couldn't have done it without you," Claudia added.

"No worries," Dara said.

Then I turned to Sly. "Thanks, Sly. For everything." I gave him a hug that seemed to surprise him.

"Uh, Jimi . . ." He tried to pull away, but I held on tighter, realizing how much I had missed him, and how much I was going to. I had a nagging sense that this could be the last time I would ever see him.

"Look," I said when I finally let go. "I know what you're doing is important, but I hope . . . I hope I see you again sometime."

"Jimi, I'm coming with you."

"Wait—what? You are?"

He smiled. "Of course I am." He laughed, then his face turned serious. "That Plan B, you weren't going to try to do all that just the two of you, were you?"

"And Kiet," Claudia said a little defensively.

"Really," he said, blowing air through his cheeks as he shook his head in disbelief.

"But what about Chimerica?" I asked. "What about your orders?"

"That's important, but right now this is more important. Big Dog's in trouble, Doc's in trouble, you two are about to be in trouble."

My mind was racing. I didn't know for sure how Sly would figure into Plan A, but as for Plan B, several ways immediately came to mind that would make it much less of a long shot.

Sly gave me a playful slug in the arm. "What kind of friend do you think I am, anyway?"

I was too choked up to answer. Luckily, Dara spoke up. "Oh right," she said. "Speaking of trouble . . ." She reached down into a duffel bag between her seat and Claudia's and pulled out two dart pistols. "Just in case, right?"

She handed one to Claudia and one to me. Sly already had one.

"Do you know how to use these?" Dara asked.

I shook my head and Sly reached over to take mine. He turned it sideways in my hand. "Safety's here," he said, pointing to a small switch on the side. "Take the safety off, point and shoot. They're good for maybe thirty yards. More than that and they lose accuracy and enough oomph to penetrate thick clothing. Other than that, line up the two sights or just point and shoot."

Dara reached back into the bag and lifted a rifle halfway out. "I don't know how much trouble you're expecting, but . . ." She raised an eyebrow, looking us each in the eye.

The three of us exchanged unsure glances. As Claudia started to reach for it, I quickly said, "No, that's okay. I wouldn't really know what to do with it."

Claudia took her hand back, and gave me a questioning look.

Dara smiled grimly as she lowered the gun back into the bag. "Yeah, you'd figure it out. But probably a wise decision. They do have a way of making situations worse instead of better."

She rummaged around in the bag one last time and came out with a small plastic box, just a few inches on a side. She handed it to Claudia. "Whoever was following you probably put a tracker on your car. Scan it with this, just hold that button as you run it over the car. If the red light comes on, it's found a device. Make sure you get rid of it before you go anywhere. And then get going, fast. These trackers are sensitive enough that even removing it from the car will be enough to alert them that you're back." Claudia nodded, then we all climbed outside except for Dara. "Okay, better get this back before it's missed," she said.

We hurried away from the copter, then watched as it lifted into the predawn sky, tilted once, and disappeared over the treetops.

Sly tucked his dart gun into his jacket, and pulled his collar tight against his throat. "Kind of forgot it was so damn cold down here, too."

He was right. It wasn't as frigid as Lonely Island, but it was plenty cold.

We set off quickly, our feet crunching the crusty ice on the side of the road. It was quiet and still. Apart from us, the only movement was the traffic light two blocks ahead, cycling through colors, oblivious to the fact that there was no one stopping or going. The Dairy Queen was several blocks past it. The back of Claudia's car was visible, right where we'd left it.

Claudia stopped walking and pointed to our right, at a darkened, run-down storefront. The plate-glass window said FRANK'S PIZZA. In the corner there was a partially peeled-off E4E sticker. I couldn't tell if it had been there so long the adhesive was failing, or if someone had tried to remove it. A set of wooden steps on the side led up to a door on the second floor.

"Kiet?" I whispered.

She nodded.

We were supposed to have met him twelve hours ago, but better late than never. The lights were off, but so were all the other lights in town.

I leaned close to Sly and whispered, "This is where Kiet lives."

He nodded. "Should we get the car first?"

I was dying to get into that car, sink into the upholstery, and crank up the heat. But I shook my head. "No, let's get Kiet first. If there's a tracker on the car, once we start moving we'll need to get it out of the way in a hurry."

Claudia nodded. "Good thinking."

As I stepped onto the sidewalk in front of the pizza shop, Sly and Claudia waited behind me. I turned to look at them.

"Knocking on a door in the wee hours?" Sly shook his head. "Probably better if it's just you instead of a couple of *mixies*. Just in case."

I couldn't argue, even with the E4E sticker in the window.

I nodded and climbed the steps to the second-floor entrance. The flimsy plywood door was peeling into layers and the wooden doorframe was rotted in places.

I knocked gently and waited a few seconds, but there was no response. I knocked a little bit harder, but still nothing. I was hoping to wake up Kiet without waking up the whole neighborhood, but finally I banged hard enough that the whole building shook.

Sly and Claudia looked small, far away, and mortified, glancing around to see if any other lights had come on.

There was still no answer. The door looked so insubstantial, I probably could have broken it in, but if the police *were* about to pounce on us, I didn't want breaking and entering added to whatever charges I had already racked up.

Almost as an afterthought, I tried the knob, and found it unlocked.

I turned to the others, shrugged, and went inside. There was a light switch by the door. The apartment was small and run-down, but tidy. There was a bed in one corner—neatly made—and across from it a small sofa and a coffee table with a neat stack of comic books. No Holovid. There was a tiny kitchenette, and one door to a closet and another door to a bathroom. I checked the bathroom and the closet, looked around once more, and left.

Sly and Claudia watched me as I came back down the wooden steps. "He's not there," I said.

Claudia frowned. "So now what?"

"Could he be working a night shift?" Sly asked.

"He never said anything about working nights," I said. "I hope he's okay."

"Me, too," Claudia said. "Should we wait here?"

Sly looked at me and shook his head.

"Sly's right," I said. "Let's get to the car and find a phone, see if there's any news on Rex, any progress on getting the word out about OmniCare. Then we can circle back here and see if Kiet's come back."

Sly smiled. "For all we know, he and Rex are probably at E4E right now, preparing for a press conference."

I couldn't muster the same optimism, and my eagerness to find Rex wrestled with my reluctance to move on without Kiet.

Then I had an idea. If I were Kiet, and I'd been looking for Devon all that time and finally found him stuck out there in the woods, I'd find some way to be out there with him. "Maybe he's in Centre Hollow," I said as we resumed walking. "With Devon."

Claudia looked doubtful. "He can't breathe in Centre Hollow."

"Maybe not with him, but near him. There were those houses on the outskirts."

"Yeah, maybe." Claudia looked at Sly, who looked at me.

"It's worth a shot," I said.

The car was just as we had left it, apart from a thin crust of ice that had laminated a note onto the windshield that read THIS IS NOT A PARKING SPACE in thick, angry green marker.

Claudia scanned for trackers and found one in the left rear wheel well.

I was afraid we were going to have to scrape the ice, and I worried the motion would set off the tracker, but instead Claudia got in and started the car. We waited outside, so as not to jostle it. In seconds, the heat from inside the car melted the ice on the windows, sending it sliding down the glass in wet sheets. She pulled the note off the window and crumpled it up.

"You ready?" she said.

We nodded, and she reached into the wheel well and pulled off the magnetic tracker, then carefully lowered it to the ground, right next to the tire. We quickly got into the car, and she backed out, careful not to disturb the tracker as we drove off, toward Centre Hollow.

CHAPTER 45

I wonder if the SmartPike's back up and running," Claudia said as we headed out of Gellersville.

Sly leaned forward in the backseat. "I meant to ask earlier—was that really you two?"

I hooked a thumb at Claudia, who grinned as she explained what we'd done. She seemed to relish the tale. I felt newly traumatized just hearing about it again.

When she was done, Sly sat back and whistled. "Man, you two are hard-core."

I almost reminded him that he had rappelled out of the bottom of a quadcopter to save us, but I didn't really feel like talking. Thinking of Kiet and Devon had got me thinking about Rex.

The SmartPike was working fine. We took it to the Belfield exit, onto Bogen Road, all without incident. The sun was fully up by then, but Claudia drove very slowly as we approached the spot where we had skidded before, carefully avoiding the raised chunks and pot-holes while I kept an eye out for the abandoned road that led to Centre Hollow.

"There it is," I said, pointing to a vague suggestion of a gap in the trees. Centre Hollow's Main Street, or what was left of it, covered with leaves and snow.

Sly leaned forward and squinted out the windshield. "Are you sure?"

"Yeah, that's it," Claudia said. "What there is of it." She started to turn the car toward it, and I turned to her.

"You're going to *drive* there?" I said, vaguely alarmed.

"Yeah," she said. "It's not much worse than the road we're on."

I glanced back at Sly and he shrugged.

The tires slid on leaves and ice for a second as we started up the hill, but they gained traction as the road leveled out. We passed the wrecked VW and the WELCOME TO CENTRE HOLLOW sign. The little cluster of houses was just ahead.

I knew it was safe to breathe here, that this was where Devon and his friends had dragged us, where we had recovered. But as the road started downhill, I worried about driving much farther into Centre Hollow. I was about to suggest maybe we should walk the rest of the way, when a figure looked out from one of the houses. The place was little more than a shack. The glass was missing from the windows, but tattered red curtains still flapped in them.

"There he is!" I said, pointing. "It's Kiet!"

Claudia stopped the car. She and I got out and ran toward him. "Kiet!" I called out.

"Hey!" He smiled as he emerged from the doorway, but his eyes looked tired and hollow, like he was happy to see us but not happy about much else. "What happened last night? Did you go back to Philadelphia?"

"We never made it," I said.

"What happened?"

Claudia started to answer, but I cut her off. "Long story, but we're okay," I said. "Kiet, have you seen Rex? We were told he'd been bailed out, but no one seems to know who did it, or where he is."

He nodded, looking down. "Right after work. I saw Rex come out of the police station with two men. They were laughing and smiling, but I recognized them. They work for Charlesford."

I felt my entire body invaded by a dark, cold dread.

"I tried to get to him, to tell him," he said. "I ran over, but they got into a van and drove off before I got there."

I couldn't breathe. "So . . . Rex is at *OmniCare*?"

"I think so, yes. I'm so sorry, Jimi."

I nodded, trying not to let panic overwhelm me. Claudia put an arm around me.

"What about E4E?" I said. "Have they been out here at all? At the hospital? Their lawyers or anything?"

Kiet shook his head. "I haven't seen any sign of them."

I turned to Claudia. "Then I guess it's Plan B."

Claudia nodded, her face somber.

"What are you going to do?" Kiet asked.

"We have a plan," I said. "A plan and some tools." I opened my jacket to reveal the dart gun Dara had given me. Sly and Claudia did the same. Kiet's eyes widened, and in them I saw a trace of excitement and optimism.

"But we're going to need your help," I said. "And we're going to need to talk to Devon, too."

Whatever light I had seen in his eyes went out, like a candle pinched between wet fingers. "Devon's not well," he said quietly.

"He's sick?" I tried to sound more sympathetic than alarmed, and more surprised than I was.

"Yes," he said. "And it's getting worse, so if your plan depends on him you need to change it."

"We just need to talk to him. It's important."

"Okay," he said, reluctantly. "You'll have to keep it short, though. He's exhausted."

"Of course," I said.

He glanced at his watch. "And I have to leave for work soon so I'm not late for the morning deliveries."

He turned and we followed him, the ground sloping down in front of us toward the clearing outside Centre Hollow. Along the way, we introduced Sly and Kiet to each other.

Then Kiet seemed to think of something and he flashed us a grin, brief but so genuine it seemed almost jarringly out of place. He shoved his hand into his pocket and said, "There is *some* good news."

CHAPTER 46

Kiet held up a little metal tube encased in a plastic holder. I knew right away what it was.

"Oh my God," I said. "Is that a splinter inhaler?"

He nodded, staring at it with a mixture of disgust and reverence.

He handed it to me, and I turned it over in my hands. On the front it said SUSTAINED PLASMID INFECTION NANOSPEAR THERAPY RESPIRANT (SPLINTR). A sticker on the back said SUSTAINED AAV REINFECTION—90 DAYS. REAPPLICATION NOT RECOMMENDED DUE TO ACQUIRED IMMUNITY.

I read it again and again, trying to remember exactly what Doc had said about nanospears being used to deliver AAV, adeno-associated virus, how it was different from somatic splices, like chimeras get, and germ-line splices, which get passed down from generation to generation.

Sly reached for the mister and I gave it to him. "So . . . so is this what they use to . . ."

"To maim those poor miners so they can't breathe air?" Kiet said, finishing his sentence as he took it back. "Yes. New. Unused. Unopened. Full."

"Kiet, that's great!" Claudia said.

"It is," I said, turning to Sly. "No one's going to believe us about OmniCare without proof, but this could change everything."

"And get Doc out of jail," Claudia added.

I was about to ask Kiet how he got it, but he held up his hand to stop us and called out, "Rajiv!"

The clearing was just ahead of us, and on the far side it, at the bottom of the hill, Rajiv appeared from behind a slight rise.

"Hey," he called out.

Kiet hooked his thumb at Claudia, Sly, and me. "They need to talk to Devon. Can you get him?"

Rajiv looked doubtful. "I'll see how he's doing." Then he turned and we watched him disappear further down into the hollow.

"You never told me what happened to you last night," Kiet said.

Claudia launched into it, as if she was glad to fill the silence. She told a good story, and it had been an eventful time. When she got to the part about shutting down the SmartPike, Kiet said, "Wait, that was *you*? Man, they've been looking for you. They think you're the same terrorists behind the H4H bombings."

"We're not *terrorists*," Claudia shot back. "We were running for our lives."

He put up his hands. "Hey, I'm glad you got away. I'm just telling you what they were saying."

We told him about getting saved or extracted or whatever, and ending up in the Chimerica camp.

"Chimerica?" He snorted. "I didn't think that was a real place."

"It's real," Sly said. "But it's not a place."

"What is it, then?"

"A group, kind of. A secret organization, kind of. Not many people know about the actual details."

"A secret group? Are you with them?"

Sly nodded.

Kiet's eyes narrowed slightly. "Oh my God, are *you* the ones behind the bombings?"

"No," Sly said, indignantly. "That's, like, the opposite of what Chimerica is all about."

"Okay, good." Kiet shook his head. "I mean, I want to fight back against H4H, too. But these bombers are doing a lot more harm than good."

"What do you mean?" Claudia asked.

"I mean the H4Hers are riled up big-time. In the last twenty-four hours, Wells has been all over the news and support for H4H is going through the roof. A bunch of other states are fast-tracking their versions of GHA. The Pennsylvania Supreme Court has said they're not going to hear the case."

"You mean they're letting it stand?" I asked, horrified. "E4E's legal challenge lost?"

"Afraid so."

"They don't even know chimeras are behind the bombings."

He nodded. "They do now. It's a group called CLAD, Chimera Liberation and Defense. They took responsibility last night."

"*Idiots!*" Sly said, shaking his head. "I mean, there's no way the US Supreme Court is going to let GHA stand. I can't see that happening. But meanwhile, these morons are turning the tide against us, just when we were making progress against those H4H lunatics. That's why Chimerica is—"

He stopped suddenly as Devon appeared at the bottom of the hill.

Devon coughed, holding onto Rajiv for support, but he winked at Kiet and said, "Did you miss me?" Then he seemed to notice the rest of us. "You're back."

"We need your help," I said.

He coughed again, and put his hand against a tree, shifting his weight away from Rajiv. "I don't feel like I could be much help to anybody right now."

"We're going to break into OmniCare, into the mine. We're going to get everyone out of there and shut that place down. Today."

Devon shook his head. "I don't think you quite understand. Everybody down there has already been splintered. That mine is the only place they can breathe. That's part of the reason they only need eight guards for eighty or ninety prisoners, remember? No one escapes, because they can't breathe anywhere else."

"You breathe here in Centre Hollow."

"Yeah, but it's too far. They'd never make it."

"It's too far on foot, but not driving." I turned to Kiet. "If Kiet can steal the hospital truck, once it's empty."

Kiet took a step back. "*What?* I can't do that on my own."

I was about to reassure him that he could, but Sly raised a hand. "I can help with that. I'll go with you."

Claudia opened her mouth as if to object, and I totally understood. I had several ways in mind that Sly could help us with our plan, and none of them involved helping Kiet take the truck, but I caught her eye and shook my head. Kiet seemed like he was still getting used to the idea, and I didn't want to put him off again. She closed her mouth but looked at me, confused.

"Yeah, okay," Kiet said finally. "That could work."

Devon was slowly nodding. "And you're going to bring them here?"

"Yup. By truck, we can get everybody from the mine to Centre Hollow in less than ten minutes. Way less. We'll time it just right. Kiet said the truck has to be empty by ten thirty. We could have it at the mine entrance by ten forty-five and have everyone here, safe, by eleven o'clock. Today."

"How are you going to get into the mine?" he asked.

"We have dart guns," I said. "We can dart the guards and take their exosuits and their breathers." If we needed to, the plan was to press the buzzer on the door and dart them when they answered. We were hoping that wouldn't be necessary.

Devon raised an eyebrow. "You know how to use an exosuit?"

"Claudia does," I said.

She nodded. "My dad's company has a couple. He let me try one of them. It freaked my mom out but they're actually pretty simple to use. Designed to be intuitive."

"Once we have a suit, we can sneak up and dart the next one, then the two after that, and the two after that. When the truck arrives, we'll load everyone on and bring them here."

"It sounds so easy," Devon said. His tone was sarcastic, but his eyes twinkled. "It might be doable. It's a simple layout inside, and those exoguards think they're invincible in those suits. They don't really expect anyone to try to escape, much less to attack from the outside. But at the first whiff of trouble, they'll just lock the place down. I've seen them do it. There's lockdown switches throughout. And there's cameras, so they'd totally see you. If anyone hits the lockdown, you're screwed, along with everyone else down there."

Claudia and I glanced at each other. "That's why we need your help," she said.

Kiet stiffened.

"What kind of help?" Devon asked.

"We just need a map," I told him. "You said there's a master switch for the doors, and one for the cameras. You know where they are. Couldn't that override a lockdown?"

He thought about it for a moment, then slowly nodded his head. "Yes, it would. Plus it would open the dorm, the processing unit. Everything. But the master switch is in the processing unit. You'd never get in there."

"You said you saw it."

"Yeah, but that was from the vent."

"Right," I said. "We need you to draw us a map of the vent, a diagram, so one of us can get there."

I wasn't looking forward to climbing down into that vent, but I felt a wave of excitement and relief. I saw it reflected on Claudia's face, and Sly's too. When I looked back at Devon, though, I saw something very different.

"What?" Sly asked him. "What's wrong?"

Devon shook his head. "The ventilation system has all sorts of branches and turns. Even if I could draw you a map that was close to accurate or made any kind of sense, you'd never find your way. And even if you could, you wouldn't be able to breathe. Even with a breather, you wouldn't have time to find the control panels, much less get back out."

I knew Devon was just thinking this through, that he was only trying to help. But the frustration and anxiety and stress and all the other emotions came bubbling out before I could control them.

"Then *what*?" I cried out. "What are you saying we should do? How can we get down there? How can we open the doors and get those people to safety?"

Devon shook his head, his face sad and resigned, but—maddeningly—almost at peace.

"You can't," he said, in a calm tone that I found even more infuriating. Then he added, "But I can."

CHAPTER 47

No!" Kiet exclaimed. "You can't go back in there!"

Devon smiled and shook his head. "I have to," he said. "It's the only thing that makes sense."

"No, it doesn't. It doesn't make any sense at all." Kiet turned to me, looking for backup. "We'll call E4E again, wait for them to get here. Why do we have to do this now, right this minute?"

"Because we can't leave those people down there any longer than they have to be," I said. "And . . . and because if Rex is down there, we need to get him out. Before they splinter him, too."

Kiet turned away from me, back to Devon. "I won't do it, with the truck. Not if it means you're going back down there."

"Yes you will," Devon said softly.

Kiet folded his arms, firm and resolute. "Why?"

"Because I'm asking you to," Devon replied.

Kiet practically crumbled. "But you could be killed. I . . . I only just got you back."

Devon smiled sadly. "I'll be back. But there's another reason we need to do this now, why we can't wait."

"You're too sick, apart from anything else," Kiet continued, having built up a head of steam. "You need to rest up, to get better."

"I'm not going to get better."

That stopped him. "You what?"

"I couldn't tell you before. I couldn't bear to. It's . . . what Henry has. We all get it before long. I'm dying."

"*Dying?*" Kiet staggered back.

Claudia and Sly both gasped. I hoped no one noticed that I didn't.

"No," Kiet said, shaking his head.

"I'm sorry," Devon said. "I wish it wasn't true. But it is."

"How do you know? Why didn't you tell me?"

"I wanted us to be happy, Kiet. To enjoy a little bit more of what time we had left."

"And what about now? What about the time we have left now?"

Devon opened his mouth to speak, but at first nothing would come out. Finally he just said, "This is important."

Kiet let out an anguished growl and stomped off into the woods, away from Centre Hollow.

We watched him go, then all turned to look at Devon. "He's upset," he said. "I am, too. But he knows deep down that this is the right thing for me to do." He turned to Rajiv. "Can you get me a breather, a rope, and some paper and a pen?"

Ten minutes later, Kiet returned, looking distraught but composed, standing at the edge of the clearing. While he was gone, Devon had drawn us a map of the mine. He handed it to me and approached Kiet. He wore the breather around his neck and he held the mask up to his face and took a deep breath before giving Kiet a long kiss.

"Let's talk," he said, then he grabbed Kiet by the hand and led him back into the woods.

As soon as they had gone, Claudia said, "That's so messed up. I can't believe Devon is dying."

Sly nodded sadly, then he turned to me and said, "Did you not want me to go with Kiet?"

"No, it's not that," I said. "We'd been thinking I would take the vent, and Claudia would take the entrance. When you said you were coming, I figured you could help Claudia."

I hadn't allowed myself to think about how much I'd been dreading climbing into that vent. I felt a claustrophobic, vertiginous wave of nausea just thinking about it.

"I could still do that," he said.

"No, it's cool," I said. "If you can go with Kiet, that would be great. With Devon taking the vent, I can go with Claudia."

Claudia snorted. "I didn't want to say anything, but I figured with you taking the vent and me ringing the doorbell like an idiot, odds were fifty-fifty we were both going to die."

"What about now?" Sly said.

She flashed him a grim smile. "At least sixty-forty."

"Stop it," I snapped, then I let out a sigh. "Sorry, that's just a little too close to home right now."

Claudia nodded, understanding. "I hear you. How's the map?" she asked.

I held it up so they could both see it, and we went over the plan.

The map was simple, but it wasn't helping my stress level. The main branch of the mine curved slightly. At one end was the entrance we had seen from the road, and not far off it were two squares labeled PROCESSING UNITS. At the other end was the main chamber, with the elevators leading up to the hospital. Just off that were a few lines labeled INACTIVE SHAFTS next to one labeled ACTIVE SHAFT, as well as a third square marked DORM. We would have to get from the entrance all the way to the main chamber, and then get all the chimeras back to the entrance in order to get them out.

Devon had explained that almost everybody would be in the active shaft and the dorm, although there might be a few in the main processing unit as well. The master switch was in the secondary processing unit, so that's where he'd be going. The plan was for him to hit the switch to open the doors and kill the cameras, then stay hidden until we got there. Once we had cleared out any exoguards, and gave him the signal—two slow knocks and three fast ones—he'd come out and we'd get him out of there with everybody else, when Kiet and Sly showed up with the truck.

If we never showed up, he'd refill his breather, go back out the vent, and make his way back to Centre Hollow.

Talking about that part of the plan left us feeling somber. When Devon and Kiet returned, Kiet looked somber, too, but Devon looked determined.

"Okay," he said. "If the timing is going to work with the truck, we should get going soon."

I looked at my watch and nodded. It was just before nine.

Devon asked for one minute. He ran over to Rajiv, and they turned and walked down into the woods on the other side of the clearing. As they disappeared from sight, I heard Rajiv saying, "Are you sure you want to do this?"

"Are you okay?" I asked Kiet.

He didn't look at me, just gave his head a tiny shake.

We heard the rattle and whoosh of the breather being refilled, and a moment later, Devon emerged from the woods with a coil of rope slung over his shoulder. He crossed the clearing with a strong, purposeful stride. Halfway across, he put on the breather.

He didn't slow down when he reached us, he just grabbed Kiet's hand and pulled him along.

At the pace Devon set, the vent was five minutes away. As we walked, the small dome of clouds appeared up ahead and the sheen of white on the ground changed, as fake snow mixed with real.

Now that I knew it wasn't snow, it seemed sinister, as if it was trying to fool us.

I saw the mudslide up ahead of us. Then I spotted the vent, the grill still leaning against the concrete rim. Fortunately, for whatever reason, this time there was nothing coming up out of it.

Devon seemed relieved.

Kiet lagged back as we got closer, but Devon pulled him along.

We formed a circle around the vent. The smell of the mines was strong. Devon pulled off his mask and looked at Kiet. He seemed oblivious to everyone except Kiet. "I'll meet you at the entrance," he said. "Don't be late."

They kissed once more, then Devon touched Kiet's cheek and stepped into the vent, climbing down the handholds and disappearing into the black depths.

We stood there for a long moment—Sly, Claudia, Kiet, and I—staring after him. Then the fake snow started up, one or two flakes at first, then a torrent, an upside-down blizzard.

I felt terrible for Devon down there in it, but as the flakes started to come down on top of us, Claudia said, "Come on. We need to go."

I put my hand on Kiet's shoulder and spoke softly. "He said don't be late."

He stared back at me with a look that felt like blame, then he took a deep breath and nodded. "Okay, let's go."

We turned and started jogging, past the clearing, back toward the car. It felt good to be moving, to be doing something.

As soon as we were inside the car, Claudia started it up and spun us around, kicking up leaves and ice, barreling down the hill past the wrecked VW and the Centre Hollow sign. As we descended, the hill grew steeper. We slid to a stop at the bottom. Claudia took a deep breath, then turned onto Bogen Road.

I studied Devon's map as we drove, trying to reconcile the underground layout with what I knew of the above-ground geography. The elevators were obviously below the hospital. At the other end of the main tunnel was the mine entrance, off Bogen Road. The vent Devon had gone through seemed to be roughly above the processing units.

The car slowed and Claudia said, "There it is."

I looked up and saw we were passing the mine entrance. The gate was down and the door was closed. It looked abandoned.

Claudia looked at Kiet in the mirror, then moved her head so she could see Sly. "This is where you're bringing the truck, right?" Then she looked at me. "Right?"

I nodded, and then felt a shudder of panic. We'd be back here in less than half an hour, waiting for the door to open, waiting for the guards to come out. Attacking the place.

My breath quickened and my heart began to race. I wasn't a commando, none of us were. What the hell were we thinking? What the hell was *I* thinking? As we picked up speed and drove away from the mine entrance, Claudia reached over and patted my knee. "You okay?"

"Yeah," I said. I gave her a smile I didn't feel.

Five minutes later, OmniCare appeared ahead of us.

The last time I'd seen it, we were running for our lives. Claudia and I had barely escaped. Rex hadn't.

We drove past the hospital and past the construction site, and Claudia pulled over just beyond the next curve. We both turned to look at Sly and Kiet, sitting in the backseat.

"No long goodbyes," Sly said. "And best not to be seen together, just in case."

I nodded and reached back with my hand. Sly gave it a squeeze. Claudia put her hand on top of his, then Kiet put his on top. It was an awkward tangled knot, and kind of a hokey gesture, but it was the closest thing to a hug we could manage under the circumstances, and it was strangely powerful.

"Good luck," I said, my voice husky with emotion.

"You too," Kiet said, nodding at us both.

"It's a good plan, *now*," Sly said, with a wink. "We'll see you in a bit."

Then they got out. Kiet started walking down the road, toward the hospital. Sly sprinted up the incline to the construction site.

Claudia and I drove a quarter mile up the road and turned around. When we came back the other way, there was no sign of either of them.

We drove past the entrance to the mine, still quiet and unattended, and pulled into a gap in the trees a hundred yards past it.

"You ready?" I asked, doubting that I was.

Claudia grinned. "Let's do this."

We got out of the car and jogged up the hill. The going was steep, but in minutes we were high above the car. We moved quickly but cautiously, parallel to the road, toward the mine entrance. When the black and yellow gate came into view, we angled down toward it and took cover behind a fallen tree that offered a perfect view of the steel door.

Despite the cold wind, we were both sweaty and warm from the trek. The exercise had helped me to focus on the matters at hand, instead of obsessing about Rex and Doc and Devon and all the miners, and the very real possibility that Claudia and I were about to die. But as we sat there and waited, the cold began to seep back in, and with it, the doubts and fears.

After ten minutes my hands and lips were going numb, but I still had enough sensation in my body to feel the ground shudder. With a low-pitched *clunk*, the door to the mine began to open.

CHAPTER 48

Claudia and I got into ready crouches, on the balls of our feet, hands on the fallen tree, watching as the door rose. When it was halfway open, we exchanged a nod and sprang over the tree trunk, half sliding down the slope with our dart guns drawn.

We were halfway to the bottom and the door was almost fully open when I saw movement in the shadows on the other side of the door. I grabbed Claudia and yanked her to the ground. She gave me a quizzical glare as we skidded to a stop on our butts, but to her credit she didn't make a sound.

I nodded toward the door and we both looked on as one of the exoguards strode out, with his oddly mechanical gait. We were barely fifty feet away from him, hiding as best we could behind a thin tree. He looked down the access road, then left and right, then he turned and bent to look at the security panel next to the door.

Claudia and I both aimed our dart guns. We had expected to encounter the guards on the inside, and even though outside was probably in some ways better, it was still a tricky situation. His breathing apparatus covered his face and the suit covered much of his body. There were plenty of gaps, including big ones under each arm, but it was still a tough shot, especially since I had never used one of these things.

We both fired, our dart guns spitting an almost simultaneous *pfft, pfft*. A clump of leaves puffed into the air as one of the darts hit the ground. The other dart made a faint *ting* as it bounced off his exosuit.

The exoguard snapped upright, and turned his head halfway in our direction.

Claudia and I both fired again—*pfft, pfft*.

This time, there was no *ting* or rustle of leaves, but he turned and looked straight at us. He raised his arm in our direction, his metal fingers clutching a massive gun scaled to his big metal exo-hand. It didn't look like a dart gun, it was a *gun* gun. And it was pointed right at us. He took two steps. Then he froze.

For a second Claudia and I did, too, crouched behind that little tree, waiting for whatever was about to happen.

But nothing did.

He wasn't taking his time to aim carefully. He was out cold. We'd hit him. Maybe twice.

Devon had said the exoguards always traveled in pairs. So instead of high-fiving and scrambling down to the entrance, we waited.

Moments later, a muffled, amplified voice called out, "Hey, Scott! What the hell's taking so long out there?" Another guard stepped through the entrance and into view, wearing an identical exosuit and yellow coveralls underneath. He walked over to his unconscious partner, saying, "Hey dumbass, what the hell are you doing?"

As he stepped around in front of the first guy, he exposed a swath of yellow through the gap on his side.

Pfft, pfft. We put two darts in him, too.

Claudia flashed me a quick grin, but I wasn't taking my eyes off the guy. He realized his partner was unconscious, and he whirled around and drew his weapon. Then he went still, too.

Every second counted, so we hurried over to the guards. It occurred to me that maybe *this* was the most dangerous part of the plan. They were completely out cold, yes, but they were standing right in front of the entrance, and right under the black bubble housing the camera. Hopefully, Devon had knocked out the cameras, but with the door wide open, anyone looking out would see us, plain as day. Claudia had assured me that getting into the exosuits would only take a second, but I felt exposed and vulnerable as we stepped out in front of the mine entrance.

It was vaguely creepy seeing the two guards, upright but unconscious, like statues, their metal suits now more like body-shaped cages. It was even creepier to see the oversized shock batons and dart guns clipped to their hips, and the empty slots where their huge pistols had been.

Claudia ran up to the first one, Scott, and reached under the plate on his chest, where the metal brackets from his hips, ribs, and shoulders intersected.

"There should be a panel under here, and a button, kind of a manual lock . . . *there*."

She pulled her hand out and stood back as the exosuit dropped the gun, then moved to a straight, upright position with its arms raised over its head. The suit clicked into position, and after a brief pause the breathing mask swung up, away from the guy's face. The brackets holding him into the suit swung open with a faint mechanical hum and he tumbled onto the ground.

Claudia hurried over to the second guy and repeated the procedure.

A few moments later, the two exosuits were empty, standing over the crumpled forms of their former occupants.

"Ready?" Claudia said.

I nodded and she bent over the first guy and began unzipping his coveralls.

She must have sensed my confusion, because she looked up and said, "If they're all wearing yellow, we need to be, too."

"Right."

Luckily, they were both wearing street clothes underneath, and the coveralls were loose enough that they came off easily. They were also way too big, and we had to roll up the sleeves and pant legs. I felt bad that we were going to leave the guards outside, unconscious in the cold, but not *too* bad.

"Okay," Claudia said, once we were in our coveralls, with our human-sized dart guns tucked inside. "Just follow my lead and do as I say. These suits are supposed to all work the same way, and they learn you, so you don't have to learn them."

We climbed up into the suits, placing our feet on the pedals in the exosuits' legs and raising our arms over our heads. I watched Claudia and followed her instructions, pressing the back of my right hand against a plastic panel in the exosuit's arm. With a faint whirr, a metal cuff moved down the arm from the exosuit's outstretched hand and onto my own.

"There's a haptic gel inside. Wiggle your fingers while it maps your hand," she said. As I did, I felt a warm, dry gel close over my hand.

"Clench your fist and the rest of the suit will close."

I clenched my fist and another cuff slid down over my left hand, then the brackets closed over my legs, arms, and torso. I felt a moment of claustrophobic panic as the breathing apparatus came down over my face, but as soon as it clicked into place, it was flooded with cool air.

"Okay," Claudia said, her voice muffled and amplified the same way Scott's partner's had been. "It takes a few seconds to get used to it, but these things are designed to feel like an extension of your body. They correct for over-compensation and actively keep you balanced, which can be weird at first." She jogged in place for a moment, did a couple of deep knee bends, and jumped up and down. Each time her huge metal feet landed, I heard a dull thud, but I couldn't feel it because of my own suit's shock dampeners. When she was done, she said, "You try it."

I ran through the same movements she just had. At first it was incredibly disorienting, as I tried to compensate for the machine's exaggerated movements, and its active sensors and servos and gears or whatever immediately corrected my overcompensation. But she was right. After a few moments that felt like my body was dancing without me, it suddenly kind of clicked, like my brain learned to speak exosuit and the exosuit learned to speak me. By the time I was jumping up and down, I felt completely at ease.

"Okay?" she said.

I nodded, twisting my wrist and flexing my fingers in front of my face, mesmerized by the movement. "It's pretty cool."

"When you need to get out of the suit, you can wiggle your arm free and use your actual fingers to push the release button under the chest plate, or just hold your right arm up, with your fingers extended, and count from five down to one, pinky first and thumb last."

We went through opening and closing the suits twice, then I looked at the ground, at the almost comically large handguns at our feet. "I guess we shouldn't leave those there," I said quietly. I had been reluctant to carry a lethal weapon before, but it seemed reckless to leave them lying there. The fact that they had almost just been used against us brought home the danger in what we were about to do. The odds were probably not in our favor, and I figured maybe I shouldn't be so casual about giving any advantage to those we'd be coming up against.

I reached down with my metal arm and closed my metal fingers around the gun lying on the ground in front of me. The feeling of the gun on my fingertips was convincing, and sobering.

Claudia raised an eyebrow—more questioning than disapproving—as I fingered the trigger, then clipped the gun into the empty slot on my hip.

"The dart guns should be our default," I said quietly.

Claudia nodded in her suit, and her mechanical hand unclipped her suit's oversized dart gun and held it up so she could look at the cartridge. "Whoa. Two-hundred-dart capacity." She turned to me. "We should test them."

I unclipped mine, aimed at a tree about twenty yards away, and hit it easily. Claudia fired at one farther away, and hit it, too.

"Not bad," she said, then pointed a huge mechanized thumb in the direction of the gaping portal beside us. "Okay, what's next?"

She knew the plan as well as I did at that point. She seemed to be saying she had done her part. Now she was following my lead.

"We go in," I said.

"Good," she said, turning toward the entrance. Then she looked back at me. "And hey, just so you know, these suits aren't made for running, but the guy in charge of them at my dad's plant said you can get up to twenty miles an hour with them, easy."

I felt a crooked smile creep across my face, even with everything else going on. The thought of running so fast with such artificial support was both appalling and exciting.

"What?" Claudia asked.

I shook my head. "Nothing." The wind gusted again, bringing a momentary barrage of sleet, and my smile fell away as I looked into the darkened opening. "Let's go."

CHAPTER 49

We stepped through the entrance and into the mine, slowly at first, as our eyes got used to the dim light. I tried not to think about the toxic atmosphere enveloping us. Just inside the entrance, a pair of squat, heavy-looking metal carts with fat tires were parked against the wall. On the wall above them was a small red box with a big red button that had LOCK DOWN printed across it.

The ground sloped down in front of us, curving to the right, just as Devon's map said it would. The walls around us were the same kind of exposed rock we'd seen in the chamber, glassy black and vaguely iridescent, with stalactites overhead and stalagmites near the walls, where they hadn't been cleared. A thin strip of lights ran down the ceiling, casting a dim orange glow that barely reached the floor.

According to the map, we were at one end of the main branch. At the other end was the main chamber, with the elevators. Based on where OmniCare sat above ground, I estimated it was maybe a mile and a half away. A hundred yards or so in front of us would be the processing units—and inside one of them, the control room with the master lock that Devon had accessed via the vent.

Hopefully, the fact that the doors opened meant he had made it there okay.

We took off at a light jog that the exosuits magnified into a sprint. It was unsettling at first, like when you first step onto a moving walkway, but again I quickly got used to it. We passed a few more mine carts, so fast it seemed like they were moving in the opposite direction.

The suits were surprisingly quiet. They must have weighed hundreds of pounds, but our feet didn't make more sound than Rex would have running in his socks.

At the thought of him, maybe up ahead, I sped up even more. Claudia quickly matched my pace.

We'd only been running for a minute or so when I noticed a rumbling, clacking sound that grew louder as we progressed. A bright spot appeared in the tunnel up ahead. I turned to Claudia and she nodded, having already seen it. I unclipped the dart gun from my hip and held it out of sight behind me. Claudia did the same.

As we got closer, I could see a second light strip intersecting with the one running down the ceiling. A wash of light came from the right, where another, brighter tunnel intersected the one we were in. Another mine cart was parked just past it. Beyond that, the tunnel seemed to level out.

We slowed to a walk, moving along the wall. The rumble had grown to a roar. We were thirty feet away when another exoguard stepped out of the other tunnel.

"Hey," he called out over the background noise. "You guys figure out what's up with the doors?" Next to his head was another lockdown button. Hopefully Devon had disabled them, but I didn't want to find out.

I raised my hand in greeting, taking a few more steps before I risked taking a shot.

"Did you find anything?" he said.

I fired my dart gun and heard Claudia's fire as well, followed by a single *ting* as one of the darts hit metal.

"Hey, what's the matter with you guys?" he said. In the dark, in the exosuits, he hadn't yet realized we weren't his coworkers. Then he did. He clamped one mechanical hand onto his gun while the other one slapped the red lockdown button. Then he went still.

One of the darts had hit him.

Claudia stepped up to him, closed her mechanical thumb and forefinger around the control panel on his chest, and crushed it, so he was trapped inside the suit.

As we peered around the corner, down the adjacent tunnel, the machine sounds doubled in volume. This tunnel was shorter and smaller that the main branch, about ten feet across and roughly thirty feet long. At the other end of it, hopefully, we'd find Devon. But we knew there was another exoguard around, and he was probably down there, too.

At the end of the hallway were two large doorways, one on the left and a little bit farther, one on the right. As we crept toward them, we saw they were both still open. Meaning the lockdown had failed.

The closest door had a small sign that said PRIMARY PROCESSING UNIT. We both peered around the edge of the doorway, into a large chamber filled with industrial-scale vats and tanks and grinders, all connected by conveyor belts and ducts and pipes. There was a row of carts, like the one by the entrance, filled with piles of the glassy black rock we'd seen being mined. One of the carts had been raised by a metal arm and was being emptied into a grinder. A pair of massive metal rollers studded with teeth ground the rock into powder. A conveyor dumped the powder into a huge vat connected to a complex tangle of pipes. The din was brutal on our ears.

Dust hung in the air, and the room was hot. Seven chimeras of different types were working on the floor, their faces covered with black powder and gray dust, except for where their tears or snot or sweat had cleared it away. Up on a big catwalk, three people in coveralls who didn't appear to be spliced were monitoring equipment. They wore ear protectors and breathing masks. There was no exoguard.

One of the chimeras looked up at us, and I held up a metal finger in front of my mouth.

We darted the three technicians. As we waited for the darts to take effect, a few more of the chimeras looked over at us, saw our dart guns, then looked up at the technicians as they collapsed—one, two, three—onto the catwalk.

On the far side of the room, a huge tank rumbled and groaned. It had two pipes coming out of it. The large one, a couple of feet across, was pumping gray dust into a huge vat set in the floor. The smaller one, maybe four inches across, rattled as a small chunk of shiny silver metal tumbled from the end of it and into a gray box.

The metal looked just like the yttrium the interviewer had held up while grilling Howard Wells. The box looked just like the ones the exoguards had carried out to the truck the first time we walked past the mine. It even had the orange square surrounding a bold, black Y.

This was where they were extracting the yttrium from the slag.

All the chimeras were looking at us now. Their eyes were haunted and wary.

I held up my finger again, telling them to wait one minute. Then Claudia and I crossed the tunnel to the doorway on the other side, at the very end of the tunnel. A sign next to the door said RECLAMATION PROCESSING UNIT.

Peering inside, we saw a room much like the primary processing unit, with a maze of ducts and conveyors.

But there were differences, too, differences so horrifying that if it hadn't been for the exosuit I would have fallen to my knees.

CHAPTER 50

The vat producing the yttrium was vented into a large duct that ran across the ceiling of the chamber and out through a hole in the wall. The duct was buckled and split in a few places, and the broken seams released pale smoke that rose to the ceiling, and a cascade of soft white flakes that settled to the floor. Like snow.

And instead of glassy black rock, the conveyor belt was carrying a body. A chimera.

As we looked on, stunned, the body reached the top of the conveyor and fell into the grinder, which fed into a vat marked SOLVENT BATH, and from there into the maze of pipes and tanks at the bottom, and at the top, the duct that vented the snowy flakes to the surface. The conveyor stopped, and down below, the tiny pipe spat two tiny, silvery pellets into a container. Devon's words came rushing back to me. *I probably absorbed thirty bucks worth of yttrium when I was down there.*

Claudia took a step back, looking nauseous, her exosuit trying to compensate for her sudden unsteadiness as the awful truth of that room hit her.

I felt nauseous, too, but I wasn't the one who had caught a fake snowflake on my tongue—a flake that was clearly some sort of residue from this horrifying process that *dissolved* the people these bastards had altered and enslaved and worked to death. And it was all driven by greed. Howard Wells's insatiable need to extract the last little bit of precious yttrium from these miners' broken bodies.

As Claudia stumbled back into the corridor, clawing at her face plate, I spotted an open door on the far side of the room with UTILITY ROOM written across it. Through it I could see a bank of industrial-type electrical panels.

I turned to look at Claudia, standing out in the hallway with the top half of her exosuit and her breathing apparatus thrown open as she vomited onto the floor. Tears streamed down her red, blotchy face. I wanted to comfort her, to pat her back and hold her hair out of the way and tell her everything was going to be okay.

But when I turned back inside, I saw the other exoguard emerging from the utility room.

"Man, I hate coming in here," he said. "Place gives me the creeps. And it's gonna freak them mixies out, having that door open. We're going to have a hell of a time getting them settled down."

In the exosuit and the breathing mask and the coveralls, he hadn't realized I wasn't his partner.

"Any word on that?" he said, as he reached into the cart and lifted out a body. "The doors?" He dropped the body onto the conveyor, which automatically started moving again.

In that moment, there was a part of me that wished the gun in my hand was a real one. Part of me thought that if ever there was a time to shoot to kill, it was now. If ever there was someone who deserved to die, it was him.

But I was holding my dart gun, and for the most part, I was glad. I was raising the dart gun when his head turned and he looked at me. "One of the master breakers is busted off in there," he said. "You think that could be it?"

Our eyes locked for a moment, and just as I squeezed the trigger, he ducked away and whirled, crazy fast, pointed his gun, and fired.

Sharp pain ran up my arm. For a second I thought I'd actually been shot, but the suit had absorbed the worst of the impact—that and the dart gun I'd been holding, which was now shattered and useless.

The exoguard was closing on me, his face snarling behind his breathing mask. I fumbled for my gun, but he smacked it out of my clip, then he grabbed me by the arm and threw me against the exposed rock wall. Again, the suit absorbed the bulk of the impact, but there was plenty left over to jar my body and leave my brain spinning in my skull.

As he closed on me again, I saw that he still had his gun.

He was just a few steps away from me, and I was trying to climb back onto my artificial feet, when a loud clatter erupted from the utility room behind him.

The duct work running across the ceiling had collapsed and smashed onto the floor. Emerging from the jumble of pieces was what looked at first like a ghost: paper-white from head to toe except for a dozen vivid red trickles from the nicks and cuts that covered him, and with eyes almost as red from rage and tears.

It was Devon.

He jumped out of the pile of broken ductwork and charged, straight at the exoguard. He had a wrench in his hand and he threw it. The wrench bounced harmlessly off the metal frame of the exoguard's arm, but it drew his attention from me. He swung his gun in Devon's direction.

I still hadn't managed to get back on my feet, but I kicked out my foot and connected with the exposed side of his thigh.

The exoguard screamed and his shot went high. The bullet pierced a set of pipes and conduits running along the ceiling, releasing jets of hot gas and a shower of sparks that cascaded down onto the floor.

The exoguard pivoted on his good leg, so he was standing right over me. He pointed his gun at my face, but before he could pull the trigger, the rage melted from his face and his body went still.

Claudia stood in the doorway leading to the corridor, dart gun in her hand. Even through her breathing mask I could see that her face was almost as white as Devon's.

"Thanks," I said.

She nodded, but didn't seem ready to talk.

Devon shook with a deep and violent cough. "Glad you made it," he said. Then he ran to the wall and hit a switch that shut down the conveyor.

I had already been impressed with his willingness to come back down here, but I hadn't fully appreciated it. Not even close. I knew he'd been returning to confront a nightmare, but it was a nightmare infinitely worse than I had imagined.

"Devon, I'm so sorry," I said. "I didn't know."

He shook his head, wiping the ashy flakes off his face, brushing it off his clothes. "It's okay. You couldn't have known. I didn't tell you. . . . I couldn't tell you."

"Can we get away from here?" Claudia asked, her voice hoarse.

Devon sniffed the air, and looked back at the gases jetting from the pipes behind us. I couldn't smell anything other than the canned air I was breathing. "Yeah, we better get going quick," he said, pointing at one of the ruptured pipes. "That stuff is incredibly flammable."

Before I had a chance to ask if anything could even burn down there, in that atmosphere, he pointed at the ruptured pipe next to it and said, "And that's pure oxygen."

We turned to go, but stopped to look at the guy in the exosuit, still standing there with his gun aimed where my head had been. His name tag said SEBASTIAN.

"Sebastian," Devon said, looking up at him with disgust. "He's a mean, sick bastard."

Claudia wiggled her arm out of her exosuit and reached her bare hand under Sebastian's chest plate. The exosuit and breathing mask sprang open, and Sebastian crumpled to the ground. His leg was bent where I had kicked him, where it should have been straight.

"Do you know how to work these exosuits?" Claudia asked Devon. Her voice was flat and quiet.

"I've seen them enough." Then he looked down at Sebastian. "If you take him out of there, he'll suffocate."

Claudia shrugged. "You're going to need that suit to keep up with us. Besides, he"—she spread her arms to indicate the ghoulish scene behind her—"was doing this."

Devon nodded, thinking. "The breather comes off," he said. "I don't need it."

"You'll be more conspicuous without it."

Devon thought another moment, "Give him the mask."

Claudia shrugged. "It's up to you."

She unhooked the breathing apparatus and handed it to Devon. He placed it over Sebastian's head. Then he said, "Okay, show me how this works."

CHAPTER 51

Claudia's color returned as she gave Devon an abbreviated version of the exosuit tutorial she had given me. When we turned to leave, the chimeras from the main processing unit were standing in the doorway watching us.

"Who are you?" demanded one of them, a woman with intense eyes and a long neck, faintly patterned like a giraffe.

"I'm Devon. One of you," Devon said. "I got out, and I came back."

"You came back?" said one of the others, not quite believing, and maybe not approving.

Devon smiled. "Crazy, right?" He gestured at Claudia and me. "These are some friends of mine. We've got a plan to get you out of here."

"You *are* crazy," said the woman with the giraffe splice. "There's no place for us out there."

Devon nodded. "There is. Not far. It's an abandoned town that's poisoned by the gases seeping up from this mine."

"Centre Hollow?" said a voice from out in the tunnel. "I've heard of that."

"I've been living there the last couple months," Devon said. "We're going to get you out, and we're going to shut this place down."

They regarded him for a moment and looked us up and down in our exosuits. Then the woman shrugged and said, "Okay, then. How can we help?"

Devon told them about the truck and the rest of the plan. Together, they decided the best thing would be for them to wait in the main tunnel, as close to the open entrance as they could and still breathe easily, and far enough away from the processing units that if there was a fire, none of them would get hurt. They'd keep an eye out for any other chimeras who came that way, and tell them the plan. Claudia and I gave them the dart guns Dara had given us, which we had tucked in our coveralls, in case they ran into trouble.

As they filed past the exoguard we'd left standing out in the main tunnel, each one of them gave him a murderous glare. Then they hustled off toward the entrance.

I grabbed the exoguard's oversized dart gun to replace the one his partner had destroyed. Then we hustled off, too, farther down the tunnel.

Devon coughed a few times as we ran, a tired, wheezy rattle. Claudia and I slowed so he could keep up.

We passed a series of three huge metal doors, set into the rock wall to our left, labeled w1, w2, and sw1. They looked ancient, sealed with corrosion and dirt. "I forgot to put those shafts on the map," said Devon, falling into the rhythm Claudia and I set. "I think they're the tunnels that extend under Centre Hollow. Anyway, should be about a mile to the dorm, then the main chamber and the active branch."

The codes Claudia had been making fun of when we accessed the mines through the hospital suddenly made sense. The other branches were ne1 and ne2 and these were w2 and sw1. I realized they were directions: Northeast 1 and Northeast 2, West 2, and Southwest 1.

We'd been running another minute when I heard a clattering noise.

"What's that?" I whispered, cringing as my voice was amplified by the suit.

We all stopped to listen. It seemed to be coming from up ahead, but with the curve of the tunnel, we couldn't see very far.

"Sounds like a cart train," Devon said, slowing to talk. "There'll be one or two exoguards and a handful of miners pushing a line of slag carts to the processing unit."

"One or two?" Claudia said. "I thought they always traveled in pairs."

"Usually," he said with a shrug. "Never in threes."

"There's three of us," Claudia replied.

"And you don't have a breather," I said. "You should get behind us. We'll see if we can dart them before they notice you."

Devon nodded and lagged behind. We ran until the carts actually came into view. Then we slowed to a walk, holding our dart guns behind our hips.

The train was a line of ten carts, unattached, each pulled by a chimera. A lone exoguard was walking three-quarters of the way back. As we approached, he poked one of the chimeras with his shock baton. It must have been set at the lowest setting, to prod instead of stun, but in the dim light of the tunnel, the blue-white flash was vivid.

The chimera pulling the first cart was tall and wide, with tiny horns on his head and muscles bulging everywhere else. He glanced up at us with eyes that were hollow and defeated. He quickly looked away, as if he knew staring could get him shocked or worse. But then his eyes came back to us, staring anyway, turning his head as we walked past. Each of the others reacted almost the same way, one by one, looking up at us as we passed. I scanned them in turn, hoping and dreading that I would see Rex, relieved and dismayed that I didn't. I realized that even in a worst-case scenario, he wouldn't be down here yet.

"Is that Carl?" said the guard as he approached us. "Those guys get the doors straightened out yet?"

We fired, all three of us. He reached for his gun, but froze before he got it unclipped.

"Holy crap," said the big guy at the front of the line, now turned to watch us. "That's Devon."

"Hi, Gus," Devon said with an emotional smile.

The smile spread among the other chimeras, and several of them said, "Devon!" in awe as they recognized him, as they realized he had escaped and survived.

One of them said, "You came back for us."

"I did," he said. "And we need your help." Then he turned to me, choking back another cough. "And my nonk friend here . . . will tell you how."

Gus swiveled his head in my direction. "Okay, nonk. What's the plan?"

"Does this guy have a partner?" I asked, pointing at the unconscious exoguard.

"Yeah, he's back at the dorm."

"Okay, good." I thought about trying to get one of the miners into the exosuit we now had at our disposal. No such thing as too many in a situation like this. But time was the more pressing concern. "Um . . . we're meeting our ride outside the mine entrance in twenty-five minutes." *Crap,* I thought. *Twenty-five minutes.*

"We can't go out there," Gus said, shaking his head. "We can't breathe."

"I know," I said. "But there's a place just a few minutes away where you can. A truck is coming to take you there."

He looked at Devon. "You found Centre Hollow? It's for real?"

Devon nodded. "It's a bit of a dump but better than this."

"We need to go and get the others," I said. "Are there any that won't be able to get to the entrance on their own?"

"There's some in the dorm. A few working who shouldn't be. Not many, though. Anyone down for more than a day or two gets sent to . . . reclamation."

His voice faltered as he said it and Claudia lost some of the color she had regained. I tried not to think of the horror behind that word. "Are there more carts down there?" I asked.

Gus laughed. "There's carts everywhere."

"Okay good. The mine entrance is open. There's others already waiting. Get as close to the entrance as you can but stay where you can still breathe easily. We'll meet you there."

Gus looked at Devon, who nodded, then he turned to the others and waved his arm in the air. "Okay, let's go."

As they hustled for the entrance, we headed farther down the tunnel.

"That's five exoguards down," I said as we ran. "That means there's three left."

"And three of us," Claudia said. "Our odds are getting better."

"I don't know how you took out the first few guards," Devon said, "but we've been pretty lucky with the last two." He gave us a grim look. "You shouldn't expect much in the way of luck down here."

Half a minute later, we saw another doorway up ahead.

"That's the dorm," Devon said.

As we approached the doorway, Devon's warning about our luck running out was at the front of my mind. From ten feet away, I could see through the entrance to the dorm. An exoguard was standing just inside it, with his back against the wall.

But I realized our success so far wasn't all luck. Part of it was definitely because the guards were focused almost entirely on keeping people in, not out. And the people they were keeping in knew they would die if they went outside.

The yellow fabric of the exoguard's coveralls was clearly visible in the gap under his arm and along his ribs. I looked back at the others and shrugged, then aimed carefully and landed two darts.

We waited a few seconds, then approached him.

As with the others, the guard was unconscious, but standing up. He was alone, looking out over a cavernous room with six long rows of sleeping mats, each with a thin, grimy sheet on it. I counted eight chimeras sleeping on them. As we walked into the room, the closest of them got up on one elbow to look at us. She was sleek and thin, reminding me of a mink or a ferret, but her eyes were dull and lifeless—until they fixed on Devon.

"Everyone else is in the mine?" he asked.

She nodded and said, "You're Devon."

He smiled and went over to her. "Sorry," he said. "I don't know you."

"I'm Elena. You left just after I got here," she said. "You're still alive."

He smiled, stifling a cough. "Yeah, I am."

"And you came back."

He nodded. "We're here to get you out. Can you walk?"

Her eyes had widened and brightened, but then they fell. She pulled back the sheet to reveal a filthy bandage around her ankle. "A little."

I tapped a metal finger on Devon's metal shoulder, and when he turned, I pointed at an empty mine cart out in the tunnel. He nodded and turned back to the girl.

"Well, don't worry, we'll get you out. Can you get the others ready to go, quietly?" he asked. When she nodded, he said, "We'll be back to get you in a few minutes."

As we turned and headed back down the tunnel again, I hoped he was right.

CHAPTER 52

The main chamber was just ahead of us, along with the active branch of the mine, where we'd seen the chimeras laboring. There, almost surely, we would encounter the remaining two exoguards and close to a hundred imprisoned chimeras. My thoughts and emotions were entirely focused on what would happen when we got there. But as we followed the curve of the main branch, the first thing to come into view was the elevator doors in the main chamber. At the sight of them, I felt a jolt to my heart. This was one of the last places I'd seen Rex, minutes before he was taken. And now, as far as I knew, he was on one of the levels above us, maybe already splintered, or about to be. An elevator ride away. Right on the other side of those elevator doors, in a way.

As we moved forward, the tunnel widened out into the main chamber, and the doors to the mine branches came into view one at a time, along the wall to our left. I pushed Rex from my thoughts, trying to regain my focus on the task at hand.

The first three of the doors, marked SE1, E2, and E1, looked as ancient and undisturbed as the other inactive branches we'd passed. The door to the last one, NE1, was open.

Devon stayed back as Claudia and I inched forward and peeked around the edge of the doorway, then ducked back.

The place looked much as it had when we saw it the first time: long and dark, sloping downward into the distance. Dozens of chimeras, clustered in groups of six or eight, every twenty or thirty feet along the left-hand wall, were working with picks and shovels, breaking up the glassy black slag that coated the walls, and loading it into carts.

As we expected, the remaining pair of exoguards were keeping an eye on them. One stood by the door. The other was way at the back, past the chimeras, a hundred yards away or more.

There was plenty of noise from all the picking and shoveling, but even so, when Devon coughed behind me, the guard by the door turned and looked over at me. He stepped through the door, out into the main chamber.

"What's the latest on these doors?" he asked.

I gave him a thumbs-up with one hand and squeezed the trigger half a dozen times with the other. He went for his weapons, but stopped halfway.

A few chimeras in the cluster nearest the door stopped working and looked over at us.

I glanced back at Claudia and Devon, and said, "The other guard is all the way at the other end of the shaft."

When I peeked around the doorway, he looked right at me. If someone looking like an exoguard didn't get back in there soon, any chance of a surprise would be gone.

"Crap," I said. "He saw me." I stepped through the door and tried to mimic the guard's posture.

"Shoot him!" Claudia said in a loud whisper.

"He's too far for the dart gun," I hissed back, not looking at her, keeping my head facing straight ahead.

"Then use your other gun," she said, louder this time.

The chimeras closest to the door stared at me intently, and so did the remaining guard. He began slowly walking in my direction, like he knew something was up. I had to get into dart-gun range before he realized what. I started walking toward him, feeling the slope of the floor impelling me forward, even through the exosuit.

As I passed the chimeras, they slowed down or stopped working entirely to watch me.

"What's going on?" the guard called out as we drew closer.

I didn't answer. My voice would give me away immediately.

He slowed to a stop, but I kept moving. Then he tilted his head, as if he was looking over my shoulder. I glanced back and saw that Claudia had entered the shaft. She was fast approaching behind me.

All of the chimeras seemed to notice, now, that something was up. Devon had told us the exoguards traveled in pairs, never in threes. Maybe that's why the guard I was headed for suddenly stepped back and raised his gun.

"Shoot him!" Claudia yelled, and I saw she had her gun in her hand. She pulled the trigger and there was a deafening *boom*. It sounded like it was right next to my head. The chimeras around us all crouched down low, recoiling from the sound. In the distance, past the guard, several glassy black stalactites shattered and fell away from the ceiling.

The guard fired back, another explosive blast.

I fired my dart gun, but even in the dim light I could see the dart arc and fall ten yards in front of him.

"Use your gun, dammit," Claudia said as she fired and missed again.

Instead I ran forward and fired two darts, aiming higher, hoping the arc would take them farther, but they landed even shorter instead.

The exoguard aimed and fired again, at Claudia. The muzzle flashed and the shoulder of Claudia's exosuit jerked violently back, her entire torso twisting as she fell backward onto the ground.

"Shoot him, Jimi!" she cried out again, grimacing as she tried to get back onto her feet.

But I hesitated.

I knew that what we were doing was right. And what we were fighting against was evil. The guard in front of me was a part of a scheme that had already taken many lives. He personally had probably done some of that killing. But still, shooting a human being, taking a life . . . I didn't know if I could live with myself afterward. I didn't know if I could do it at all.

The guard fired at me, but I ducked, and thanks to the exaggerated movements of the exosuit, he missed. As he aimed again, one of the miners closest to him jumped onto his arm, jarring it just enough that he missed again.

I kept charging forward, closer and closer to dart-gun range, even though I knew the seconds it would take for a dart to knock him out were seconds in which he could kill us all.

As I slipped the dart gun into my left hand and reached for my gun, the guard whipped his arm and flung the woman against the wall. She crumpled and dropped to the ground, motionless and bleeding.

Another miner sprang, swinging a pickaxe into the guard's right arm, piercing his flesh and locking the elbow mechanism in place.

"Shoot him!" the miner yelled, his large, lemur-like eyes wide and frantic. "Use your gun! Shoot him!" The guard was reaching around with his left arm, trying to grab him.

I was still out of dart-gun range, and I knew it was way too late for that. As the guard's metal fingers closed on the pickaxe and ripped it out of his arm, I raised my gun. Even in my exosuit's grip, it felt heavy.

The miner looked into my eyes, pleading, as the exoguard's metal fingers closed on his leg. A scream tore through the mine as his leg snapped.

Claudia was still on the ground, screaming *"Shoot! Shoot!"* and trying to twist around to aim her gun.

I pointed my gun and told my finger to squeeze that trigger. But it wouldn't.

The guard pointed his gun at me with one hand while his other raised the injured, screaming chimera high over his head.

And still I couldn't move.

Then a blast erupted behind me and I felt a breeze go past my head. The guard stumbled and looked down. His midsection was shredded, a mass of red where the belly of his yellow coveralls had been. He looked back up, his eyes white hot with rage and pain. His metal fingers shifted on the grip of his gun, but before he could fire, another explosion erupted behind me, the breeze this time brushing my neck. The guard's head jerked back in its metal frame as his breathing mask and his face disappeared in a cloud of plastic shards and red.

I turned and saw Devon behind me, his gun raised, still smoking. His eyes had a deadness I hadn't seen in them before, and I felt a wrenching guilt. He had insisted on leaving the breathing mask with the other guard, Sebastian, because he hadn't wanted to take a life, not even then. But he had shot this guard because I'd been unable to. Once again, I'd forced him into a position where he felt he had to do something he dreaded.

"I'm sorry," I said, quietly.

He nodded but didn't look at me. Claudia didn't either, as Devon reached down and helped her to her feet. "We need to get out of here," he said. "We need to get going."

The guard was still standing in his exosuit where Devon had shot him, his face and his midsection bleeding out through it, onto the rock floor. The miner who had attacked him with the pickaxe, one of two who had saved my life, was still clutched in his metal hand, high overhead, moaning in pain.

Claudia ran over and reached under the exosuit's bloody chest plate. She stepped aside and raised her arm. "Hold onto my hand," she told the miner. The suit assumed its ready position, spilling the dead guard onto the bloody floor as the metal hand released the injured chimera. He clung to Claudia's arm, wincing as she gently lowered him to the ground.

The miner who'd been flung against the wall was sitting up, groaning and holding her head.

The rest of them were staring at us, wondering what was going on. I turned to Claudia and Devon, but neither of them seemed ready to speak.

"We're here to get you out of here," I announced. Even amplified, my voice sounded feeble and inadequate. "We need to get to the main entrance of the mine. Then we'll get you all to safety."

None of them moved. They stared at me for a moment, then they turned to Devon.

He was oblivious at first, staring at the ground, then he seemed to feel their eyes on him, and he looked up at them. "It's okay," he said. "She's right."

"We can't breathe out there, Devon," one of the chimeras said. "You know that."

He nodded, then cleared his throat and started coughing. When he resumed talking a few moments later, his voice was loud and strong. "We're getting you out of here. There's a place nearby, an abandoned town called Centre Hollow, where the air is like it is in the mine, so you can breathe there. It's not far. We're going to take you all there. Then we're going to shut this place down, and we're going to find the people that put us here and make them pay."

They nodded and murmured and smiled at each other, but they still seemed full of doubt.

Devon looked at me, unsure what to do. Before I could say anything, Claudia came up beside us. "Okay," she said, her voice booming. "Anybody who wants to stay is welcome to, but for anybody who wants out, our ride will be here any minute. It's time to go. *Now!*"

CHAPTER 53

The chimeras who weren't injured or sick or weak carried the dozen or so who were to two of the mine carts. As I tipped the unconscious exoguard into a third, I sensed Devon and Claudia staring at me.

"I don't want them to just wake up and walk away from here," I said. "They need to pay for what they've done. And testify against Charlesford or Wells or whoever they were doing it for." But I also didn't want to simply leave them there unconscious, to die when their air ran out. We left the dead guard where he lay.

Devon and Claudia each got behind one of the carts with the chimeras and started pushing, fast. The other chimeras ran along behind them. I got behind the cart with the guard, but before I started running after them, I raised my right hand, extended my fingers, and folded them down, one by one. The suit assumed the start position, the brackets released, and the breathing mask swung up and away from my face. Without stepping out of the legs, I leaned over and reached into the cart, checking the exoguard's pockets. It was vaguely intimate, reaching into his clothes like that, and repulsive in every way imaginable.

I checked his breast pocket, then the two front pockets around his hips, where I finally found what I was looking for: his ID card. I slipped it into my own pocket, resumed my position in the exosuit, and pressed my wrist against the plastic panel in the arm.

I wanted to let out a sigh of relief as the arm cuff slid down onto my hand, but I couldn't breathe just yet. I wiggled my fingers in the dry gel, then clenched my fist. By the time the suit closed around me once more, and the breathing mask closed onto my face and began pumping air, my lungs were aching and I was fighting off the beginnings of panic.

I took a deep, grateful breath, and began pushing my cart after the others. I almost caught up with them at the dorm, where they had stopped as several of the stronger miners began pushing the carts with the injured from the dorm. I dragged out the other unconscious exoguard and dumped him into my cart with his comrade. Devon and Claudia looked back as I did. So did some of the chimeras. I couldn't tell if they approved or not—the nonchimera saving the nonchimeras who had been imprisoning the chimeras. I'd understand if they didn't.

Once again I almost caught up, but stopped to collect the exoguard who had been watching Gus and his crew. I tipped him in on top of the other two.

I finally did catch up just as we were approaching the processing units. The ground shook, and dust and small stones fell from the ceiling.

"What was that?" I said as I came up behind Claudia and Devon.

Devon shook his head. "Doesn't sound good."

Even pushing the carts, Devon and Claudia hadn't been running at close to the suits' top speed, holding back so that the miners on foot could keep pace. I looked back at them, sweaty and exhausted. But we sped up anyway, urging them faster.

For all we knew, Kiet and Sly were already waiting for us, sitting ducks in a stolen truck, visible from the road.

The closer we got to finishing the whole thing, the more I felt that it could all come apart any moment. The ominous rumbling added to that feeling, and as the side tunnel to the processing units came into view, it grew even stronger. Devon and Claudia seemed to be feeling something similar, but probably even more intense.

There were still people in there, two guards and a half dozen technicians. I didn't want to leave them behind to escape or die, either, but right now, we had to focus on getting the chimeras to the truck and getting them safely to Centre Hollow. The processing unit was close enough to the entrance that I could come back for them afterward.

Each of us cast a glance down there as we passed. Debris littered the ground outside the reclamation unit. A steady cloud of smoke was seeping out, creeping along the ceiling and making its way out into the tunnel.

"What's that place?" one of the chimeras asked. "I've never been up here."

No one answered.

As we hustled past, Devon pulled ahead, outpacing the miners. He looked back and motioned for Claudia and me to catch up with him.

As we put some distance between us and the rest of the group, he said, "That second unit is coming apart." He choked back a cough. "If it explodes, it could destabilize the entire mine. Especially if it triggers an explosion in the other unit, as well."

The miners were running out of steam, especially as the slope of the floor steepened, but when the curve of the main tunnel finally revealed a pale gray rectangle of light in the distance—the tunnel's main entrance—they seemed reenergized.

About halfway between us and the entrance, Gus and the other miners we had encountered earlier were huddled against the wall.

Beyond them, through the entrance, I could see the black and yellow gate still in place. No truck.

The ground shook with a loud boom, more violent this time. Looking back, I saw heavier black smoke coming out of the processing units, clinging to the ceiling and blotting out the lights.

As we approached Gus and the other waiting chimeras, we slowed to a stop.

"Sure is good to see you folks," Gus said, as the floor rumbled again. "And there's definitely a ride coming, right?"

The other miners looked terrified, caught between the explosions and mayhem on one side, and the world of fresh air that was poisonous to them on the other. Gus might have felt the same way, but he was doing a much better job of hiding it.

A faint, cool breeze rolled in from the open entrance. The chimeras in Gus's group inched farther away from it as we all turned to look. A strong wind was blowing snow horizontally, and I hoped that wasn't going to complicate things. Then the black and yellow gate rose, and a white truck pulled in underneath it.

"Thank God," Devon whispered.

"Okay, everyone," Claudia called out. "Looks like our ride is here. Once they have the back open and I say go, take a deep breath and run your asses off. You just get yourselves into the back of that truck, don't worry about how crowded it is, don't worry about what you're breathing, just get in there. It might not be pleasant, but we'll get you away from here and take you to Centre Hollow."

The air was thick with a palpable mixture of excitement and fear, hope and anxiety as the miners contemplated freedom, but freedom that could kill them.

Out in the blowing snow, two figures got out of the truck. One stood by the driver's-side door, rubbing his hands against the cold, while the second one went around to the back and opened the door.

"Okay," Claudia said, "Let's *go!*"

Claudia and Devon and I ran forward, pushing our carts. After a half-second pause, the other chimeras followed.

Outside, the wind died down for a moment, and I slowed a step, halfway there.

The chimeras streamed around me as I squinted into the gray light outside. Claudia turned to look back at me.

"Wait!" I called out.

She and Devon slowed a step, too, looking back and forth between me and the entrance. Some of the other chimeras paused as well.

"What is it?" Claudia asked.

I squinted, trying to make out the details of what I was looking at, trying to be sure.

"That's the wrong truck," I said. I couldn't see it clearly, but it wasn't as big as Kiet had described it. And the guy standing by the driver's-side door wasn't Kiet or Sly. But he did look familiar, with blond hair shaved on the sides and a matching blond tuft on his chin.

"Oh, no," I said, then I shouted, *"That's not them!"* I charged forward, pushing my cart through the crowd of chimeras, shouting, "Get back! Everyone, get back!"

The guy outside, the guy who'd been driving the truck the day we first walked past the mine, was crouching and squinting at us through the mine entrance.

I got out ahead of all the chimeras and turned, with my arms thrown out. "No!" I shouted, stopping so suddenly that my feet slid on the dusty stone floor. "Go back! They work for OmniCare. They work for Wells!"

CHAPTER 54

As I stood there for a moment with my arms flung out, watching the entire group—even Claudia and Devon—disappear back down the tunnel, back toward the smoke now billowing out of the reclamation unit, I was more devastated than afraid.

For a moment it had seemed like we were going to make it. Now everything was falling apart.

I heard a distant pop, and a bullet bounced off the ceiling over my head, sprinkling me with rocks and dust. I turned and saw the two men outside, both pointing guns in my direction. I heard another pop, and a small stalactite shattered to my left.

A wave of fury washed over me, not just at the men outside who had cut off our retreat, not just at Charlesford and Wells and whoever else was part of this evil scheme, but at fate for getting us so close to success, and then dashing our hopes.

But fate wasn't available for me to rage at. Neither was Charlesford or Wells. The only ones at hand were the two men shooting at me. As I stared at them for a moment longer, feeling my adrenaline surge, I saw another truck swerve onto the access road behind them.

This time it *was* the truck from the hospital. This time it was Sly and Kiet.

Before I knew what I was even doing, I started running, pushing the cart in front of me as fast as I could. With three exoguards in it, the thing must have weighed close to a ton.

My motion definitely got the men's undivided attention. They fired once more. The first bullet pinged off one of the exosuited legs sticking up out of the cart. The second passed close enough to my head that I heard it go by.

My fury was in no way diminished, but my fearlessness was gone. I was scared. I didn't want to die. But I didn't want my friends to, either. I hunkered down behind the cart as low as I could.

A couple of bullets slammed into the cart, and a few more sailed overhead. I hoped the people behind me were out of the line of fire.

I, obviously, was not. And yet I hadn't fired my gun. In spite of everything that had happened, everything I'd witnessed, after having forced Devon to act in my place, I still dreaded using it. I'd been pushing that cart so long, I figured pretty soon I'd be close enough to run over them, if I lived that long. But if I was nearly within striking distance with my cart maybe I was close enough to do something else.

I gave the cart a final shove, and as it rolled away from me—taking my cover with it—I drew my dart gun and straightened up to aim.

They were less than twenty yards in front of me. One was looking right at me, and I fired two darts at him, *pfft, pfft*. The other guy was turned, looking behind him, at the other truck. I fired three darts at him, *pfft, pfft, pfft*. I was running the whole time, but the suit's stabilizers steadied my aim.

As the first guy fired back at me, I ducked, so fast and so low I lost my balance and went sprawling across the stone floor of the mine. I heard the gunshot, close and loud, then the crash of the mine cart slamming into something.

I clawed at the floor to stop myself skidding across the ground, and panicked as I came to a stop right at the mine's entrance. As I struggled to get to my feet, the exosuit tried to help, guessing what I was trying to do but getting it totally wrong.

I had already decided that if I hadn't darted them both, it would be time for bullets. Before they could kill my friends, or me. But if I couldn't get to my feet, I wouldn't have the chance to act on that decision.

As I struggled to get to my feet, my skin crawled with the certainty that any second those two goons would walk up to me and shoot me dead. Then they'd go kill my friends. And they'd go on killing chimeras—abducting them and altering them and imprisoning them underground, working them to death and then dissolving their bodies to extract whatever precious minerals had been absorbed during the brutal last months of their lives.

I heard footsteps approaching. Terrified, I finally managed to get my toes underneath me, and from there, to get myself upright.

As I stood up straight, I heard the familiar *ting* of a dart bouncing off metal, and I saw Kiet lowering his dart gun, looking mortified.

"Jimi!" he said. "Oh, crap, sorry."

Next to him was Sly, grinning wide. He gestured at the two men sprawled unconscious on the snow next to the upended mine cart and the three unconscious exoguards. "Good thing your aim is better than Kiet's."

I lifted my breathing mask and smiled. "Sure is good to see you two."

But there wasn't time for more small talk than that.

"I'll go get the others," I said. As I turned to run back inside, an ominous trickle of black smoke slid out of the top of the entrance and curled up over the rocky lip before dissipating on a gust of wind. Inside, I could see it slithering like a black snake along the ceiling.

"Okay let's go!" I shouted. "Take a deep breath, then run!"

This time there was no hesitation. The chimeras in the tunnel surged forward, streaming toward the trucks outside.

I slid my breathing mask over my face and watched as Devon and Claudia followed with their carts of injured miners from the dorm. The first ones to reach Sly and Kiet's truck were coughing already, and I swallowed against the lump of fear and guilt growing inside me. I had known all along that this was going to be uncomfortable and dangerous for them.

Grabbing an empty mine cart, I ran back inside.

I slowed to a stop next to the guard we had left in the tunnel, the one whose exosuit Claudia had disabled. Steadying the cart with one hand, I tipped him into it with the other. He went in upside down, so he was resting on his head with his huge metal feet sticking up into the air. I didn't bother straightening him out.

The cart almost tipped over as I turned down the side corridor toward the processing units. The smoke sliding across the ceiling was thicker and lower and darker. I was glad I had a breathing mask.

I left the cart in the corridor and ran into the reclamation unit, trying not to look around me, trying not to look at the bodies in the cart, on the conveyor. I grabbed the guard we had left on the floor, the one I had kicked in the leg. His knee was oozing blood, and it flopped as I dropped him into the cart. Then I went next door. As I was piling unconscious technicians into the cart, the reclamation unit let out another loud rumble, followed by a clang of falling pipes. When I got back out into the corridor, it was rapidly filling with smoke.

I grabbed the cart and pushed it back into the main tunnel. Rounding the corner, I almost plowed into Claudia.

"What the hell are you doing?" she yelled at me. "We need to get out of here!"

"Here," I said, pushing the cart forward until she put her hands on the edge of it. "More witnesses." Behind me, the processing unit rattled and rumbled again. I was already stepping away from her, back down the tunnel. "I need you to get them out of here."

"What? Wait, where are you going now?" she called out across the growing distance between us.

The ground shook hard enough that I stumbled as I turned back to yell, "I'm going to get Rex!"

CHAPTER 55

The ground shook violently as I ran. Chunks of ceiling came down around me, clanging off the exosuit and littering the ground in front of me. Devon's words about how unstable the mines were came back to me, and while the suit itself handled the uneven terrain just fine, I was terrified that one misstep would leave me stuck on my back as the entire mine came down around me. Behind me, all I could see was black smoke, filling the tunnel, erasing the ceiling lights as it came my way.

I ran as fast as I could, worrying the whole time about all the people on their way to Centre Hollow, telling myself they would be okay because the people taking care of them, Claudia and Sly and Kiet and Devon were all brave and smart and competent and better equipped to do what needed to be done for the miners than I was.

The smoke disappeared behind the curve of the tunnel as I sprinted away from it, but another explosion rumbled behind me. As I dodged more falling debris, I observed with dread that a crack had opened in the ceiling, several inches wide. Now, Claudia's words came back to me about how the coal columns left by the original miners to hold up the ceiling had been liquefied and pumped out.

A minute later I passed the dorm, then the inactive branches of the mine. Then I was back in the main chamber. I slowed to a stop in front of the elevators and slipped my arm out of its cuff and into the pocket on my coveralls to retrieve the ID card I had taken from the exoguard. I swiped the card through the slot and pressed UP, the only button on the panel, then slipped my arm back into the relative safety of the exosuit.

Then I waited, heart pounding, looking around at the cavern, at the open entrance to the NE1 mine shaft, at the main tunnel that now seemed to be in real danger of collapsing. As far as I knew, there was no one else in the entire mine complex. No one else alive, anyway. I felt isolated and utterly alone, just me and—increasingly as the seconds ticked by—a swarm of doubts and fears.

Suddenly I heard a voice, surreally calm, absolutely unfazed by the chaos. It said, "Air supply, ten minutes. Please change canister."

It took a moment to register that it was the exosuit's automated warning system. I cursed the voice and the news it delivered, but the worst of what I said was drowned out by a thunderous boom that echoed down the main tunnel, shaking rocks and dust loose from the ceiling of the main chamber. I looked up in time to see a massive stalactite, at least thirty feet over my head splinter and come away from the ceiling.

As I threw myself to the side, the exosuit's exaggerated movements slammed me against a wall, but probably saved my life. The stalactite came down right where I'd been standing, like a missile, exploding on impact and pelting me with chunks of rock. Another one came down in the middle of the cavern, taking with it a section of ceiling lights, which shattered on the ground. I was wondering if the whole thing was going to come down on top of me, when I heard a thunderous crack—not some distant explosion, but nearby, all around me—and the ceiling over the mine branch entrances split, spilling rock and debris onto the floor and raising a dense, dark cloud of dust that rolled toward me. It was pulsating and undulating, like something out of one of the cheesy horror movies Kevin and I laughed at when we were little.

But I wasn't laughing now. I was terrified. I got to my feet and moved away from it, watching over my shoulder as the cloud rolled toward me, all the while picturing myself dying alone, underground, in the blackness. The crack in the ceiling widened, releasing more debris.

I reached the elevator door as the dust cloud was about to envelop me. Then the rest of the ceiling lights detached and blinked out, plunging me into absolute blackness, a total absence of light that made my terror complete.

I froze, unsure where to go, knowing the dust was all around me, pressing in against my breathing mask. I heard the light fixtures hit the ground, and I jumped. Other things crashed to the ground, too, and I pictured more needle-sharp stalactites raining down around me.

My face was wet, and I realized I was crying. Buried underground, knowing I was going to die, knowing Rex was going to die and Doc was probably going to die in jail, I felt utter and absolute despair and, for a brief moment, something almost like peace, as I considered giving in to the feeling.

Then, loud and clear, I heard a bright, almost cheerful *ding*, like on an old-fashioned quiz show when someone got the right answer. For an instant, that's what I thought it was, and I pictured God as some cruel cosmic game-show host, telling me I got the right answer: dying alone in the darkness underground was *exactly* what was going to happen.

Then something rumbled behind me and suddenly a glow from behind cast my silhouette in front of me, as a widening rectangle of light penetrated the churning dust and debris.

I turned, half expecting some supreme being beckoning me to the afterlife. Instead, I saw the elevator doors, wide open.

I stumbled inside and reached out to press the CCU-C button for the floor above when more of the ceiling came down, sending the dust cloud tumbling onto the elevator with me.

As the doors began to close, I noticed a sign on the wall, small but emphatic: IN CASE OF FIRE DO NOT USE ELEVATOR.

I took a step back as a handful of fist-sized rocks tumbled through the door, denting the rear wall.

Finally the doors closed, but the elevator didn't seem to be moving. As the seconds stretched out, I became increasingly concerned that it wouldn't—that the explosions and shaking had damaged the mechanism. I cursed myself for even hoping that the thing might have still been working.

The doors began to open again, and my hand shot out for the CLOSE DOOR button, desperate to keep out whatever was happening in the chamber. But light streamed in through the opening doors, revealing white floors and white walls.

I realized I was on CCU-C. The exosuit must have corrected for the motion of the elevator, so I hadn't felt it move.

After so long in the mine, and outdoors before that, it felt strange being in such a relatively clean and orderly environment. But across from me, I could see that the window set in the wall was cracked. And beyond it, a couple of IV stands lay across the floor.

The beds were all empty. This would have been the last stage of the process, before the splintered chimeras were moved down to the mines. I wanted desperately to find Rex, but I was glad I hadn't found him there.

As the elevator doors started to close, I briefly wondered if I should use the stolen security card to enter the room, or use my exosuit to smash my way in, to see what I could discover beyond the two doors on the other side of all those empty beds. But as desperately as I wanted any information that could exonerate Doc and incriminate Charlesford or Wells, it was all a distant second to finding Rex. And with the mayhem below, I didn't know how long the elevators would be running. I had to hope the SPLINTR inhaler and the testimony of dozens of altered chimeras—and a handful of captured accessories—would be enough.

I pushed the button for the next level, CCU-B, and when the doors opened again, the floor looked much like the previous level, except there were no beds at all, the window was intact, and the IV stands were all upright.

As I pressed the button for CCU-A, the relief and anxiety I had felt upon not finding Rex on the lower levels returned twice as strong: on one hand, maybe he hadn't been altered at all; but on the other hand, maybe I'd never find him.

But then the doors opened, and I spotted him right away.

The beds on that level were three-quarters filled with chimeras. Rex was the largest of them, lying halfway down the row to the right. He seemed unconscious—they were all unconscious—but he looked healthy and hale. None of them had that gray tinge. And nothing in the room looked broken or dislodged, as if the tremors from below hadn't reached this level.

I'd been standing there just a moment, planning my next move, when a door on the far side of the room opened, and a woman in scrubs wheeled in a bed with a chimera strapped to it.

The chimera—a wolf splice by the looks of him—was barely conscious. His eyes were half closed, and his head lolled from side to side as he seemed to be trying to get them to focus.

The woman in scrubs had fake-looking red hair, and I realized I'd seen her earlier, examining the chimeras. She didn't seem alarmed in any way, or even aware of the explosions going on below. In fact, she wore that same vaguely disgusted expression as before. Maybe it wasn't because of the chimeras; maybe that was just how she always looked. But I think that said something, too. She wheeled the bed into the next empty space, a few spots down from Rex. She wasn't wearing a breathing mask, and neither were any of the chimeras. They were breathing the same air.

As I looked on, she took out a syringe and held it up to tap it. Then she looked past it, right at me.

In this light, and from this distance, I knew she could tell I wasn't a real exoguard. She glanced at a phone on the wall, but I moved before she did, vaulting across the small vestibule with all the force the exosuit provided. I obliterated the door and crossed the room in three strides, jostling several of the unconscious chimeras as I did.

I got to the phone just before she did, and I slammed my hand against it, spraying us both with bits of plastic and metal. She closed her eyes against the barrage, then opened them to look up at me, clearly terrified.

She still had the syringe in her hand, and I grabbed her wrist with my metal fingers, willing to risk the possibility that the exosuit's augmented strength would crush her arm to pulp. Apparently the suit had a light touch, so I squeezed a little tighter, making her wince.

"What's in that syringe?" I asked. Her name tag said DR. REIVIK, and under that, SENIOR MEDICAL STAFF.

"Just a . . . a sedative," she said, like she was having trouble breathing.

"Have they been splintered? With the inhalers?"

She gave her head a jittery shake. "No. Not yet."

I flipped up my breathing mask. "Wake them up," I said.

Her eyes widened, as if she was suddenly scared of more than just me. "I can't do that."

I squeezed harder, making her yelp. "I don't believe you."

I felt like I was being watched, and I looked down and saw the chimera she had just wheeled in staring up at us, his eyes in focus now.

"Okay, okay," she said. "Let go."

I released her wrist and she cradled it in her other arm.

"It can be quite unsettling," she said. "For the patient. Coming out of it so quickly."

As she spoke, I heard a dull rumble and the rattle of unseen glass and metal objects vibrating against each other. She looked mildly concerned, and confused, like she didn't know what it was. But I had some idea. I was pretty sure the situation down in the mine was getting worse.

"Do it."

She nodded and turned to the door next to the one through which she had entered.

"Wait," I said, and she stopped, looking back at me over her shoulder. "What is that door?"

"It's a supply closet," she said. "That's where the counter-sedative is. You want me to wake them, right?"

I looked down at the chimera strapped on the gurney. Our eyes met and he gave me a shrug. "What's your name?" I asked, stepping closer to him and yanking the restraints so they no longer held him to the bed.

"Ben," he said, sitting up, still woozy as he undid the buckles and removed them.

"Okay," I told Reivik. "Go ahead." I wrapped my hand around one of the IV stands next to us and bent it between my metal fingers. "And don't try anything."

She turned her bruised wrist away from me, and nodded. As she opened the door, I tensed, ready to spring into action in case it led to a room full of rentacops. But it was a closet, just like she said.

She grabbed a box of glass vials and a fistful of syringes. As she came out with them, I said, "What is that?"

She held up the box. "Flumazenil." She shrugged. "That's what we use."

"What about him?" I said, gesturing toward Ben.

"He doesn't need anything. He'll be fine in a minute."

I nodded and stepped back, bumping into a tray table. I felt big and bulky and clumsy in the small space, at a disadvantage because I didn't know what she was doing, what Flumazenil was. "Okay."

"Where are we?" Ben asked me quietly as we watched Reivik put the box of vials and the syringes on another tray table.

"Under the hospital," I told him.

Reivik picked up a syringe and filled it from the vial.

"What are they doing here?" he asked.

I eyed Reivik coldly and explained as briefly as I could. "They were going to alter your lungs so you could no longer breathe air, only the toxic gases down in the mines, deep underground. They were going to send you down there as slave labor."

His eyes went from shock, confusion, and disbelief to understanding and rage.

Reivik made a point of not looking at either of us as she crossed to the nearest bed and gently lifted the wrist of the chimera lying there, a dark-haired young woman with a feline face and tufted ears, like a bobcat or a lynx.

She undid the woman's restraints, then removed the IV and taped a square of gauze where it had been. Reivik's movements seemed deft and competent, a serious medical professional attending to a patient. It struck me as strangely incongruous, since she was a party to such inhumanity, such cruelty. I reminded myself she was a murderer.

"But you're getting us out of here?" he said.

"We're getting out together."

"Thanks."

"We're not out yet."

Reivik swabbed the girl's arm with alcohol, stuck in the needle, and pushed down the plunger.

The girl flinched, then went still, then opened her eyes wide and gasped, suddenly wide awake. She looked at Reivik and scrambled away from her, falling off the gurney.

Reivik looked on coldly as Ben slid off his gurney and went to comfort the girl, who moved to the far end of the room and stood with her back to the wall, breathing heavily, freaked out despite Ben's efforts to reassure her.

"What's your name?" I said.

"Louisa," she said. "Who are you?"

"I'm here to help," I told her. "How do you feel?"

She looked to Ben and he nodded. "Okay, I guess," she said. Her breathing had slowed, almost to normal. "Confused. But . . . I'm okay. What's going on?"

As Ben explained the situation, the floor rumbled again. I turned to Reivik and pointed at Rex. "Him next."

CHAPTER 56

Reivik shrugged and moved over to Rex. I positioned myself on the other side of him. I wanted to tear off the exosuit and hold him, kiss him. I could feel myself trembling, and I was grateful that the suit corrected for it instead of exaggerating it. But I knew I had to focus. Now wasn't the time to be getting all emotional. Not yet. Instead I made sure Reivik saw it when I unclipped the gun from my hip.

She looked at it, then at me, then at Rex.

"He's big," she said. "He might not come out of it so easily."

"Just don't screw it up." I pointed the gun at her.

On the other side of the room, Ben finished explaining the situation to Louisa, whose eyes had cleared and filled with anger.

"You're making me nervous," Reivik said, nodding at the gun.

"I'm already nervous," I replied. "Don't do anything to make it worse."

As she undid the restraints and pulled Rex's IV, I took a step back.

"Is he a friend of yours?" she asked, as she filled the syringe.

I raised the gun higher, so it was pointed at her head. She nodded and slid the needle into Rex's arm.

A tremble ran through him, just like with Louisa, but nothing happened after that. I looked away from him and glared at Reivik.

"I told you, he's big," she said.

I started to say something but she held up a hand to silence me. "Just . . . give it a second."

The floor shook again, followed by a rumble, louder than before. I put the gun in my left hand and pulled out the shock baton.

"Just . . . just wait a minute," she said. She was scared of me, and I found that both gratifying and chilling. I had never before wanted to be scary.

Then, with a snort and a cough and several blinks, Rex woke up.

Ben was still a little woozy, but by that point Louisa was perfectly fine. I handed her the shock baton and pointed at Reivik. "Don't let her move a muscle," I said.

Reivik rolled her eyes, exasperated, but she eyed the baton with trepidation as Louisa took it from me and moved closer, pointing it at Reivik's midsection.

I wiggled one arm out of the exosuit, and put my bare hand on Rex's cheek. He was confused and disoriented, but at the touch of my hand he settled down, like he knew right away it was me. Then he looked over and startled at the exosuit, but immediately realized it was me after all, and he smiled, shaking his head.

"Kind of a new look for you," he said, his voice reverberating through me, touching every nerve.

I laughed, and started to say something equally witty, but I was crying so hard I would have flubbed the delivery.

Rex looked around as the place shook again. "What the hell is going on?" he asked. Then his head snapped back toward me and he clasped a hand to his chest. "Did they . . . ?"

I shook my head. "No," I said, "they didn't." I could see the relief in his eyes, and it intensified my own sense of relief. I wanted to hug him and cry and bask in the fact that he was okay. Instead I said, "But we need to get out of here."

He nodded and I stood back, slipping my arm back into the exosuit.

"Okay," I said, turning to Reivik. "Do the rest of them. Quick."

To her credit, she did, one after another, in such rapid succession that the chimera she revived after Rex was still coming out of it by the time she had revived the last of them. Ben and Louisa helped them, reassured them, explaining to them what was going on while I told Rex a slightly fuller version.

He smiled when I was done. "You got them out of the mine? All of them?"

"We got them out, but I don't know for sure that they got to Centre Hollow. And there was an explosion down there. The mine's collapsing. I'm worried it's going to take the hospital with it."

As if to emphasize the point, the place shook again, this time violently enough that I could feel it even in the exosuit. In the opened closet, several bottles fell off shelves and smashed on the floor. For the first time, I smelled the faintest trace of smoke. I wondered if it was from the mine or if the tremors had caused a fire somewhere in the hospital.

Rex slid off his bed, onto his feet. In the exosuit, I was the same height as him. There was a lot of hardware around my head, but he found an angle that worked and tilted his head just right to kiss me. As handy as it had been, I was getting sick of wearing that damn exosuit.

The building shook again, and we pulled away from each other. "We need to go," I said, and he nodded.

I went over to Reivik and snatched her ID card from her waist.

"You can't just leave me here," she said.

"No," I said. "You've got too many answers to too many questions, and I know too many people who are going to want to talk to you."

I tied her hands and feet with IV tubing and gagged her with gauze and tape. Then I slung her over my shoulder.

She wiggled and complained, but just for a minute. Then she went quiet, I guess realizing that the alternative was to be stuck down there.

We packed into the elevator and I pressed the top button, for BASEMENT. As we started to rise, my mind was racing. I thought about Sly and Claudia and Devon and the others, hoping they were far from OmniCare and safely in Centre Hollow.

I also thought about all the innocent patients being treated upstairs for normal things, like in any other hospital, oblivious and not complicit in any of this. We needed to tell someone the hospital was in danger.

But then the elevator stopped and the doors opened.

The basement was a pandemonium of red lights flashing and alarms blaring. Smoke hung in the air, along with the smell of chemicals and burned plastic. Water trickled from fire sprinklers in the ceiling, down onto the floor, which was covered with puddles. I looked at my feet and saw the water pouring down into the gap between the elevator and the floor.

I figured the people in the hospital probably already knew something was up.

For a half a second, no one moved. As we stood there, stunned, taking it in, a guy in a janitor's uniform ran past us and burst through the doors into the stairwell across the hall. The building shuddered violently and Reivik whimpered. I passed her over to Rex. He took a step back, as if he was going to protest, but then he nodded and slung her over his shoulder with a sigh.

I peeked out and looked both ways. There was no one else in sight.

I nodded at Rex, then turned to the others. "Come on," I said, and I clomped across the floor to the stairwell. In the moments that I stood there, holding the door open and waving the others over, the smoke thickened perceptibly. Rex came over and took the door, while I climbed the steps to the first landing, to the doorway we had escaped through the first time. I swiped Reivik's card through the slot and opened the door.

The wind had picked up considerably, and it pushed the blustery cold into the stairwell. I held the door open and waved the others outside.

"Run straight across, past the construction site and into the woods," I told them. "Get as far from here as you can."

They streamed past, wide awake now, some of them still sick or injured with whatever had brought them to the hospital in the first place, but all of them desperate to get away. I thought back to the first time we'd come through that hospital, before we had witnessed what was going on in the conversion units and in the mines. What had brought us there in the first place was Doc, and the hopes of finding something to exonerate him. Hopefully we'd done enough, and had exposed enough, to bring down OmniCare and Wells and everything they were trying to do. But knowing H4H, knowing Wells's resources, I now began to worry it might not even be enough to get Doc released, let alone topple OmniCare.

The last few of the chimeras ran past me, then Rex brought up the rear, still carrying Reivik. He paused in front of me, looking concerned, as if he could sense what I had in mind.

"Time to get out of here," he said, edging toward the door. Outside, the other chimeras were sprinting across the snowy grass. Smoke rose from several of the basement windows.

I crossed to the other side of the stairwell and peeked through the door leading to the lobby. It was a mess. The floor was strewn with papers, broken glass from windows, and odd bits and pieces of medical equipment. Water still trickled from the sprinklers, and the haze of smoke pulsed in the flashing red lights. A handful of medical staff were clustered at the front entrance, pushing a few patients on rolling beds. They seemed to be the last ones. The parking lot out front was jammed with patients in beds and people milling around, plus cars and ambulances and school buses.

I turned to Rex. "Get everyone to safety," I said. "Including your*self*."

"Let's get you to safety, too," he said.

"I will. But I need to do something first."

"What are you talking about?"

The building shuddered violently, and outside, half a dozen windows fell from the upper floors, shattering on the icy ground. Reivik squirmed and made frantic muffled noises, which we ignored.

I went over to Rex and tilted my head, finding just the right angle so I could press my lips against his. He put his hand—warm, soft, strong—on the side of my neck, holding me there.

"I'm two minutes behind you," I said as I pulled away. Then I ran up the stairs.

CHAPTER 57

As I rounded the steps and headed for the next floor, Rex called after me, "Jimi, no! We don't have two minutes!"

I knew he might be right. I hoped he wasn't.

As I passed the second floor, two older men in business suits ran down the steps past me. They both glanced up at me, then back at their feet, focused on more pressing matters than how strange it was to see a seventeen-year-old girl in an exosuit running up the steps while they were fleeing the building.

Smoke seemed to be following me up the stairs.

When I reached the fourth floor—the top floor—I swiped Reivik's card through the slot. This time, though, the panel flashed red, and the words ACCESS DENIED scrolled across. I cursed under my breath. Reivik's name tag said SENIOR MEDICAL STAFF, goddamn it.

The smoke from below curled against the ceiling, languid, unhurried, but inexorable. I stepped back, making sure I wasn't too close to the steps, and kicked the door as hard as I could.

The boot of the exosuit smashed through the door easily, sending chunks of it skittering down the marble floor of the elegant hallway.

It was different up there, as different from the hospital floors as they had been from the mines. Even doused in water from the sprinklers and bathed in flashing red light, the luxury was obvious: paneled walls hung with paintings, heavy wood doors, floors covered with marble tile and thick carpet.

To my right was a receptionist's desk, to my left a plush seating area, and straight ahead a short hallway, all of it soaked and dripping. The floor trembled and a large window in the seating area cracked and fell inward, letting in a gust of cold air that somehow smelled even stronger of smoke.

I trotted down the hallway, past doors left open to reveal wet, chaotic-looking offices, strewn with paper as if they had been abandoned in a hurry. At the end of the hallway, there was a thick glass wall with a glass door set in it, both beaded with water. The door was etched with the words DR. DAVID CHARLESFORD, PRESIDENT AND CEO in an elegant white font.

Beyond the glass wall was another reception desk and seating area, even more luxurious than the first, and a double set of dark wooden doors.

I pushed on the glass door, but it was locked. Then I pushed harder and it shattered easily, littering the wet carpet with a million tiny shards that crunched underfoot. I shoved the wooden doors with both hands, and they split and swung open.

The office inside was huge, with windows on three sides, and what probably would have been an amazing view if not for the low clouds and the black smoke sliding up the outside of the building.

A single red light was flashing on the ceiling.

Against the wall across from me was a four-drawer steel file cabinet. And standing next to it, stuffing files into a courier bag, was Dr. David Charlesford, President and CEO. He paused, holding a folder halfway between the open file drawer and the bag, staring at me the same way he had before, with his head tilted slightly down and his eyes looking up, as if the Wellplant was looking at me, too, like a third eye.

I got the sense he was considering his options, calculating them. When he let go of the files, I knew he would only do that so he could grab something else. And I knew it wouldn't be anything good.

The courier bag dropped to the floor and I crossed the space between us in two strides, reaching him just as he was raising a gun. Without thinking, I backhanded it out of his grasp.

The gun flew across the room so hard it dented the wall before bouncing onto the floor. Charlesford's features melted into a grimace of agony and anger, and I realized the force of my slap had mangled his hand. He clutched his wrist with his good hand, unable to utter a sound until he finally managed a strangled whisper. "You . . . little shit." He looked up at me—with his eyes this time. "I'm . . . a surgeon."

I tried not to picture what kind of surgery he did, but I was pretty sure I wouldn't feel bad if he couldn't do it anymore. "You're a murderer," I said.

He snorted and sneered through his pain, then a strange calm fell over his features. "A temporary conversion on a bunch of punks? Please."

"You killed them. Dozens of them. I saw them."

I stepped toward him but he backed away, now dipping his head again. "A small price to pay," he said evenly, "for the next level of human development."

He dove for the gun, grabbed it with his good hand, and came up with it, pulling the trigger. But it was as ruined as his hand, managing only a feeble *click*.

Several things happened then, all at the same time.

The building heaved and shifted, and the floor between us split, the carpet tearing as the crack opened several feet wide, releasing a billowing column of black smoke. Charlesford spun and threw himself against the wall behind him, which opened, revealing a perfect rectangle with gray daylight painting the wall behind it. A secret door.

I vaulted over the crack and pushed through the door after him.

It led to a narrow staircase up to the roof. It was a tight fit in the exosuit. I had to turn sideways to get through it. As my metal foot hit the first step, I heard the roar of a quadcopter and I knew I was probably already too late. I continued anyway, pushing myself sideways, bracing myself with one hand as my legs pushed me upward.

I reached the roof just in time to see the copter lift unsteadily into the fierce winds and the swirling black curtain of smoke rising on all sides. Ice crystals assaulted my face.

In the distance, emergency copters were headed toward us, their flashing lights a stark contrast to the dark gray sky.

I turned and dropped back down the stairwell into Charlesford's office, now quickly filling with smoke. The chasm that bisected the floor had doubled in width. A side chair tumbled into it.

I closed the breathing mask over my face and hopped over the hole in the floor to the file cabinet. The suit announced, "Air supply, five minutes. Please change canister."

There were a half a dozen files in the courier bag on the floor, and a few more sticking up from the top drawer. They all seemed to be patient files but my metal hands were too big to flick through them. The other three drawers were locked.

I felt like I needed to think, to be smarter than I was. What should I be looking for, specifically? The thickening black smoke, the flashing red light, and the almost constant trembling of the rapidly disintegrating building did not help me concentrate.

I clenched my metal fists, almost paralyzed with frustration. The exosuit was incredibly formidable, but what I needed now was brain power. Brute strength was no help.

Or maybe it was.

I grabbed the courier bag and stuffed it into the open drawer, slammed it shut and tapped the button to lock it.

Then I picked the whole thing up, jumped across the gap in the floor, and started running.

The floor splintered under my feet. Behind me, the crack widened, and the half of the room where I had just been standing seemed to tilt. Then it slowly pulled away from the rest of the building.

I ran through the doorways I'd smashed open, and into the main lobby of the fourth floor. The file cabinet wasn't heavy enough to test the exosuit's strength, but it was an awkward size and shape to carry, especially while running through a building that was coming down around me.

I was almost back to the stairwell when another crack appeared, a couple of feet in front of me. I skidded to a stop and watched in horror as it yawned open, spouting oily black smoke lit from below with a hellish shade of orange.

I looked back toward Charlesford's office as that side of the building fell away completely. Swirls of black smoke and red embers wrestled with wind-driven snow. I ran to the seating area and put the file cabinet down next to one of the windows that had fallen in.

As I leaned through the window, smoke streamed out beside me, whipping away on the harsh wind. The parking lot was packed with people, loading the patients onto school buses and ambulances. A string of vehicles were already rushing away, up Bogen Road toward the SmartPike. A pair of fire trucks were coming toward us from the opposite direction, to join the two that were already spraying water on the far side of the building. A few people were standing on the grass, but luckily they seemed to be at a safe distance. Then I looked directly down, and saw a lone figure, much closer to the building than anyone else. Much bigger than them, too.

I flipped up the breathing mask. "Rex!" I cried out, waving my arm.

He looked up and waved back frantically. "Jimi!" he called out, his voice faint from the distance, barely penetrating the din of background noise from the fire and the sirens and the wind and the groaning of the building.

He came even closer and I moved both arms to the side, mimicking the motion of pushing something away. "Get out of the way!"

He waved back, and then beckoned with both arms, like he was telling me to come. I couldn't make out what he was saying.

"Get out of the way!" I shouted again, still motioning with both arms for him to get out of the way.

Again he waved back, but didn't move. The smoke was getting thicker and darker around me. I could feel heat on my back, even as I felt the cold air on my front.

I couldn't think of a way to get the message across, and I was running out of time for being subtle.

I flipped the breathing mask back down over my face and withdrew from the window, back into the smoke-filled building. The suit's voice announced, "Air supply, two minutes. Please change canister." Hefting the file cabinet with both hands, I lifted it to the edge of the window.

I could still see Rex, getting closer and closer. With a quick prayer that my aim would hold true and that I wouldn't hit him, I heaved it outside.

For a second Rex just stood there, and then he flung out his arms and widened his stance, like something from an old cartoon, as he gauged the file cabinet's trajectory. When it was halfway down, he darted to the left.

The cabinet hit with a thunderous but truncated *gong*, as it embedded itself into the icy mud.

Before Rex or anyone else could run over to see what it was, I squeezed through the window and threw myself out, too.

CHAPTER 58

As I fell, I thought about Galileo, about the experiment we had studied in physics class, where he dropped two spheres of different weights from the Tower of Pisa, proving, *he said*, that just because an object has more mass doesn't mean it will fall any faster. We would have to agree to disagree on that, I thought, because as I plummeted through the air in that five-hundred-pound exosuit, it seemed like the ground was coming up at me pretty damn quick.

I twisted and contorted, trying to maneuver the suit so my feet were under me, so they could absorb as much of the impact as possible when I landed, and so I could roll forward, the way skydivers do, the way you're supposed to do when you land from a great height and don't want to break every bone in your body.

I did manage to land on my feet, but that was about it. I hit the ground with a massive, violent jolt, and a chorus of breaking, snapping, cracking, tearing sounds that I hoped were all coming from the exosuit and not from me. The suit did its best to absorb the force of the impact, and I guess it did a pretty good job, considering I wasn't completely splattered, but I definitely still felt it.

I tried to go into a roll, my muscles remembering the plan even as my brain was focused on ringing like a bell. But the suit was dead, and I couldn't move at all. My legs were embedded shin-deep in the mud. I was facing away from the hospital. I could see the edge of the parking lot to my right, the people staring at the hospital. But I couldn't see anybody else.

Then the exosuit started to shift, almost imperceptibly at first, but then it was undeniable: I was tilting forward. A sucking sound came from my feet, and I toppled like a tree.

The ground came at me slower this time, but it was closer, and this time the exo-feet didn't absorb the impact. As the my face approached the mud I thought, *Thank God I've got this breathing mask on.*

Then I hit, and everything went black as the mud blotted out all light.

I took a deep, calming breath and told myself not to panic. Then a cheerful voice told me, "Air supply depleted. Please change canister."

Frantically, I tried all the hand gestures Claudia had shown me: I wiggled my fingers in the gel, clenched my fist and counted up and down with my fingers. But nothing worked. I tried to slip my arm out of the exosleeve so I could try to find the release button under the chest plate, but I was pinned against the mud.

It was cold and wet and dark. The mud seeped through the coveralls and into my clothes. I could feel my tears gathering inside the mask. After all I had just been through, it appeared that I was going to suffocate in a pile of mud.

Then I started to rise, tilting sideways. The mud sucked at me, like it didn't want to let me go. But something else was lifting me up—like it didn't want to let me go, either.

The ground came into view through my muddy breathing mask, then the trees and the flashing lights of police and emergency vehicles. I saw the crowd in the front parking lot and the hospital, fully engulfed in flames that totally outmatched the arcs of water from the fire hoses now trained on it. Then I saw the sky, buzzing with all sorts of copters and drones. And finally I saw Rex, his face red and his muscles bulging and shaking as he lifted me and turned me over. His jaw was clenched with effort, but as he eased me to the ground, his eyes caught mine staring at him. He smiled despite himself.

Maybe I distracted him, or maybe it was just the mud, but at that moment, his foot slipped. He dropped me the last few inches, back onto the cold wet mud, with a thud that was totally unmitigated by any servos or shock absorbers. He landed on top of me, his face just an inch from mine.

He pulled off my breathing mask, and I smiled. Without the mud pressing in from the front, I was able to pull my arms out of the exosleeves. I put one muddy hand on the back of Rex's neck and said, "Well, this is convenient."

He smiled as I pulled him closer, and we kissed. For a while. Until I remembered we were surrounded by several hundred staring strangers. And that we had to get to Centre Hollow. Immediately.

I put my hand on Rex's cheek and pushed him away.

"What?" he said. Then he looked up at the crowd gathering around us. The flashing lights seemed closer. A few of the copters even seemed to be circling us instead of the hospital.

"I'm freezing," I said. "And we need to make sure everyone got to Centre Hollow okay. And I'm a little worried the ground is going to give way under us. But before any of that, I need to get out of this thing."

He nodded, then frowned. "How do you do that?"

I reach under the chest plate and held my breath as I pushed the release button, hoping it would work.

It did, kind of. With a raspy mechanical whir, the chest plate and the shoulder brackets retracted. But the brackets on my lower legs, the ones holding my feet in place, had more trouble. They both made a series of noises—*whir, clunk, whir, clunk, whir, clunk*—but failed to disengage.

The snow was starting to come down harder, driven sideways by the wind. Squinting up through it at Rex, I said, "It's jammed. From the impact."

A section of the hospital collapsed and the ground shook. A murmur rose from the crowd and they backed away as smoke and sparks billowed into the sky. They weren't staring at us anymore.

Several cars with angry flashing lights were driving toward us over the muddy lawn. I sat up as best I could and put my lips near Rex's ear. "We've got company," I said.

He looked over at the approaching cars, then turned back to me. "Try it again," he said.

I reached back under the chest plate and pressed the button. As the leg brackets did their *whir, click, whir, click* thing, Rex grabbed the brackets on either side of on my left leg and pulled. With a sound of tortured metal they came apart and I pulled my leg out. We did the same thing again, on the other side, and then I was free. Muddy and freezing, but free.

I scrambled to my feet. It was strange to be outside the exosuit. I felt weak and small and vulnerable. My body didn't seem to be working quite right.

I looked up at Rex. "Where's Reivik?"

"I had to let her go."

"You what?"

"I have her driver's license, her address. She swore she would testify if I let her go. I couldn't just hold her captive."

The cars with the flashing lights pulled up right next to us. Rex put his arm around me as we turned to face them.

One of the copters drifted over as well, a big one, hovering directly above us. It didn't have any flashing lights on it.

All six of the front doors on all three cars opened simultaneously, and six men in uniform got out. They all wore shades, even though it was a dark, gray day. They all had guns drawn, and they all had Wellplants—the new ones. Their cars were facing us, with the headlights on, so I couldn't see what was printed on the sides.

One of them came forward. "You're under arrest," he said.

"What for?" Rex asked.

The guy smiled coldly. He glanced back at the hospital, then down at the broken exosuit on the ground. "I don't know if I can think of any charges I *couldn't* throw at you, but let's start with stealing and destroying that exosuit, and burning down the hospital."

He stepped forward, then the others did, too.

"You're not cops," I said, and they stopped.

"Excuse me?" said the leader.

I looked around and realized it was just us and them. Everyone else had withdrawn to a safe distance, over by the road. "You're not police," I said. "You're private security. You're rentacops."

He smiled again. The same smile. "We are empowered by the state to enforce the law and arrest perpetrators within the OmniCare facility."

The copter above us was hovering lower, and the rentacop in charge glanced up at it, annoyed, like he had the situation under control and he didn't need anybody stepping on his toes.

"We're not *in* the OmniCare facility," I said. "In fact, there's not much OmniCare facility left. And we didn't burn it down."

"Well, young lady, you're going to have to explain that to the judge."

I could feel Rex tensing beside me, like he was getting ready to fight it out with them. I glanced down at the exosuit. The dart gun was gone, but the shock baton was still clipped on. Next to the gun. I wondered if I could make either of them work with my tiny bare hands.

The rentacop in charge seemed to read my mind. He laughed. "Sweep harp, I would lub to add rejisting arresh to the long lips of cha-chas."

CHAPTER 59

The other rentacops seemed confused as they looked at the one doing the talking. Their heads tilted forward, staring at him the same way Charlesford had stared at me, as if their Wellplants were studying him.

He glanced back at them, irritated, but confused as well. Then he turned back to Rex and me. "Amb I'd lub to subub, bub . . ."

"What the hell . . . ," Rex muttered. But I'd seen this before. I squinted up at the copter hovering over us, then looked back at the rentacops in front of us.

With their shades on I couldn't tell what was going on with their eyes, but the one in charge swayed and fell sideways. His comrades watched him fall, then they fell, too, one after the other, all in a row.

Rex still looked confused, but I nudged him with my elbow and pointed up at the copter.

"Is that Dara?" he said, squinting at the figure waving out the side door of the copter.

"What about your orders?" I called up to her as she descended.

She shrugged. "I got new orders."

As Dara touched down, the last section of the OmniCare building still standing let out a loud, grinding noise that sent the firefighters backing away. It toppled over in a column of sparks, settled for a moment, then let out a loud groan, like the last gasp of some horrible dying beast. It folded in on itself as it sank into the earth, then all that was left of it was a glowing red hole and a stream of bright embers, rising into the sky like snowflakes from hell.

We were all quiet for a moment, watching the spectacle in awe. Then I turned to Dara. "Just so we're clear, we didn't do *that*."

"That's actually reassuring," Dara replied. "What about the miners? Did they all get out okay?"

"They got out," I replied. "But I don't know if they're okay." I turned to Rex. "We need to get to Centre Hollow."

Rex nodded. "Can you give us a lift?"

A gust of wind twisted the column of smoke and sparks into a corkscrew.

"Sure thing," Dara said, with a nervous laugh. "But we better hurry up. That storm front from last night is catching up with us. It could be a rough ride."

Dara wasn't delighted when I pointed at the filing cabinet embedded in the mud and told her we needed to take it with us. Even with the three of us, the cabinet was hard to lift. It was frustrating, after having carried it by myself with no problem. I got the sense that some in the crowd gathered on the roadside were watching us again, but they were at quite a distance, and none of them seemed interested in coming any closer to see what we were doing.

We finally managed to slide/roll/walk the cabinet onto the copter, but by the time we were in the air, the snow was coming down harder. We had to fly just over the treetops to see where we were going.

From the sky, the fiery pit where the hospital had stood looked like a portal to hell, which in a way it had already been. The last of the school buses and ambulances were gone, all the patients presumably in transit to other hospitals—hopefully ones that didn't engage in forced medical experiments or slave labor.

I told Dara generally where we were headed, what direction and what landmarks to look for. We flew roughly along Bogen Road, looking for the break in the woods where the old Main Street led down into Centre Hollow.

On our way, I got out of the mud-soaked coveralls, leaving me in the semi-mud-soaked clothes I'd been wearing underneath. There was a blanket in the copter, and Rex wrapped it around me. He wasn't even wearing a coat, but he didn't seem cold.

We flew over a couple of places where the ground had collapsed or split open, including one where the angry red glow from the underground fires reflected off the snow, melting it in places. I worried about the fires spreading underground, but with no coal left to burn and no air to support combustion, the only fire was the fire from the chemicals in the processing units. That and the hospital.

But I also worried about the instability undermining Centre Hollow itself. The branches of the mine under Centre Hollow hadn't been touched by OmniCare's operation. They were still sealed off. And the liquefaction that took out the supporting coal columns had happened years ago. But there was no guarantee that the geological instability that took down the hospital wouldn't spread anyway.

Off to the side, I spotted what looked like a short chimney in the middle of the woods, spouting black smoke. The trees around it were either burned or blackened with soot.

As the wind buffeted the copter and the snow came down harder, I pointed at it and leaned close to Rex. "That's the vent."

He looked at me quizzically and I realized he hadn't been there for any of that. He hadn't seen the awful fake snow coming out of it, or talked to Devon, or seen what had been going on below it. He moved his face close to mine, brushing my hair away from my eyes as he stared into them. "Are you okay?" he asked.

I nodded and wiped my eyes. I'd tell him about that someday, when he told me about whatever horrors he had been enduring these last few days. But not right now.

I leaned toward Dara. "It should be just to the southeast of here. Less than a mile."

"Good." She gave me a sober look. "This wind is getting too dangerous to fly so low."

She adjusted course, and thankfully we didn't see any other signs of fire or geological instability. A minute later, we spotted Main Street. We flew over the WELCOME TO CENTRE HOLLOW sign and the wrecked VW, then the clearing where Devon and Kiet had reunited. Beyond that, down in the hollow, the faint outlines of the buildings of Centre Hollow came into sight through the snow: the school, the post office, the old stores lining Main Street, and the houses on the street that crossed it. Then I spotted the truck. It appeared suddenly right in front of us; one second there was no sign of it, then there it was, a big, long white box, almost invisible against the snow.

"There's the truck!" I called out, pointing. "They made it!"

Rex put his hand on my shoulder and squeezed, but as I reached up to put my hand over his, I stopped. There was something dark lying in the snow next to the truck. As we got closer, I spotted two more. Three. Six. Twelve. I grabbed Rex's hand and squeezed it tight. "Oh, no," I whispered.

They were bodies.

CHAPTER 60

Put me down there," I told Dara.

"Are you sure?" she asked, concerned. "There's no place to land. You'd have to go down on a rope. I wouldn't recommend it in this wind."

"No," Rex said. "You can't go down there. It's inside Centre Hollow. You can't breathe down there."

His words stopped me. He was right. And I didn't have a breather.

"There's a clearing, west of here. We just passed it," I told Dara. "It should be big enough to land, easily."

Rex shook his head. "Even that's not safe. Not for long."

Dara looked back and forth between us, while keeping one eye on the copter's controls and displays.

"Why isn't it safe?" she said. "Explain."

We told her how the clearing was like a no-man's-land between the area where the miners who had been splintered could safely breathe and the area where the rest of us could safely breathe.

"We can breathe on one side, they can breathe on the other side. It's not perfect for anybody, but you can breathe in the middle there for at least a few minutes," I told her. "And if you stay at the western edge, you'll be fine."

She gave me a dubious look, then looked at Rex. He shrugged and nodded.

"Okay," she said. "Tell me where."

The wind grew worse even in the few seconds it took us to find the clearing, and by the time Dara put down, I think she was more worried about the storm than any toxic gases.

"I can't wait here for you," she said. "If the wind gets any worse, I won't be able to take off."

"I have one more favor to ask," I said,

She raised an eyebrow, dubious but ready to listen.

I told her about Doc, and about Cornelius, aka Bennett Thompson, and how Doc's predicament was what sent us out there in the first place. "Doc's still in jail," I told her, "and I'm pretty sure there are documents in that filing cabinet that should prove him innocent and get him released, and also reveal what was going on at OmniCare." I asked her to take it to New Ground Coffee Shop in Philadelphia, that Jerry would know what to do with it. "Plus," I said, feeling slightly ridiculous, "can you ask him to let my mom know I'm okay?"

Dara smiled and said she would, but her smile was cut short as another gust of wind rocked the copter.

We said our thanks and goodbyes, then we opened the side door.

Driving snow whipped into the cabin, stinging our faces and swirling everywhere.

"This is nice," Rex shouted, holding his arm up to shield his face as we stepped out of the copter.

The snow was only a few inches deep in most places, but drifting so much it was hard to get good footing.

As we approached the middle of the clearing, he said, "The moment you start showing any signs of confusion or whatever, I'm getting you out of there." He had to raise his voice over the sound of the wind. "Even if I have to carry you kicking and screaming."

I stopped. "What about you? What if you pass out?" I didn't have my exosuit anymore. "If you pass out, I won't be able to carry you out."

"I'm not *that* heavy," he said, laughing. He wasn't very convincing. "Come on, let's go."

"*No!*" I shouted. "You wait here, where we know it's safe. I'll go over to the truck to see what's going on. If I'm not back in five minutes, you come and get me."

He looked at me with his clear, somber, deep brown eyes, studying my face while he considered my plan. "Okay," he said finally. "Three minutes."

"Four."

"Okay, four."

He grabbed me by the elbows and kissed me, filling me with a warmth that I sorely needed.

It took me almost a minute to cross the clearing and make my way through the woods to the truck. The first chimera I came to was half covered with snow and unconscious, but alive. His breathing was fast, shallow, and loud. I shook him, but he didn't respond. The next one was in the exact same state, and the one after that as well.

A nagging horror grew in the back of my mind, a terrifying suspicion that regardless of our intentions, somehow we had killed them all. I knew we all shared responsibility, the whole group, but I couldn't help the feeling that if it all went wrong, it would be all my fault.

As I ran from one crumpled figure to the next, my brain seemed to fragment, part of it trying to figure out what could have happened, part trying to figure out what I should do now, part of it focusing more than a little energy on despising myself for my hubris—for thinking I had all the answers, when in reality I couldn't even figure out what the questions were.

The idea struck me that maybe I could somehow get them all back onto the truck, get them back into that awful mine. Or even back to the hospital, to the underground CCU units, where at least they could breathe.

But those were no longer options. They'd all been destroyed.

There had been plenty of times in my life when I had wished I were different in some way or another, when I embarrassed myself or felt lonely or pathetic. But I had never hated myself before, and at that moment I did, with an intensity that scared me.

I heard a groan near the front of the truck, and I ran over there. One of the chimeras in the snow was moving, just a bit. I brushed the snow off his face and saw that it was Gus, the big guy with the horns we had encountered in the tunnel.

"Gus!" I said. "What happened?"

He looked up at me with half-closed eyes. "Don't know," he answered. "We got here okay. The folks here were helping us. Then the storm moved in and they all got sick."

"Where's Claudia? Where's Devon?"

He shook his head and coughed.

"Hey!" a voice called in the distance. I assumed it was Rex at first, and I turned, ready to argue that it hadn't been four minutes yet, but it was someone much smaller.

"Help me!" he cried out, breathlessly. "Help!"

"Henry?"

"Oh, it's you," he said. "Thank God! Help us get these poor bastards out of the cold."

"Us?"

He was a cold, wet, disheveled mess, but he looked healthy, worlds better than the last time I'd seen him, when he couldn't even get out of bed. "Yeah, there's a couple others who are doing okay."

"What happened? And did you get *better*?"

"I don't know what happened out here. They came from the mine, in that truck, and they all got sick. Everybody else, too. Everybody but me. I was lying in bed, damn near dead, listening to the wind whistling through the house and wondering if the cold was going to get me before the sickness. Then I just . . . started feeling better, just like that. I came outside to tell someone, and I saw these folks collapsing onto the ground."

Something was starting to click into place in my brain, but I couldn't quite put my finger on it.

"Thank God Claudia showed up a minute later in her big exosuit."

"She's here?"

"She's been helping me get them to shelter, but we could use a hand." He grabbed my sleeve and gave it a shake. "So, can you help us or what?"

I ignored him for a moment, trying to let my thoughts arrange themselves into something comprehensible.

"I said, can you help?" Henry tugged at my blanket. "They're going to freeze to death out here."

"Jimi!" boomed another voice. This time it was Rex for sure, trudging toward me through the snow. I held up a hand, letting him know I heard him, but that I needed a moment to think. "Jimi!" he called again as he got closer. "It's been five minutes."

"I know," I told him, closing my eyes, trying to concentrate, wondering if the toxic gases were making it difficult to think. But they weren't. I could think just fine.

When Doc had mentioned AAV therapy he said it only changed one generation of cells at a time, but that people were trying to extend that using viruses that re-infected the new cells as they arose. I thought back to the label on the SPLINTR inhaler: SUSTAINED AAV REINFECTION 90 DAYS. REAPPLICATION NOT RECOMMENDED DUE TO ACQUIRED IMMUNITY.

A gust of wind whipped around me as the shock of realization hit. I hadn't understood it then. But now I understood it meant the treatment could only be applied once. Each new generation of cells would be reinfected, but after ninety days, the patient would be immune.

When Devon had told me about the sickness, he said the treatment not only changed their lungs, it killed them after three months. And in the mines, it did. In Centre Hollow, it did. But it didn't have to. I opened my eyes and looked over at Henry, who was scowling at me for not helping him. He seemed perfectly healthy now, and I realized it was because of the storm, because he was breathing fresh air.

"Henry!" I said, grabbing him by his sweater. "The SPLINTR treatment isn't fatal, it's *temporary*. It only kills you if it wears off when you're still in the mines, or here in Centre Hollow."

We both looked at the chimeras lying on the ground as the wind lacerated our faces.

Rex grabbed me. "We've got to get out of here, before we pass out," he said.

"No," I told him. "It's fine. The air's fine. That's what's killing them."

"*What?*"

"Holy . . . ," Henry said, suddenly getting it. "It's the storm. The wind blew away all the gases, even down in the hollow." He took a deep breath, smiling just for an instant as he savored the fact that he'd just been given his life back. Then his smile fell away.

"So what can we do for them?" Rex asked.

"We need to find someplace still safe," I said. "where the wind can't get to. Like a basement without windows."

Henry's head whipped around. "The school basement. It's big and it's deep, and depressing as hell. No windows at all."

Rex and I nodded and all three of us sprang into action. As we each grabbed one of the fallen chimeras, a figure emerged through the snow and the trees, a big one. It was Claudia in her exosuit. She must have come on foot. "Jimi!" she called out. "Rex!" She sounded breathless. "Thank goodness. You've got to help us get everyone out of the snow."

"Claudia!" I ran over to her. "We need to get them to the school, into the basement."

"What?" Her breathing mask was plastered with snow and ice, but I could see her face, confused and exhausted beneath it. "Why aren't you wearing a breather? Oh, God, did you get splintered?"

"No, I'm fine. Where's Devon?"

"He's fine. We got him out of the snow, but everyone else—"

"I know," I said, "the wind has blown all the mine gas out of the hollow. We can breathe here," I told her. Then I pointed at the chimeras lying on the ground. "But they can't!"

CHAPTER 61

most of the chimeras were already indoors, having either walked there before the storm hit, or been carried or dragged there by Claudia and Henry. But with hardly a window intact in the entire town, indoors didn't count for much. The intense winds had flushed out all the mine gases and replaced them with fresh air, so even those inside were still in danger.

"If we can breathe here, I should go get Sly and Kiet," Claudia said. "They're waiting on the outskirts of town, where they could breathe safely."

"There's no time for that," Henry said, shaking his head vigorously. "We need to get these folks to that basement, *now*!"

We started with the people still out in the snow. Our main worry was asphyxiation, but exposure was a serious concern as well. Henry and I each grabbed someone and started dragging. Rex carried Gus, and Claudia carried two others, one over each metal shoulder. Luckily, the school was one of the closest buildings in town, a hundred yards or so through the woods to Main Street and then a block up the hill.

Close to twenty chimeras were already there, just inside the door, lying on the dirty floor, coughing and shivering in the snow that had blown in through the missing windows. A faded banner hung in tatters on the wall: HOME OF THE FIGHTING BOBCATS.

Henry led us past them, down the hallway to a set of stairs that led to the basement. Henry lifted his chimera and carried him carefully down the stairs, but I didn't have the strength left. The girl I was carrying was no bigger than I was, but it was all I could do to try to minimize the bumping and not drop her as I lugged her down the stairs.

The basement was dark, lit only by the dim gray light from a row of glass-block windows set high in one wall. We were well below ground level, so they must have looked out onto window wells. We rested the chimeras next to each other against a wall, then hurried back upstairs.

As we ran out past the chimeras in the hallway, I saw that one of them was sitting upright against the wall. It was Devon.

"Devon!" I said, as I crouched down in front of him. "You're okay!"

He looked up at me and coughed. "Jimi," he said with a smile. Then he looked left and right, at the other chimeras. "I don't think we are. What's going on?"

"I don't have time to explain it," I said, placing my hand against his cheek. "But you're going to be okay. All of you."

He looked up at me, his eyes looking like they couldn't focus. "How?"

"I'll explain later," I said. "Just try to rest."

As I headed for the door, I wondered again if we should have stopped and moved them downstairs first, but as I stepped out into the wind, I knew we couldn't leave the anyone outside any longer than we had to.

I caught up with Henry, but Rex and Claudia had pulled way ahead of us. They passed us coming back before we were three-quarters of the way there.

When we got back to the truck, Henry and I each grabbed someone, but as we dragged them to the school, I struggled to keep up with him. I was exhausted, and mad at myself because of it. I couldn't bear the thought that I might not be able to keep going, even when there were lives at stake, lives that *I* had put in jeopardy.

My legs were aching, but I increased my pace anyway, drawing close enough to Henry that the door to the school was still closing when I got there. But I didn't actually catch up with him until I got down to the basement.

He was standing at the bottom of the steps, slowly shaking his head. As I came down next to him, struggling to hold a slender kid who felt like he weighed two hundred pounds, Henry said, "I'll be damned."

The chimeras Rex and Claudia had just dropped off were lying against the wall, looking much as they'd looked outside. But the others, the ones we had brought on the first trip, were already sitting up, blinking and looking around, confused but seemingly healthy.

Gus looked at us and said, "Where the hell am I?"

"In the basement of the abandoned school," I told him, stunned, as I put the kid I'd been dragging right next to him.

"You should be able breathe down here," Henry said. "That's why we brought you."

"Oh, thank God," Gus said with a short laugh. "For a moment I thought I was back in high school. As if being stuck in that mine hadn't been hellish enough." Seeing them doing so well gave me enough strength that I felt like I could make one more trip, and hopefully get the last of those still out in the snow.

As I headed back to the truck, I heard Claudia in the distance calling out to Henry that she was going to get Sly and Kiet. He replied that some of the people in the basement were already well enough to help bring the others at the school downstairs.

When I reached the truck I circled it twice, making sure no one was covered with snow or hidden in a drift. When I was positive no one was there, I took a moment to reflect on it, to be grateful. I could feel the adrenaline fade away, and the burning in my limbs turn to a dull ache. Then I started trudging back to the school.

I slipped in the snow, and landed hard. My hands were numb and my arms and legs exhausted. I barely had the strength to get back on my feet.

Then a few steps later I slipped again.

I knew that even though there was no one left out in the snow, there were people in other buildings, still in danger, who needed to be moved into the basement so they could breathe. But I also knew there were other people working on that, and they probably had the situation well under control. Besides, I thought, as I closed my eyes against the snow coming down, I needed to rest my arms and legs. Just for a second.

CHAPTER 62

I woke up in a shack with tattered red curtains flapping in the broken windows. I recognized it as the place Kiet had been staying. I was bundled in dirty blankets and warmed by Rex, who was asleep beside me, on top of the blankets but with his arms and legs wrapped around me. He woke up as soon as I stirred, his big eyes right next to mine.

"Good morning," he whispered, resting his hand gently against my face. The sun was out, and through the torn curtains I could see the painfully bright blue of a winter sky the day after a snowstorm.

"Good morning," I whispered back.

"You had us worried," he said.

"How long have I been asleep?" I asked.

"About eighteen hours," he said.

"Eight—"

I heard a cough and realized we weren't alone. I turned over, startled to see Doc and Claudia, sitting in chairs pulled up next to the bed with a chessboard between them, mid-game.

"You're awake," Doc said, adjusting his glasses. "That's good."

"Doc?" I said, stunned. "What are you doing here?"

He shrugged. "That trove of OmniCare documents your friend Dara brought to E4E headquarters yesterday is very interesting stuff, from what I'm told. They'll be trying to make sense of it all for some time. But they found Cornelius's file right away, and that was enough to get me released. Jerry brought me up here this morning, so I could thank you in person. And to make sure you didn't die."

Claudia yawned and stretched. "He also brought blankets and other supplies for the miners." She smiled. "And a chess set."

I saw my clothes hanging on a line, and I lifted the covers to see that under them, I was wearing a baggy sweatshirt and under that my bra and underwear.

Claudia snorted and raised a hand. "I did that. We had to get you out of your wet clothes."

"I found you passed out in the snow," Rex said. "I don't know how long you'd been there amid all the confusion of getting everyone into the basement."

Doc leaned forward. "You should have been in a hospital. But apparently, the only one nearby is, um, no longer an option."

"What about everyone else? Are they okay?"

Doc nodded. "Mostly, yes. A couple had hypothermia, but they warmed up okay, like you did. One young man seems to have a nasty lung infection."

"Devon," Rex added.

"It's not looking good, and I can't figure it out. He said you told him he was going to be okay."

"He is," I said. I sat up, grabbing the covers as they fell away, feeling suddenly cold and exposed.

I explained to Doc about Henry and what I knew about the AAV treatment, what I'd read on the SPLINTR inhaler. "I think Devon's not getting sicker, he's getting better. He just has to make it through the transition."

Doc sat back and thought for a moment. "Hmm. That's good news, but it's tricky. How does one treat someone whose lungs are transitioning from processing one medium to another?"

"You're the doctor," I said. "But Henry survived it, so you should talk to him. Maybe a mixture of air and CO_2 or mine gas or whatever." I told him about the CCU wards we'd seen under the hospital and suggested the files might have some helpful info. By the time I was done, I felt wiped out again.

Doc nodded. "That's what I'm hoping. Interesting. I'll consult with some of my old colleagues and maybe we'll try that. Matter of fact, I should go check on Devon and the others." He stood up, then added, with a wink, "Of course, I'll have to be careful no one catches me practicing without a license."

Claudia got up, too. "Glad you're okay," she said, stopping to put a kiss on my forehead before turning to Doc and gesturing toward the chessboard. "Should we finish this later?"

Doc paused, looking down at the board. He moved one of the pieces and said, "Checkmate."

Claudia tilted her head, studying the board. "That's just mean."

Doc laughed and she followed him outside. Then I was alone with Rex. "Glad you're okay, too," he said.

"I'm glad *you're* okay," I said. "I was really worried about you."

He smiled. "To be honest, for a minute there, I was, too."

"Where's Sly?" I asked.

He smiled, then started laughing.

"What?" I said.

"I'm not supposed to say."

I growled and shook my head, but then he kissed my cheek and squeezed me tight. His warmth penetrated the blankets, and I wondered how warm it would be if the blankets weren't between us.

CHAPTER 63

Kevin did write that note to my mom. It was messed-up, but I understood why he did it. I did not get to it before she did, and from what Aunt Trudy tells me, Mom was every bit as furious as I thought she'd be. Luckily, I wasn't there for that.

There wasn't a phone in Centre Hollow, but Doc told me that the message that I was okay had been delivered the day before—maybe a little premature and unjustifiably optimistic, but ultimately more or less accurate.

In a stroke of genius, Jerry got Marcella DeWitt to deliver the message. That helped a lot, I think—not only getting word to my mom so she knew I was okay, but having it delivered by a semi-high-powered lawyer for Earth for Everyone, in the context of "Your daughter helped strike an important blow for the human rights of chimeras today and exposed and helped end an evil, oppressive, and murderous plot, saving the lives of scores of young people." Oh, and by the way, she might be late for dinner.

DeWitt did a bang-up job of softening her up before I got home, and while I didn't want to set a precedent of involving a lawyer in every interaction I had with my mother, I decided I'd keep DeWitt's phone number, just in case. Mostly, though, I wanted it because I realized I had initially misjudged her. DeWitt was pretty awesome, and even hilarious in her no-nonsense, get-stuff-done kind of way.

After I got dressed, Rex and I visited the school basement.

I didn't want to make a big deal out of it or anything, I just wanted to see for myself that people were okay. When I came down the steps, I got kind of choked up at the sight. Everyone was grimy and exhausted, wrapped in blankets, but talking and laughing, giddy at being out of the mine and alive.

I put my hand over my mouth, trying not to cry, and Rex put his hand on my shoulder and squeezed. I smiled up at him and nodded. I'd seen what I needed to see. It was time to go. But as we started up the steps, a voice called out, "Hey! There's the nonk!"

I froze, mortified. Part of me wanted to just keep going, but before I knew it, I was spinning on my foot and going back downstairs, ready to have it out with some Roberta-like jerk.

But instead, when I looked back, I saw everyone in the basement grinning up at me. Standing at the front was Gus, and I realized he was the one who had shouted out.

"Claudia told us what you folks did. And what you personally did back there, after we got out." He winked, his eyes twinkling with humor. "We just wanted to say thanks."

"Yeah, thanks, nonk!" someone called out from the back. The room erupted in laughter at that, then cheers.

Standing up on the steps, looking down at them, it kind of felt like the moment demanded that I say something better than "You all take care." But nobody wanted a speech, least of all me. Besides, I was a bit of a blubbering mess.

Rex put his arm around me as we walked back upstairs and out into the sunshine. He took me to where Devon was set up, a windowless but semi-above-ground basement under an old hardware store.

Kiet and Henry were sitting at the top of the steps, taking turns running down to check on him.

"He's still pretty sick," Kiet said, "but . . . we're both ecstatic that he's actually going to get better."

Henry smiled. "I keep telling him, soon he'll be as healthy as me."

"That's great," I said.

Devon looked terrible, but he grinned when I came down to see him.

"How are you doing?" I said.

"Getting better, I'm told," he said with a laugh. "Imagine that." He struggled not to cough as he said those last two words, but afterward he was overtaken by it, a deep, wracking cough that lasted for over a minute and left him looking wiped out.

By the time he was done, I felt wiped out, too. I'd been feeling woozy even before I went down there, and I didn't know how much of it was from the hypothermia and how much was that the hollow was filling up with mine gas again now that the winds had died down.

"You'd better get out of here," he said when he was done.

I nodded. "Yeah, I should. I have to go, anyway. You get better, okay? And next time I see you, maybe we'll go for another walk in the woods."

"Sounds good," he said. "Just not these woods. I'm a little sick of these woods."

After a tearful goodbye to Kiet, we left. Claudia insisted on driving, and she also insisted that Rex sit in the back with me, which was very nice. We didn't talk all that much, any of us, and that was fine, too. We were tired, numb, and traumatized. And especially considering what was waiting for us when we got back to Philadelphia, it was great to have an hour to listen to the radio and drive with my friends in a kick-ass car.

But after an amazing string of two songs I loved for every song I hated, a news break told us briefly about the fire at OmniCare, and the related story of how Earth for Everyone had released copies of some of Charlesford's files. It was back to music after that, but the mood in the car was different then. We all had a lot to think about.

Mom was pretty freaked out when I got home—relieved to see me, furious at me, and flustered by all the reporters and cops and lawyers waiting to speak with me. Yet again.

I talked to some, and we shooed away the rest. By the time everyone cleared out that night, she didn't have the energy to be upset with me. Physically, I was fine. And as it turned out, I hadn't actually missed any school while I was gone. The storm that tore through Centre Hollow also hit Philadelphia pretty hard, so we actually had a snow day.

But I did take a couple more days off after I got home. I was tired and still recovering, and really, I didn't want to waste the hypothermia excuse, complete with doctor's note from our family physician.

That's not to say Mom and I didn't have it out—we did. Many times.

She would usually start out by saying something like, "It shouldn't have to be a seventeen-year-old girl doing all this," sounding only slightly less annoying than Kevin. And I would reply, "Yeah, you're right, it shouldn't have to be, but what are you supposed to do when no one else is doing anything about it?"

Then we'd go back and forth with her talking about schoolwork and college and my safety and the importance of keeping in touch, and me talking about all the messed-up stuff in the world, and eventually she'd hug me and tell me how I got all that from my father's side of the family, and that she was proud of me. And I'd apologize—not because I was sorry for what I'd done, but because I really was sorry that I had hurt her or scared her. Then, before long, one of us would inevitably say something that brought it all up again, and we'd go through the whole conversation once more.

Who knows, maybe on some level it was therapeutic.

On the third day of my convalescence, the FBI came to talk to me. Luckily, DeWitt was there, too. I found out later from Claudia that they questioned her as well, but she had one of her parents' lawyers present.

There were two different teams, or rather, a lone agent to ask me about the horrible things that Charlesford had been doing at Omni-Care Gellersville, and an entire team to ask about something else.

"What do you know about CLAD?" the lead investigator asked. Her name was Special Agent Ralphs, and she looked at me with a stare that she obviously thought was serious and penetrating. She seemed like a bit too much of a badass, like maybe she'd watched too many old action movies.

"CLAD?" We were sitting at my dining room table: me, my mom, DeWitt, Ralphs, and her team of two other agents who didn't even introduce themselves. My mom had made us all hot chocolate.

"The terrorist group Chimera Liberation and Defense."

"Just what I've heard on the news. I heard they'd claimed responsibility for those H4H bombings."

"That's right. Do you know anyone involved with them?"

My mom and DeWitt both looked alarmed until I said, "No! Of course not."

"What was CLAD's involvement in the destruction of OmniCare Gellersville?"

I snorted. "None. The place went down because the people running it built it on an unstable mine, so they could use chimeras as forced labor, to—"

Ralphs held up a hand to stop me. "My colleague is investigating those allegations. You can tell all that to him in a minute. But you're saying unequivocally that CLAD had nothing to do with destroying that hospital?"

"Yes, that's right."

"And you are not involved with CLAD in any way?"

"Absolutely not. Why do you even keep asking that?"

"Because they've been involved in a number of serious incidents and they are a top priority. And because we've intercepted communications between CLAD members that included mentions of you. By name."

I snorted, reflexively, because it was so ridiculous. "What?"

Instead of repeating herself, she sat back and slowly nodded. My mom looked alarmed again. As Ralphs's words sank in, I may have looked alarmed, too. I was still kind of freaked out that apparently

Wells and his people had been following me. And Chimerica had been, too, for that matter.

Ralph's leaned forward again. "Ms. Corcoran, what do you know about the terrorist group Chimerica?"

I think she expected that to throw me, but she was finally asking a question I'd kind of been expecting.

I smiled. "Everybody says Chimerica isn't real."

Her already cocked eyebrow moved even higher, and she stared at me, waiting for me to crack.

"Okay," she said, leaning back in her chair. "I guess that's all we have for now." She put her business card on the table.

When they left, the next agent, O'Dowd, came in and asked the more relevant and important questions, about Charlesford and OmniCare and Wells. I told him everything I knew, and he took his time, asked insightful questions, and made sure he thoroughly under- stood all of what I was telling him. I glossed over any references to Chimerica, and said there were some sympathetic nonchimeras who had helped, whose identities I didn't know and whose descriptions I could only give in the vaguest terms.

He was not a badass at all. He seemed like a good guy, smart and sincere, like he understood the gravity of this, took it seriously as the horrific crime that it was.

Doctor Reivik, whom I'd last seen slung over Rex's shoulder, was cooperating fully in exchange for reduced charges. She had told O'Dowd plenty, but he knew and I knew that the cards were stacked against him. Charlesford was gone. Within days of his disappearance, there was a sighting in Belize and one in Norway, less than twelve hours apart. After that, nothing.

Howard Wells was undeniably implicated, this time more directly than in Pitman. He was a major shareholder in OmniCare, and Well- plant Corporation was the sole customer of OmniCare's yttrium extraction subsidiary. There was a lot of speculation that Wells had been so desperate for yttrium, he had moved ahead with the Omni-Care plan even though GHA wasn't settled law. But there was no direct evidence tying him to the SPLINTR operation, or at least not enough to charge him.

That didn't mean he got off scot-free.

Wellplant was in trouble. Not only had the company lost its supplier of yttrium, meaning thousands of orders were going unfilled and thousands of buyers were mad as hell and filing lawsuits, but it also came out that there had been growing stories about malfunctions in the new Wellplant models that had already shipped. A recall was even imposed, which Wells was fighting in court. Oddly enough, he was joined in the suit blocking the recall by thousands of Wellplant wearers who didn't want to give up their Wellplants, and didn't want them altered in any way—which I sort of understood. I'd probably be reluctant to have something yanked out of my head, too. But maybe even stranger was that, while new orders for Wellplants plummeted, orders for upgrades from existing users were stronger than ever, even with the recall.

And while Wells had so far escaped criminal prosecution, there was a huge civil suit in the works, filed by E4E on behalf of those who had been imprisoned in the mines, and the families of those who had died down there. It was complicated by the fact that, under GHA, it wasn't clear if chimeras had the right to sue, but the burden of proof was much lower in civil court than in criminal court. Wells might have escaped prosecution, but he could stand to lose billions, even trillions, if the suit was allowed to proceed.

Rex kept me posted on the progress in Centre Hollow. Apparently, as happy as everyone was to be out of the mines, there was some grumbling at first about trading life in one pit for life in another. The basement in Centre Hollow wasn't the easiest place to exist. But the storm left behind calm, clear weather, and as soon as the winds fully died down, the gases seeped up through the cracks in the rock again, filling the hollow. Within a couple of days, the people there had the run of pretty much the entire town, such as it was.

Doc set up a tent for Devon and controlled the atmosphere, a mix of mine gas and fresh air, tweaking it every day with a little more air and a little less mine gas. At the end of ten days, Devon was breathing plain air, and his lungs had cleared up completely.

Based on that success, over the next several weeks Doc set up a series of tiny tent clinics, from the middle of town to the outskirts, and as each of the chimeras from the mine fell ill, he put them in the first clinic and cared for them, moving them from one clinic to the next, carefully controlling what they were breathing, until their lungs were clear and they were breathing fresh air. In light of Doc's legal troubles, everyone in Centre Hollow made sure to keep the whole thing quiet. Over the next three months, one by one, every single one of them got sick, and then got better, until there were none, and Centre Hollow went back to being a ghost town.

Rex and I went through some acclimation of our own, getting used to the luxury of being around each other a lot. We got used to that part pretty quick. But we also had some work to do.

It might seem a little overly analytical to say you have to work on a relationship when you're seventeen. It seems more of a thing you do when you've been married ten years.

But we'd had some issues before everything went down with OmniCare. Issues with secrecy. It didn't bother me as much now—in part because there were fewer secrets—but still, I wanted our own air cleared, so to speak.

One night, about a month after we got back from Centre Hollow, we were at Rex's apartment. We'd been seeing each other almost every day at that point, and on this one night, we had just come back from dinner at my house, with my mom and Kevin and Trudy. It wasn't the first time Rex had been over, but it was the first time it hadn't been *excruciatingly* awkward.

Sure, Kevin—being Kevin—had felt the need to share with everyone his Rex impersonation for the thousandth time. But Rex responded with a dead-on Kevin. I didn't know there was such a thing, because Kevin was so boring and nondescript, but Rex nailed it with a "Yo, doofus, stop hogging the potatoes," or something like that. For the next ten minutes the two of them stayed in character while Mom, Trudy, and I just about died laughing.

It felt different after that. A new level of . . . well, not normal. I didn't even *want* normal. But healthy and real.

Maybe it was because of that, or maybe in spite of it, that I wanted more than ever to have an honest conversation about things.

We were sitting on his sofa, exactly where I wanted to be, with his arm around me and my fingers intertwined with his.

"You know," I said, "I don't condone CLAD or any of their actions. . . ."

"But?" Rex asked.

"But it's kinda nice not having that H4H logo staring back every time you look out the window."

"I'm just glad no one was hurt."

"Me, too," I said quickly. "I just—"

"I know."

He smiled and looked at his lap for several long seconds. It was great having him right next to me, but all day, it had seemed like a part of him was far, far away.

"What's on your mind?" I said, looking up at him.

He didn't meet my eyes. "Nothing."

"Okay," I said. I took a deep breath. "Now that I've been to Lonely Island, I think I kind of get it more now, Chimerica and what it's about. And I know there're things Martin couldn't tell me, that you can't tell me, about what Chimerica is up to or who is in charge and everything. Like I said, I understand. But why don't we try this: if there are things you can't talk about that are bothering you, you can still talk to me about the fact they're bothering you, even if you can't tell me what they are. We can at least do that, right? And try to stay a little more in tune with each other?"

I expected him to say "I know" or "Okay," and then we'd move on. And I was ready to move on.

But instead, Rex crossed his arms and sat there for a moment, looking thoughtful. Then he said, "Sometimes there are things I want to tell you, but I don't because I don't want to dump it on you."

"What do you mean?"

"Keeping secrets is hard. For me, at least. It's a burden. It sucks. And maybe there's stuff I *do* want to tell you, but I don't want to weigh you down with it, because it's a secret and then you'll have to deal with it and you won't be able to tell anybody."

"Rex," I said, patting his cheek, maybe a little condescendingly, maybe because I thought *he* was being a little condescending. "I'm not a little kid. I can keep a secret. Whatever it is, I'm pretty sure I can handle it. And you'll probably feel better when you get it off your chest."

He stared at me for a long moment, thinking, then he said, "Okay, well . . . you remember before OmniCare, when you were asking who was in charge of Chimerica?"

"Yeah?"

He paused again, staring and thinking. I felt bad for him that he was grappling so hard with this, and I was about to tell him, *Look, if it's that big a secret, maybe you should just keep it to yourself.*

Then he blurted out, "It's your aunt. That's who's running Chimerica. She's the one who started it and conceived of it. . . . She's behind *everything.*"

I rolled my eyes, and let out a sigh. We'd had a lot of fun at dinner, but I was trying to be serious here. Then again, it was a pretty funny thought. "That's hilarious, Rex. My Aunt Trudy is the head of Chimerica. Haha. Thanks—I needed that."

"No, Jimi, not Trudy," he said, his voice earnest. "Your Aunt *Dymphna*. She's the head of Chimerica. Dymphna Corcoran."

"Aunt *Dymphna*?" I felt my eyes widen in shock. Aunt Dymphna, whom I'd basically just found out about after not knowing about her for my entire life?

"Yeah, it's crazy, right? I honestly don't know much about how she runs things, but everyone says she's great. And she's totally brilliant. Turns out she practically invented the whole splicing procedure."

I was stunned. Rex's voice seemed so far away, it felt like it was taking several long seconds for his words to even start sinking in.

What did this mean? How could this be true? So many things suddenly made sense, and so many more things suddenly didn't. I wanted to run home and interrogate my mother, my Aunt Trudy, demand they tell me what they knew about this.

But I couldn't.

Because it was a secret.

I turned to look at Rex, my jaw slack as the implications washed over me.

His head was back and his eyes closed. His shoulders looked relaxed. He let out a long sigh and slowly grinned as he put his arm back around my shoulders. "Wow," he said. "That was really weighing on me. But you know what? You're right—I do feel a lot better now that I've shared it with you."

ACKNOWLEDGMENTS

There are many people I'd like to thank for their help, their enthusiasm, and their support, who have championed *Spliced*, and whose wisdom informed *Splintered*. First off, in all things, is my wife Elizabeth, who is essential to my writing, and also to my being. As always, I'm grateful to Stacia Decker: super agent, brilliant creative partner, and dear friend. I'm also grateful for the insights, the commitment, and the friendship of my amazing editor, Kelly Loughman, as well as the entire team at Holiday House.

Spliced was my first young adult novel, and since its release, I've learned a lot about YA (and how much I hadn't known about it previously) and a lot about the YA community (and how wise, welcoming, and wonderful the people in it are). When *Spliced* came out, I felt like an absolute newbie in the world of young adult fiction. And while I still feel like one now, I'm not anymore, really, thanks to all that I've learned from so many authors, bloggers, teachers, librarians, and of course, YA readers, both teen and adult.

I'd particularly like to thank the amazing Laurie Halse Anderson, who has been a gracious and invaluable source of wisdom and support, as has my friend and champion Eric Smith—author, agent, and many-other-book-related-things extraordinaire. I'd also like to thank Alex London and Katherine Locke and the wonderful folks I've met at Low Groggery, plus all the people I've met at KidLitCon, Rochester Teen Book Festival, ABC Children's Institute, NCTE, ALA, PLA, and PaLA.

A lot of people helped with my research into the science behind this book, including petroleum and chemical industry expert

Dan Lundeen; Veronica Coptis, from the Center for Coalfield Justice; and Amy R. Sapkota, PhD, MPH, from the University of Maryland School of Public Health. A lot of others provided critical support for the writing. I'd like to thank my pals in the Philadelphia Liars Club, especially my cohosts on the Liars Club Oddcast—Merry Jones, Keith Strunk, Greg Frost, and Kelly Simmons, whose wisdom I absorb each week, even as I pepper them with stupid jokes.

The response to *Spliced* has been tremendous, and tremendously gratifying. I have thoroughly enjoyed visits to schools and libraries, teen writing groups and book groups, and Skype visits around the country. I look forward to doing more, and I thank those librarians and teachers who have invited me into their classroom, and who have championed my books. Special thanks to librarians Cheri Crowe, Tracee Yawger, and Dena Heilik for all their support.

The relationships that I've forged haven't been limited to the world outside my books. One of the great joys of writing is the people you meet, including the ones on the page. I had a blast writing *Spliced*, and getting to know the characters in it, and *Splintered* has been no different. So, to the characters who have come to mean so much to me, and especially Jimi Corcoran: Thanks for letting me write you, and for living in the pages of my books, and, hopefully, in the hearts and minds of my readers as well as in my own.

Finally, *Splintered* is a work of fiction, and the struggles of the characters within it are fictional as well, but they are most assuredly based on the realities of many, many people facing many different struggles, people who must fight to be who they are and to live their lives without persecution. I am grateful to them for their bravery and persistence as they lead the efforts to make this world a place where those fights are no longer necessary.

A plan for peace becomes a fight for survival

READ THE THRILLING CONCLUSION
OF THE ACCLAIMED
SPLICED TRILOGY